A Mother's Secret

Katie Flynn is the pen name of the much-loved writer, Judy Turner, who published over ninety novels in her lifetime. Judy's unique stories were inspired by hearing family recollections of life in Liverpool during the early twentieth century, and her books went on to sell more than eight million copies. Judy passed away in January 2019, aged 82.

The legacy of Katie Flynn lives on through her daughter, Holly Flynn, who continues to write under the Katie Flynn name. Holly worked as an assistant to her mother for many years and together they co-authored a number of Katie Flynn novels.

Holly lives in the north east of Wales with her husband Simon and their two children. When she's not writing she enjoys walking her two dogs, Sparky and Tara, in the surrounding countryside, and cooking forbidden foods such as pies, cakes and puddings! She looks forward to sharing many more Katie Flynn stories, which she and her mother devised together, with readers in the years to come.

Keep up to date with all her latest news on Facebook: Katie Flynn Author

Katie Flynn

A Mother's Secret

PENGUIN BOOKS

PENGUIN BOOKS

UK | USA | Canada | Ireland | Australia
India | New Zealand | South Africa

Penguin Books is part of the Penguin Random House group of
companieswhose addresses can be found at global.penguinrandomhouse.com

First published by Century in 2024
Published in Penguin Books 2024
001

Typeset in 11.08/14.11 pt Palatino LT Pro
by Integra Software Services Pvt. Ltd, Pondicherry

Printed and bound in Great Britain by Clays Ltd, Elcograf S.p.A.

The authorised representative in the EEA is Penguin Random House Ireland,
Morrison Chambers, 32 Nassau Street, Dublin D02 YH68

A CIP catalogue record for this book is available from the British Library

ISBN: 978–1–80494–245–1

www.greenpenguin.co.uk

To Tara
for making Sparky whole again

Prologue

Sweat pricked Libby's brow as she heard the old man's belt buckle hit the floor. If she didn't make a move soon, he would be on top of her, and if that happened she would be powerless to stop him. Summoning every ounce of courage she possessed, she swung her legs out of the bed, but before her feet could touch the floor he had pushed her back down with one hand whilst pulling his grimy undergarments down with the other. Screaming for him to get off her, Libby kicked out with her feet, but the weight of his body was too great.

'My, but you're a feisty one,' he said, his tone heavy with perverse amusement. 'Like it rough, do yer?'

'I've changed my mind!' Libby sobbed. 'Please stop.'

His beady black eyes bored into Libby's. 'There's no changin' yer mind cos I've already paid yer. Now stop playin' silly beggars and give me what I'm owed!'

Tears streaming down her face, she glimpsed his purple-headed member as he forced her knees apart. Crying out for Jack to come and save her, she used all

1

the strength she could muster to repeatedly hit out with her fists, but no matter how hard she tried she failed to make a single connection. Desperate to make her escape, she continued to strike out, only stopping when she became aware of someone speaking in earnest yet reassuring tones. Pausing as she strained to hear what the woman was saying, she felt relief flood through her body as she recognised the voice. It was Margo! But what on earth was she doing here? Unless . . . *I'm havin' another nightmare,* Libby told herself. *I've got to wake up.* Praying that she was indeed dreaming, she felt a sense of relief as her eyes met Margo's, and saw that her friend was gazing at her with deep concern.

'It's all right, Lib, no one's goin' to hurt you,' Margo soothed. 'It sounded as though you was havin' another one of them bleedin' nightmares – which will make it the fourth one this week.'

Libby grimaced apologetically, pushing her hair away from her face. 'It's the same old scenario every time. I can't fight him off for love nor money, and Jack's nowhere to be seen,' she mumbled. 'I feel awful that my nightmares keep disturbin' your sleep. Perhaps I should bed down in one of the stables; at least that way one of us would get a decent night's kip.'

'You'll do no such thing!' Margo scolded. 'Besides which, I wouldn't get much rest knowin' that you were relivin' that hell night after night without anyone to wake you from it.'

'Thanks, Margo. I'm sure I'll grow out of them eventually, although why I'm havin' them now after all this time is beyond me.'

'I've been wonderin' the same,' admitted Margo. 'All that business happened the best part of a year ago. It doesn't make sense that they've started again since you moved to the farm – unless the two are related somehow.'

Peering over Margo's shoulder to make sure that Suzie – one of the other girls who was working at Holly-bank Farm in return for bed and board – couldn't hear, Libby carried on speaking in hushed tones. 'They must be, because I was fine when we was livin' on Walton Road, but I can't fathom for the life of me why the move's causin' me to have such awful nightmares.'

'It's ever so quiet here come the night time,' supposed Margo, 'summat which we're not used to, bein' city gels. I reckon all this peace and quiet is allowin' yer mind to wander and that's what's givin' you nightmares.'

Libby hugged her knees. 'I think you might be right, cos as soon as me head hits the piller I start wonderin' how much sleep we'll get before the siren goes off, and then I remember that we're not in the city any more, and we don't have to worry about the Luftwaffe as much as we did when we was down by the docks.'

'If you're thinkin' about the Luftwaffe then why aren't you havin' nightmares about the day you lost yer parents? That would make more sense than dreamin' about that old perv.'

The thought of repeatedly watching her parents' bodies being removed from the rubble of their old house caused the colour to drain from Libby's face. 'I've no idea, but I'd rather dream of anythin' other than that.' She felt a shiver run down her spine as she

3

unwillingly saw herself identifying their bodies. 'Maybe that's why the nightmares are about him and not them.' She rubbed her hands over her pale face. 'I'm absolutely shattered, but I don't want to go back to sleep, not if I'm going to dream about Mum and Dad this time.'

'Sorry, Lib. I didn't mean to put thoughts in yer head,' Margo apologised, adding in brighter tones, 'I know. Why don't you think of summat positive before you go to sleep – like the day you and me left London for Liverpool?'

'I'll try, but what's the bettin' my mind starts to wander back to what could've been had I not escaped when I did?' She sighed irritably. 'I honestly don't know why I do it to myself, I really don't. It's as though I'm determined not to be happy!'

'D'you think you're scared of bein' happy?'

Libby stared at her in disbelief. 'Why would I be scared of that? Surely everyone wants to be happy?'

'If you think about it, you were happy when your parents were movin' from London to Norwich, but then the Luftwaffe came and took it all away. You were the same when you found your mother's side of the family . . .'

'Until I learned they were worse than me Uncle Tony,' interjected Libby.

'Exactly! Every time you find happiness summat comes along to take it away – or at least that's the way you perceive it.'

'So, you think my mind's stoppin' me from bein' happy?'

4

'Jack proposed the day we came to Hollybank,' said Margo. 'Maybe you're worried summat's goin' to happen to take your happiness away like it did the last time you were truly happy.'

Libby stared at her open-mouthed. 'You don't think it will, do you?'

'No!' cried Margo, a little louder than she had intended; lowering her voice, she spoke in hushed tones. 'But I think you might be worryin' about it deep down, and it's playin' out in yer dreams. After all, had you gone ahead with you-know-what . . .'

'Prostitutin' meself,' supplied Libby plainly. 'There's no sense in beatin' about the bush, because that's what I was goin' to do before I changed me mind.'

'Had you not, you'd never have met Jack, and Gawd only knows what sort of a future you'd have had – not a happy one, that's for certain.'

'I'd never have considered it had I had the money to pay for me parents' funeral,' said Libby dully.

'I know, and we're all grateful that you changed your mind. Cos if you hadn't, Jack would never have met the woman of his dreams, and I'd still be workin' the Whitechapel Road as a shoeblack whilst me dad picked the pockets of me customers.'

'And had Jack not come to me rescue, I'd have drowned in the Thames, forever remembered as a thievin' tart.'

Margo glared at her friend. 'You're not a thief, cos you gave the perv his money back, and you're not a tart cos you never did nothin'.'

'But if Jack hadn't rescued me, I'd never have had the chance to give the man his money back, and if you'd seen the clothes I was wearin' when he pulled me out of the river, you'd know they were those of a scarlet woman.' Libby envisaged the stallholders who'd worked alongside her parents down Petticoat Lane. 'The thought of Pete and the rest of them findin' out what had become of me . . .'

'But they didn't,' said Margo, 'and they never will. Those days are gone, and you have to embrace the future, cos it's goin' to be bright, Lib, I know it is, so please stop torturin' yerself with what could've been.'

Libby gave her a rather wan smile. 'I hope you're right . . .' She hesitated as the slumbering figure of the only other person who shared the barn with them stirred in their sleep. 'What I'd give to sleep as soundly as Suzie.'

'You could do with takin' a leaf out of her book,' remarked Margo, 'cos she doesn't let anythin' bother her does that one.'

'She certainly seems to take everythin' in her stride. I'd be beside meself if I'd found out that me mum was alive after years of believin' her to be dead.' She stifled a yawn behind the back of her hand, and continued sleepily, 'If we don't get some sleep we'll be dead on our feet come the mornin'.'

Margo also yawned. 'You're right there. Just remember, only happy thoughts!'

Libby pummelled her pillow into a roundish shape. 'G'night, Margo. I promise I'll not think of anythin' that could give me more nightmares.'

'Glad to hear it. G'night, Lib.'

Closing her eyes, Libby turned her thoughts to the day she and Margo had arrived at Hollybank less than a week before. Having each secured a job working for Mr Soo in the laundry on the first day they set foot in Liverpool, they had been happy with their lot until a ruptured gas pipe meant they were unable to return to their flat or continue their work. With other accommodation in short supply, the girls had been advised to try Hollybank Farm as an alternative form of bed and board until the pipe was deemed safe enough for people to move back into the area.

Jack had offered to drive the girls to the farm, and Margo's boyfriend, Tom, had come along as moral support for Margo, who was uncertain about the move. Upon arriving at the farm, they had been greeted by a friendly land girl by the name of Adele, who had given them a quick tour of the stables before leaving them to settle into the barn which had been set up to house those in need.

Libby had no idea that Jack was thinking of proposing until the words had left his lips, but that hadn't stopped her from accepting his proposal without hesitation. Now, as she lay in her bed, she remembered that Jack and Tom were coming to take her and Margo out to the cinema the next day, and replayed the image of Jack pushing the ring onto her finger as he smiled lovingly at her, his sparkling green eyes made all the brighter by contrast with his thick, dark curly hair. *If I'm to dream again tonight,* she thought, *I shall dream of Jack, and the life we shall share as husband and wife!* And with that thought still in the forefront of her mind, Libby drifted off into a peaceful sleep.

Chapter One

Despite their restless night, Libby and Margo were up betimes the following morning to milk the cows and put them out to pasture before continuing with the rest of their chores.

'I'm sure the pigs would prefer it if we left the muck be,' said Libby as she transferred the dirty straw from her fork to the wheelbarrow. 'Why else would they say "happy as a pig in muck"?'

Margo had opened her mouth to agree with her friend when Adele came racing into the stable. Hastily checking to make sure that she wasn't being followed, she closed the door before turning to the girls, wide-eyed.

'You're not going to believe what I've just heard!'

Libby's face lit up expectantly. 'Have we won the war?' she asked, her fingers crossed.

Adele grimaced apologetically. 'I'm afraid not. I'm talking about Suzie and Bernie having a blazing row in the milking shed just now. He was calling her all sorts, saying that she was an evil little bitch, and a backstabber, and that he should chuck her out on her ear.'

Libby was shocked to hear that Bernie had behaved in such an ungentlemanly way, and said as much to Adele. 'What on earth has Suzie done to make him act in such a manner? I know she can have a bit of an attitude sometimes, but I thought she and Bernie got on like a house on fire.'

'They do – or rather, they did,' corrected Adele. 'It's because of her attitude with the land girls – and Roz in particular – that everything's gone pear-shaped.'

'Why Roz?' asked Margo curiously. 'She seems nice enough to me.'

'Me too,' agreed Libby.

'That's because she is,' said Adele. 'Suzie's angry at Roz because she thinks she's in cahoots with her mum.'

'Has this got summat to do with Suzie thinkin' her mum was dead before she came to Hollybank? Cos that's hardly Roz's fault,' said Margo, who was peering through the top half of the stable door.

'It's more complicated than that,' said Adele. 'You see, Suzie's father – Callum – is a right nasty piece of work, and when Joyce disappeared the whole community – including Suzie and her gran – thought that he'd thrown one punch too many and got rid of the evidence, as it were.'

'He obviously hadn't, though,' Margo pointed out.

'Only because Joyce ran away before he had the chance,' said Adele.

'I don't blame her,' said Libby, moving the wheelbarrow to the far side of the stable. 'Better that than a one-way trip to the bottom of the Mersey.'

Adele agreed before speaking in hushed tones. 'Did you know that Suzie's gran died during the bombings?'

'Joyce said summat about it when we first got here,' Libby confirmed.

'Well, from what I've just overheard, Callum was the one responsible for her death.'

Margo gasped out loud, but Libby was sceptical.

'You can hardly accuse Callum of foul play if it's the Luftwaffe that took her out,' she said fairly.

'Under normal circumstances I'd agree with you, but Suzie reckons her dad forced her gran to stay at home in case someone tried to steal his loot while he was out on the rob.'

Libby stared at her aghast. 'Well, that's a different kettle of fish entirely. If it's true then Suzie's right: he as good as murdered his own mother.'

'Evil – there's no other word for it,' breathed Margo, 'and, considerin' what her father's like, I fail to see why Suzie's angry with her mother for runnin' away.'

'She probably felt abandoned, and I can't say as I blame her,' said Libby. 'But these things are rarely black and white, and I'm sure there's a perfectly good explanation for Joyce leaving her behind.'

'I suppose she must've been desperate,' said Margo, and went on curiously, 'What I don't understand is why Suzie singled out Roz in particular.'

'That's a much bigger story, which is best told from the beginning,' said Adele. She went on to tell the girls how she had met Roz and Felix whilst waiting to board the ferry which would bring them from Holland to England.

'I didn't know you were a Jewish refugee!' Margo cut in abruptly. 'You don't sound in the least bit German to me.'

'That's because I'm not; I'm English born and bred. My father was sick of not having permanent employment so he moved us out to Germany, where he was promised regular work. I hated it at first because I missed my friends, but I soon made new ones and given time I grew to love my new life. Indeed, everything was perfect until *he* came to power. I was too young to understand why our neighbours were concerned about the new leader, especially given my parents' optimism that things couldn't be as bad as they seemed. But when people began smashing the windows of Jewish shopkeepers, it became clear that we were in real danger. My parents were desperate to get me back to England but reluctant to travel themselves for fear that the Nazis might accuse them of being spies – the soldiers would use any excuse to cart you off to one of their camps – so they agreed to follow me when it was safe to do so.'

Libby stared at Adele, horror-struck. 'So where are your parents now?'

Adele shrugged. 'As far as I know they're still in Germany, but I try not to think about it too much, because I don't like to get my hopes up, or imagine the worst.' Her features darkened as she fell momentarily silent before pressing on. 'Where was I? Oh yes, the ferry! I began chatting with Roz and Felix and that's when I learned that Roz wasn't meant to be on the train.'

'How come?'

'Her parents had visas to get out of the country legally, but they were involved in a car crash on the way to the station, and when Roz came to she found herself on board the Kindertransport with no knowledge of her parents' whereabouts.'

Libby leaned against the fork handle. 'Poor Roz, she must've been terrified.'

'She was, but she's made of stern stuff – she'd have to be to put up with Suzie's family.'

Margo rubbed her brow with the back of her hand. 'How on earth did she end up with them?'

'Slave labour,' said Adele simply. 'The Haggartys saw the refugees as a good way of making money for nothing, so offered to give her a home.'

'That man really is the lowest of the low,' snapped Libby. 'How could anyone prey on innocent children like that?'

'It's more common than you'd think; there were many taken in like Roz. Felix and I were two of the lucky few.'

'If Roz was livin' with the Haggartys, how come she wound up as a land girl?' asked Libby curiously.

'Luckily for Roz, Callum chucked her out.'

'How come?'

'She's no idea, but she's just glad he did, because it gave her the opportunity to join the Land Army with her friend Mabel. They started off working at Glasfryn farm high up in the Welsh mountains, where Mabel still works, but with Hollybank being desperately short on land girls Roz came to us.' She arched a single eyebrow. 'Bernie fell for Roz as soon as she arrived, but

Roz was in love with Felix, and that was the end of that – until Suzie arrived.'

'What's Suzie got to do with the price of fish?'

'As you can imagine, it came as a huge shock to find that her mother was still alive, but when she saw that Roz was also here, she got it into her head that they were laughing at her behind her back.' She heaved a sigh. 'The silly girl stormed off, vowing never to return, leaving Joyce in bits.'

'What made her come back?' said Libby.

'She had nowhere else to go,' said Adele simply. 'Which is why she came to Hollybank in the first place.'

'It must've been a bitter pill to swallow, comin' back when she'd made such a dramatic statement,' Margo supposed.

'She certainly didn't want anything to do with any of us,' said Adele, 'which is why she insisted that Bernie be the one who showed her the ropes, or she really would leave for good.'

'But that's ridiculous!' cried Margo. 'In fact, I'm surprised he agreed.'

'Ah, but Bernie only agreed because Roz persuaded him to and Roz only did that because Joyce couldn't bear to lose her daughter after only just getting her back.'

'Good job he was sweet on Roz,' said Margo. 'I bet he wouldn't have agreed otherwise.'

'And therein the trouble lies,' said Adele ruefully. 'You see, Bernie thought that by doing this favour for Roz, he might be in with a chance of forming a romantic relationship with her.'

'Even though he knew Roz was in love with Felix?' asked Libby, somewhat disapprovingly.

'I'm afraid it's not as straightforward as that,' said Adele. 'You see, there did come a time when it looked as though Roz and Felix's relationship was on the rocks, something which Bernie knew about – and I rather think he hoped things might swing in his favour if he and Roz spent some time alone.'

'Unfortunate,' conceded Libby, 'but that was hardly Suzie's fault.'

'Only it was – because Suzie knew how keen Bernie was on Roz, and *she* was the one who led him to believe that he could win her heart if he headed her off at the station this morning.'

'But isn't Roz going to spend Christmas with her pal Mabel?' said Libby, a line creasing her forehead.

'Along with Felix,' said Adele, nodding darkly.

Margo's jaw dropped as the realisation dawned. 'Suzie set him up!'

'Hook, line and sinker.'

'Poor Bernie! No wonder he's angry. He must've felt a real fool.'

'So that's why he threatened to chuck her out on her ear,' said Margo.

'Yes, but that was before he heard everything that Suzie had been through with her dad,' said Adele.

'It's Roz I feel sorry for,' said Libby. 'She was only tryin' to make the peace between Suzie and her mum.'

'Exactly what I was thinkin',' agreed Margo. 'So why would Suzie be so spiteful to her?'

'Jealousy, that's why.'

'Of what?' cried Libby.

'Roz!' said Adele. 'She might have lost everything when she came to this country, but in Suzie's eyes Roz had everything she didn't.'

'Like what?' demanded Libby, who could hardly believe that anyone could be jealous of a refugee.

'She had loving parents who had moved heaven and earth to get her to safety, and good friends who stuck by her through thick and thin, which was a lot more than Suzie had.'

'I s'pose if you put it that way,' conceded Margo. 'Where's Suzie now?'

'She's gone to the station to see if she can patch things up between Roz and Felix.' Adele breathed out a staggered sigh. 'I hope she's successful, cos those two have been through too much to risk losing it all over some petty act of jealousy.'

Libby glanced fleetingly at Margo. 'And you thought livin' on a farm was goin' to be borin'!'

'We'll certainly have a lot to tell the boys when they pick us up later this evenin'. Talkin' of which, we'd best get a move on if we're to finish on time.'

'And I'd better get back to work if I don't want people to think that I'm standing around gossiping! Even though I am,' said Adele. 'See you later, girls.'

Libby and Margo bade her goodbye before returning to the task at hand.

'Suzie doesn't know how lucky she is to have a mother,' said Libby. 'I'd be cock-a-hoop if someone told me that it had all been a big mistake, and my parents were still alive.'

Margo smiled sympathetically. 'Sometimes we don't always know what we've got until it's gone. Suzie's blinded by the pain of her mother's leavin', rather than seein' the bigger picture.'

'I know. I just find it so frustratin' at times,' said Libby. A half-smile formed on her lips. 'I'll say this, though: we never had owt as excitin' as this happen when we were workin' down the laundry. The closest we came to a scandal was when we found that pair of gentleman's undergarments in the widow Thompson's washin'.'

Margo grinned. 'Poor mare blushed to the roots of her hair when I asked if she knew whose they were.'

'It didn't help matters that you couldn't keep a straight face,' said Libby. 'And we never did find out who they belonged to.'

'Rumours and gossip are only excitin' if you're not the one who's bein' talked about,' said Margo. 'I bet Suzie doesn't find any of this in the least bit excitin'.'

Libby put the last of the muck into the barrow and rested the fork on top. 'Probably not. Mind you, it does explain her petulant attitude when it comes to her mum and the rest of the land girls. I know she's rushed off to see if she can fix things between Roz and Felix, but do you think she only did that in order to smooth things over with Bernie?'

'It does seem a tad fishy to have had such a big change of heart in a relatively short space of time,' agreed Margo.

'Or maybe hearin' a few home truths has made her realise how unreasonable she was bein'.'

'Possibly,' said Margo as she closed the stable door behind them. 'Funny thing is, if someone were to ask which one I thought to be the refugee between Roz and Suzie, I'd have picked Suzie every time.'

'Because she walks around lookin' like she's found a penny but lost a pound,' said Libby as they began to walk towards the muckheap.

'Exactly! Which doesn't make sense considerin' she found her mother to be alive and well, whereas Roz has no idea if her parents are dead or alive.'

Libby pushed the barrow up the plank and tipped the contents onto the top of the muckheap. 'If you look at things from her point of view, it's easy to see how she could feel as though Joyce had deserted her – made a fool of her, even. And seein' her with Roz probably exacerbated the situation.'

'Roz had everythin', includin' Suzie's mum,' said Margo. 'I suppose that does make sense if you look at it from Suzie's point of view.'

'Believin' yer mother to be dead for all them years must've been dreadful, especially if you think your own flesh and blood was the one that done her in. Seein' her years later, not only alive and well, but livin' a lovely life on a farm in the heart of the country, must've been a real kick in the teeth.'

'Only that wouldn't have been how it was for Joyce at all,' said Margo. 'It must've been heart-wrenchin' for her to leave Suzie behind.'

Libby wheeled the barrow back down the plank and they headed towards the rest of the stables. 'I hope Suzie forgives her, cos she's not the one Suzie should be angry with.'

17

'From what Adele's just told us it sounds as though their relationship is well on the road to recovery,' said Margo. She jerked her head in the direction of the barn. 'C'mon, let's have some lunch before we start on the afternoon chores.'

After a hearty lunch of cheese and pickle sandwiches, the girls had continued with the rest of their chores, and a few hours later were on their way back to the house after putting the last of the animals out to pasture.

'I'm so looking forward to seeing Jack tonight,' Libby enthused. 'I know it's only been a few days since I saw him last, but it feels like so much longer.'

'We've learned a lot since then,' said Margo, continuing with a touch of pride, 'I can milk a cow – which is summat I never thought I'd get the hang of – and I'm not afraid to herd them to and from the pasture like I was in the beginnin'.'

'I can still see yer face when you realised we weren't goin' to be leadin' each one by hand,' chuckled Libby. She pulled a shocked expression as she imitated her friend. '"You mean they're goin' to be *free*? What happens if they try and run away?"'

'How was I to know they were pretty much domesticated when it came to bein' herded around the farm? Besides, you weren't much better with the pigs.' She giggled as she recalled the image of Libby temporarily riding on the back of one of the sows.

'Touché!' said Libby. 'I'll admit I was naïve in thinkin' they'd be easier than cows cos they were half the size.'

'Maybe half the size,' said Margo, 'but four times the character.'

Libby grinned. 'Between the farm and everythin' that's gone on with Suzie, the boys will be lucky if they can get a word in edgewise.'

'I know she's been a proper troublemaker, but I kind of feel sorry for her after everythin' she's been through,' said Margo. Seeing the look of disapproval on Libby's face, she quickly added, 'Not that I'm sayin' she was right to set the cat amongst the pigeons between Roz, Felix and Bernie, but—'

'But nothin',' said Libby firmly. 'Suzie had no right to do what she did, no matter the reason. Your father's a right so-'n'-so, yet you wouldn't dream of treatin' someone badly just to make yerself feel better.'

'There are differences,' said Margo, 'the main one bein' my father never killed anyone.'

'Even if he had, you still wouldn't do it, because you haven't got it in you to do so,' said Libby loyally. 'The two of you are cut from a different cloth, it's as simple as that.'

'I still think a person's circumstances have a lot to do with it,' said Margo, 'but that's summat we'll only find out if Suzie really does turn over a new leaf.' Tilting her head to one side, she fell silent as she tried to remember something Adele had mentioned earlier. 'You know how Adele said that Suzie's father was called Callum?'

'What of it?'

'I can't help thinkin' I've heard that name before. Does it ring any bells with you?'

Libby was about to shake her head when a vision of her Uncle Donny talking to a man in the Grafton entered her mind. 'Wasn't Callum Haggarty the name of that dodgy feller we saw talkin' to me uncle when we were at the Grafton?'

Margo's features sharpened. 'Of course! That was the night we discovered your aunt and uncle had been tellin' porkies about their past.'

'Talk about a small world,' mused Libby. 'Although they do say that birds of a feather flock together!'

'I know yer aunt and uncle can be a bit dodgy what with all the hooky gear they've got stashed in their house, but that's a world away from murderin' old grannies. Do you think they know what Callum's true colours are?'

'I doubt it. People like that tend to hold their cards very close to their chest, and my aunt and uncle are no different. Let's face it, other than the fact they're my aunt and uncle we know very little about them.'

'My dad was the same,' said Margo. 'He never told no one nothin' for fear the bluebottles might come buzzin'.'

'They're quick at thinkin' on their feet an' all,' said Libby. 'That's how me Uncle Tony come up with that bill of sale – which was a pack of lies – just moments before the bomb hit.'

'The one showing he bought your father's business?'

Libby nodded. 'If he didn't have that, I'd have him bang to rights, but either way I know he got the business by foul means not fair. I just don't have the proof.'

'You don't need proof, not as far as I'm concerned,' said Margo firmly, 'because I know that you're tellin' the truth, as does everyone else.'

'I just wish the bluebottles would see it that way.'

'Your word should have been good enough,' said Margo.

Libby smiled appreciatively. 'You're a diamond, Margo Fisher, I hope you know that.'

Margo waved the comment away. 'As are you.'

'Me? What've I done?'

'If you hadn't persuaded me to not go back to London, I'd still be livin' hand to mouth in Blendon Row whilst dodgin' backhanders off my miserable excuse for a father.'

'It works both ways. If you'd have gone back, I'd have had no choice other than to live with me Auntie Jo and Uncle Donny.' Libby shuddered theatrically. 'A fate worse than death.'

'Are you sure about that?' queried Margo. 'Only when we first met, you said you'd return to London if things didn't work out with your mother's side of the family.'

'And if you hadn't have stayed with me, that's exactly where I'd be, back in London,' Libby reminded her. 'And if that had happened, I'd never have found me mum's diaries, which means I'd never have known about the affair.'

'I don't know whether that's such a bad thing,' muttered Margo quietly.

'The news that the man who raised me for sixteen years might not be my father came as one heck of a shock – as well you know – and I don't think I'll ever come to terms with it, but I'd rather know the truth, no matter how painful it is.'

'Only you'll never know the truth, not really,' Margo pointed out, but Libby was adamant.

'Not only do the dates in her diary tally up, but my parents were wed for three years before they had me. Quite frankly, how much proof do we need?'

Margo remained doubtful. 'It still could be one heck of a coincidence.'

'Then why has my Uncle Tony always treated me and me mum like outcasts? Never comin' round to see us on Christmas Day or birthdays when invited, and yet never an explanation as to why. I'm almost positive he knows summat, and that's why he's kept his distance. The only thing I can't work out is why he never told my father.'

'If he did suspect summat – and I'm not sayin' he did, mind you – then he's in the same boat as yourself,' said Margo. 'Cos knowin' summat is one thing, provin' it another. Even if he told your dad of his suspicions, it would be his word against your mum's, and if your father didn't believe him it would be the end of their relationship.'

Libby sidestepped a puddle which had formed earlier that morning. 'If my Uncle Tony really believes I'm not his niece, I suppose it's hardly surprisin' that he didn't want me to inherit his brother's business.'

'He's got no proof, though,' said Margo, 'the same as you with the bill of sale.'

'Apart from the story he made up about winnin' big on the horses – which I don't believe for one minute. Never mind a coincidence – it would be a miracle for him to have won the money the same day we were leavin' for Norwich.'

'Findin' those diaries has opened up a real can of worms . . .' Margo began, but she stopped talking abruptly as the sound of someone weeping softly caught her attention. Lowering her voice, she whispered, 'Did you hear that?'

'It sounds like someone cryin',' confirmed Libby. Holding a finger to her lips, she walked cautiously towards the sound, beckoning Margo to join her. As they neared the rear of the stable block she called out tentatively, 'Hello? Is everythin' all right?'

Scrambling to her feet, Suzie wiped her tear-wet cheeks on the backs of her hands whilst keeping her head lowered. 'I was just checking on the pigs.'

Libby and Margo both glanced at the empty paddock. 'Is there anythin' we can do to help?' ventured Libby.

Suzie shook her head miserably. 'No one can help me, not this time.'

Forgetting that they had only learned of Suzie's recent activities through gossip, Margo spoke without thinking. 'Oh heck, does that mean you didn't make it to the station on time?'

Suzie stared blankly at Margo before the penny dropped. 'Oh, you mean Felix?' Barely pausing for breath, she went on, 'No, this has nowt to do with him – or Roz, come to that.'

Thinking that Bernie might have had a change of heart and decided to follow through with his threat to throw Suzie out, Libby continued cautiously, 'Then why the tears?'

'Whilst I was at the station, I caught me dad picking someone's pocket.' She gave a short snort of contempt. 'I've not seen hide nor hair of him since the day Gran died, yet there he was bold as brass like he hadn't a care in the world, doing what he does best.' She pushed her hands deep into her dungaree pockets. 'I was so angry to see him carrying on as though nothing had happened, I reached out and grabbed his hand before I had a chance to think it through.'

Having once brought attention to her own father's wrongdoings, Margo blew her cheeks out. 'I should imagine that didn't go down too well.'

Suzie's eyes widened. 'He certainly wasn't happy to see me, not surprising given the circumstances, but even so I'd have expected him to welcome me with open arms, thankful to know that I was still alive. But instead he just stared at me, angry that I'd stopped him from pinching the feller's wallet. I could tell just by looking at him that he couldn't give a fig whether I was alive or dead. All he cared about was nicking stuff what didn't belong to him. It really made my blood boil, so I decided to hit him where it hurts.'

Margo's eyes popped until Suzie put her straight.

'Not like that! A punch in the goolies wouldn't hurt anywhere near as much as what I did.'

'Which was?'

'I shouted a warning to the folk around us to keep their hands in their pockets if they wanted to keep what was rightfully theirs.' She paused as she recalled her father's furious reaction. 'Now, that *really* didn't go down well. He was practically spitting feathers, asking me what the hell I thought I was doing.'

'What did you say?' asked Margo, engrossed by Suzie's tale.

'I told him that it's wrong to steal stuff that people have worked hard for.' She wrinkled her nose in disgust. 'Judging by the state of him he's been sleeping rough, because he doesn't look or smell like he's had a bath or even a wash in months.' She let out a staggered breath. 'Maybe I shouldn't have pointed that out, because that's when things really started to go downhill.'

'Did he hit you? Cos if he did . . .' Libby began sternly.

'Nothing like that,' said Suzie. 'He turned it on me by suggesting I ask whoever I was living with to take him in too, because I'd obviously landed on my feet.'

'As if you'd do that!' gasped Margo, although Libby could tell by the look on her friend's face that she wasn't altogether certain Suzie would not.

'He even implied that we could go back to the way things used to be, with me begging down the market whilst he went out on the rob.' Suzie hesitated before continuing sadly, 'Not once did he mention Gran.'

'Pig of a man!' snapped Libby. 'I hope you told him to sling his hook?'

'I certainly did,' said Suzie, 'but not before telling him I thought he was a thieving liar and a rotten father to boot and that I'd never go back to the way things were.'

'Good for you!' cried Margo, but Libby could see by the tears glistening in Suzie's eyes that things were about to take a turn for the worse.

'And what was his response?' she asked hesitantly.

'He said I should be grateful that he never beggared off like me mam did, and that she'd only gone because she couldn't stand the sight of me.' She stopped speaking as the tears began to fall. 'I told him that I'd seen me mam and she'd told me that she was tired of him using her as a punchbag. He called me a liar saying that I'd not seen her, and that was the straw that broke the camel's back. I was so angry that he'd accused *me* of lying, I made a point of telling him that I saw her every day. I shouldn't have done that.'

Margo was looking confused. 'Why on earth not? There's nowt wrong with what you said, or not so far as I can see.'

'By saying that I saw me mam on a daily basis, I practically told him that she was back in Liverpool,' said Suzie, as another tear escaped down her cheek. 'All those years of her successfully hiding away, and I've basically handed her to him on a plate.'

'What did he say?' asked Libby, who could see the enormity of Suzie's words.

'That me and Mam were like peas in a pod, only out for ourselves and not giving a rat's arse about anybody else. Which was rich considering what he'd done to Gran, so I told him straight that the only person who was out for themselves was him, and that it was his fault Gran died during the air raid.' She rubbed her throat absent-mindedly. 'That's when he really lost it. He grabbed me by the throat

26

and clapped his hand over me mouth so that people couldn't hear what I was saying. He was squeezing that tight, I don't know what I'd have done had Felix not stepped in.'

Libby gaped at her. 'When did he turn up?'

'He was waiting for the train to take him back to his barracks.'

Margo tutted sadly. 'Does that mean he's not forgiven Roz?'

Suzie was about to speak when she shot both girls accusing glances. 'Hang on a minute. How do you know about Roz and Felix?'

Rather than land Adele in it, Libby pretended that they had overheard the row between Suzie and Bernie themselves. Suzie instantly relented. 'I can't say I'm surprised; I wasn't exactly worried about people overhearing me at the time.'

'Never mind that,' said Margo, keen to move on, 'what happened next?'

'Dad let go of me, and some feller started shouting as to how his wallet had been swiped. I knew it must have been down to Dad, so I searched his pockets whilst Felix had hold of him. I found three wallets and a watch – none of which were his. The man who'd had his pocket picked recognised one of the wallets, and when other people checked their pockets there was quite the commotion, what with people saying that they too had been robbed. All this caught the attention of Charlie – he's one of the local scuffers – who came along to see what was going on, and that's when all hell broke loose.'

Margo grimaced. 'This doesn't sound good.'

'At first Charlie tried to arrest me, assuming that I was acting as decoy for my dad, but the others soon put him straight, although he did take a bit of persuading. I think he only truly believed me when I told him everything, including Gran dying in the flat. That's when the doo-dah well and truly hit the fan!'

'I bet it did,' chorused Libby and Margo together.

'Dad tried to make a run for it, but Charlie was too quick for him.' She shrugged. 'Of course, Dad being Dad, he gave Charlie every excuse in the book – as I knew he would – and it looked as though Charlie would have no choice other than to let him go, so I said I'd go with them down the station and make a statement saying that I'd taken the stuff out of his pockets.' She hung her head in shame. 'I hope you don't think it dreadful of me to grass on a member of my own family, but he can't keep getting away with everything all the time.'

'Not at all,' said Libby. 'In fact I admire your courage, cos I shouldn't imagine he took it lyin' down.'

Suzie's eyes widened. 'Too right he didn't. He was throwing out threats left right and centre all the way, saying that if I went through with it I'd have to spend the rest of my life looking over my shoulder, because he'd make sure that everyone knew I was a grass. I told him I didn't care, because I wasn't that person any more, but he just laughed in my face and said that I'd always be a Haggarty no matter what. He even called me a Judas, and said that I had a nerve turning on the man who'd put food in my belly and a roof over my head, and that if I went ahead with the statement he'd make me rue the day of his release.'

'Didn't it cross your mind to walk away?' asked Libby in hushed tones.

'No. Too many people – including me – have been giving in to my father all his life, and if I did the same I know that nothing would change. I honestly don't see that I had any choice, although I dread to think what he'll do to me and Mam when he gets out.' Suzie's bottom lip trembled as she wrung her hands in despair. 'We're going to have to leave Liverpool for good, and it's all my fault.'

'Let's not panic,' said Libby, partly to Margo, who was looking nervously around her as though she expected Callum to jump out at any moment. 'I know you told him that you'd been back in touch with your mother, but you didn't tell him where she was, did you?'

'No, but like I said, he knows now that she's in Liverpool and he won't stop until he hunts her – or rather us – down.'

Libby looked doubtful. 'Even after all this time?'

'*Especially* after all this time. Dad's had years of people whispering behind his back, saying he'd bumped her off. He'll want to make them eat their words by proving them wrong and he can only do that if he shows people that she's still alive.'

'I guess no one likes bein' accused of summat they haven't done,' said Margo. 'Do you have any idea how long he'll be locked up for?'

'Not a clue. I know they're keen to throw the book at him, because they've been trying to pin him down for donkey's years. But that's just it – he's as slippery as an eel when it comes to getting off the hook, and it wouldn't surprise me if he wasn't back on the streets this time tomorrer.'

Libby stared at her open-mouthed. 'But what about your gran? He practically *murdered* . . .'

Suzie held her hands up in a placating fashion. 'I agree with you, but when all's said and done, it wasn't me dad who dropped the bomb. The only thing they can really do him for at the moment is picking pockets on the platform.'

Margo appeared deep in thought. 'How many people know your mother's here?'

'Not many. The only time Mam went into the city was during the May blitz, and if someone had seen her I'm sure Dad would've got wind of it before today. On the other hand, I've been doing the milk rounds with Bernie for some time now, and if just one of Dad's cronies has seen me they'll know that I'm working at Hollybank.'

'Practically speaking, you can't run, cos you've nowhere to run to,' said Libby plainly. 'But havin' said that I reckon you should be safe enough here as long as you stay on the farm, cos there's more than enough of us to see him off should he decide to come callin'.' She jerked her head in the direction of the stables as she continued, 'And should he need a bit of persuasion, I reckon a prod up the backside with a pitchfork will do the trick.'

A small smile fleetingly touched Suzie's lips, before collapsing. 'Do you really think the Lewises would want to get involved after my recent escapades?'

'Not a doubt in my mind,' said Libby. 'Bernie's a decent feller, as are his parents. They'd not turn their

30

backs on someone who's in trouble, especially given the circumstances.'

'And as we don't know how long your father will be inside, I think it best if we go and see them now and let them know what's what,' said Margo.

Suzie brightened. 'We? Does that mean you're going to come with me?'

Libby arched a single eyebrow. 'Unless you'd rather go on yer own?'

'I'd rather not.' She hesitated briefly. 'Does that seem cowardly?'

'Not at all. Especially not after the day you've had. If you ask me, you should cut yerself some slack, cos standin' up to yer father like that took guts.' Libby placed an arm around Suzie's shoulders. 'I'll go and round up the troops, while you and Margo wait in the kitchen of the main house.'

With less than an hour to go before the arrival of Jack and Tom, Libby and the others were waiting patiently for Bernie to arrive, and Libby could tell by the look on his face as he walked through the door that he was concerned at seeing the gathering in the kitchen, especially when his eyes settled on Suzie.

'Dare I ask?'

Holding her hand to her stomach, Suzie related everything that had transpired after she arrived at the station, finishing with an apology. 'I'm so sorry. I never meant for any of this to happen, and I'll understand if you give me my marching orders after this morning's shenanigans.'

Bernie's mother Helen, who had remained stiff-lipped, softened. 'You couldn't possibly have known he was going to be there, and at the end of the day, you only did what was right.'

'But I've brought trouble to your door,' said Suzie. 'I seem to be quite good at that.'

Helen looked to Joyce. 'You know him better than anyone here. What do you think?'

'Callum's only brave if he's picking on people that can't fight back. He knows that farms are run by farmers.' She glanced at Bernie and his father Arthur, both of whom were considerably larger and stronger than her husband. 'So, he'll not come here.'

'He'll also be worried that you might call the police on him for trespassin', and he'll not want to risk that when he's fresh out of the nick,' said Margo.

Suzie's bottom lip quivered as she looked to her mother. 'I thought you'd be angry with me.'

'What for?' cried Joyce. 'You only did what any decent person would've done. Angry? I'm *proud* of you, Suzie, because I know how hard it is to stand up to a man – and I use that word loosely – like your father.'

'Your mother's right,' said Adele. 'A lot of people in your position would've walked away.'

Not used to such praise, Suzie felt her cheeks colour. 'You've all been ever so kind,' she said, and turned to Libby and Margo. 'Thanks for listening. Just talking has already made everything heaps better.'

Libby waved a nonchalant hand. 'That's what friends are for . . .' As she spoke, her gaze fell on the clock above the large wooden mantel. 'Cripes! I didn't realise that was the time.' She began to trot towards the kitchen door, closely followed by Margo. 'Sorry to dash, but we have to get a move on if we're to make it to the cinema on time.'

Helen took the kettle off the stove. 'I do love the flicks. What are you going to see?'

'*The Adventures of Robin Hood*,' said Margo, placing her hands to the side of her face in a prayer-like fashion and fluttering her lashes. 'With Errol Flynn.'

Helen's smile broadened. 'Errol Flynn! Now you're talking!'

Arthur tutted loudly. 'Real men don't wear tights!'

Laughing, Margo and Libby bade everyone a quick goodbye before hurrying across the yard to the barn, where they had a brisk wash before getting changed into their frocks.

'I'm glad we managed to sort things out for Suzie,' said Libby thickly, a hairgrip between her teeth.

'Me too,' agreed Margo. 'She certainly seems a lot happier than she did a couple of hours ago.'

'It certainly appears that way,' agreed Libby. She fished her engagement ring from under her pillow and placed it proudly on her finger. 'I still can't believe that I'm engaged to be married!'

'Have you thought about a date yet?' said Margo, quickly pressing on with an impish grin, 'Are you goin' to ask your Auntie Jo to be yer maid of honour?'

Libby inhaled sharply, causing her to cough. 'Am I heck as like! Could you imagine her in a bridesmaid's dress with a fag hangin' out the side of her gob?'

Margo chuckled. 'Yes, I could!'

Libby wagged a chiding finger. 'Don't you be givin' me nightmares, Margo Fisher, I have enough of them as it is.'

'Does that mean Donny's not goin' to be Jack's best man?' teased Margo, quickly ducking to avoid the pillow which Libby threw at her.

Libby sat down on her bed with a whump. 'You might well joke, but I can see them now, floggin' knockoff gear to our weddin' guests; the very image is givin' me palpitations!'

Margo tried to hide the smirk which was threatening to tweak her lips. 'I can just see the vicar fishin' the fag ends out of the font, just like I did with me cup of tea that day, d'you remember?'

Libby turned green at the very thought. 'How could I forget? It still turns my stomach and it wasn't even my cup!' She rested her elbows on her knees. 'What am I goin' to do, Margo? I can't not invite them, but I can hardly say please behave yerselves, because I don't want to risk offendin' them.'

'Ignore me, I'm only teasin'. I'm fairly certain they wouldn't do anythin' to embarrass you on yer big day,' said Margo, although Libby noticed that her friend was crossing her fingers as the words left her lips.

'Maybe not intentionally, but they never miss an opportunity to make a few quid, and they'd use the excuse that they were tryin' to save the guests some money . . .' She stopped speaking as the sound of tyres on gravel reached her ears. 'They're here!'

'How do I look?' Margo asked as slid her arms into the sleeves of her coat.

Libby eyed her friend from her golden locks down to her patent leather shoes. 'Perfect, as always. How about me?'

Margo glanced at the dark, wavy, shoulder-length hair pinned away from Libby's face before giving her the thumbs-up. 'Ditto.'

Jack beamed at Libby as he opened the back door of the car. 'How's tricks?' he asked before giving her a quick peck on the cheek.

'We've got heaps to tell you,' said Libby, sitting down.

'Sounds intriguing.'

Margo joined Libby on the back seat. 'Life's certainly more excitin' here than it was in the city,' she said.

Jack waited for Tom to get in before turning the car around. 'Muddy yes, dirty yes, but I never imagined farm life to be excitin',' he said as he began the descent down the drive.

Leaning forward, the girls took it in turns to tell them all that had happened that day.

'And there I was thinkin' you'd be safer livin' in the country!' said Jack, his eyes connecting with Libby's in the rear-view mirror.

Libby waved a dismissive hand. 'Joyce doesn't think Callum'll come anywhere near the farm, and I tend to agree with her. He's nowt but a big bully who picks on folk what can't stand up for themselves.'

'Well, I certainly hope she's right, but what about after the war? Joyce and Suzie can't stay on the farm for ever.'

Libby stared out of the window at the barren hedge-rows. 'I suppose they'll have to cross that bridge when they come to it, but as I can't see the war endin' any time soon they should have plenty of time to think it through.'

'Talkin' of the future,' said Margo with a wicked grin, 'me and Libby have been chattin' about yer upcomin' weddin'.'

Jack twinkled at Libby in the rear-view mirror. 'Can't wait, eh?'

'Margo's been windin' me up about havin' Donny as best man and Jo as maid of honour, sayin' that they'll be stumpin' their fags out in the font.'

Jack and Tom both roared with laughter.

'It's not funny, Jack!' cried Libby, although she too was laughing. 'I'm in a rare old pickle, cos I can hardly tell them I'm gettin' wed without at least invitin' them to the weddin'. And they're bound to say yes, cos they'd do anythin' for free grub.'

Coughing into his hand, Jack regained his composure. 'Perhaps it'd be better if we tell them we don't want a weddin' gift. I don't fancy bein' banged up for receivin' stolen goods on me weddin' day.'

Libby's face fell. 'Oh Gawd, I hadn't even thought of that!' She hesitated. 'I wonder if that's what they did for me mum and dad's weddin' gift?'

Margo stared at Libby. 'I bet yer Uncle Tony would've done the same.'

'No doubt about it. I know me mum was hardly whiter than white, but—'

Jack cut her off without apology. 'But me no buts! There's a great deal of difference between someone like yer mum – who made one mistake – and yer Auntie Jo who breaks the law for a livin'.'

'It may've been a one-off,' said Libby, 'but just look at the ramifications.'

'I don't think she thought about the repercussions for a second,' said Margo softly. 'It sounded more of a spur of the moment thing to me, a mistake if you will.'

Libby stared into space. 'Like me.'

Margo wagged her finger in a chiding fashion. 'Don't go sayin' things like that, Libby Gilbert. Your mother might have had one hell of a cross to bear, but that don't mean to say she loved you any the less.'

Jack pulled the car up alongside the kerb. 'You shouldn't go passin' judgement when you've only read a couple of pages. You should read the rest if you want the fuller picture – just like I did.'

A look of revulsion crossed Libby's features as she accepted Jack's hand out of the car. 'A couple of pages was more than enough, thank you. I'm happy not knowin' the ins and outs of my mother's personal life, which is why I asked you to read it for me in the first place.'

Jack closed the door behind her. 'But that's the trouble with only knowin' half the story. If you'd read more, you'd know that yer parents were desperate for a child, so much so that your dad told yer mother she should divorce him and find herself a real man who could give her children. Accordin' to yer mum, things got so bad they were barely speakin'.'

'Which is awful,' said Libby, 'but still no excuse . . .'

'I know it's no excuse, but yer mother grew increasingly lonely, which I'm guessin' is what made her finally succumb.'

'Succumb?' repeated Libby. 'You make it sound as though the man was houndin' her.'

'She was definitely bein' pressured by someone,' said Jack, 'because she made reference to him not takin' no for an answer.'

'So she'd told him no?' said Libby.

'Very much so. And on more than one occasion, too.'

'But she doesn't say who?'

'Sorry, but no,' said Jack, adding as an afterthought, 'and whilst I can't recall everythin' she wrote, I do remember her writing about how he'd told her not to worry and that she should do as he suggested if she wanted to save her marriage – or words to that effect.'

Libby's features grew stern. 'It sounds to me as though he was pressurin' her to sleep with him or risk losin' me dad!'

'I can't think what else it could mean,' Jack admitted.

She glanced up at the underside of his chin as he placed his arm around her waist. 'I bet he badgered until she finally gave in.'

Margo gave Libby a sidelong glance. 'I wonder if the feller concerned knows you could be his.'

Libby gave a snort of contempt. 'I've no doubt he ran for the hills when he found out that Mum was pregnant.'

'It's hard to tell without havin' the next diary in line,' said Jack.

She glanced up at him. 'Why didn't you tell me any of this before?'

'Ever heard the expression "Least said, soonest mended"?'

'Of course I have.'

'That's what I figured when it came to your mum's diary, but it seems all I really did is allow yer imagination to run wild.'

'That's not your fault, though,' assured Libby. 'Not when I was the one who'd asked you to read them in the first place.'

'Even so, I should've been more forthcomin',' said Jack. 'Your mum was a good woman. I can tell that by readin' her thoughts.'

'She was,' agreed Libby, 'but I still find it hard to forgive her for what she did.' She held up her hands in a placating manner before anyone could object. 'I know it's unfair of me to judge because I wasn't the one goin' through it, but I can't help thinkin' about me dad and how devastated he'd have been had he known the truth.'

'But he didn't, did he, and that's a good thing, because I don't think yer mother made it a habit to sleep with other men,' said Margo.

Libby's eyes nearly left her skull. 'Of course she didn't!'

'Then why hang her for one mistake?' said Margo. 'Cos whether you were born from it or not, that's all it was, a stupid mistake which she rued until the day she died.'

'I s'pose if you put it like that . . .' Libby began, but Margo continued.

'How else can you put it? Either yer mother was a loose woman who didn't give two figs about yer father, or she was a loving wife, who fell under pressure.'

Libby lowered her gaze. 'I've been lettin' my emotions cloud my judgement.'

'Only because you were hurt,' said Margo. 'I'm sorry if my words upset you, but sometimes it's easier to see things when you're on the outside lookin' in.'

'I couldn't see past her betrayal,' said Libby grimly.

'I know, but you have to move on, because there's no sense in beatin' yerself up when you could well be your father's daughter anyway,' said Margo. 'All that pain and sufferin', and for what?'

'I knew there was a reason why I asked you to stay in Liverpool with me,' said Libby. 'You might be a bitter pill to swallow, Margo Fisher, but you've done me the power of good.'

Margo linked arms with Libby as they joined the queue of people waiting outside the Rialto. 'I hope this means you're not goin' to say owt to yer Uncle Tony, cos I know you were plannin' on askin' him whether he knew about the affair at one stage.'

'No chance. He'd be crowin' it from the rooftops if I told him about the diaries, and you can bet yer last penny he'd not see things from me mum's point of view. He'd be callin' her all sorts, and she doesn't deserve that.'

Jack kissed her softly on the cheek. 'You'd only have given him ammo to have a go at her, and he's taken enough from you as it is.'

Libby smiled up at the three of them. 'I'm lucky to have friends like you.'

He coddled her hand in his before letting go. 'Wait here whilst me and Tom get the tickets.'

'He's a diamond,' said Margo as they waited for the boys to come back.

'He really is,' agreed Libby, 'but so are you.'

Margo winked at her. 'You're not so bad yerself, Libby Gilbert.'

They saw the boys gesturing for them to follow the usherette, who guided them to their seats, and Jack jerked his head at the velvet curtains still covering the screen as they sat down. 'Have you seen this 'un before?'

'No, but everyone knows the story of Robin Hood and Maid Marian.' She nestled her head against his chest. 'You reminded me of Robin Hood, the way you saved me from the river.'

Jack chuckled softly. 'I love you dearly, but it'll be a cold day in hell before you catch me wearin' tights!'

Libby conjured up an image which caused her to emit a shriek of laughter, before stifling her giggles behind her hand. 'I can't see the RAF makin' it part of the uniform, can you?'

'Only if they get us mixed up with the WAAF.'

Having overheard the conversation, Margo leaned forward eagerly. 'I think Errol Flynn looks dashing in tights.'

Seeing the way Tom rolled his eyes, Libby tried her best not to giggle. *Only these three could cheer me up when*

I was feelin' low. They really are the best friends a girl could have! Libby thought as she watched the lights flicker across the screen.

By the time the film had come to an end, Libby found herself wondering what her own wedding would be like in comparison with Maid Marian's. *Obviously, I wouldn't be able to afford anythin' anywhere near as extravagant as Marian's weddin' dress, but does that really matter in the grand scheme of things? Cos if truth be known, I'd rather get wed in dungarees surrounded by my friends and family than a posh frock in a room full of strangers.* Libby imagined herself in the register office on Brougham Terrace with Jack, his father Gordon, Margo, Tom, Jo and Donny. *I suppose I could ask the girls from the farm,* she thought; *I know I don't know them that well, but it'll be a pretty sparse weddin' otherwise.* She then imagined what her wedding would've been like in London. Her father would have marched her proudly down the aisle, whilst her mother dabbed the tears from her eyes. The stallholders from Petticoat Lane would have moved heaven and earth to ensure they could attend her big day, just as they had the day of her parents' funeral. *They'd all be dressed in their Sunday best,* Libby mused, *and Dad would insist everyone have jellied eels followed by spotted dick and custard.* She compared the two scenes side by side, and quickly came to a decision. *I can't get married in Liverpool with people who barely know me. I have to go back to London. The market folk are like family, much more so than Auntie Jo and Uncle Donny – Uncle Tony too, come to that – and if anyone should be at my wedding then it's them.*

When she had first moved to Liverpool she had made up her mind to make it her home, believing that there was nothing left for her in London. But as she sat in the cinema she found herself beginning to question that decision. Liverpool had made her happy because it was many miles away from the horror she'd lived through in the capital, and at the time she had wanted to be somewhere where her parents had only known happiness, but after finding the diaries she realised that her mother had been at her lowest ebb whilst in Liverpool, which was why they'd moved to London in the first place. *I came to Liverpool hopin' to recreate a sense of family, but I'm no better off here than I was back in London. Auntie Jo and Uncle Donny only want me because they're convinced that I'm goin' to come into a large inheritance, but one of these days they'll realise that's never goin' to happen, and when they do I daresay they'll drop me like a hot cake.*

As the lights of the auditorium went up, Margo leaned across Tom to talk to Libby. 'What a smashin' film. I'm glad we picked this over Laurel and Hardy. I know they're funny, but nowt hits the spot like a good bit of romance.'

Tom raised his brow in a speculative manner. 'A bit far-fetched though, don't you think?'

'Everyone knows Robin Hood's a myth . . .' Libby began, but Tom was shaking his head.

'I was referrin' to all that runnin' he was doin' through the forest without once snaggin' his tights,' he said, much to the amusement of Jack, who winked at Libby.

'You never know, should the RAF see this film, tights might well become part of the uniform.'

43

Tom grinned as they left their seats. 'Nah, they'd not spend extra on the gusset; you'd only get stockings.'

Jack roared with laughter. 'That'll go down well with the fellers in the Navy.'

Tutting loudly, Libby slapped his bicep in a reprimanding fashion. 'Honestly, Jack, you can't make assumptions like that.'

Stretching in an exaggerated fashion, Jack allowed his arm to loop over Libby's shoulder as they walked out onto the pavement. 'I'm only messin'.' He rubbed his stomach hungrily. 'Does anyone else fancy fish 'n' chips? I'm famished.'

Tom rubbed his hands enthusiastically. 'Count me in. We could go to the one on Aigburth Street if you like. It's not far from here, and they do the best batter.' With everyone in agreement they began the short walk to the fried fish shop.

Sliding her arm around Jack's waist, Libby voiced her recent thoughts. 'Watchin' that film made me think about our own weddin'.'

'Oh aye?'

'I didn't think it bothered me where I got married, but seein' Maid Marian and Robin surrounded by their friends made me realise that's the sort of wedding I want, and even though I've made some wonderful pals here in Liverpool, it's not the same as people who've known me all my life.' She glanced at him shyly. 'I'd particularly like Pete to be there because he means the world to me, he truly does, and not just because he's known me my whole life, or that he was really close to Mum and Dad when they worked down the market. It's everythin' that he did for me after they died. If it wasn't for him rallyin' the troops and organisin' a collection, I'd never have been able to pay for their funeral, never mind the cars and the wake! They were all marvellous, though, and I did think about invitin' everyone up here, but if it's anythin' like my parents' funeral the whole market will want to attend, which is why I think it might be easier if we got married in London.'

Jack kissed the top of her head. 'I don't mind where we get married just as long as we do.'

'I'd also dearly love to ask Emma to come, but with her bein' in Ireland, and me not knowin' her address, findin' her would be like lookin' for a needle in a haystack.'

'Weren't you goin' to get in touch with the landlord of the Norfolk property you were movin' to, to see if he'd received any mail from her?'

'I was, but with one thing and another I never seemed to get round to it.'

'How about puttin' an ad in some of the Irish newspapers, asking Emma to get in touch?' suggested Margo. 'It'd be a shame for her not to be there, what with her bein' yer oldest friend an' all.'

Libby mulled this over. 'I s'pose it wouldn't harm to give it a go.'

Tom held the door to the chippy open whilst they all trooped through. 'It might be worth tryin' some of your old neighbours as well,' he said as they waited their turn in the queue. 'I bet Emma's tried writin' to at least one of them askin' if they know why you haven't replied to her letters.'

Feeling her heart rise in her chest, Libby tucked her arm through Jack's. 'What a good idea! Because it wouldn't surprise me at all if you were right.'

Jack ordered four portions of fish and chips and settled back to wait. 'It would be wonderful if you could find her.'

'The icin' on the cake,' agreed Libby. 'I miss havin' someone to reminisce with.'

Jack's nostrils flared as the scent of hot battered fish mixed with salt and vinegar invaded his senses. 'That smells good!' he told the girl who was wrapping their meals in the pages of yesterday's *Echo*.

'Best this side of Liverpool,' said the girl as she handed the portions over.

Having paid for their meals, they headed away from the chippy to find a suitable wall to sit on. 'There's nowt better than fish and chips on a cold and frosty night,' Margo said as she took care to unwrap her chips without losing any. 'They warm yer hands and yer tummy at the same time.'

'The perfect end to an excitin' day,' agreed Libby, hurriedly adding, 'although I probably shouldn't say that considerin' everythin' Suzie's been through.'

'Poor kid's had a rough old ride thanks to her dad,' said Jack. 'It must've been even harder without any pals to turn to – cos I'm guessin' she can't have had any real friends with a man like that for a father.'

'Not from what I can gather,' said Libby, 'which is why I thought it might be nice if I went on the milk round with her tomorrow mornin'; show her that we're true to our word when we say we'll stand by her.'

Margo spoke thickly through a mouthful of fish. 'Good idea. I know Bernie's drawn a line under the whole thing, but she's bound to feel awkward after all what's gone on – I know I would.'

Tom licked the salt from his fingers. 'Are you sure it's a good idea for her to be doin' the milk after the whole business with her father? He might be banged up but I bet word's already begun to spread.'

'That's a point...' Margo began, but Libby was quick to intervene.

'Suzie needs to send out a clear message to Callum as well as his criminal pals that she won't be bullied, and she'll not be doin' that if she hides away. Besides, they'd have to be stupid to do owt when she's with Bernie and Goliath.'

An image of the large Suffolk Punch entered Margo's mind. 'Goliath would plough straight through them like they was skittles.'

'If they're anythin' like my aunt and uncle they probably won't get out of their pits till gone ten o'clock, and we're back from the round well before then,' said Libby. 'And even if they were up and at 'em, do we really think they'll want to get involved when Suzie's already proved she's not afraid to grass?'

Margo smiled slowly. 'No chance! As far as they're concerned, she's a loose cannon, which makes her dangerous. If anythin', they'll want to keep out of her way. After all, it's Callum Suzie's got a beef with, not them, and they won't want to give her reason to dob them in to the police.'

'That makes sense,' considered Tom. 'I reckon the only person Suzie has to fear is Callum himself, and he'd be daft to try summat when the scuffers have him under their watchful eye.'

Libby scrunched her chip paper into a ball. 'It wouldn't surprise me if he decided to leave Liverpool until the dust settles, like my aunt and uncle did when they needed to lie low for a while.'

Margo collected everyone's chip paper and looked around for a bin. 'All that tosh about movin' to Ireland when they'd really been hidin' in Blackpool.'

'They probably told people they'd moved to Ireland to throw whoever it was they were tryin' to get away from off the scent,' said Libby.

'Do you think your grandparents are in Ireland, or . . .' Jack left the question hanging.

'They'll be in Ireland all right. Jo and Donny would've used them as a smokescreen.'

'That's the trouble with tellin' porkies,' said Margo. 'Once you start you can't stop, and they always come back to bite you on the bottom!'

Libby took Jack's hand in hers as they began the walk back to the car. 'Talk about weavin' a wicked web. I'm amazed they managed to keep it secret what with my grandparents workin' cheek by jowl with them down Paddy's market,' she said. 'I know the folk from Petticoat Lane would've smelled a rat straight away had my parents tried to pull a stunt like that.'

'Which makes me wonder why only one of the stall-holders had heard of your grandparents. You'd think they'd be well known throughout the market what with them havin' had a stall there,' mused Margo.

Tom answered Margo's question with ease. 'Paddy's market stretches across Great Homer Street and Cazneau Street, so it depends which one her grandparents were on.'

'Not that it makes any difference, not any more,' said Libby casually.

As they approached the car Jack turned to Tom. 'Do you fancy takin' a turn at the wheel?' In answer Tom opened the driver's door and took the crank handle out. Margo gaped at him.

'I didn't know you could drive!'

'Who do you think was drivin' the van when I smuggled you off the mail train?' chuckled Tom.

'I forgot about that! It seems like a lifetime ago now.'

Jack opened the door for Libby. 'The time's flown by since me and Lib got together. I can't believe it's been nigh on a year already.'

Libby snuggled up to him as he joined her on the back seat. 'I wish we could spend Christmas together again.'

'As do I. I did ask my corp, but he said I had more chance of flyin' to the moon.' He withdrew a small package from his jacket pocket. 'I know it's a bit early, but I'd rather give you this before Christmas than after.'

Libby smiled as she unwrapped the small bar of scented soap. 'Lily of the Valley, my favourite – Mum's too, come to that.' She opened the clasp of her handbag and handed Jack an equally small gift. 'Great minds think alike. I hope you like it.'

Jack kissed her on the cheek. 'Shaving soap, and just as mine was running low, too.'

'I know there's nothin' you can do about Christmas,' conceded Libby, 'but how about New Year?'

Jack tucked the shaving soap into his pocket. 'I'm afraid I'm on shift for both, but if it's any consolation, I thought we could go and spend some time with my dad in London – when I manage to get some leave that is. We won't have to fork out for a couple of hotel rooms, so it shouldn't cost much.'

Libby's eyes sparkled as she gazed up at him. 'Oh, Jack, what a wonderful idea. It'll give me a chance to catch up with Pete as well as everyone else.'

Jack lifted her hand so that he could see the engagement ring. 'Dad couldn't believe it when I told him that Mum's ring fit you like a glove.' As he finished the sentence, his lips brushed against hers, and Libby was lost in the warmth of his kiss. So much so, she didn't notice the large animal that dashed across their path as Tom pulled onto the drive which led to the farm.

'Bloody hell!' Tom exclaimed as he swerved to avoid it. 'You never said you kept bears!'

Margo stared wide-eyed in the direction the beast had taken. 'What on earth was that?'

Broken from Jack's embrace, Libby peered out of the window. 'You didn't hit it, did you?'

Tom pulled the handbrake up and swivelled in his seat to face her. 'The car would be knackered if I had! Didn't you see the size of it?' Seeing the sheepish grin on Jack's cheeks, he turned back to face the front. 'I see!'

Libby peered into the darkness. 'Perhaps it was a cow?'

Margo shook her head fervently. 'I'd say it looked more like a dog, but you don't get dogs that big.'

Libby opened the car door and stepped out. 'Well, whatever it was, I'd wager the poor thing's probably scared out of its wits!'

Calling for her to come back, Jack hastily followed her out of the car. 'Where do you think you're goin'? That thing – whatever it is – could be dangerous for all you know!'

Libby waved a dismissive hand. 'Don't be daft. We're in Liverpool, not Africa – it's not as if I'm likely to bump into a lion.'

Tom rolled down his window. 'Not since they closed down Walton Zoo, at any rate.'

Presuming he was joking, Libby laughed, but Tom remained straight-faced.

'I didn't know Liverpool used to have a zoo. Why did it close?' Libby ventured as she took a step back towards the car.

'Cos the animals were allus escapin'. . .' Tom began before being cut off by the sound of slamming doors as Libby and Jack threw themselves back into the car.

'Please tell me you're jokin',' said Margo, looking nervously out of her car window.

'The zoo closed down in the eighteen eighties, so I'm pretty sure we'd have heard by now if any of the animals were still roamin' free.' Tom rubbed his chin in a thoughtful manner. 'How old do lions live to be, do you think?'

The four of them peered into the dark. 'Even if they lived a fair while, they'd be in their sixties by now,' mused Margo, 'although I suppose they could've had kittens, or whatever it is they call baby lions.'

'Cubs,' Libby supplied. 'And it would be a lot easier to see what it was if we could have proper lights on the car.'

Tom selected first gear and began to creep forward, making sure to take his time in case the beast cut across his path again.

'With a bit of luck, it'll be long gone by now—' Margo broke off with a shrill squeal. 'It's there! Right by the door to Rose Cottage.'

Libby leaned over to Jack's side of the car in order to get a better view of the mystery animal. 'That's not a bear!'

'It's a bullmastiff,' said Jack, 'and a big 'un to boot.'

Margo stared in wonderment at the huge dog. 'I ain't never seen a dog that big in my life! Do you think it bites?'

Tom looked at her expectantly. 'Weren't you the one that said that all animals bite?'

Margo paled. 'I've just had a thought! What do you think it'll do if any of the girls decide to come out of the cottage unexpectedly?'

Her words were drowned by the sound of Libby's door closing, closely followed by Jack's as he too leapt out of the car. 'What on earth are you playin' at?' he cried as he stepped in front of her.

'They're as good as sittin' ducks in there, cos they haven't a clue what's waitin' for them on the doorstep,' protested Libby, 'and I for one am not goin' to sit around waitin' to see what happens should one of them decide to come outside. Although havin' said that, I shouldn't imagine he'd do much. He certainly doesn't look vicious to me.'

Jack stared at her in disbelief. 'How do you know it's a he?'

Libby raised her brow, a small smile lifting her cheeks.

Jack held a hand to his forehead. 'Forget I asked,' he said, 'but what makes you think he doesn't look vicious?'

'His hackles aren't raised, and he's not growlin' or snarlin'. If you look closely, you can just about see the tip of his tail wagging ever so slightly. If anythin', he's wary, which is understandable considerin' he nearly got run over just now.'

'My dad always said you should never approach a dog what's scared or backed into a corner,' said Jack.

Libby walked around him, and slowly began to approach the dog. 'We never had a dog, but a couple of the market traders did; they used to let me take them for a walk after school.'

The door to Rose Cottage opened suddenly, sending the dog rushing towards Libby, and Adele appeared in the doorway, spatula in hand ready for the attack. She relaxed as her eyes met Libby's. 'Blimey, Lib, we thought you were Callum.' She called over her shoulder to the others, who were right behind her armed with various kitchen implements. 'It's all right, it's only Lib and . . .' her eyes fell to the dog. 'Oh no, not you again!'

Suzie appeared in the doorway behind Adele. 'Eh?'

Adele nodded towards the dog. 'It's that dog from earlier on.'

Libby looked from the dog to Adele. 'You've seen him before?'

'He was hanging round the yard when I went to check on the cows. I thought I'd scared him off, but obviously not. Where did you find him?'

Getting out of the car, Margo gestured towards Tom. 'Tom nearly ran him over on the drive.'

'No I didn't,' objected Tom. 'It was the dog that nearly ran into me.'

53

Suzie approached the dog with caution, offering him the back of her hand. 'Poor thing must be lost, cos he's in too good a condition to be a stray.'

'Well, he can't stay here, not with the livestock . . .' Adele began before being interrupted by Suzie.

'But you've already tried shooing him away and that didn't work. I think it'd be better all round if he stayed in the barn with us, cos then we wouldn't have to worry about him messing with the livestock.'

'Suzie's got a point,' said Margo. 'It's senseless to shoo him away when we know it doesn't work, and even if it did, we wouldn't be able to point his owner in the right direction should they come lookin' for him.'

There was a short sharp flushing noise before the door to the outside water closet opened and Joyce stepped out. Walking briskly towards them, she grimaced as her eyes settled on the dog, which was being petted affectionately by Libby, Suzie and Margo.

'I see he's back.' She glanced at Adele. 'Although he probably never left in the first place.'

Suzie stared up at her mother. 'I didn't know you'd seen him before?'

'I was with Adele when we tried shooing him out of the yard. I did think it a bit of a long shot cos he was obviously reluctant to leave, but what can you do?'

Jack patted the dog's broad head. 'I don't think the Lewises would want him wanderin' amongst the livestock, but it's a bit late to be callin' the dog warden, beside which we all know what'll happen to him if he winds up in the pound.'

Suzie, Libby and Margo formed a protective ring around the dog. 'He's not goin' to the pound,' said Margo fiercely. 'He's a lovely dog who's done nowt wrong bar get lost, which is hardly his fault! What's more I'd wager he must be hungry, yet he never attacked the livestock.'

'I didn't want to feed him because I didn't want to encourage him to stay,' said Adele, adding over her shoulder as she walked into the cottage, 'but I'd rather he had a full tummy than looked for food elsewhere.' When she reappeared a few seconds later, she was holding a couple of rounds of bread smeared thinly with margarine. She approached the dog, who immediately sat down and offered her his paw.

With cries of 'Aww' and 'What a good boy' from the girls, Adele broke the meagre portion into pieces and held it out for the dog, who took it with unexpected gentleness.

'He's ever so well behaved,' said Suzie. 'I reckon he'd make a brilliant guard dog.'

Joyce wagged a warning finger. 'Don't go pinning your hopes on him staying permanently. This is a one night only deal; tomorrow we find his owners.'

Jack pulled his sleeve back to look at his wristwatch. 'I'm afraid I'm goin' to have to fly.'

Libby walked over to him. 'I forgot about you having to be back by a certain time. I'll give you a bell tomorrow.'

He kissed her on the cheek. 'You can let me know what Bernie said.'

'Bernie?' she asked, puzzled.

He grinned. 'After Suzie and Margo have begged him to let the Hound of the Baskervilles stay on as a sheep dog.'

Libby laughed. 'Collies are quick and nimble. This 'un doesn't look as though he could catch a cold, let alone a sheep!'

'He certainly wasn't bred for speed,' said Jack as he started the car, 'although I wouldn't fancy bein' chased by him.'

'Which is why he'd make a brilliant guard dog,' said Margo as Tom got into the passenger seat. 'We might know he's not got a bad bone in his body, but an intruder wouldn't.'

'If you take him on the milk round with you, word'll soon get back to Callum and he won't dare come near the farm,' said Jack as he inched the car forward.

'Good idea!' said Libby, before calling out, 'Merry Christmas!'

Waving his hand through the open window, Jack called 'Merry Christmas' back before driving out of the yard.

Waving until the car had gone from view, Libby turned her attention to the dog. 'I don't know what we're goin' to feed you, because I'd wager you eat like a horse.'

As if on cue, Suzie came out of Rose Cottage with a bowl of scraps, all of which were gratefully snuffled up by the hungry hound. 'My dad would run a mile if he saw this 'un coming towards him,' she said as the dog checked the bowl for any bits he might have missed.

'I think Jack's right when he says your dad wouldn't dare come to the farm,' said Margo, 'and what's more I don't think any of his lackeys will have a pop at you either.'

'That's not what he thinks,' mumbled Suzie.

'He might like to think they'll rally round, but why would they say owt to you when they know you're not frightened to go to the scuffers? I could be wrong, but I doubt they're that stupid.'

Suzie lowered her voice so that only Libby and Margo could hear what she had to say. 'I might put on a brave face, but deep down I'm worried sick, cos even if they don't threaten me directly, that won't stop them from hurling abuse or spitting in me face, and Bernie shouldn't have to put up with that sort of thing on my account.'

'They wouldn't,' said Libby, if somewhat hesitantly.

'I reckon they'd have Bernie to answer to if they did,' put in Margo, 'cos he won't put up with that sort of behaviour.'

'But he shouldn't have to get involved,' said Suzie.

'I'd already made my mind up to come with you on the round tomorrow,' said Libby, 'because I'd understand if you felt awkward with it just bein' you and Bernie.'

'I would a bit,' Suzie admitted, 'especially if someone did have a go at me.'

Libby folded her arms across her chest. 'If they get out of their beds just to spit at you, then they're in for a nasty surprise.'

'But what can we do about it?'

'Goliath's bound to leave the locals a parting gift at some point on the round,' said Libby. 'Anyone spits at you, and they'll be wearin' it!'

Suzie gasped. 'Oh, Libby, you wouldn't?'

'Damned right I would. Fight fire with fire, that's my motto, and even though I wouldn't stoop as low as to spit at someone, I'm a dab hand at dealin' with manure!'

Suzie beamed as she ruffled the dog's ears between her fingers. 'I can't believe how much my life has changed in just a few hours. I started off the day without a friend in the world, yet here I am with two of the best pals a girl could wish for.'

'I don't think we've done that much . . .' Libby began, but Suzie was quick to intervene.

'You've stuck by me even though I didn't deserve it, and I can't tell you how much that means to someone like me who's always been seen as trouble to be avoided at all costs.'

'Not you, your father,' Margo corrected her. 'Had anyone realised my father was tryin' to pick their pockets whilst I was shinin' their shoes they'd have tarred me with the same brush as him, so there but for the grace of God go I.'

'I don't think I've ever smiled so much as I have today,' said Suzie happily.

'And this is only the start,' said Libby.

'The beginning of a new life,' said Suzie, 'and I'm not going to let anyone – especially my father – stand in my way!'

Chapter Two

Eager to catch Bernie before he happened across the dog, the girls made sure that they were up earlier than usual the following morning so that they could get the work done before explaining the dog's presence and pleading his case.

'He's such a sweetheart, and a gentle giant to boot,' said Margo as they brought the last of the cows in. 'I don't understand how he could've wandered off without his owner knowin', but even if that's the case, how come he hasn't just made his way back home?'

'A lot of merchant ships carry dogs to guard the cargo,' said Suzie knowledgeably. 'He probably went missing whilst they were unloading, and as they're only allowed so much time in the docks they wouldn't have had any other choice than to set sail without him; as the saying goes, time and tide wait for no man – or in his case dog.'

Libby juggled the dog's enormous jowls affectionately. 'We should take a gander down the docks to see if anyone recognises him.'

'They can't have cared for him much,' said Margo defensively, keen to nip the suggestion in the bud. 'I know I'd not let him out of my sight if he were mine, and I'd certainly not let him wander around the docks on his own, what with all them men shoutin' and hollerin' to each other, not to mention the wagons tootin' their horns and the cranes swingin' the cargo around like it was a feather. It's scary enough for me, never mind a dog, not to mention dangerous.'

Libby cast her friend a shrewd glance. 'I knew it was a bad idea lettin' him sleep on your bed.'

'That has nothin' to do with it,' Margo said, somewhat stiffly. 'I just don't want him to go back to someone who never really cared about him in the first place – after all, he might not be so lucky the next time.'

Suzie paused in her milking to gape at Margo. 'You let him sleep on your bed? Where did you sleep, the floor?'

Margo turned her gaze from Suzie to the cow she was tethering. 'He doesn't take up that much room, and I could hardly leave him to sleep on the bare floor where he'd be all cold and lonely.'

Hearing someone clear their throat, the girls turned to see Bernie leaning against the doorframe shaking his head in an admonitory fashion. 'I can see he's played the three of you like a fiddle.' He jerked his head towards Margo. 'You in particular.'

Feeling as though she'd been caught with her hand in the till, Margo began to gabble an incoherent explanation, before Suzie cut her off. 'We would've told you sooner, but he didn't come back to the farm until late yesterday evening and we thought it better for him to bunk down with us for the night rather than make a fuss.'

'We didn't want him roamin' free, cos he could've caused a hell of an accident if he'd wandered onto the road,' added Margo. 'He's really hard to see in the dark, which is why Tom nearly hit him in the first place.'

Bernie looked at the cows in the milking shed. 'You're early with the milking. I don't suppose this would be your way of trying to butter me up?'

'No . . . well, not exactly,' said Margo.

'We wanted to speak to you first so that you knew we weren't trying to be disrespectful by having the dog on the farm without your permission,' said Suzie. 'We would've taken him to the dog warden, but we were worried he might . . . you know.'

Bernie straightened up. 'You acted with your hearts, which is a good thing, cos you need a kind heart when it comes to working with animals, and whilst I agree with you about not taking him to the pound, I do think we should at least try to find his owner before you girls get too attached – if you haven't done so already,' he added, glancing pointedly at Margo.

Encouraged by the thought that they might be allowed to keep the dog should an owner not come forward, Margo voiced her main concern. 'We don't have to take him down the docks, do we?'

'Why? Is that where you think he came from?'

'More than likely,' said Libby, 'because it's easy to see how he could've got lost in the general hustle and bustle.'

'So you think his ship has sailed?' Bernie concluded.

'We reckon so,' said Margo, 'but that wouldn't stop some docker from sayin' the dog was his just so that he could sell him on, or even use him in a dog fight.'

Bernie sank into deep thought before finally coming to a decision. 'We won't take him down the docks, but we will take him on the milk round with us this morning, and if no one recognises him we'll call in at the police station on our way home to see if they've any reports of a missing dog.'

Margo crossed her fingers behind her back. 'And if not?'

Bernie heaved a resigned sigh as the girls eyed him pleadingly. 'Then he'd best start earning his keep – and he'll be your responsibility, *not* mine.'

Grinning from ear to ear, Margo patted the dog's head enthusiastically. 'I promise you won't know he's here.'

'Don't go counting your chickens before they've hatched,' warned Bernie, 'and remember, if someone does come forward we can't refuse to hand him over just cos you don't like the look of them.'

'I know,' Margo said solemnly, although Libby noticed her friend's fingers remained crossed.

'Then let's get this show on the road!' he said. Turning on his heel, he went off to fetch Goliath from his pasture.

'I hope no one recognises him,' said Margo as she finished tethering the cow and placed an empty pail beneath its udders.

'We should be fine as long as we steer clear of the docks,' said Suzie. 'And the quicker we do the round the less chance we'll have of someone claiming him.'

'That's a point,' said Libby. 'We need to get a move on if we're to keep him.'

When Bernie took the milk cart out a short while later, he was accompanied by all three girls, all of whom wasted no time in getting the customers served before moving on to the next street.

'My heart's in my mouth every time someone comes over, cos I'm convinced they're goin' to either say he's theirs or they know who he belongs to,' Margo confessed to Libby.

'I was the same at first, but I spoke to one of the women and she reckons a lot of people are abandonin' their pets because they can't afford to feed 'em.' She stroked the dog's ears as she continued to speak. 'And let's face it, a dog his size isn't goin' to be cheap to feed.'

'We'll manage somehow,' said Margo, in a voice loud enough for Bernie to hear. 'I don't mind givin' him some of my food if it comes down to it.' Libby saw Bernie shake his head with a smile as Margo's words reached his ears.

'I know you've got your heart set on keepin' him,' she said, 'but have you thought about what you're goin' to do when the laundry reopens?'

'We'll cross that bridge when we come to it,' said Margo, quickly adding, 'I wonder if Mr Soo likes dogs?'

'It can't harm to ask,' Libby supposed.

Suzie poured some of the milk into a jug and handed it to Libby. 'I didn't realise you were thinking of leaving Hollybank?'

Libby shrugged. 'We're only at the farm because of the gas leak. Once they've made it secure there's no reason why we shouldn't go back.'

'Apart from the fact that it's safer in the country,' said Margo, 'which is precisely why Tom and Jack wanted us to move to the farm in the first place.'

'I know, and I can understand their concern,' conceded Libby, 'but my heart's in the city, much like yours.'

Margo pulled a doubtful face. 'Before we came to Hollybank I'd have agreed with you one hundred per cent . . .'

Libby looked at her in surprise. 'Are you sayin' that's no longer the case?'

Margo stroked the dog's head in an absent-minded fashion. 'Yes. Despite my initial fears I've found the animals to be sweet-natured, even the pigs, and they all have different personalities – includin' the chickens.'

Bernie laughed. 'All they want is to be looked after. They don't care who feeds and waters them, as long as someone does.'

'That may be so,' said Margo, 'but I kind of feel like they're my responsibility now, almost as if they're my children.'

Libby jumped down from the wagon, ready to pour the milk into whatever vessels the women brought out. 'I didn't realise you felt that strongly.'

'Neither did I until now, and if you were to go back to the city I'd go with you, because we're a team.' She turned hopeful eyes to her friend. 'But I think it only polite that we stay until they find someone to replace us, after them takin' us in an' all.'

Libby felt her tummy lurch guiltily. 'When I said I was a city girl, I wasn't exactly talkin' about Liverpool.'

'Oh?'

'Sorry, Margo, but deciding to get married in London made me realise how much the folk of Petticoat Lane actually mean to me. I suppose I've always known it deep down, but I guess with my parents dyin' and my uncle desertin' me I looked for solace elsewhere, even though that was never goin' to cut the mustard when my heart belonged in London.'

'I thought you said there was nowt left for you in London?'

'And there wasn't at the time, or at least I didn't think so. But with hindsight I reckon I was chasin' rainbows. I was desperate to replace my useless uncle with a proper family, people who were more like my mother, but Jo and Donny have turned out to be just as bad if not worse than Tony, so I'm no better off here than I was back in London. Truth be told, Pete and the rest of 'em down the market are more like a family to me than my aunt or uncle could ever be. In fact, the longer I've been in Liverpool the more I realise what an idyllic life I had in London before Hitler took it away. Leavin' London might've eased my pain at the time, but it also left me with a big hole in my heart.'

'You're really thinkin' about goin' back, aren't you?'

'I rather think I am.'

'Are you *sure* you'd be makin' the right decision? To go back I mean?'

Libby poured some milk into a vase which was being held out to her by a young girl. 'If I'd thought my Uncle Tony would welcome me with open arms, then I'd have gone back as soon as I'd spoken to Jo and Donny. It was his frosty attitude that made me think I had more in Liverpool than I did in London, but that's because I was seein' family just as blood relatives. I realise now that family is far more than that.'

'Do you have any idea as to when you intend to head back?'

Libby took some money off one of the women and handed it to Bernie. 'I'm not rushin' into anythin' quite yet, and as I was the one who persuaded you to stay in Liverpool, I certainly won't be leavin' you in the lurch.'

Margo waved a dismissive hand. 'Don't worry about me. I'll be right as rain as long as I've got my Tom.'

'Are you sure you're not just sayin' that to make me feel better?'

Margo smiled at her kindly. 'We're not joined at the hip, and I'd rather you were happy in London than felt you had to stay in Liverpool because of me. I'm a big girl now, and my future is here.'

'I wish I was as brave as you,' said Suzie, who had been handing out milk nearby. 'I'd leave Liverpool in a heartbeat if only I had the guts.'

Bernie moved Goliath on with a click of his tongue. 'You fended for yourself for a fair while after the May blitz. What makes you think you've not got the guts to go it alone when you've already done so?'

'It's easy to do it in a city which is familiar, and if I had family in London then I'd be off like a shot, but starting a new life in a strange city isn't the same when you're on your tod.' She glanced at Libby. 'Am I right?'

'Very much so,' agreed Libby.

Margo walked beside the cart. 'If you go back to London you won't see Jack anywhere near as often, have you thought about that?'

'Yes, but at the same time Jack could be posted hundreds of miles away at the drop of a hat, so there's no sense in stayin' put on those grounds.'

'True, but what would you do for work?' said Margo. 'I'm not tryin' to put a spanner in the works, I just want to make sure you've thought things through.'

'I've got experience in laundry work, and when I've saved enough money I shall open my own stall down Petticoat Lane.'

Margo pulled a sceptical face. 'Could you really stand to work on the same market as yer uncle?'

Libby gave this due consideration. Working in the same market as the man who stole her parents' stall would be a tough row to hoe, but seeing as he'd practically run said stall into the ground before she'd left for Liverpool, as well as putting the other stallholders' backs up by dealing with the spivs, she very much doubted he'd still be there. She then imagined a complete stranger standing where her father used to do his trading. Would she be able to stop herself from interfering if she thought they weren't doing as good a job as her parents? She turned to Margo. 'Do you think I'm goin' off half-cocked?'

'I think you might be seein' London through rose-tinted specs the same way as you did Liverpool, and we haven't even addressed how you'd feel about seein' yer uncle again knowin' what you know about yer mother's diaries,' Margo finished darkly.

They had been so deep in their conversation they had almost forgotten about the mastiff when a woman approached the cart. Holding her hand out for the dog to sniff, she patted his broad head. 'Hello, my beauty.'

Margo froze, hoping against hope that the woman wouldn't say the dog was hers, and seeing the look on her friend's face Libby crossed her fingers as she asked the dreaded question for her. 'Do you know him?'

'You must be jokin'!' the woman laughed. 'I don't know the sort of folk who could afford to keep a rabbit, lerralone a magnificent beast like this.'

Margo sagged with relief as the woman left with her quota of milk. 'That's the end of the round, so it looks like we've got ourselves a guard dog.'

Bernie turned Goliath in the direction of the police station. 'Not so fast. We've one more stop to make.' He turned his attention to Suzie. 'Do you want to come in with me? See if there's any news on your father?'

Suzie's face dropped. 'You don't think they'd hang him for what he did to me gran, do you? Only I had the most awful nightmare last night.' She shuddered as the image of her father walking to the gallows re-entered her mind. 'I know what he did was really bad, but I don't think he seriously thought our place would get a direct hit.'

Libby squeezed Suzie's hand. 'Your dad's as slippery as an eel, remember?' Suzie nodded, and Libby continued, 'It's just your conscience weighin' heavy on yer mind. I'm sure things won't go that far, especially without any evidence, and there's no way the scuffers are goin' to start searchin' through the rubble when they'd never be able to prove that any loot they may or may not find was put there by him.'

Suzie felt her cheeks redden. 'I know he's a bad man, but he's still my dad.'

'Don't worry, Suzie, I feel the same way about my old man,' said Margo. 'He may be an inconsiderate, selfish swine, but he's my inconsiderate selfish swine.'

Suzie grimaced. 'I just feel so guilty.'

'We can see that,' said Libby, 'but why you're the one that's feelin' guilty when it's your father what's in the wrong is beyond me. Anyone would swear it was your fault he'd wound up in jail.'

'But it is,' said Suzie. 'Had I not made a statement he'd be out on the streets.'

Libby folded her arms across her chest. 'Had he not taken what didn't belong to him in the first place it wouldn't matter what you said. There's only one person to blame for his incarceration and that's him, and you mustn't let him convince you otherwise!'

'Hopefully, a good spell in the cells will make him see sense,' said Bernie. 'From what I've heard the courts are coming down hard on people who've looted bombed-out buildings, and whilst he won't be on the end of a noose, I can't see him getting out any time soon.'

'So he'll have longer to sit and fester,' said Suzie, a rueful look on her face.

Libby tutted impatiently. 'Any normal person would vow never to steal again.'

'Not my dad,' said Suzie. 'He'll just make sure he doesn't get caught next time.'

'There's no helpin' some people.' Libby hesitated. 'I know you said yer dad made yer gran stay behind, but why didn't she tell him to take a runnin' jump? Or was she just as worried about the loot?'

Suzie tutted miserably. 'They'd had a row. She accused him of being greedy when it came to selling the loot on, and that's when Dad really lost it. He said he never actually nicked the stuff but found it on the ground fair and square, and that she ought to feel what it was like to be out in the middle of things instead of tucked away down a shelter. I begged him to see sense, because I knew she couldn't get down the steps without one of us helping her, but he was adamant that she should learn a lesson.'

The three of them stared at Suzie.

'But she was only tellin' the truth,' whispered Margo.

'Which is exactly what I did when I turned him in,' said Suzie grimly.

'Only you're not a defenceless old woman,' said Bernie, 'and neither are you on your own, summat he'll learn when we go into the station.'

'We could all go in,' suggested Margo. 'I daresay he won't see us, but the policeman's bound to mention you comin' in with a bunch of your pals, as well as a big dog, and some feller.'

'It can't do any harm,' said Suzie.

Bernie pulled Goliath to a halt, and they all jumped down from the cart, with Suzie being the one to lead the dog into the station. As they approached the desk Suzie felt the butterflies enter her stomach. It was all very well to put on a brave front, but the thought of hearing that her father was already out soon brought her back down to earth.

Looking up from his position behind the desk, the constable who'd booked her father the day before smiled welcomingly. 'I didn't expect to see you back so soon.'

Suzie patted the counter to encourage the dog to jump up. 'We were wondering if anyone had reported this 'un as missing?'

The constable petted the dog's large head. 'Not that I've heard of.' He turned to the policeman next to him, who shook his head.

'Not a sausage – and I'd wager he could get through a fair few of them given the chance!'

Margo was grinning like the cat that got the cream. 'So does this mean he's ours to keep?'

Bernie chuckled softly. 'No, this means he's yours to keep, remember?'

Margo squealed with delight. 'You're ours now, Thor.'

Bernie blinked. 'Thor?'

'Cos when he growls it sounds like thunder,' said Margo, continuing in lowered tones, 'not that I've heard him growl, mind you, but I reckon it would sound just like that if he did.'

'I'm glad to hear it's not cos he moves like lightning,' chuckled Bernie. 'Cos that would be an out and out lie.'

Libby arched an eyebrow. 'He certainly sounds like thunder when he's snorin' his head off come bed time.'

Suzie cleared her throat, regaining the policemen's attention. 'Can anyone tell me what's happening with my father?'

The constable glanced towards the back of the station. 'He won't be leavin' here any time soon if that's what concerns you.'

Suzie relaxed a little. 'I know he's done wrong, but I honestly don't think he intended my grandmother to die. He just wanted to make her see how dangerous air raids are when you're not down a shelter.'

'Lemme guess. You're frightened he'll be on a murder charge?'

'Will he?'

'Not as far as your gran's concerned, cos it was the Luftwaffe what took her out, not your father. Lootin' from the deceased, on the other hand, carries a lengthy sentence – providin' they find the stuff he stored up the chimney, of course, and I've no doubt they will given the fullness of time.'

Suzie remained quiet. There wasn't a doubt in her mind that her father would have robbed from the dead as readily as he would from the living, if not more so.

Libby jerked her head in the direction of the cells. 'Does he know about this?'

'He certainly does, which is why he's itchin' to be released, cos if some poor sod turns their toes up before we find the stuff he'll be in real strife.'

'You think he's intending to retrieve his loot before people go looking?' Suzie asked.

'Nah,' replied the constable complacently. 'He'll not bother takin' the risk. If you ask me, he'll be out of Liverpool before you can say knife.'

A wave of relief washed over Suzie. 'Do you really think so?'

'I wouldn't have said so otherwise,' he told her. 'They're all the same. As soon as things get tough, they run for the hills. No one wants to be constantly lookin' over their shoulder more than they do already, especially when they're on the rob.'

Suzie visibly relaxed. 'I thought he might come after me and me mam.'

'He was threatening all kinds when he was in here, but that's just hot air. They all do that. He wanted to stop you signing the statement, nothing more.'

'I hope you're right.'

'You see?' said Libby. 'We told you you had nowt to worry about.'

Nodding, Suzie thanked the constable for his help before leading the way out of the station.

One by one they got back onto the cart, sitting Thor in the middle. 'My first dog, and what a beauty he is,' said Margo happily.

'And I can tell me mam that we needn't worry about me dad for a long time yet,' said Suzie.

'All's well that ends well,' said Libby.

Settling onto the back of the cart, Suzie felt a smile form on her cheeks. She was free for the first time in her life, and it felt good!

***

It was the day of Roz's return from Glasfryn and Libby and Suzie were herding the cattle back to the field.

Aware of Roz's imminent arrival, Suzie rubbed her hands together anxiously as she voiced her concerns to Libby. 'I wasn't this nervous when we called in at the police station!'

'What's done is done. All you can do now is apologise and try to move forward.'

'That's going to be easier said than done if they're no longer together because of me,' said Suzie miserably.

Libby patted one of the cows on the rump to encourage it to keep moving. 'If Felix loves her as much as he says he does, then he'll have gone after her, and if he didn't then you have to ask yourself whether he really loved her in the first place.'

Suzie waited for the last of the cows to pass through into the field before closing the gate behind them. 'But men can be such proud creatures, and it can't have been easy seeing Bernie standing there large as life,' she said ruefully. 'I knew what I was doing when I set the cat amongst the pigeons, so I've no one to blame but myself.' She glanced up the track as the sound of tyres crunching on gravel reached her ears, and looked back to Libby wide-eyed. 'She's here.'

Libby gave her an encouraging smile. 'There's no time like the present, and the sooner you clear the air the better.'

Suzie took a deep breath. 'Here goes nothing.' Her stomach fluttering apprehensively, she strode over to Roz, who turned to face her as the taxi pulled away. 'I'm so dreadfully sorry,' Suzie blurted, 'and I don't blame you if you hate me, because I deserve it.'

Roz fixed her with a stern glare, before relenting. 'I won't deny that I was angry at first, but Felix told me what you said on the platform, and at the end of the day I did bring a lot of it on myself.'

Suzie shook her head fervently. 'No you didn't. All you did was try and help my mam because I was behaving like a spoiled brat—' She broke off as Roz's words caught up with her. 'You've spoken to Felix?'

A small smile touched Roz's lips. 'I have indeed.'

Suzie felt a sense of hope begin to rise in her chest. 'Does that mean . . .?'

Roz's smile broadened. 'After you and he spoke, Felix realised he was cutting his nose off to spite his face, so he hopped on the very next train to Glasfryn – with my mother.'

Thinking she had misheard, Suzie repeated, 'Your mother?'

'They met on the platform whilst he was waiting for the train.' Roz eyed Suzie seriously. 'If Felix had got on the train with me as originally planned, he'd never have met my mother, and goodness only knows when we'd have been reunited. All in all, I suppose you could say that everything worked out for the best.'

Wondering why Roz's mother hadn't come to Holly-bank with her, Suzie voiced that very question, finishing tentatively with: 'You've not mentioned your father?'

Roz's smile faded. 'That's because we don't know where he is. He got separated from my mother when they were in Holland and she's not seen or heard from him since.'

Suzie blushed at her own ignorance. 'Where's Holland?'

'It borders Germany, so whilst he's out of the trees he's not far from the woods, if you get my meaning.'

'You must be worried sick,' said Suzie. 'Is there anything I can do to help?'

'It's very kind of you to offer, but my mother's got everything in hand. She spent a large part of Christmas either on the telephone or down the local police station, establishing who she is and what she can do to help the British in their fight against the Nazis. In return she's hoping they'll help her to find him.'

'They will,' said Suzie confidently.

Roz held up her fingers, which were crossed. 'Let's hope so. I said I'd join her just as soon as they find someone to replace me here.'

Hearing Roz talk about her parents brought home to Suzie how badly the Haggartys had treated the refugee. 'I'm embarrassed and ashamed at the way my family behaved towards you, myself included. When people say the Haggartys are the scum of the earth, they're merely speaking the truth.'

76

Roz placed a comforting hand on Suzie's shoulder. 'I won't deny that's the case when it comes to your father, but you really shouldn't include yourself in that statement, because we both know what would've happened had you tried to defy him.' Her features darkened. 'Felix told me what your father did to your gran, and whilst Lilith and I didn't see eye to eye I never wished her any harm. He also said that you were going to the station to make a statement against your father. Did you go through with it?'

'Too right I did! He had a damned nerve standing there like nowt had happened whilst I'd been going out of my mind with worry.'

'That was a very brave thing to do,' Roz told her.

'I don't think bravery came into it,' confessed Suzie. 'I was that angry I didn't care about the consequences. For the first time in my life, I was seeing things as they truly were.'

'How do you mean?'

'That my father was a liar, a thief and a bully. Of course, I suppose I always knew it deep down, but it was easier to blame everyone else than admit the truth.' She hung her head in shame as she continued, 'Mam reckons I was horrible to you because I was jealous, and she was right.'

Roz's brow shot towards her hairline. 'You were jealous of *me*?'

'You had wonderful parents who loved you very much, and I was stuck with a rotten father who cared more for money than he did for me.' She tutted beneath her breath. 'You came to this country with nowt, yet you still had more than I did.'

Roz was left temporarily speechless. 'I never thought for a minute that you were acting out of jealousy.'

'Your parents did everything they could to get you to safety because they love you, while my dad sent me out begging or on the rob – hardly the act of a loving father.'

'I'm certain he does love you in his own way, but with Lilith for a mother he didn't exactly have the best of examples. I mean, what sort of mother encourages her son to steal? Not a good one, that's for sure.'

'That's true,' conceded Suzie. 'Did you know that it was Gran's idea to take in a refugee?'

Roz pulled a downward smile. 'No, but it does explain why Lilith was so chatty and you and your father had faces like a wet weekend.'

Suzie gave an embarrassed laugh. 'We didn't see the point, but she insisted.' A sudden thought entered her mind. 'I can't believe I never asked what happened to your parents when you got separated from them in Germany. Did your mother know that you'd boarded the Kindertransport?'

'She certainly did. You see, my mother knew our plans were scuppered and that if she didn't act quickly we'd be stuck in Germany, so she told a passerby that I was one of the orphans bound for England and that I'd been hit by a car whilst crossing the road.'

Suzie gaped at her. 'She asked a stranger to send you to London on your own?'

'She had no choice. If anyone realised that she was my mother, the game would've been up and I'd have been refused passage.'

'My father would never do anything like that for me,' Suzie said miserably, but Roz wagged a chiding finger.

'I know you think that, but if that were true he'd have left you with your gran instead of insisting you go to the shelter.'

'He didn't leave me with Gran cos he knew I'd have got her out of there,' Suzie said, adding glumly, 'although I bet he wishes he did now.'

'I highly doubt that.'

'He said that I'd have to look over me shoulder every time I left the house if I signed the statement.' She jerked her head in the general direction of the farmyard. 'The others don't think he'll dare come to the farm, but I have my doubts.'

'I'm sure they're right, but you and I both know what your father can be like when someone's rattled his cage, so how about I give you something that'll make him stay away for good?'

'What is it?' Suzie asked, intrigued to know what could wield such power over Callum.

'When your father threw me out, I took a bit of insurance with me in the form of a ration book in the name of a Sheila Derby.' Roz waved a nonchalant hand. 'He'd given it to me a couple of days before, to use when I was doing the shopping, but I wasn't going to do that when it was obviously stolen . . .' Seeing the look of complete horror on Suzie's face, Roz stopped

79

speaking. 'Are you all right? You look as if you've seen a ghost.'

'The ration book,' said Suzie breathlessly. 'Can I see it?'

'Of course. I'll fetch it now—' She broke off as the penny dropped. 'You know who she is, don't you?'

Suzie had lost all the colour from her cheeks. 'I really hope not.'

Roz jerked her head in the direction of Rose Cottage. 'Come on.' Suzie followed her, her mind racing as she hoped against hope that she wasn't correct in thinking that her father had done the unthinkable.

Sheila Derby's father, Bill, was a brutish man with a fearsome reputation. She had only met him a handful of times, but even so, the scars that crossed his face had left Suzie in no doubt that his cut-throat reputation was well earned.

Now, as they entered Rose Cottage, Suzie recalled the fateful night when Bill had lost his beloved daughter to the Luftwaffe. The funeral had been heavily attended by the darker side of Liverpool – all keen to show their allegiance to the Derbys – and Callum had insisted the Haggartys join them, despite Suzie's determination to stay away.

'But I hardly knew Sheila!' Suzie had wailed as her grandmother dragged a comb through the knots in her hair.

'That won't matter to him,' growled Callum. 'If we don't show our faces, he'll see it as a sign of disrespect, and I ain't gettin' on the wrong side of a man like Bill Derby.'

'I ain't stopping you and Gran from going,' Suzie insisted, but her father wasn't having any of it.

'Bill values family, and if I turn up without me daughter, what does that say about our family?'

Suzie had mumbled an incoherent objection below her breath, causing her grandmother to tug the comb even more viciously. 'Don't you go backchatting your father! He's only doing what's best for the family!'

Suzie had hoped they would sit at the back of the church, but Callum had insisted they sit at the front where they could be easily seen. It had seemed to Suzie as though the service would never end, and she was relieved when the vicar led the way out of the church, followed closely by Bill and the rest of his family. She was about to head in the direction of the church gates when Callum waylaid her.

'Where do you think you're goin'?' he hissed.

'We've done our bit,' said Suzie, but Callum was shaking his head.

'We've still to bury her, not to mention the wake.'

Reluctantly, Suzie followed her father to the grave, where, to her horror, Bill fell to his knees. Callum had been one of the first to help the burly man back to his feet, and Suzie had seen him nodding vigorously as Bill gripped him by the shoulder and spoke privately into his ear. Lilith had waited until they were out of earshot of the rest of the mourners before asking her son what Bill had said.

'He wants me to search through the rubble of his old house to see if I can find summat what belonged to Sheila, cos he's got nowt to remember her by.'

Lilith eyed him sternly. 'I take it you said yes?'

Callum rolled his eyes. 'Course I did. I ain't stupid.'

81

He had searched through the building as best he could, but had returned saying that he was sorry, but everything had perished in the fire. Suzie had worried that failure might mean repercussions for her father, but Bill had been grateful that Callum had done his best, and said his loyalty would be repaid.

Now, Suzie sank down on one of the kitchen chairs whilst she waited for Roz to return. Would her father really have pocketed what little Bill had left to remember his daughter by in the hope that he might profit from her death? The answer to her question came in the form of a blue ration book which Roz handed to her wordlessly. Her eyes rested reluctantly on the name and address of Bill's daughter. Taking a deep breath, she handed the book back to Roz, explaining as she did so just who Sheila Derby was.

Tapping the book against the palm of her hand, Roz remained quiet whilst she sought for the correct words. Eventually, she settled for: 'I'd really hoped this would buy you some security from your father, but after what you've just told me I don't think we can do anything other than to give it back to Bill. It may not seem much to us, but it'll mean the world to him.'

Suzie paled. 'And admit what my father did?'

Roz shrugged. 'I don't see that we have much choice, do you?'

'I could say I found it in the street.'

'And do you think he'd believe you?'

Suzie's heart sank. People like Callum and Bill never believed a word that left anyone's lips, because they knew what liars they were themselves. 'No,' she said quietly.

'So, you can do one of two things. You either hand it over, or keep shtum. I can't say I'd blame you for keeping quiet if that's what you choose to do.'

Suzie turned her mind to how broken Bill had been on the day of his daughter's funeral. 'He'd want it, I know he would.'

'I could come with you if you like?' Roz volunteered.

'No!' said Suzie firmly. 'This is my father's doing, so I shall be the one to put it right.'

Roz passed the book back. 'You'll be needing this.'

Suzie pushed it into her pocket. 'I'll let the dust settle on Dad's arrest before I speak to Bill. It'll give me a bit of time to think about what I'm going to say. There's no doubt he'll be pleased to get the book back, but he's going to ask questions for which I don't have the answer – well, not ones I can give him anyway.'

'He'll know it was your dad . . .' Roz began, but Suzie was shaking her head.

'Dad couldn't use a child's ration book bearing a girl's name, and neither could Gran. If Dad didn't try and sell it on then there's only one other reason for him to keep it.'

'But he gave it to me to use, not you.'

'Only because I'd've known where it came from,' said Suzie, 'and if I were Bill and I had to take a punt on who Dad had given it to I'd choose me every time.'

'Which is why I should come along,' Roz insisted, 'so that I can tell him the truth.'

'No, you've done enough already. Leave it with me; I'll think of summat to say.'

'If you change your mind, you know where to find me.'

'I'm glad you're back,' said Suzie as she headed for the door.

'Me too,' said Roz. 'It's been good to clear the air—' She stopped speaking as Suzie opened the door and Bernie came into view, his knuckles poised to knock.

He smiled briefly as he came through to the kitchen. 'Ladies.'

Roz blushed. 'I'm glad you still think that.' She waited until Suzie was out of earshot before stepping straight into an apology. 'I should've put you right on my relationship with Felix. No matter my intention, keeping it quiet was the wrong thing to do, for which I'm sincerely sorry.'

Bernie sat in the seat which Suzie had just vacated. 'I'll admit I was furious at first, but once I'd had a chance to cool down I realised I shouldn't be mad at you. It's not as if we were an item, or owt like that. If you'd come back and said you'd made it up with Felix whilst you were away, I'd be disappointed, but I wouldn't have held it against you. It was Suzie who made me think we had a shot at being a couple and it's my fault I listened to her.'

Roz slid her hands over her face before resting the tips of her fingers under her nose as if in prayer. 'But if I'd told you that Felix and I were going to Glasfryn together you'd never have turned up at the station, no matter what Suzie said.'

'Swings and roundabouts, as my mother would say, but at the end of the day there's no sense in crying over spilt milk,' said Bernie. 'How did it go with Felix? Did you manage to make amends?'

'It took a while – understandably – but we got there in the end.' She smiled. 'I've found my mother.'

Bernie gave a small whoop of joy. 'Now that *is* good news.' He hesitated. 'Unless of course it means you'll be leaving the farm. Are you?'

'Not until you find a replacement.' She lit the stove. 'Cup of tea?'

'Not quite champagne, but it'll do. Now how about you tell me where your mam's been all this time . . .'

***

Libby and Margo were en route to Jo and Donny's house, discussing how to break the news of the upcoming wedding.

'Tell them the truth,' said Margo: 'that you've not set a date, and the weddin's goin' to be in London.'

'I don't know why I'm so worried, cos I don't think they'll give a monkey's that I'm gettin' married, never mind where. Same goes for me Uncle Tony,' said Libby dully. 'What a family!'

'I reckon they'll be interested, if only for the free food,' Margo supposed.

Libby laughed sceptically. 'Not when they'd have to pay a train fare in order to get some.'

'Unless they're expectin' you to pay for it.'

Libby gawped at her. 'How on earth do they expect me to pay for that, along with everythin' else?'

'Your inheritance, remember?' said Margo wryly.

'If they thought that, they'd try and talk me out of it. Why waste my money on a poxy weddin' when it could be spent on them?' Libby sighed. 'I'm only tellin' them cos they're family, but I reckon if my mum were here she'd tell me not to bother, and my dad would suggest I gave 'em the two-fingered salute.'

Margo gave a snort of laughter. 'I wish I'd met your parents – especially your father. He sounds like a right card.'

Libby grinned. 'He was always up to summat – much to my mother's dismay.'

'A loveable rogue,' said Margo warmly.

Libby clapped her hands together, startling Margo. 'That's him to a tee! I know he dabbled in the black market, but only so that he could help those who didn't have enough. He wasn't a spiv or owt like that.'

'Not like his brother, or your mum's sister come to that.' Margo chuckled before adding, 'Imagine if the two of *them* had married . . .'

'A match made in heaven,' groaned Libby. 'Cos they're like peas in a pod. How she had the audacity to run me Uncle Tony down when she's no better is beyond me. In fact, I'd say she's probably worse, judgin' by the amount of contraband she's got stashed in her house; you can barely get down the hallway without bumpin' into boxes containin' goodness only knows what.'

'They make Suzie's father look like an amateur,' said Margo. 'Do you reckon he was tryin' to sell them some of his loot that night we seen him in the Grafton?'

'I'd say so. They're definitely the bigger fish compared to Callum.'

'Do you think they know about his arrest?'

'Bound to,' said Libby. 'I wonder if they know that Suzie was the one who grassed him up.'

'If they do, it might put Suzie's mind at rest regarding payback from his cronies,' said Margo.

'Indeed, but how can we ask without raisin' their suspicions?'

'We can always say we heard some of the women gossipin' whilst we were out deliverin' the milk.'

'Good idea!' said Libby. Turning into the court, she automatically covered her nose with her hand. 'I don't think I'll ever get used to the smell.'

Margo, who'd lived in a similar place in London, shrugged. 'You'd be surprised what you get used to over time.'

Striding to the top of the court, Libby knocked on the Murphys' door and stood back, hoping her aunt would come quickly so that they could get inside away from the foul odour.

'Who is it?' yelled Jo from the other side of the door.

'Libby and Margo,' Libby called back. Hearing the sound of approaching footsteps, they watched as the door opened a crack and Jo peered through suspiciously. Blowing a plume of smoke in their faces, she replaced the cigarette holder between her teeth and opened the door just enough for them to fit through. Quickly closing it behind them, she hurried up the hallway ahead of them, taking care to flip down the lids of open boxes which lined the walls as she passed them by.

Leading the way into the parlour, she half-turned to speak to them over her shoulder. 'What brings the two of you here?'

Libby smiled as she heard Margo mumble 'It's good to see you too' beneath her breath. 'We thought it would be nice to have a bit of a catch-up,' said Libby. She cast an eye around the room and its everlasting turnover of hooky goods, from bottles of whisky and nylon stockings to tins of fruit. The parlour was an Aladdin's cave of procured wonders.

'Oh aye,' said Jo uninterestedly. She picked up a few unlabelled tins from the Chesterfield two-seater sofa and stacked them haphazardly on top of more tins labelled *Ox Tongue*.

Brushing the seat free of bits with the palm of her hand, Libby sat down. 'We've been meanin' to pop by ever since movin' to the farm,' she fibbed, 'but we haven't had time what with one thing and another.'

'Been busy, have you?' Libby could tell by the sound of her aunt's tone that she had no wish to hear about their life at the farm.

'Very,' she said, 'otherwise I'd have dropped by to tell you the good news earlier.'

Jo eyed Libby hungrily as she abandoned her efforts to conceal a box of brandy beneath an old blanket. 'Have you heard from your parents' solicitors?'

Libby frowned as she held out her hand to show off her ring. 'No, I have not. I'm engaged.'

Jo's face fell in an instant – this clearly wasn't what she thought of as being good news. Forcing her lips into a false smile, she glanced fleetingly at the ring. 'Congratulations.'

Annoyed at the older woman's lack of enthusiasm, Margo spoke up. 'Well, I think it's wonderful news.'

'As do I,' replied Jo, albeit half-heartedly.

I've told her over and over that I haven't a penny to my name, thought Libby as she stared at her aunt, *yet she clearly thinks I'm lyin'. Why else would she ask if I'd heard from my parents' solicitors?*

Jo picked up a couple of mugs, whilst fishing out a third from under some newspapers. 'Cuppa tea?'

Seeing the mould swimming in the third mug, Margo shook her head. 'Not for me, thanks.'

Jo shrugged. 'Suit yourself.' She looked to Libby, who tried to stop herself from grimacing.

'Yes, please.'

Margo scowled at Libby as Jo went off to make the tea. 'She could at least have pretended to be happy for you, the miserable so-'n'-so.'

Libby agreed. 'It's obvious that she thought the solicitors had unearthed some forgotten fortune, which is why she was lookin' disappointed.'

Margo rolled her eyes. 'When is she goin' to give up that particular ghost?'

'I don't think she ever will.'

Jo came back into the room with two cups of tea, and Libby could tell by the feel of the mug and the colour of the tea itself that she hadn't bothered to make a fresh brew. Tentatively sipping the lukewarm liquid, she turned the conversation to a different subject.

'Is it true that Callum Haggarty's been banged up for killin' his mother?'

Spluttering as she choked on her tea, Jo wiped the liquid from her chin. 'Where the hell did you hear that?'

'When we were deliverin' the milk,' said Margo. 'Everyone's talkin' about it, so it must be true.'

'Someone said his daughter had summat to do with it,' continued Libby, who was unsurprised to see her aunt showing more interest in Callum Haggarty than in her own niece's wedding.

Jo's face crumpled in disgust. 'Turnin' on your own family. I call that bloody disgustin'. He should've given her a damned good beltin' when she were still young enough to learn right from wrong.'

A small disbelieving laugh escaped Margo's lips before she could stop it. *Talk about the pot callin' the kettle black,* she thought. *Jo couldn't tell the difference between right and wrong if it slapped her in the face!*

'So, it's true then?' said Libby, hoping her aunt would elaborate on the matter.

'I'm not sayin' that, and neither will you if you know what's good for you, especially when the likes of Callum Haggarty are involved. But if the rumours are to be believed, and I'm not sayin' they are, mind you, then that Suzie should watch her back.'

Libby felt her heart quicken in her chest. 'Why would she need to do that if Callum's locked up?'

'Because he won't be locked up for ever,' said Jo. 'He'll be out sooner or later and when he is he'll want them that sent him away to pay.'

Remembering she was meant to be ignorant as to the ins and outs of the arrest, Libby had to stop herself from remarking that Callum probably wouldn't get out for some time yet.

'I'm surprised he hasn't got someone to have a word in her shell-like,' said Margo. 'See if they can persuade her to retract her statement.'

Libby froze, waiting for her aunt to question how Margo knew so much, but she didn't seem to notice. 'Puttin' the screws on someone what would squeal on their own flesh and blood?' she cried, her eyes rolling in astonishment. 'He ain't got a cat in hell's chance of doin' that, not when the girl's got a gob like a foghorn.'

Margo and Libby exchanged glances. It was the answer they had been expecting, but it was still good to hear that Suzie was safe whilst her father remained behind bars.

***

Callum roared with anger as the judge passed a six-month sentence on what Callum thought of as petty crimes.

'I didn't even nick 'em,' he spat as he shoved the constable who was trying to escort him from the court-room. 'I've been set up by that ungrateful brat and that tart of a mother of hers. They won't be happy till they see me on the end of a rope, and I can prove it too if you'd let me out of these cuffs.' He scowled at the two constables who had come forward to help the first. 'Get yer bleedin' hands off of me!' He tried digging his heels in, but three against one was too much. *Six months for stealin' a few poxy watches*, thought Callum as he was half-shunted, half-dragged back to his cell. *If the judge thinks six months is a justifiable amount of time for a pickpocket, what'll he give me if they find the stuff I had stashed up the chimney?* His throat bobbed nervously. He knew for a fact that some of the items belonged to people who'd died in the bombings, because he'd seen their bodies with his own eyes. Sweat pricked his forehead as he recalled someone he'd come across whilst looting one of the buildings. The victim had been mostly buried beneath the rubble, but there had been a hole just big enough for them to look out of. As their eyes met Callum's, he knew he must act swiftly, so he'd bricked over the gap, knowing that they'd never be found, at least not alive. The memory washed over him like detritus entering the drains. *It's payback*, Callum thought now; *they're reachin' out from beyond the grave to make sure I hang.* He paused as another, more hopeful, thought entered his mind. What if they were alive? He'd assumed they hadn't survived, but what if they'd been rescued in the nick of time? He'd not be done for stealing from the dead, and . . . he felt the bottom drop out of his stomach. They'd tell the court how he'd bricked them up before leaving them to die. He could hope they'd not remember what he looked like, but if the court really wanted to make an example of him there might be a picture of him in the *Echo*, which could just be enough to jog the person's memory.

He grimaced as the image of a noose flashed before his eyes. *And all because Suzie opened her big mouth,* he thought bitterly. *Well, she ain't goin' to get away with it, not whilst there's still breath in my body!*

***

Libby and Margo stepped out of the taxi and were immediately greeted by an anxious Suzie.

'How did it go?' she asked, wringing her hands in anticipation. 'Is he out, or . . .?'

Libby grinned. 'Six months!'

Suzie whooped for joy. 'I never dreamed he'd get that long.'

'Neither did Callum,' said Margo darkly. 'He was spittin' feathers when they led him away.' She glanced at Joyce, who was standing nearby. 'He was callin' the two of you all sorts, sayin' you'd not be happy until you saw him on the end of a noose!'

Joyce rolled her eyes. 'Typical Callum, blamin' everyone bar himself.'

Suzie wrinkled her brow. 'But what's me mam got to do with him picking pockets?'

'Goodness only knows, but he appears to be holdin' the two of you accountable for his wrongdoings,' said Libby.

'This is all my fault,' said Suzie miserably. 'I wish to God I'd never seen him on that bloomin' platform.'

Roz picked up the wheelbarrow they'd just filled. 'Thank God you never gave Sheila's ration book back.'

Joyce nodded sternly. 'As a parent myself I know how much that book would mean to her father, but we'd be giving up the only bargaining chip we have.'

'But what will we say?' asked Suzie. 'Cos he's going to be mad as fire when he knows we've still got it.'

Roz smiled slowly. 'Don't you worry about that. He gave the book to me, so I'll be the one that does all the talking.'

Suzie was shaking her head. 'I'm not going to let you put your neck on the line,' she began, but Roz cut her off.

'I've never had the chance to tell Callum what I think of him, and this would give me the perfect opportunity.'

'Me too,' said Joyce firmly.

'You aren't going without me,' said Suzie.

'We'll all go,' Roz decided.

'But what will we say?' Suzie asked for the second time.

'That unless Callum leaves Liverpool we'll take the book to Bill and tell him exactly where we got it from,' said Roz simply. 'That way the ball's in his court. He can either agree to our terms or suffer the consequences.'

'And what if he does the latter?' Adele put in.

'Then he'll be leaving Liverpool anyway,' said Roz, stony-faced.

'Callum might be a fool, but he's not stupid,' said Joyce. 'He'll take the easy route out, just as he always does.'

Relief swamped Suzie. 'Thank goodness you saw fit to keep that book, because we'd be knackered without it.'

'If it's any consolation, Bill Derby is a vile thief who wasn't past raising a hand to the women in his life – including Sheila, I might add,' said Joyce sombrely, 'and whilst I feel for his loss, there's not a doubt in my mind that he would've tried to use her coupons for his own benefit had your father handed it over.'

'I know they say all's fair in love and war, but using your dead daughter's ration book? That's despicable,' Adele said reprovingly.

'Are you sure Bill would be angry with Callum if he was goin' to do the same thing himself?' said Libby.

'I reckon so,' said Margo. 'Bill would see it differently, cos Sheila was his daughter.'

Libby whistled softly. 'Callum will rue the day he ever lied to Bill, that's for certain.'

'He'll be furious when he finds out, but there won't be a damned thing he can do about it,' Suzie agreed.

Joyce was beaming. 'I'm sorry to say it, Suzie love, but this has to be the best day I've had in years.'

'Don't mind me,' said Suzie. 'I'm as relieved as you are!'

'Then why don't we do summat to celebrate?' Margo suggested.

Joyce's smile broadened. 'Such as?'

'How about we all have a bite to eat at Lyons?' suggested Adele, who very much enjoyed the pastries there in particular.

Margo licked her lips. 'Their penny buns are simply the best!'

Joyce gazed into the distance wistfully. 'I don't know the last time I went to Lyons for a penny bun, but it must've been before I met your father, because he never took me, that's for sure.'

Suzie eyed her mother curiously. 'How did the two of you meet?'

Joyce chuckled softly. 'I suppose it must be hard for you to imagine how I was ever attracted to someone like Callum, but he was very different back in the day, or at least I thought he was at the time. You see, I was running some messages for my parents when I bumped into Callum in one of the shops. I'd just got to the till when the shopkeeper accused your father of stealing a bottle of summat or other, I can't remember what. Of course, Callum denied it to the hilt, saying he'd never do such a thing and that the older man must've imagined it.'

'I doubt it,' said Suzie pessimistically.

'Quite,' Joyce agreed, before continuing, 'The man insisted on searching him, and Callum allowed him to do so, knowing full well that he wouldn't find anything because he'd already got rid of it.'

'How do you know he'd nicked summat if the man never found owt?' Margo asked.

'Callum was waiting for me when I got out of the shop. I thought he wanted my opinion on what had just happened, but it turned out he wanted to look in my bag.'

'Why?' chorused Libby and Adele, but Suzie already knew the answer.

'That's where he dropped the bottle, wasn't it?'

Joyce pulled a face. 'I was horrified at first, and told him he should take it back, but he said he'd only nicked it to pay the man back for accusing him unfairly.'

'What stopped you from turning him in?' asked Roz curiously.

Joyce blushed. 'I know I should have, but he had the most handsome smile, and he looked at me with them big brown eyes of his as though I were the only woman in the world.'

'But he was a thief!' cried Suzie.

'I know! But he was also a risk-taker, someone who flew by the seat of their pants, who wasn't afraid to do what they wanted when they wanted. In short, he was everything I wanted to be and I was besotted with him.'

Suzie's lips parted. 'You wanted to be a thief?'

'No, I wanted to be able to make my own choices without worrying what my parents were going to say, but most of all I didn't want to marry Walter Winthorpe.'

'Who's Walter Winthorpe?' asked Libby.

'He ran a stall down the Greatie. My parents thought he was the bees' knees cos he went to the same church as them, but I couldn't bear him. He believed a woman should be kept in her place and he wasn't shy as to who knew it. Callum treated me as an equal – or he did at the time.'

'He included you in his act, which made you feel special?' hazarded Roz.

'It sounds stupid, of course it does, but I was a sixteen-year-old girl who knew nothing of the world. Callum was full of charm and confidence and I believed every word that left his lips because he made me feel special.'

'But if your parents wanted you to marry that awful Walter feller, how did you get them to agree to let Callum come courting?'

She grimaced. 'They'd never have let me go out with a feller like Callum, so we met in secret. It was thrilling to sneak around behind my parents' back, and Callum was very attentive, which I mistook for love.' She blushed to the roots of her hair. 'I was a stupid fool who fell for good looks and a silver tongue, but getting pregnant out of wedlock was the last straw for my parents, and they threw me out. In my naïvety I ran to your father in the hope that he'd be supportive, but needless to say Callum didn't want to be lumbered with a pregnant woman. He saw me as a burden who'd got pregnant on purpose just to escape my parents. But he took me in – albeit begrudgingly – and when he agreed we should wed I honestly believed everything was going to work out just fine. Only married life wasn't for Callum, or not marriage to me, at any rate. I tried to get him on the straight and narrow, but that only riled him because he said I was trying to change him and he'd never let any woman do that. I did hope that things might be different once you were born, but he didn't show any interest in you until you could walk. The moment he realised you could get through gaps that he couldn't, he used to take you out on the rob with him, and you soon became the apple of his eye.'

'I remember those days,' said Suzie softly. 'Dad used to tell me that I was the best at getting into small spaces, and he couldn't do his work without me by his side. I felt so special.'

'Your father's good at making women feel that way – but only when it suits him.'

'Couldn't you have gone back to your folks?' asked Margo, her voice hoarse with sympathy.

Joyce reeled at the very thought. 'It was bad enough I caught out of wedlock, but to marry a common thief? My father would've gone to hell first, and Callum knew it.' She sighed. 'I eventually realised that it was never going to work out, and things went rapidly downhill from that point on.'

'How?'

'Callum knew I disapproved of him and the way he was bringing you up, and it quickly got to the point where we couldn't stand the sight of each other. I only had to look at him the wrong way and I'd get a backhander straight across the chops. He said he'd made the worst decision of his life by marrying me, and it suddenly struck me there was only one way out for him.'

Suzie swallowed. 'You really think he might've murdered you?'

Joyce shrugged. 'I didn't know, and I wasn't hanging around to find out.' She smiled sympathetically at her daughter. 'If I could've taken you with me, I'd have done it in a heartbeat, but with no job or money I couldn't look after myself, never mind a child, and I had no reason to believe your father would ever mistreat you the way he did me. If I'd've taken away his special little girl, who knows what he'd have done to me?'

'I can guess,' said Suzie, 'and I don't blame you.'

Roz clapped her hands together, startling everyone. 'This is a time to celebrate, not dwell on the past. If we get a move on, we'll soon have the farm work done and dusted, and be in the city in time for tea and whatever else takes our fancy.'

'We could go dancin' at the Grafton,' suggested Margo.

Joyce's face lit up, but only briefly. 'I'd love to, but I can hardly go dancing in dungarees.'

Libby beamed. 'Margo and I have a few dresses between us. One of them's bound to fit you – Suzie too, come to that.'

'Only I can't dance,' said Suzie.

Libby tucked her arm through Suzie's. 'Not to worry. It's as easy as countin' to three!'

It had been with great enthusiasm that the girls got ready for their evening out, and it hadn't taken Suzie long to get into the swing of things.

Libby sank down beside Margo. 'Isn't it good to see Joyce and Suzie having so much fun?'

'They certainly danced circles round the rest of us,' noted Margo. 'I got a stitch in my side just watchin' them.'

'I can't believe Joyce has had to hide away all these years because of Callum,' said Libby. 'How can one man hold so much power?'

'He had her over a barrel, but all that's changed now that they have Sheila's ration book, may she rest in peace.'

'It makes you realise how lucky we are to have men like Tom and Jack,' said Libby. An image of Margo running through Petticoat Lane market to escape her father entered her mind. 'Real men don't hit women; my father wouldn't have dreamed of raisin' a hand to me or Mum.'

Margo watched as Suzie and Joyce danced a quick-step. 'Do you think your father ever brought your mother here?'

'I know he did,' said Libby, 'because I've started to read her diary from the beginning.'

'I thought you weren't going to do that, in case you read summat you shouldn't?'

Libby smiled fleetingly. 'And look where that got me! Imagining all sorts of scenarios that just weren't true.'

'And are you pleased that you changed your mind?'

'Definitely; in fact I wish I'd done it sooner. I'd assumed that Mum and this feller had been sneakin' round behind me dad's back for ages, but nothin' could be further from the truth. It really was a spur of the moment thing – just as Jack suggested – and I know that she instantly regretted her behaviour, sayin' it was an act of desperation in a time of deep depression.'

'At least you know that she never saw him again.'

'No, I don't, I can only *assume* she never saw him again, but I'll never know for certain unless I find the rest of her diaries.'

'If you're right about your uncle knowin', how do you think he found out?'

'Do you remember when I told you that Tom had the hots for you, and you asked me how I knew?'

'You said it was the way he looked at me,' said Margo.

'Exactly! I think Uncle Tony probably noticed the way they were around each other.'

'Do you think he ever confronted her?'

'If he did, she must've denied it, else my father would've found out.'

'So why d'you think he didn't believe her?'

'My mother was a true-blue churchgoer, who believed you should always tell the truth. There's no way she could've lied convincingly, so Uncle Tony would've seen straight through her.'

'Surely your father would've noticed that summat was awry as well?'

'I think he was too caught up in his own misery to see what was goin' on under his own nose,' said Libby sadly.

'I bet Tony was dyin' to say summat to yer dad.'

'Absolutely, but how could he without any evidence?'

Seeing Suzie approach, the girls drew their conversation to a close. Sitting down with a whump, Suzie indicated her mother, who was now dancing with Adele. 'I don't know how she does it. She's running rings around me!'

'Around all of us,' agreed Libby. 'Where did she learn to dance, I wonder? I can't imagine Callum takin' her out to tread the boards.'

Suzie tutted loudly. 'The only dance he does is with the devil. Nah, it was Elsa – the woman who helped her to escape from him – what taught her how to dance.'

'Elsa must be one heck of a good friend,' said Margo, 'keepin' your mother's whereabouts secret all them years.'

Suzie fanned her face with her hand. 'It took guts to do what she did, cos let's face it, Dad would've given her a right good hiding if he'd found out she'd helped me mam to get away from him.'

'Now that you know you have nothin' to fear from your father or his cronies, what do you think you'll do? Stay at the farm? Or maybe find work in the city?'

102

Suzie laughed sarcastically. 'I may've escaped my father, but I'm still a Haggarty, and I'll never escape that whilst living in Liverpool. I only have one option: as soon as peace is declared I shall leave Liverpool for good.'

'What about your mum?'

'Mam's been saving for a smallholding, but that's not for me. I wanna do summat different with my life.'

'Like what?'

'I dunno, cos I've never really tried my hand at anything bar begging and thieving.' She grinned. 'And as I don't plan on making either of them my career, I'll probably have to try my hand at a few things before I find summat I like.'

'Jack seems to think that there'll be plenty of opportunities once the war's over,' said Libby, 'especially for someone who's not afraid of hard work.'

Margo paused before taking a sip of her drink. 'Have you thought about where you'll go?'

'Wherever the wind takes me,' Suzie said happily.

'Now doesn't that sound good!' sighed Libby.

***

The next day, Suzie was still revelling in her new-found freedom. 'Dancing's got to be the best thing in the world!' she told Libby and Margo as they walked down to the meadow to bring the cows in for milking.

'It's even better with a feller,' said Margo, causing Libby to laugh. 'Well it is!' Margo persisted.

'I very much doubt any feller would want to ask me to dance,' murmured Suzie.

'Because you're a Haggarty?' Libby ventured.

'No. Because of this,' said Suzie, drawing an invisible ring around her face.

'What do you mean by that?' asked Margo, confused.

'That I'm no oil painting,' Suzie said simply.

'Whatever makes you say summat like that?' asked Libby sternly. 'There's nowt wrong with the way you look.'

'When Dad used to send me and Roz out begging he said that Roz should do the talking because the punters preferred someone with a pretty face.'

'That was just your father bein' spiteful,' scowled Libby, ''cos you're pretty too.' Seeing the disbelief radiating from Suzie, she decided to elaborate. 'You're both pretty but in different ways. A woman once told me that there's a cover for every pot, meanin' that everybody likes summat different. Not all men like blondes, just as not all women like big muscular men, no matter what Hollywood tries to tell us.'

Margo grinned. 'Just as there's a Tarzan for every Jane, there's a Robin Hood for every Maid Marian.'

Suzie looked perplexed. 'You've lost me.'

'Johnny Weissmuller plays Tarzan the ape man. He's big and strong and wears nowt but a pair of briefs made from leather, whereas Errol Flynn – who plays Robin Hood – is a more refined character who—'

'—wears tights,' cut in Libby with a giggle. 'I know which one I'd prefer.'

As Margo said 'Errol', Libby said 'Johnny', which made them all laugh. 'So don't be listenin' to the likes of yer dad,' Libby went on, 'cos he doesn't know what he's talkin' about.'

'Why am I the only one with a rotten father?' said Suzie.

'You're not,' said Margo. 'My dad used to force me to dress as a boy so I could work as a shoeblack.'

Suzie ran an eye over Margo's beautiful golden locks. 'How on earth did you pass for a boy?'

Margo piled her hair on top of her head. 'I used to wear me hair under a cap, and Dad used to smear boot polish on me cheeks cos he said it was the sign of a good shoeblack.'

Libby opened the gate to the meadow and they stood to one side, allowing the cows to filter through. 'Your mother's parents didn't sound like nice people either,' she said to Suzie.

'Worse than my dad in my opinion,' Suzie agreed. 'How anyone could turn their backs on their own daughter – especially when she'd got preggers out of wedlock – is beyond me.'

'My uncle was the same after my parents died,' Libby told her. 'He made it plain he didn't want any-thin' to do with me – still doesn't, for that matter. My Auntie Jo might not be my idea of an aunt, but she did take me and Margo in after our first flat got bombed.'

'Your first flat? How many flats have you had?'

'Just the two,' said Margo. 'We got bombed out of the first, and as you know our current flat's out of bounds because of the ruptured gas pipe.'

Suzie looked fearfully towards the farm. 'They say these things come in threes . . .'

'My old house in London got flattened by the Luffwaffe,' said Libby, 'so that's my three.'

'You're like a cat with nine lives,' said Suzie. 'How do you know your current flat is still unsafe?'

'I suppose we don't,' said Libby. She continued thoughtfully, 'Come to think, it's probably safe by now, considerin' we've been here over a fortnight.'

'So why haven't you gone to look?'

Libby quickly fielded a cow who'd decided to go to a different meadow. 'That's a bloomin' good question, Suzie,' she called out over her shoulder.

'So what's the answer?'

Libby headed back towards them. 'That we're comfortable here,' she said, much to her own surprise. 'Which is odd, because I never thought I'd prefer it to the city.'

Margo made a clicking noise with her tongue, bringing Thor to her side. 'If I go back, I won't be able to take Thor with me. Not only that, but I don't particularly want to go back to the laundry. I like the girls, and I'm ever so fond of Mr and Mrs Soo, but there's a real feelin' of comradeship here, and you don't get that livin' in a city.'

'What I don't understand,' said Suzie, 'is why you came here rather than go back to your aunt's?'

A grin split Margo's cheeks. 'You've obviously never met Libby's aunt; you'd understand why if you had.'

'Can't be any worse than my old man,' said Suzie. 'Didn't she feel put out when she heard you were coming here instead of going to her?'

'No, because she knew we were out of work and would have no money to contribute to the household like we did last time.'

'Contribute?' cried Margo, her brow rising swiftly. 'I reckon we were payin' the whole of the rent, not to mention all the grub we provided. We must've saved them a small fortune by movin' in.'

'That's true.'

'And we done all the cookin' and cleanin'. The place was unrecognisable when we left. Not that it took them long to turn it back into a hovel,' Margo went on glumly.

'Are you goin' to stay on the farm, then?' Libby asked.

'For the time bein'.'

'And the future?'

Margo spread her arms wide as they herded the cows into the shed. 'Can any of us truly say what we're goin' to do in the future when we don't know what tomorrow will bring?'

'I s'pose not,' Libby conceded. 'But after bein' made homeless three times, I know there's always a tomorrow whilst there's breath in yer body.'

'You're right,' Margo said, tethering her nearest cow to a ring. 'Deal with each problem as it crops up, and don't worry about tomorrow until you get there.'

'I was adamant I wanted to move back to London,' said Libby, picking up a milk bucket and placing it beneath the nearest cow, 'but who knows what'll happen given the fullness of time?'

'Do you not like it in Liverpool, then?' asked Suzie as she deftly dodged a cow which had chosen to relieve itself in front of her.

'I love Liverpool and the people in it,' said Libby, 'but it doesn't hold any memories for me, not like London. When we first came here, I hoped I might be able to work for my grandparents on their stall, because it would make me feel close to my parents again, but Paddy's market isn't Petticoat Lane. I don't know any of the traders and they don't know me. Market tradin' is in me blood; it's all I've ever wanted to do. I love everythin' about it, from the quirky customers to the smell of chestnuts roastin', not to mention bein' yer own boss.'

'Your own boss, eh? Now, that does sound good,' sighed Suzie wistfully. 'I'd like to do summat like that. No one to answer to . . .'

Worried that she might've given Suzie the wrong impression, Libby quickly broke in. 'It's not quite that simple: you still have to keep the market inspector sweet, cos he's the one who gives you a pitch. So, while you are yer own boss, you can't turn up just when you fancy and do as you like or he'll give your pitch away to someone else . . . unless you're my Uncle Tony, of course, in which case you can do as you bleedin' well please as long as you pay the inspector to turn a blind eye.'

Suzie passed her bucket to Margo, who poured the contents into one of the churns. 'How do the other traders feel about that?'

'They don't like it,' said Libby grimly, 'but they don't say owt cos they don't want to upset the people Tony deals with.'

'Spivs,' said Suzie wisely.

'I reckon some of them are worse than spivs,' Libby replied darkly.

'How on earth did he get a job working on the market in the first place?' Suzie asked, before jumping to the wrong conclusion. 'Or did he give the inspector a backhander for that an' all?'

'Even worse,' said Libby, and went on to explain everything that had happened after her parents' demise. 'I know he's lyin',' she finished, 'because his story about winnin' the money on the gee-gees was the stuff of fantasy.'

'So why did you leave him to run the stall if you don't believe he bought it fair and square?' asked Suzie.

'Cos even though I'm positive he got Dad to sign the paperwork before he'd handed over the readies, I've no actual proof.'

'But why would your father do that?'

'Because Uncle Tony strung Dad along until the day we were leavin', knowin' that Dad would either have to agree to his terms then or leave London with the business unsold.'

'Sneaky beggar,' said Margo. 'He knew what he was doin' all right.'

Suzie unleashed the cow she'd finished milking. 'Aren't you furious?'

'I was beyond furious,' admitted Libby. 'So much so, I couldn't stand to be in the same city as him knowin' what he did, but not bein' able to prove it.'

'If he said he paid your father for the business, why didn't you ask where the money had gone?'

'I did. He said it must still be at my parents' house. I called his bluff, sayin' I'd happily search the rubble meself just to prove him a liar, and guess what happened a couple of days later?'

Suzie shrugged.

'Someone torched the house, and it doesn't take a genius to work out who did it. Of course he denied it, even convincing folk the money must have been burned because someone found two charred five bob notes amongst the debris.'

Suzie was shaking her head fervently. 'That is exactly the sort of thing my father would do.'

Libby choked at the very suggestion. 'Set fire to his own money?'

'If it meant he got summat at a knock-down price – yes. And while you say that it was two notes, how do you know it wasn't one note torn in two which he'd deliberately scorched to make it look as though they'd been in the fire?'

Libby stared at Suzie. 'It never even occurred to me.'

'That's because you don't think like they do,' said Suzie, hurriedly pressing on, 'and neither do I, but after living with me dad for as long as I have I know how their minds work. Devious as the day is long, and sharp as a tack when it comes to money. There's not a doubt in my mind that your uncle's responsible for the fire as well as the charred money, cos no one else had anything to gain from setting fire to a pile of bricks.'

Libby staggered a breath. 'I wish the other stallholders had believed me instead of takin' his side. He played them like a flamin' fiddle, makin' me look like the bad one.'

'That's what they do,' said Suzie.

'And it worked,' said Libby. 'Even though I tried to fight my corner, the weight of everyone else takin' his side . . .' She shrugged helplessly. 'It was pointless for me to continue accusin' him when it was fallin' on deaf ears.'

Margo shook her head angrily, her blonde curls bouncing around her shoulders. 'I don't know how that man sleeps at night.'

'Cos it's like water off a duck's back to folk like that,' said Suzie. 'I'm pretty sure Dad ended up believing his own lies half the time.'

'You didn't, though – believe his lies, I mean,' said Libby.

Suzie pulled a rueful face. 'I'd like to say I didn't, but what are you supposed to do when you've only got one person's version of events?'

'I can see that with your mum,' said Margo, 'but you must've realised it was his fault that your gran died.'

Suzie lowered her gaze. 'I blamed my mam for Gran's death.'

Libby looked at her aghast. 'How on earth could you blame yer mother when she wasn't even there?'

'I blamed her *because* she wasn't there,' said Suzie, much to the confusion of the girls. 'You see, as far as I was concerned everything was all right before me mam left. Dad never blamed me for owt, or sent me begging, but only because Mam was there to take the blame. But after she left, no one was allowed to mention her name, and if he heard me so much as ask any of the neighbours if they'd seen her he'd fly into a rage – saying

111

that I shouldn't ask questions and that I was to forget about me mam.'

'Which made him look guilty,' said Libby.

'Exactly. From that day on, I took the blame for anything that went wrong whether it was my fault or not. He never hit me, mind, but you could tell he wanted to.'

'So how do you think your mother's presence would've changed what happened to yer gran?' queried Margo.

Suzie shrugged. 'I don't think it would, not really. I guess I just needed someone else to blame.'

'You're better off without him,' said Margo, adding by way of explanation, 'just like me with my dad.'

'I know that now,' said Suzie, 'but everything's clearer with the benefit of hindsight.'

'You're right there,' said Margo. 'I know my parents only had me to try and save their marriage, which is ludicrous considerin' my mother was an alcoholic and my father was up to his eyeballs in debt.'

Their conversation was interrupted by Bernie, who called out a cheery 'Mornin', ladies' as he entered the shed. 'I hear you spent last night dancing your cares away.'

'We certainly did,' said Suzie happily. 'It was the best night of my life.'

'It does you good to let your hair down every now and then,' he said, hefting Goliath's harness over his shoulders. 'How far away are you from being ready to load up?'

Libby did a quick head count of the cows left to milk. 'We'll be ready by the time you are.'

'Good-o. Who do I have for company this morning?'

'Just me – unless you'd rather one of the other girls come with you?' said Suzie hesitantly.

He winked at her. 'You'll do just fine.'

Smiling to herself, Suzie tethered the next cow in line. 'Shan't be long.'

When the last of the cows had been milked, the girls helped Suzie and Bernie load the cart and waved them off. Sliding the bolt back on the milking shed door, Libby stood back as the cows made their way out.

Following behind the cattle, Libby gave Margo a sidelong glance. 'What Suzie was sayin' about my uncle havin' set fire to his own money has given me cause to pause.'

'I'm not surprised, cos it makes perfect sense, but why do you suppose the others believed him over you – especially when they knew what he was like?'

Libby recalled the conversation she'd had with her uncle the day after the fire. He had allowed her to rant and rave, throwing all kinds of accusations at him whilst the rest of the stallholders stood by. *He knew what he was doin' by stayin' silent*, Libby thought now. *He was guidin' me into a trap of my own makin', and no one else could see it, not even me.* Going ahead of the cows, she opened the gate for them to pass through. 'I must've looked as though I'd lost my mind, accusin' someone of settin' fire to a ruined buildin',' she said, 'and with him not mentionin' the singed money I just dug myself further in.'

Margo's eyes narrowed. 'But if he didn't tell you about the money who did?'

'One of the other stallholders,' said Libby. 'You could've knocked me for six when he told me they'd found two charred notes, and when I said I still didn't believe me uncle, it made me look as though I was actin' like a petulant child. Thinkin' back, that was the straw that broke the camel's back. I wanted to get as far away from Uncle Tony and his disgusting lies as I possibly could, and using my mother's family was a perfect excuse to do just that. Cos if I really wanted, I could've telephoned the police stations in Liverpool and asked them to pass on the news.' She shrugged. 'I said I wanted to tell them face to face because it wasn't right for them to hear in a letter or over the phone, but why would I feel that way about people who'd treated us like lepers?'

'Do you think you made a mistake by leavin'?'

'No. I had to get away in order to clear my head, and I couldn't do that livin' in the same city as *him*.'

'So, what now?' said Margo.

'I'm not sure. Part of me wants to march up to my uncle and demand my stall back, but the realistic side of me knows I haven't a leg to stand on. I'm goin' to have to think this through carefully.' She clicked her tongue to encourage the last cow to enter the meadow before closing the gate. 'My biggest concern about goin' back is you.'

Margo's eyes grew wide. 'Me? Why me?'

'I wouldn't be a very good pal if I left you on yer tod now, would I?'

Margo waved a hand dismissively. 'As I told you before, I'll be fine as long as I've got my Tom.'

'I know, but that doesn't stop me from feelin' guilty.'

'Well, it should, Libby Gilbert, because you've not got owt to feel guilty about, besides which I'm a woman grown and I know how to look after myself. It was my decision to stay in Liverpool, and I'm glad I did, cos had I not I dread to think where I'd be now.'

'What'll you do if I do go back?' said Libby. 'You can't afford a place on yer own, and you can hardly shack up with Tom.'

'I shall cross that bridge when I come to it, cos, as we've already learned, summat always comes along in the nick of time.'

'I feel a bit better knowin' that Tom won't be called on to join up,' Libby said. 'Thank goodness for fallen arches, eh?'

'Don't let Tom hear you say that.'

'Why not? It's hardly his fault,' Libby began, but Margo spoke over her.

'He hates the fact that he can't join up, cos he wants to do his bit. To make it worse, he's had folk accusin' him of cowardice.'

Libby's expression turned to a look of disgust. 'Why on earth would they do that?'

'Folk see a fit young lad who's not in uniform and assume he's a coward.'

Libby eyed her cautiously. 'Has someone said somethin'?'

Margo's features sharpened. 'Some silly cow tried to give him a white feather.'

'She *what*?'

Margo kicked a stone with the toe of her wellington, causing it to bounce down the track ahead of them.

'She held it out and told him to stick it in his cap for all to see.'

Libby's cheeks flushed with anger. 'Poor Tom! What did he say? I hope he put her right.'

'He tried to tell her that he couldn't join because of his flat feet, but she didn't want to listen.'

'Well, he doesn't deserve that,' said Libby. 'I hope that woman thinks twice before gobbin' off in future.'

'Some people have too much time on their hands,' said Margo, 'and she was obviously one of them.'

'My mother used to hate people who judged others,' Libby said, 'although with hindsight, perhaps that's not so surprisin'.'

'I'm afraid it's human nature,' said Margo. 'We did the same with Suzie.'

Libby grimaced. 'I know, and I feel awful about it now, but you have to go off face value until you've got to know someone properly.'

'True, otherwise Joyce would never have fallen for Callum.'

'Talkin' of Callum, I wonder if she and Suzie have thought any more about payin' him a visit in prison?'

Margo shuddered. 'Rather them than me. Those places are horrible.'

'Needs must,' said Libby, 'and the sooner they do it the better.'

'They've got six months,' said Margo. 'What's the rush?'

'The longer they leave it, the harder it'll be,' said Libby, 'and if anythin' should happen to that ration book, they won't have a leg to stand on.'

'What on earth's goin' to happen to it?'

'It only takes one raid for it to go up in flames, and then where will they be?'

'Ooo, I never thought of that,' said Margo. 'But you're right, it'd be sod's law for summat like that to happen.'

'It's why I started takin' my mother's diaries and photo albums down the air raid shelter when we were in the city,' Libby reminded her. 'It's too late to cry afterwards, and that book is the key to their freedom!'

Chapter Three

Jack adjusted his tie as he checked his reflection in the mirror for what felt like the hundredth time. He didn't know why his tie was bothering him so much when he had bigger things to worry about. Sighing heavily, he pulled the knot loose before starting again. Everything had been fine until a few hours ago. In fact, he corrected himself, it had been better than fine. He'd entered the services thinking he'd be lucky if he got to see Libby more than twice a year, and hadn't been able to believe his luck when he received his first posting to RAF West Kirby. *I should've realised it was too good to be true*, he thought now as he slid the new knot into place. The last thing he wanted was to see her upset, but the matter was out of his hands. He gazed at his mirrored face as he replayed the conversation in his mind.

Jack had been making his way from the NAAFI when he was waylaid by his sergeant, who handed him a piece of paper. Reading the instructions, he'd barely got to the bottom before looking up sharply. 'Biggin Hill? But that's miles away!'

'I thought you'd be pleased!' said his sergeant. 'Most men would give their right arm to be posted so close to home.'

'Not me!' said Jack firmly, adding with a hint of hope, 'Is there any chance you could send one of the other lads in my stead?'

'No there bleedin' well isn't,' snapped the sergeant, 'so stop your bellyachin' and be grateful you're not bein' sent overseas – cos that really would give you summat to whinge about.'

Jack's heart skipped a beat as the sergeant's words washed over him. He might not like the idea of being in Biggin Hill, but it was a lot closer to Libby than Africa.

Now, he slid his feet into his highly polished shoes and fastened the laces. *At least I'll be close to Dad, which is better than bein' sent to somewhere like Lincoln, away from everyone I know and love.* He turned his mind to how Libby would react when he told her of his new posting. She wouldn't be happy, that was obvious, but she would look on the bright side, probably saying that they'd be able to arrange a date for the wedding a lot sooner with him being based so close to London. He grimaced as a less positive thought entered his mind. *Unless the bloomin' RAF see fit to move me again, of course . . .*

Taffy – one of the Welsh mechanics who worked on the same planes as Jack – opened the door to the hut and smiled broadly. 'Is luvver boy ready?'

119

In answer Jack took his wallet off his bed and tucked it into his pocket before following Taffy to the waiting lorry and jumping into the rear of the vehicle, which was all but full of personnel waiting to go into town. Taffy took the seat opposite him, and the driver secured the tailgate before taking his place behind the wheel.

Taffy stared at Jack thoughtfully as the engine stuttered into action. 'Why the long face? I thought you was lookin' forward to takin' your fiancée dancin'?'

'I'm still takin' her dancin', but I can't say I'm altogether lookin' forward to it,' Jack said dully. 'Not after findin' out that I'm bein' posted in a few days' time.'

'I see,' said Taffy. 'Oh dear.'

'Oh dear indeed,' said Jack ruefully, 'cos I can't say as I'm lookin' forward to breakin' the news.'

'Tears before bedtime,' said Taffy in the manner of one who'd been there before. 'Where's the new postin'?'

'Biggin Hill, which isn't too far from my old stompin' ground. I probably sound like an ungrateful sod, cos a lot of folk would be thrilled if they were to be posted closer to home, and my father'll be cock-a-hoop when he hears the news.' He fell silent, leaving Taffy to fill in the blanks.

'But you'd rather be closer to your belle than your old feller.'

'Exactly,' said Jack. He held on to the seat as the lorry lurched into motion. 'I feel sorry for me dad because he's on his tod, but . . .'

Taffy finished Jack's sentence. 'He's not Libby.'

'Does that make me a bad son?'

'Nah. I reckon most men would be the same in your position – unless they've been married for a long time, of course,' he added with a chuckle.

'It's Libby I feel most sorry for,' said Jack. 'She's expectin' a fun night out, oblivious of the news that lies ahead.'

Taffy looked up sharply. 'Hang on a mo, didn't you once tell me that she was a cockney, same as you?' Seeing Jack nod, he continued, 'Couldn't she move back to London too?'

Jack shot him an incredulous glance. 'Not when the bloomin' Luftwaffe are makin' it their main target she can't. And what if they choose to send me to Lincoln next, or even further afield? God forbid.'

Taffy steadied himself as the lorry bounced over a pothole. 'There is that.' Determined to look on the bright side, he gave Jack a grim smile. 'Absence makes the heart grow fonder?'

'Let's hope so,' said Jack, 'cos I'd rather that than out of sight out of mind.'

Feeling the lorry begin to slow, Taffy looked out through the tailgate. 'I seem to remember you sayin' summat about her wantin' to get married in London; surely it'll be easier to set a date once you're in Biggin Hill?'

'That's the only silver linin',' Jack agreed. 'I just hope Lib doesn't use it as an excuse to up sticks and join me down south.'

'Do you think she would?'

'I'd hope not, but she has been talkin' about London with a fondness I've never heard from her before,

121

which makes me think she might be feelin' a bit homesick.'

'Now that really is a case of absence makin' the heart grow fonder,' said Taffy knowingly. 'She's forgotten how bad things are down south, and it's up to you to remind her that livin' in London is a different kettle of fish to livin' up north.'

Jack locked eyes with the other man. 'And how can I do that, when I'll be tryin' to persuade her that I'm goin' to be perfectly safe in Biggin Hill, which isn't that far from the city itself?'

Taffy pulled a rueful face. 'I see your dilemma.' He fell into silent contemplation before shrugging. 'Surely it's got to be safer in Biggin Hill than the centre of London?'

Jack stared out of the back of the lorry. 'They might be able to fight back, but they've had their fair share of attacks *because* they're so close to the capital.'

'Still better than the city though,' said Taffy contentedly. 'A bright girl like Libby will see the sense in that – cos I'm presumin' she's got a sensible head on her shoulders?'

A smile creased Jack's cheek. 'She certainly has, and while she can still be a bit of a wild card at times, she's not reckless.'

'Sounds like you've got a good 'un,' said Taffy.

'The best,' said Jack softly, adding in the privacy of his own head, *and I'll do anythin' I can to protect her.*

When the lorry pulled up outside St George's Hall, Jack and a few others made their way over to the bus which would take them to the Grafton. Taking a seat near the front, he tried to envisage himself telling Libby of his new posting, but imagining the pained look in her eyes was too much for him to bear. *There isn't a good way of breakin' news like this, so I shall just have to bite the bullet and tell her straight off the bat.* He sighed inwardly as the bus pulled away from another stop. He hoped that telling her in this way would be as easy in practice as it was in theory, but somehow he doubted it.

When the dance hall loomed into view he scanned the pavement, but Libby was nowhere to be seen. Stepping down from the bus to wait for her to arrive, he tried to think of a gentle way to break the news.

With the farm well and truly in the grip of winter, Libby's least favourite activity was breaking the ice on the troughs.

'I swear me fingers have gone through most of the colours of the rainbow!' she cried as she pushed her hands back into her mittens.

'Use a hammer,' said Margo. 'That's what I do.'

'As do I, but you can't use a hammer to get the chunks of ice out of the water,' Libby pointed out. 'And mittens aren't waterproof!'

'You'll forget all about the cold when you have your bath later,' said Margo.

'I've never looked forward to a hot bath as much as I have livin' here,' Libby said, trying to stamp the life back into her toes.

It was much later the same day and Libby was sitting on the bus, excited for her evening with Jack. Dancing with the girls was all well and good, and even though she'd thoroughly enjoyed their evening out she knew it would pale in comparison to spending time with her beau. She sighed wistfully as she imagined his strong arms holding her close, guiding her effortlessly around the dance floor. *Firm, yet gentle, and not a foot out of place*, Libby thought as she sat on the bus, *the perfect dance partner.* A chuckle escaped her lips as she pictured Margo, who would keep forgetting that she was meant to be the one leading, resulting in many trodden toes on top of countless apologies.

As the bus neared the Grafton, she spotted Jack standing on the pavement waiting for her to arrive. Eager to be in his arms, Libby left her seat and was walking towards the back of the bus before it had come to a complete halt. Descending onto the pavement, she trotted towards him. 'Have you been waitin' long?'

Shaking his head, he eyed her from head to toe, giving a low whistle of admiration. 'The belle of the ball as always! Is that a new dress?'

Blushing under his praise, she treated him to a twirl. 'It's one of Margo's. It's cheaper to share clothes than buy second hand.'

'Now that's what I call usin' yer head,' said Jack, hooking his arm through hers and leading her into the Grafton. He knew it would be better to broach the subject of his posting sooner rather than later, but he couldn't bring himself to cast a damper on the evening before it had even started, so he decided to buy himself some time by asking her how things were going at the farm.

Libby chattered merrily away, telling him about Suzie and Joyce and the outcome with Callum whilst Jack listened with half an ear, wondering when would be the right moment to break his news. When she got no response from him as she finished her tale, Libby squeezed his fingers. 'What's up? Only you appear to be somewhat distracted.'

He rubbed the back of his neck with the palm of his hand. 'I'm sorry to say this, Lib, but I'm bein' posted to Biggin Hill.'

Libby stared at him, temporarily stunned by his revelation. 'But Biggin Hill's not far from London.' She barely paused for breath before asking the question that she most dreaded. 'When?'

He grimaced apologetically. 'I leave on Friday.'

'This Friday?' she gasped.

'I'm afraid so. If it's any consolation I only found out myself a few hours ago.'

'But why you?' asked Libby, who was trying her hardest to not sound petulant.

'I haven't the foggiest. I did ask if they could send someone else, but the answer was a resounding no.'

Determined not to let the news ruin their evening, Libby began to unbutton her coat. 'I've been hummin' and harrin' about goin' home, so maybe this is fate's way—'

But Jack was shaking his head vehemently. 'No, Lib. I know what you're goin' to suggest, and even though I'll miss you like crazy I'd rather you stayed in Liverpool where you'll be safe.'

'But things have gone a lot quieter since Hitler decided to attack Russia.'

Cupping her cheek in the palm of his hand, Jack twinkled lovingly into her eyes. 'Maybe up here, but he's still got his sights very much on London, make no mistake about it. If I thought it were safe for you to

125

return then I'd say so in a flash, but Dad reckons it's as bad there as it ever was.'

Trying to find a way around her dilemma, Libby slipped her coat from her shoulders and handed it to the coat clerk. 'I know what you're sayin',' she told him as they made their way to the dance floor, 'but I reckon it's pot luck as to whether your time's up. Had Margo and I not been down the shelter when the bomb hit our flat, we'd be goners.'

'But that's what the shelters are for. It's the difference between standing outside the tiger's cage and inside it; some people make their own fate,' said Jack reasonably.

Remembering how Jack's mother had taken her own life when he was still a baby, Libby clapped a hand to her forehead. 'Oh, Jack, I'm so sorry. I didn't think . . .'

Jack looked puzzled before realisation dawned. 'You thought I was talkin' about me mum?'

'Weren't you?' asked Libby, glancing up at the underside of his clean-shaven chin.

'Not intentionally, although you do have a point. What I was tryin' to say is there's a deal of difference between Liverpool and London, both geographically and politically. If Hitler conquers London, he's conquered Britain, which is why London will never be safe – not whilst we're still at war with Germany.'

She very much wanted to argue with him, but he had a point, and a good one at that. 'But if I can't come to London, when on earth are we goin' to see each other; and what was all that talk about the two of us stayin' with yer dad next time you got some leave?'

Jack grimaced. 'Bein' in Liverpool makes it easy to forget how bad things are for them down south, but a quick phone call with my dad soon put me right on that score.' Seeing the forlorn look on her face, he quickly added, 'But Biggin Hill's nigh on an hour's drive from London, which makes it a lot safer than the city itself, and there's bound to be a hotel or B&B nearby that you can stay at.' He smiled encouragingly. 'It'll be like a little holiday.'

Relieved that he wasn't going to dismiss the possibility of a visit out of hand, Libby gazed up at him. 'I quite like the idea of us havin' a little holiday together.'

He kissed her softly. 'That's my girl!'

She nuzzled her cheek against his chest as the band struck up a slow waltz. 'I'm goin' to miss this.'

Holding her so close that there wasn't a sliver of air between their bodies, Jack breathed in the perfumed soap which he had bought her for Christmas. 'That makes two of us.'

Determined to make the most of every second, Libby couldn't believe it when she found herself applauding the band, who had just played their last number.

'It doesn't seem as though we've been here more than five minutes,' she told Jack as he helped her into her coat.

'That's the trouble with enjoyin' yerself,' said Jack. 'Time always flies by when you're havin' fun, but it makes you hungry too. What do you say to a fried fish supper?'

Libby fastened the buttons of her coat as they walked outside. 'When have you ever known me turn down a fish supper?'

Jack hailed an approaching bus. 'Fair point. Have you anywhere particular in mind?'

She waited until they had taken their seats on the bus before giving him her reply. 'I don't mind where we get them, but I would like to eat them on the overhead railway. It's lovely to look over the docks whilst you're havin' yer supper.'

Jack paid the clippie, then turned his attention back to Libby. 'Sounds like the perfect end to a perfect evenin'.'

'Perfect except for your news,' said Libby, sliding her hand into his. 'I'm tryin' my hardest to put your postin' to the back of my mind, because I don't want to spend our last evenin' together in tears.'

Taking her hand to his lips, he kissed her knuckles. 'It's not goin' to be for ever.'

'Too right it's not,' said Libby. 'I'll be comin' down to Biggin Hill whenever time allows, especially as I've now decided to stay on at the farm.'

'What difference does it make where you work?' asked Jack. 'I mean, I'm glad to hear you've decided to stay at Hollybank, but . . .'

'It makes a huge difference,' said Libby. 'By stayin' on at the farm I won't have to fork out for rent like I would if I went back to the laundry.'

'Will you have to become a land girl now you're staying?'

She shrugged. 'I dunno. Suzie hasn't, so maybe I won't have to either. To be honest, I'd rather not, because I'd like to be able to come and see you in London as often as possible and I don't think I'll be able to do that if I'm formally employed as a land girl.'

'You certainly have a lot to think about,' said Jack, getting to his feet. 'C'mon, this is our stop.'

He held her hand as she alighted from the bus and they headed for the nearest fried fish shop, where Jack ordered two portions of fish and chips.

'Have you thought about goin' back to the market stall where you found your mum's diaries?' he asked as he pocketed the change.

Surprised at the sudden change of topic, Libby stared at him. 'What on earth makes you ask that?'

'Because if any more have turned up they could give you the answers you're lookin' for.'

'What makes you think I'm not happy with my lot?'

'Because I know you too well, Libby Gilbert.' He took the parcels of food and handed one to Libby. 'You won't rest until you've learned the whole story, I know you won't.'

'You're right, of course, but I don't want to build my hopes up just to have them come to nought.'

'And will that stop you tryin'?'

'I doubt it.' She cast him a sidelong glance. 'Do you really think they'll turn up?'

He shrugged. 'You won't know if you don't take a look.'

They reached the overhead railway and broke off the conversation whilst they paid for their tickets and boarded the train. 'But what if I read summat bad,' ventured Libby, beginning to unwrap her parcel of food.

'Or what if you read somethin' that puts your mind at rest?' suggested Jack as he, too, unwrapped his food.

129

'She might actually name the man in question; for all we know he could be dead.'

Libby looked startled. 'Blimey, Jack, you don't mince yer words, do you? It never occurred to me that he might be dead – not that it makes any difference either way.'

'Maybe not, but it's all part of the puzzle.'

Libby broke off a piece of fish, releasing the delicious scent throughout the carriage. 'Not knowin' is the worst,' she said, 'and try as I might, I can't stop the questions from runnin' through my mind. Did he know he might be my father? And if he did, did he threaten to tell me dad, and is that why she wanted to move to London, to stop Dad from findin' out?'

Jack swallowed his mouthful before replying. 'Which is why I think you should go back to the market where you found the diaries, and see if any more have turned up.'

'I will,' Libby assured him, before adding, 'We came on here to admire the view whilst eatin' our supper and I've not so much as glanced out of the window!'

'Oh, I don't know. I reckon the view's just as good from this angle.'

Blushing, Libby nudged him playfully. 'Give over!'

'I'm serious,' grinned Jack. 'Best view in the world is this.'

With the blush deepening, Libby turned her attention to her chips. 'You could charm the birds out of the trees with that silver tongue of yours, Jack Durning.'

'Only speakin' the truth,' said Jack. 'There's nothin' wrong with that.'

Her cheeks burning, Libby deftly changed the subject. 'What d'you suppose we could have for our weddin' breakfast?'

Jack held up one of his chips. 'Fried fish supper?'

Coughing on a chip which she had inadvertently inhaled, Libby's eyes widened. 'You must be plannin' on winnin' the pools, cos fish and chips for that many would cost us a fortune!'

Jack stifled a chuckle with the back of his hand. 'How many people are you plannin' on invitin'?'

Libby promptly began to tick them off on her fingers. 'There's your dad, my aunt and uncle – includin' Uncle Tony because I know me dad would be hurt if I didn't invite him, then there's Pete, Luke the feller from the hardware stall, and Mrs Pratchett, and . . .'

'The entire market, I bet,' said Jack, still chuckling.

'They forked out for my parents' funeral whilst my own family didn't chip in so much as a penny. I wouldn't dream of not invitin' them to the weddin'.'

Jack squeezed her hand. 'I'm only teasin'. This is your day, and you can invite the entire city if it makes you happy. We'll find a way to feed folk, even if it's just finger sandwiches.'

An older woman who'd only been pretending that she wasn't listening joined in the conversation. 'Pardon me for eavesdroppin', but you could allus ask folk to bring a contribution.'

'Ask them for money?' gasped Libby, clearly aghast at the very notion.

The woman laughed. 'Good God no! I meant food. That's what me and my Alby did. Each of the guests brought summat different so that there was a wide variety and plenty for all.'

'That's an excellent suggestion,' said Jack, screwing his wrappings into a ball. 'I'm sure people would understand, what with the war an' all.'

The woman beamed, happy that her idea had been well received. 'When's the big day?'

'We've not decided on a date yet,' said Libby. 'I'd like to have my best friend with me, but I've no idea where she lives now that she's moved to Ireland.'

The woman shot them a shrewd glance. 'Time and tide wait for no man, and it's the same when it comes to war. I understand you want your bezzie there, but I'm sure she wouldn't want you to wait on her account.'

'She'd insist we go ahead, but it won't be the same without her there.' She glanced at Jack wretchedly. 'I know I've said it before, but I'll telephone the landlord in Norfolk just as soon as I get back.'

'I thought you'd already done that?'

She shook her head. 'I keep meanin' to, but this is my last resort. If he says he's not heard hide nor hair from her, I'll know I've reached the end of the line, and I don't think I could bear that.'

'On the other hand, he could have her address in his possession,' said Jack.

Libby gave him a look of pure yearning. 'Wouldn't that be wonderful?'

'Indeed, but you won't know the answer unless you ask.'

'You're right!' said Libby determinedly. 'I shall really do it this time, cos I've been silly holdin' out for so long.' She stared idly out of the window to the docks below. 'We were as thick as thieves when we were growin' up, always in each other's pockets. My dad used to say we may as well be joined at the hip, and he was right, because we used to share everything!' She smiled. 'We had our wedding days planned down to the last detail, from the flowers we'd have in our bouquets to the way we'd style our hair.' Her smile faded. 'I always took it for granted that my mum and dad would be a huge part of my wedding day, and the thought of gettin' married without them there is almost incomprehensible to me.' A line creased her brow. 'I have no choice when it comes to my parents, but I'm determined to do everythin' I can to make sure that Emma's part of my weddin'.'

'Then you must make that telephone call your priority,' said Jack.

Remembering the older woman's warning that they shouldn't rest on their laurels, Libby nodded. 'I will, and we must set a date as soon as possible, because even though I'd love for Emma to be at the weddin', I can't see her makin' it back to Blighty before the end of the war.'

'You never know yer luck.'

She coddled his hand in hers. 'You always manage to cheer me up.'

'Good, cos I don't like seein' you unhappy.'

She gazed at him affectionately. 'Just think, in a few months' time I could be Mrs Jack Durning.'

'Mrs Jack Durning! Now doesn't that sound good?' breathed Jack, a sloppy grin stretching his cheeks.

'It does indeed; I just wish my parents were here to see it. Dad would be proud as a peacock to walk me down the aisle, and Mum would be goin' through hankies like there was no tomorrow.' She looked out of the window as the train came to a halt. 'They may not be present physically, but I know they'll be with me in spirit.'

As the other passengers began to leave the train Jack leaned forward; his lips meeting hers, he kissed her gently at first, but as the kiss deepened his passion increased until Libby felt the depth of his love engulf her in its entirety. So lost were they in their embrace they didn't realise that they were the only ones left in the carriage. Jack glanced at his wristwatch.

'Crikey, is that the time? I'd better get a move on if I don't want the lorry to leave without me.'

The thought of him missing his ride would've been music to Libby's ears had she not known how much trouble he would be in if he did. Holding his hand as they left the train, she fought back the tears as they hurried towards the pick-up point. Hearing the lorry toot its horn to announce its imminent departure, Jack brushed his lips over hers. 'Trust them to be on time,' he whispered. 'Although perhaps it's just as well they're here, because I don't know how much longer I can keep my gentleman's honour.'

Libby ran her hand up his neck to cup his chin, and he leaned into her touch. 'Is there no chance of us seein' each other again before you leave?' she asked hoarsely.

He turned his head to kiss the palm of her hand. 'I won't be able to come to you, but if you could come to me . . .?'

'Of course I can come to you!' cried Libby. 'Just tell me when.'

'Ring the NAAFI tonight; I should know somethin' more concrete by then,' said Jack. His eyes sparkled as they gazed into hers, and Libby was reminded of the day he had come to her rescue over a year before.

Hearing the driver toot the horn impatiently, Jack murmured, 'I'll see you on Friday,' before pressing his lips against hers for one last kiss.

The driver revved the engine of the lorry, and Jack broke away to jump into the back, where he waved goodbye to Libby from his seat. She felt her stomach lurch as she fought back the tears. Hugging herself, she began to walk to the bus stop. Jack had kissed her many times before, but never with as much passion as he had that evening. Remembering how her body had tingled in his embrace, Libby wondered whether this was what it felt like before you made love. As the thought entered her mind, she came to the sudden realisation that making love was all part of being married, something she might be doing in just a couple of months' time. *He'll expect us to do it*, Libby thought now, the sweat beading her brow, *because that's what every married couple does on their wedding night, but what if I'm no good at it, or I do it wrong?* It was at times like these that she wished she had some-one like her mother to talk to. Not that she'd want to discuss the matter at length, but she could have asked Orla what would be expected of her. *I know that Jack will be gentle with me*, Libby told herself now, *and I'm glad that he'll be my first, because I wouldn't want to do it with anyone else.* An unwelcome image of her mother looking up at a man other than Reggie entered her thoughts. *How could she have lain down with someone she didn't love?* thought Libby. *I'll find it nerve-racking enough with Jack, never mind someone I'm not in a relationship with.* The answer came to her without hesitation. *Because she was at the lowest point in her marriage and she needed to feel loved, and no matter how much I disagree with what she did, we all deserve that.* She recalled how her mother had once told her that marriage wasn't a bed of roses, something which Libby hadn't understood until now. Marriage didn't guarantee a fairy-tale ending, and Libby knew two examples of that, first her parents, who had found it nigh on impossible to conceive, and then Jack's father Gordon, who'd tried everything he could to save his wife, only to find that he was too late. *If we're to be happy, we're goin' to have to work at our marriage, because communication is the key. Had Mum and Dad spoken more, she might never have sought affection from another.* She paused in her thoughts. Jack's mother was proof that some people couldn't be helped no matter how much you loved them or how hard you tried. *Mum's indiscretion might actually have saved their marriage, so maybe it's better that she did what she did, otherwise not only would I not be here, but she and Dad might have ended up goin' their separate ways regardless, and who would that have benefited? Seeing as Mum wasn't the one who was having difficulty conceiving, she might have moved on to pastures new and had a family, but what about Dad?* She pictured him living as a bachelor alongside his brother. Her bottom lip trembled. *He'd have been miserable.* She swallowed. Hard as it was to acknowledge, Libby was glad her mother had turned to another man for comfort, because it had worked out well in the long run. *I've been so caught up in Mum betrayin' Dad, I never looked at the bigger picture. I wish I could let her know that I understand what she did, and that I'm glad she did it, because no matter how hard it must've been for her to live a lie, she made Dad the happiest man in the world!*

***

It was the day of Jack's departure, and Libby was waiting for him outside the gate to his base. She had arrived in plenty of time, but even though she'd been there for a good ten minutes Jack was still nowhere to be seen. Worried that something might have happened to prevent him from meeting her, Libby was about to ask the guard if he could find out where he was when she saw him jogging towards her.

'Sorry I'm late, I got held up,' he said, taking her in his arms. His eyes locked with hers as their lips met. Losing herself in the kiss, Libby was disappointed when he pulled away.

'I wish we had just one more day together,' she said, and glancing past Jack to the guard on the gate she murmured, 'and somewhere a little more private wouldn't go amiss neither.'

Jack cupped his hands around her face so that she was partly hidden from the guard, who was pointedly looking anywhere but at the two young lovers. 'I'm sure Bert doesn't want to watch us smoochin', and when you come to visit me in Biggin Hill we'll have all the privacy we need.'

Libby fixed him with an accusing look. 'I hope you're not thinkin' what I think you're thinkin', Jack Durning.'

Flashing her a mischievous grin, he leaned in as though to kiss her again before turning his head at the last second and tracing a series of small kisses along her neckline until he reached her ear, when he whispered in a seductive manner, 'Oh yeah? And just what might you be thinkin'?'

'You know full well!' chuckled Libby. Taking his chin on the tips of her fingers she guided his lips back up to meet hers.

'I shall be as good as gold,' murmured Jack as he kissed every part of her mouth, 'Scouts' honour!'

'Have you ever actually been a Scout . . .' Libby began, only to be silenced by his kiss. Melting into the warmth of his embrace, she felt the tears seep between her lids. She had promised herself that she wouldn't cry, but now that she was actually saying goodbye, no number of promises could've stopped the tears from forming.

Breaking away, she lowered her head as she dabbed the tears with the handkerchief Jack had fished from his pocket. 'I'm sorry,' she mumbled quietly. 'I didn't mean to put a damper on our last day.'

He chucked her under the chin. 'You could never do that. Seein' you only ever brightens my day, which is why I ain't half goin' to miss that beautiful smile of yours.'

Libby started as she suddenly remembered the photograph she had in her handbag. She opened the clasp and handed it to Jack. 'It's the photograph we had taken when we went to the flicks with Margo and Tom, do you remember?'

His eyes danced as he studied the photograph. 'I do indeed. We were in Lyons café not long after I came to West Kirby. You, me, Margo and Tom.'

'I've kept a copy for myself,' said Libby, 'so that we've got one each.'

Jack carefully placed the photograph in his lapel pocket. 'Here's what we'll do. Every night at precisely twenty-two hundred hours, I shall take this photo out and say goodnight to you. If you do the same, it'll be like we're together, even if it's just for a minute or so.'

Libby leaned up on her toes and pecked him on the lips. 'That's a smashin' idea, and I promise to do it every night without fail.'

Jack rested his forehead against hers. 'Till we meet again, Libby Gilbert.'

'Goodbye, Jack, and good luck.'

Libby watched as Jack walked back through the gates to his base. With every step that he took, Libby wondered if he would turn to look back, but he only did it the once, touching his cap briefly as he did so. Libby was grateful that he had continued to walk, because she couldn't bear to say goodbye for a second time.

Only when he was completely hidden from view did she turn to walk the short distance to the bus stop just outside the gate. Already feeling lost without him, she tried to focus her thoughts on when she would see Jack at Biggin Hill and how wonderful their reunion would be. *And it'll be all the sweeter if you sort your own life out first*, Libby told herself. Seeing the bus approach, she held out her hand and waited for it to stop. Taking a seat near the front, she began to plan out the rest of her day. *I shall find Margo as soon as I get back to Hollybank so that I can tell her about my decision to stay on at the farm; after that I shall go and see Helen to set the wheels in motion – whatever they may be – and finally . . .* she felt her tummy flutter with anticipation . . . *I shall phone the landlord in Norwich and ask him if he's received any mail addressed to me. What I do then will depend on what he says.*

The bus journey was arduous, with many diversions and changes of route due to fallen buildings or craters, and Libby was grateful when they were free of the city and trundling along the road which led to the farm. As the bus pulled up at her stop, she thanked the clippie before jumping down and walking up the drive. Wishing that Jack wasn't being posted elsewhere might be fruitless, but that didn't stop her from doing so. *I know I promised I wouldn't move to London*, Libby thought now, *but I don't see why I couldn't live on the outskirts. Anything's better than not seeing him for goodness knows how long, and I could easily get work . . .* She stopped as a sudden thought entered her mind. What would she do for work? It wasn't feasible to imagine that she could travel in and out of the city on a daily basis, not with the Luftwaffe causing endless detours as it did in Liverpool.

'Wotcher!'

Libby looked up to see Margo waving at her from the yard. Waving back, she walked to meet her. 'I've been doin' some thinkin',' she said, 'about the future and what I want to do with it.'

Margo looked crestfallen. 'Please don't tell me you're plannin' on movin' to London to be with Jack.'

Libby shook her head, although she made sure not to look Margo directly in the eye. 'I mean about stayin' on at the farm. I've decided it's what I want to do.'

'I can't say I'm not relieved, because I am,' Margo said plainly. 'Just the thought of spendin' night after night crammed into a public shelter with Gawd knows how many others – some of whom smell worse than the pigs – whilst keeping my fingers crossed that the vibrations from the bombs don't bring the roof down makes me shudder.'

'Me too. How on earth we used to go and do a full day's work after spendin' the night down a shelter is beyond me. We must've been like the walkin' dead,' said Libby.

'We didn't have a choice at the time, not when we had bills to pay.'

'Which brings me to my next question. Do we join the Land Army, or ask if we can stay on as we are?'

'That's goin' to be up to the Lewises to decide,' said Margo, 'but given the choice I'd rather join up as a land girl, because we'll get proper wages, even if they aren't up to much, although I'm hopin' a bit more than the pocket money the Lewises give us.'

'I wouldn't be able to go and see Jack as often as I could if I were a volunteer.'

'You'd have more chance of that as a land girl than you would down the laundry, though,' Margo pointed out.

'I know, which is why I'll join the Land Army if that's what Helen would rather.' Libby jerked her head in the direction of the house. 'Talkin' of Helen, I'm goin' to ask if I can use her phone to ring the landlord in Norwich. Do you want to come with me so that we can tell her of our decision?'

Margo looked towards the orchard. 'I promised to help Suzie with the hens, so if you don't mind speakin' on my behalf . . .?'

'Not at all,' said Libby. 'I'll let you know what she says.'

'How did it go with Jack?'

'As well as can be expected, only he got held up so it was short but sweet.' She pulled a rueful face. 'That's the trouble when you're in the services: yer time's not yer own.'

'It's a shame you didn't have as long as you'd have liked, but at least you got to say goodbye.' Hearing Suzie call, Margo waved in response. 'I'd best be off. Good luck with the landlord – I'll keep my fingers crossed for you.'

'Thanks, Margo.'

Libby went across the yard and knocked briefly on the door of the farmhouse. Hearing Helen call 'Come in', she stepped into the warmth of the kitchen, where Helen had temporarily stopped rolling pastry to dust it with flour.

'Hello, Libby luv. What can I do for you?'

'I was wondering if I might use your telephone, please?' Libby told her.

Helen jerked her head in the direction of the hall. 'Feel free. Just pop the money in the box when you're done.'

'Thanks, Helen.' She left the older woman rolling pastry and headed for the phone, which was located

142

on a small wooden table in the hallway. Picking up the receiver, she asked the operator to put her through to the landlord. Hoping and praying that he would be in his office, Libby felt her heart leap as a man's voice came down the line.

'Is that Mr Peacock?'

'It is indeed. To whom do I have the pleasure of speaking?'

'Libby Gilbert,' said Libby. 'My father was Reggie Gilbert, and we were meant to be rentin' a flat off you, but—'

The man interrupted without apology. 'If it's about the deposit—'

Libby rolled her eyes. 'It's not about the deposit; the solicitors made it perfectly clear that you wouldn't be returning it,' she said waspishly. 'I'm telephoning to ask if you've had any correspondence for me or my parents at your office?'

'Did you not get the letter I forwarded to your father's solicitor? I know the mail system's a bit hit and miss at present, but it should have arrived by now. Good God, I must've passed it on over a year ago!'

Libby's heart began to race. 'Was it for me?'

'Yes,' came the succinct reply.

'It has to be from my friend Emma,' breathed Libby. 'She's the only person who'd write to me at your address.'

'I must say, I think it was jolly remiss of the solicitor not to pass it on,' said Mr Peacock stiffly. 'Most unprofessional, in my opinion. Not what you'd expect from a practitioner of the law.'

Libby pulled a guilty grimace. 'I'm afraid that's probably my fault. What with one thing and another I totally forgot to inform them of my new address.'

There was a short pause before he spoke again. 'Just for the record, I really was sorry to hear about your parents, and I would've returned the deposit had I had someone to take over the lease, but . . .'

Not wanting to hear his excuses for keeping money which could have made a big difference to her life, Libby cut him short. 'As I said, my father's solicitor explained the situation. I understand you have to make a living, but I couldn't even pay for my parents' funeral.'

There was a long pause before the man spoke again, and when he did he sounded sheepish. 'If it was down to me—'

'I'm lucky enough to have great friends who paid for everything,' Libby interrupted. She paused for breath. 'Thank you for sendin' the letter on. Goodbye, Mr Peacock.'

She heard him mutter a brief goodbye before replacing the handset.

Having had no intention of mentioning the money, Libby was pleased that Mr Peacock had given her a chance to voice her thoughts. *I hope he has a few sleepless nights, just as I did when I realised that I wasn't goin' to see a penny of Dad's deposit*, she thought as she placed another coin in the box and rang her father's solicitors. *Please God, don't have thrown the letter away*, she thought just as a woman answered the call. After a brief explanation as to who she was and why she was calling, it hadn't taken long to ascertain that they had indeed received the letter, and would send it on to Hollybank. Euphoric at the news, Libby went back into the kitchen.

'Thanks for lettin' me use the phone, Helen. I've put the money in the box.'

'Did you get through? I know they've been having a dreadful time, what with the lines being down so often an' all,' Helen said, turning the pastry over.

'I certainly did, and the solicitors are goin' to forward her letter on to this address.'

Helen wiped the hair from her face with the back of her hand. 'That's marvellous news, Libby luv. Is it from your friend in Ireland?' When Libby nodded, she went on, 'Oh, I'm so glad. I know how much you've missed your old pal. I bet you can't wait to read her letter.'

'It's goin' to be a bitter-sweet experience, because she doesn't know about my parents, or that I'm livin' in Liverpool.'

'She'll just be relieved to learn that you're all right 'cos she must've realised that summat was up when you'd not replied to her.'

'You're probably right,' Libby said ruefully. 'I wish I'd done this sooner.'

'Better late than never,' said Helen, deftly laying the pastry on a plate.

Libby gestured towards the pie Helen was making. 'I wish I could make pastry like you.'

'I'll teach you how one of these days.' Helen slid a knife around the excess pastry, cutting it off with ease.

'You said the letter's being sent here? Does that mean you're planning on staying a while longer? Only Bernie mentioned summat about your old flat probably being ready to move back into soon.'

'I'd like to stay until the end of the war,' said Libby, before adding quickly, 'Margo too, if that's all right with you?'

Helen was visibly relieved. 'It's more than all right! I'll not deny that I was really beginning to worry we were going to be left shorthanded, what with Roz talking about leaving to find her father and you and Margo having jobs to go back to at the laundry any time you wanted. If you all went at once, it'd only leave Adele, Joyce and Suzie, which isn't enough hands to run a farm this size.'

'Do we have to apply to become land girls, or . . .?'

'Yes, because it has to be official and above board. We'll help you with the paperwork, but there's no sense in you doing the course – such as it is – as you already know which end of a spade is which.'

Libby grinned, assuming that her hostess was joking. 'I think there's a bit more to it than that!'

Helen cast her a shrewd glance. 'You ask Roz; she'll tell you.'

'Then it's a good job we're not handlin' weapons, if that's all the trainin' you get.'

'You'd think so, but from what we've heard they've practically halved the training time for all the services, whether you're flying a plane, manning a submarine or shooting a gun.'

Libby gaped at her. 'They can't do that!'

'They can and they have,' said Helen. 'They need the men yesterday, and if that means they don't get the full training, then so be it.'

'But they have to have proper trainin',' said Libby incredulously. 'How else do they expect to win the war?'

'God knows,' replied Helen, shrugging. 'I suppose it shows how desperate a situation we're in. Your Jack's lucky he got in at the start.'

'And what a good job he did,' said Libby, 'although I very much hope the mechanics are gettin' proper trainin', cos they can't expect the pilots to fly a plane what's not fit to get off the ground.'

Helen began to ladle the pie mixture onto the pastry. 'Let's hope so.'

Libby felt her cheeks begin to warm. 'I'm happy to sign on as a land girl, but with Jack bein' posted down south . . .'

Helen finished the sentence for her. 'You were hoping to have time off to go and see him?'

Libby nodded silently.

'We'll see you right, don't worry about that,' said Helen. 'It's important to see the ones you love as much as you can, all things considered.'

'Thanks, Helen. I'll let Margo know the good news about you helpin' us to become land girls.'

'And I'll give you a shout when the paperwork arrives,' said Helen. 'It's not much, just dotting the i's and crossing the t's.'

Libby bade Helen goodbye, then headed over to the chickens to tell Margo the good news, but she was nowhere to be seen.

Seeing that Libby was looking for someone, Suzie called out as she walked towards her, 'If you're after Margo, she's taken Thor for a walk. She said to tell you she wouldn't be long.' She smiled. 'I hear you and Margo are staying put.'

'Helen's goin' to help us with the paperwork to make it official. I just hope they don't try and send us to another farm.'

'They wouldn't – would they?'

Libby shrugged. In all honesty it had only just occurred to her that the government might well move them to the Welsh hills, or even further afield should they see fit. 'They moved Roz from Glasfryn to Liverpool, and Jack from West Kirby to Biggin Hill; who knows what they'll decide to do if the fancy takes them?'

'Well, they'll have a riot on their hands if they try to move you and Margo away cos we're hard pushed as it is.' She eyed Libby curiously. 'If I'm honest, I'm not surprised Margo decided to stay, what with Thor an' all, but I got the impression you wanted to move back to London. Is that still your intention given the fullness of time, or have you decided to knock that idea on the head?'

'I'm only stayin' put until the war is over,' said Libby. 'After that I'll be on the first train back.'

Suzie brightened. 'I was rather hoping you'd say that.'

Libby's face fell. 'Have I done summat to upset you?'

'No!' gasped Suzie with a giggle. 'I meant . . .' she hesitated, 'that is to say, I was hoping you might let me come with you when you go back to London.' She swallowed. 'I know it's cheeky and a big ask but if you don't ask, you don't get.'

Suzie had never shown an interest in the capital until now, so her request had come as quite a shock to Libby. 'I didn't realise you were even thinkin' of movin' down south. Is this summat to do with yer father?'

'It has everything to do with my father,' said Suzie bleakly.

'I can understand your trepidation, but isn't that why you're goin' to show him the ration book, so that you can let him know you've got summat over him?'

'Oh, we're still going to do that,' said Suzie, 'although we'll have to wait until he gets out of the nick because he's only allowed one visitor at a time.'

'Why can't just one of you go?'

'Because we want to show him we're united on this and that if one of us should have an accident' – she formed quotation marks with her fingers around the last word – 'the other two will be there to tell the scuffers who done it and why.'

'Good idea,' said Libby, 'although I'm still not quite sure why you want to go to London.'

'To get away from my name,' said Suzie. 'Haggarty means nowt to the cockneys, and that's what I need in order to make a fresh start.'

'Well, you're welcome to come with me—' said Libby, stopping short as Suzie gave a whoop of joy.

'Thank you so much. I promise I won't be a nuisance, and I'll do everything you say.'

'What about yer mum? Will she want to come too?'

Suzie shook her head. 'Mam still wants to find herself a smallholding. She's asked me to help her run it, but much like yourself I'm a city girl to me bones.' She cast an eye around her as she continued to speak. 'It's lovely here and the people are great, but I miss the hustle and bustle of the city. I like to feel a part of things; to know what's happening in the world, and you don't get that out here.'

'Have you spoken to your mother about this?' ventured Libby.

Suzie gave her a wry smile. 'I have, and she was worried because she didn't like the thought of me going off on my own, but she'll feel a lot happier when she hears that I'm going with you.'

'I just hope London lives up to your expectations,' said Libby.

'I can't see why it wouldn't. Let's face it, there's nowt left for me here.'

'I remember sayin' that exact same thing when I was in London.'

'But your surname wasn't holding you back there like mine is here,' said Suzie. 'It doesn't matter how much I love the city itself; my name carries a real stigma, so much so it'll forever be holdin' me back, and I don't wish to die a spinster.'

'Oh, Suzie,' cried Libby, 'I'm sure that won't happen.'

Suzie's brow shot skyward. 'Really? Cos I can't see any man wanting to marry a Haggarty – or at least not anyone decent. The only fellers that'd be interested in me are the ones who like to go on the rob, and I wouldn't want to be with someone like that in a month of Sundays.' Her eyelids fluttered at the very thought. 'I don't want to lumber meself with someone like me dad.'

'I don't blame you,' said Libby. 'But I don't think we'll be goin' to London for a long time yet, not with the way the war's goin'.'

'As long as there's a light at the end of the tunnel, then that's fine by me.'

Margo approached them from behind, followed closely by Thor. 'What's this about a light at the end of the tunnel?'

'Libby's said I can go to London with her after the war,' said Suzie.

'I think that's a wonderful idea,' said Margo, huffing on her hands to keep them warm. 'And even though I know our Libby's perfectly capable of holdin' her own, it'll be good to know she'll have someone with her.'

'I'll have Jack,' Libby pointed out, 'and I'm hopin' we'll be married before then.'

'Jack won't be able to leave the RAF as soon as the war's over,' said Margo. 'He'll have to be demobbed first, and that could take months, if not years.'

Libby gaped at her. 'Years? Why on earth would it take that long?'

Margo shrugged. 'Gawd knows.'

'Well, I think it's silly,' said Libby.

'The war can't go on for too much longer,' Suzie put in. 'It's already been more than two years.'

Libby and Margo exchanged glances. 'The Great War went on for just over four,' said Libby.

'But things were different back then.'

'Yeah,' agreed Margo, continuing in a pessimistic tone, 'and they've had plenty of time to look at where they went wrong last time, and make sure they don't repeat the same mistakes.'

'But we're winning,' cried Suzie; then, seeing the looks on her friends' faces, she lowered her voice before adding, 'aren't we?'

'Rome wasn't built in a day,' Libby assured her, 'and I wouldn't say anyone was winning at the moment.'

'But we will win,' stressed Margo, 'cos the Nazis ain't got our bulldog spirit.'

'Tough as boots, us Brits,' agreed Libby, 'and when we send Hitler to hell, it'll send a message to every dictator who thinks they can do the same as him!'

Suzie smiled somewhat grimly. 'I wonder how much of Britain will be left by the time the war is over?'

'It doesn't matter, because we'll build Britain back to being better than it was in the first place, and while the men are rebuilding the city we can be doin' everythin' else.'

'Like what?' said Suzie. 'Have you a job in mind?'

'I shall get my parents' market stall back,' said Libby firmly, 'and if my uncle dares to try and stop me, I shall demand proof that he paid the money to my father in the first place.'

Margo shot her a wry glance. 'You know what he'll say, because he's already said it.'

Libby's eyes flashed. 'And if I'd have been in my right mind at the time, I'd have demanded to see the winnin' ticket.'

'But what if he says he's lost the ticket?' said Margo. 'It'd be plausible after all this time.'

'I'll ask which bookies he placed the bet at. I remember Dad sayin' summat about them havin' to keep records of all their wins, so he wouldn't be able to wriggle out of it.'

'You're right, they do,' said Margo. 'I reckon you've got him by the short 'n' curlies, and not before time.'

Suzie giggled at Margo's words. 'Serves him right, too.'

'I reckon we could get my parents' stall back to what it was in no time at all,' said Libby, continuing in excited tones, 'and we could even stock some of Gordon's carpentry – Jack's too once he's demobbed – that way it'll be a proper family business just like the good old days.'

'What'll you tell yer aunt and uncle?'

Libby shrugged. 'I don't think they'll be interested, do you?'

'Nah, it's too far away for them to try and sell their hooky gear,' chuckled Margo.

'I've heard you mention your Auntie Jo, but I don't think I know her,' said Suzie, 'which is odd when you think about it because I know most people from the wrong side of the tracks.'

'Jo Murphy,' said Libby. 'Her maiden name was O'Connell.'

Suzie fell into deep thought as she racked her brains to put a face to the name, but she couldn't think of a single person by that name. 'Murphy's a common name around here, as is O'Connell, but I can't say as I know a Jo Murphy, or a Donny Murphy come to that. Are you sure they deal in hooky gear?'

Margo erupted into laughter. 'There ain't nothin' in their house what doesn't belong to somebody else! And by that I don't mean they bought it at a jumble sale, either. You can't move for boxes full of goodness only knows what, and I've never seen so much whisky outside of a pub – not that I frequent pubs, mind you.'

'So definitely not strait-laced,' mused Suzie. 'Where do they live?'

The thought of anyone describing her aunt and uncle as strait-laced made Libby smile. 'They live in one of the courts – Back Bond Street, to be precise.'

'I know the folk from Back Bond Street of old. Do you know how long they've lived there?'

'Now therein the question lies,' said Margo. 'You see, they told us they'd been living in Ireland, with Libby's grandparents, but when we spoke to the barmaid in the Grafton she told us that Donny had been in Blackpool, *not* Ireland.'

'Come to think of it, that was the same night we saw him talking to your dad,' said Libby, 'so they definitely know each other.'

'You saw my dad?' said Suzie, stunned by this revelation. 'Where did you see him, and how did you know who he was?'

'We saw him whilst we were in the Grafton, and the barmaid told us who he was,' said Libby. 'It didn't mean much to us at the time, of course, because we were only really interested in what my uncle was doin' there.'

'Well, I know my dad wasn't there because he fancied a turn on the floor,' said Suzie. 'He'll have been meeting your uncle to do business away from prying eyes.'

'We were dyin' to know what Donny was doin' there,' said Margo, 'so when he left, Jack went to speak to your father.'

Suzie's eyes grew wide. 'He was taking one heck of a risk doing that. Dad doesn't like people asking questions – for obvious reasons.'

'That's what I said,' said Libby, 'but Jack didn't tell us what he was goin' to do until he'd already done it.'

'What did Jack say to him?'

Libby grinned. 'He said that Donny reminded him of his old priest from back in Ireland. Your dad thought it was hilarious, and told Jack that Donny had never set foot in Ireland, never mind a church.'

Suzie held her face in her hands as she tried in vain to picture Donny and Jo, but no matter how hard she tried nothing came to mind, or at least nothing feasible. There had been a few people by the name of Murphy living in the area, but none that sounded like Libby's aunt and uncle. 'They must be people that Dad never took me to see,' said Suzie, slowly, 'which is odd, because he used to take me everywhere with him.'

'It's possible they were in Blackpool at the time,' Libby supposed.

'There's an easy way to solve this,' said Margo.

Libby eyed her quizzically. 'How?'

'Take Suzie to meet yer aunt and uncle,' said Margo matter-of-factly.

'But does it really matter if I know who they are or not?' Suzie asked.

'No, but I'd like to know more about them,' said Libby, 'such as why they lied about goin' to live in Ireland when they were really in Blackpool.'

'And why they're convinced you're goin' to inherit a fortune when you've not got a penny to yer name,' said Margo.

Suzie rolled her eyes. 'Even if you did have an inheritance, it wouldn't be yours until you were eighteen. You'd need a guardian to take care of your money until then.'

Both girls stared at Suzie open-mouthed. Libby was the first to find her tongue.

'How on earth do you know summat like that?'

'My dad's Callum Haggarty, remember?' said Suzie, with a hint of sarcasm. 'What he doesn't know about extorting money from innocent people could be written on the back of a postage stamp.'

'But if that's the case, why do they think I'm gettin' anythin'?'

'Unless they think you're lookin' for a guardian to take care of yer money and that's why you came to Liverpool,' said Margo. 'They know yer Uncle Tony well enough to know that he can't be trusted, so they probably reckoned you'd come to Liverpool to entrust the money to yer grandparents, but with them not bein' on the scene . . .'

'I'm waitin' until I'm eighteen,' finished Libby breathlessly. 'No wonder she's hung on to the inheritance theory like a dog with a bone, but as if I'd ask them to look after my money when I wouldn't trust them to look after fresh air!'

Suzie was shaking her head. 'I'd love to see who they are, just out of curiosity.'

'Then that's that settled,' said Margo promptly: 'we'll take you to meet them—' She stopped short, seeing Suzie shake her head.

'I don't think my meeting them in person is the right way to go about it. If I do know them, they'll either clam up *or*, if they've really got summat to hide, get nasty.'

'From afar, then,' said Libby, 'but goodness only knows how we'll get them out of the house.'

'She's like a hermit,' Margo explained to Suzie. 'She couldn't have gone out more than a few times the whole time we lived there – quite frankly it was a miracle we met her when she was browsin' the market—'

Suzie choked on a giggle. 'If she's as bad as you both paint her, I highly doubt she was browsing the market, more likely casing the stalls for stuff to nick once the stallholder's back was turned.'

'That sounds more like it,' said Margo, 'although when you come to think about it, it does seem a bit fortuitous that we happen across Jo on one of the rare occasions that she does decide to venture out.'

'She must go out at some time during the day, if just to get the shopping in,' said Suzie reasonably.

'We were workin' in the laundry when we lived with them,' said Libby, 'so it's quite plausible for her to have done the shoppin' when we were at work – although I highly doubt it, considerin' the cupboards were always bare unless we filled them.'

'I always assumed they survived on the contraband they stored in the house,' Margo commented, 'but either way, we're goin' to have to find a way of gettin' them out of doors so that Suzie can have a good gander.'

'What about your uncle?' asked Suzie. 'Does he go out much?'

'He's rarely in,' said Libby, 'especially come the evening.'

'If that's the case it's going to be easier for you to point him out to me, rather than your aunt,' Suzie concluded, but Margo was doubtful.

'I don't see how. We haven't a clue where he goes.'

Suzie appeared to be deep in thought, before suddenly raising her head. 'The houses on Back Bond Street have two entrances; that's right, isn't it?'

'Yup. Donny's favourite escape route whenever we go callin',' said Margo, and laughed sarcastically. 'Anyone would think he didn't want to see us.'

Suzie brightened. 'And does he go out every time you visit your aunt?'

'Without fail – if he's there,' said Libby.

'Then the answer is easy. Margo and I will wait on the other side of the street, and as soon as your uncle appears Margo can point him out to me.'

A slow smile crept up Libby's cheeks. 'I do hope you recognise him, because I'd love to know more about them.'

'I probably won't be able to tell you more than you already know,' said Suzie frankly, 'but I might know summat behind the rumours of them disappearing to Blackpool.'

With hope rising in her chest, Libby began to get excited. 'If you know Jo and Donny you might know my grandparents. Jo doesn't talk about them, but then neither did my mum.'

Aware of the weight being loaded onto her shoulders, Suzie spoke candidly. 'Please don't pin your hopes on my recognising them, because I'd hate to disappoint you.'

'I know, but I can't help gettin' excited, because you *must* know who they are if your father does business with them,' said Libby. 'How about we go to their house this Saturday after work? We can make an evenin' of it by callin' in at the cinema or the Grafton on our way home.'

'The cinema!' squeaked Suzie. 'I've always dreamed of going to the cinema. It must be wonderful to see all them famous people as if they're really there in front of you.'

Margo stared at her incredulously. 'You can't seriously expect us to believe you've never been to the cinema?'

'Dad said it was a waste of money because you had nothing to show for it afterwards, so I wasn't allowed to go. He did suggest I try and sneak in for free, but that's easier said than done when every bugger in Liverpool knows who you are, cos they're watching you like a hawk – not that I blame them.'

'Well, there'll be no sneakin' in on Saturday,' said Libby. 'We'll go to the chippy first, then on to my aunt's – I'll say that I'm meetin' some pals at the cinema so won't be stoppin' long, not that she'll be bothered.'

'I'm looking forward to playing detective,' said Suzie. 'What with that and the cinema, I can't wait for Saturday!'

***

MARCH 1942

Spring was on its way and Libby had swapped her thick woolly jumper for a shirt and cardigan. Having only seen the farm under the spell of winter, she had marvelled at the beauty of the trees and hedgerows as they came into bud.

Shielding her eyes from the blazing sun, she walked over to the postman, who was holding out an envelope. 'Mornin', Lib. Just the one today,' he said as she took the envelope from his hands.

'Thanks, Dave . . .' Her smile dissappeared as her eyes fell to the official-looking typewriting. Making her excuses, she hurried to the barn so that she might read the letter in private. She was fairly confident that the RAF wouldn't write to her should something awful have happened to Jack, since they were neither married nor related, but even so she still crossed her fingers as she opened the envelope and found another within. A quick glance sent her heart soaring as she recognised Emma's handwriting. Beaming from ear to ear, she wasted no time in opening the second envelope and pulling out the letter inside.

160

Immediately, her eyes fell to the date at the top, which was the day her friend had left London; the same day that Libby's parents had died. *I lost everythin' that day*, Libby thought now: *my parents, my best friend, everythin' we owned and the future I should have had.* Her stomach clenched as another thought entered her mind. Had Emma seen fit to tell her where she was? Glancing down, her stomach settled as her eyes rested on an Irish address.

Dearest Libby,

By the time you receive this letter you'll be in Norwich and I'll be in Ireland, and even though I hated to leave London, I'll be glad when I get off this train and onto a ferry. I suppose a lot of people had the same idea as us, because there isn't room to swing a cat on the whole train. Every time we reach another station, I keep my fingers crossed that more people will get off than on, but no luck so far!

Anyway, that's enough about my stuffy train journey. How's life at the new shop? I should imagine it's very different from your dear little stall on Petticoat Lane. Have you got a till? I've always thought it would be great fun to push the buttons and count people's change out when the drawer opens. Is Norwich quieter than London by way of air raids? I do hope so, considering that was your whole motive for moving. I know it's still early days, but I hope you've got the shop up and running, and that you've plenty of customers. You've always been good at making friends, so I'm sure you've got lots of new ones, you'll have to introduce me to when I come to stay, although when that'll be goodness only knows.

Mum's dreading the trip across the Irish Sea, saying that we're as good as sitting ducks, but Dad's hopeful they won't bomb the ferry because of Ireland being neutral. Needless to say, I hope Dad's right! I'm feeling pretty anxious about making new friends. It's different when you're little, and I daresay Cathy won't have any trouble at all, but seeing as I'm not going to school, I don't know how I'll meet anyone of my own age – I know my grandparents are Irish but I'm a cockney through and through and from what I've heard the Irish aren't keen on the English, so I'm already setting off on the back foot as it were.

Running your own shop should mean you have no problem meeting new folk, and with your father being Norfolk born and bred, doubtless he'll know a few people already, which should make settling in a bit easier.

I asked Dad if he was looking forward to seeing his old school pals but he doesn't seem fussed. He said most of the lads he grew up with moved away from Ireland to find work, the same as him. I hope things have changed, because we've little to no savings and Mum said my grandparents are already struggling to make ends meet without having a family of four landing on their doorstep.

At this point in the letter the pencil jerked downwards, causing a long streak across the rest of the page. Emma explained.

Sorry about the state of my writing, but this train's swaying more than a ship on the ocean. Poor Cathy spent the first half of the trip with her head down the loo.

I'm hoping the ferry's going to be smoother than the train, but I doubt it somehow. Talking of ferries, Dad says we're nearly in Liverpool and we should get our things together.

Please write back just as soon as you can so that I know you got to Norwich safely. Here's hoping that someone does that blooming Hitler in so that we can get back to normal asap.

TTFN

Emma

As soon as she had finished reading, Libby quickly sought out paper and pencil from the chest of drawers she shared with Margo and Suzie. Holding the pencil above the first line, she stared at the empty page. She had a lot to say, so would be as brief yet thorough as she could whilst being careful not to leave anything out.

After several false starts and lots of erasing, it was some time later that Libby finished writing. Blowing rubbings from the paper, she read her letter through for the final time.

Satisfied with her efforts, she crossed her address off the solicitor's envelope and replaced it with Emma's. Glancing quickly at the alarm clock which stood atop the dresser, she used some Sellotape to re-seal the envelope and went out to the yard, hoping that she would catch Bernie before he headed into the village. The yard was empty, but when she looked to the driveway she saw the back end of the cart trundling down the track. Calling out for Bernie to wait, she ran full pelt after it waving the letter to gain his attention.

Hearing the commotion, Bernie twisted in his seat and pulled Goliath to a halt. 'Talk about being in the nick of time. D'you wanna come along for the ride?' he said, patting the empty space beside him.

Libby shook her head. 'I've got to help the girls with the rest of the chores.' She gave the letter a kiss before handing it to Bernie, along with the money for a stamp.

Bernie winked at her. 'Sealed with a loving kiss, eh?'

'Not in the way you're thinkin',' Libby laughed. 'This is more like a kiss for luck. It's been over a year since my friend wrote the letter and I'm really hopin' she hasn't moved to pastures new in that time. Quite frankly the sooner this gets to her the better.'

'Consider it done,' said Bernie. He urged the horse on with a click of his tongue. 'Trot on, Goliath, we've a mail coach to catch!'

***

Hearing her mother calling for her to come down to the kitchen, Emma appeared at the top of the stairs, an inquisitive look upon her face.

'What's up?'

Lucy waved an unopened envelope at her. 'You've got a letter!'

Thundering down the stairs, Emma took the letter from her mother and stared at the writing. 'Oh, my Gawd!'

Grinning, Lucy handed her daughter a knife from the top drawer of the dresser. 'Who'd have thought it, eh? After all this time.'

Emma took the knife and carefully slit along the edge above the Sellotape before handing it back to her mother. Taking a deep breath, she whispered 'Please don't be bad news' as she took the letter out.

Sinking onto one of the kitchen chairs, Emma read the first paragraph, her eyes growing ever wider as silent tears rolled down her cheeks. Lucy's smile faded. 'What's wrong?'

'Libby's parents died the day we left for Ireland – it must've happened whilst we were down the shelter.' She dabbed her tears with the handkerchief she'd pulled from her dress pocket. 'I can't imagine what it must've been like for Libby to go through that on her own.'

'I remember that day as if it were yesterday,' said Lucy hoarsely, as she came round to comfort her daughter. 'It had to be one of the closest calls we'd had yet, which is why your father insisted we leave on the next train.'

Emma read the rest of the letter in silence, whilst her mother placed the kettle on to boil. A hot cup of tea had always been Lucy's response to any bad news.

Taking the cup of tea, Emma handed the letter over for her mother to read. 'Lib hasn't half been through the wringer, but she seems to have come out the other side all right, no thanks to that no-good uncle of hers.'

Lucy read the letter before voicing her opinion. 'That man is a filthy, rotten, cheatin'. . .' She broke off, shaking her head angrily. 'How could he treat her like that when she'd just lost her parents? Has he no heart?'

'He was hardly what you'd call a dotin' uncle when her parents were alive,' said Emma, 'but I didn't think he'd stoop this low.'

'If it were anyone else I'd give them the benefit of the doubt, because grief does funny things to folk, but this?' She took a moment to calm herself before continuing. 'This is a disgustin' way to behave! Turnin' yer back on yer own flesh and blood as well as robbin' their livelihood out from underneath them is beyond despicable.'

'I agree,' said Emma stiffly. 'Libby always did say that he was a wrong 'un, and this just goes to prove it. Thank God for Jack is all I can say, cos I don't know what she'd have done if he hadn't come into her life. I just hope he's everythin' he seems to be.'

'Our Libby's always had a strong head on her shoulders,' said Lucy. 'She knows a pauper from a prince; if he weren't the real deal she'd soon see through him.'

'She's been incredibly lucky to have found Margo and Jack,' said Emma. 'I wish I'd been lucky enough to find good friends like them.'

Lucy smiled kindly. 'I know you've found it rough, luv, but it'll be much easier once you're in the ATS. It's just a shame your trainin' camp's nowhere near Liverpool, else you could've popped in to say hello.'

'I could always arrange to call her on the telephone,' Emma supposed. 'It would be wonderful to hear her voice again.'

'I'd wager Hollybank is on the blower if it's as big a farm as she says,' Lucy called as Emma disappeared into her room to write a response.

Turning her attention back to preparing their evening meal, Lucy mulled over their life since moving to Ireland. Emma had tried her hardest to fit in with the locals, but they had been less than willing to make friends with a girl from England, and Lucy had lost count of the times her daughter had come home in floods saying she wished they'd never left London. Distraught at seeing her reduced to tears whilst threatening to swim back to Britain, she had suggested the only thing she could think of: that Emma should join the services.

Emma had brightened instantly. 'D'you really think they'd have me?'

Lucy had cupped her daughter's chin in the palm of her hand. 'They'd be lucky to have you, but don't tell yer father until yer papers come back. You know what he can be like.'

Emma had agreed, and Lucy paused in her cooking as she recalled the argument which had ensued when Emma finally showed the papers to her father.

'What the hell was the point of me movin' you all the way out here just for you to go back?' Daniel had yelled, reading the official documents confirming his daughter's posting.

'I'm lonely over here,' Emma had said through her tears. 'I've not got one pal – even Cathy's struggled to make friends and she's a lot younger than me.'

'Friends don't keep you safe from the Luftwaffe,' growled Daniel, 'and they sure as hell don't put a roof over yer head.'

'I'd rather be with people who don't hate me just because of where I'm from than here,' cried Emma. 'You don't know what it's been like for me, Dad.'

Frustrated by his daughter's response, Daniel had fallen back on sarcasm. 'Oh, poor you, who gets to wake up every mornin' – unlike some of them we left behind. Poor you, what doesn't have to worry about food, cos there's plenty to be had. Poor—'

Lucy had cut across her husband. 'That's enough, Daniel! Your daughter is miserable, so much so that she's willing to put her life in danger just to be happier. Whilst that may be hard for you to understand, I know where she's coming from, because I've found it hard to integrate too.'

'Haven't we all!' barked Daniel. 'But you don't hear me whingin' about it.'

'It's not the same for you, cos you were born here,' snapped Lucy. 'They see you as one of their own who finally made it back home. But me and the girls are outsiders, and that's how they'll always see us.'

Daniel stared disbelievingly at his wife. 'I'm just tryin' to keep you safe.'

She softened. 'I know, and we're grateful, but that doesn't mean to say we're happy.'

The argument had gone on for several days as Daniel tried to encourage his daughter to give Ireland a little longer, but Emma had remained adamant until he had had no choice other than to back down.

She'll be happy once she's back in Blighty with like-minded girls of her own age, Lucy thought now, *and with Libby back on the scene, things are bound to get better.*

***

Jack's new posting had been a stark reminder that the war was far from over, and when talking on the telephone to Libby he had made certain to steer the conversation away from how bad it was in London, instead concentrating on the wedding and the latest news from Hollybank. Whether Libby had picked up on his subtle deviation he couldn't be sure, but she in turn had written back with news of her life in Liverpool, with the latest letter being no exception.

His eyes fell to the page in front of him, and a smile creased his face as he began to read.

My dearest darling Jack,

I have the most exciting news to impart. As you know, I recently wrote to Emma and I'm delighted to say that I received a letter from her this very morning, telling me she's joined the ATS and will be moving back to Blighty for her initial training! As I'm sure you can imagine, I was over the moon to receive such good news, as it means it won't be too long before I see her again. She was terribly upset to hear about my parents, but ever so glad to learn that you had come to my rescue and that we are going to be wed. She says she's determined to be there for our wedding and that Hitler can go hang himself if he even thinks of trying to stand in her way. I can't tell you how wonderful it was to hear from her, and I'm really looking forward to reliving the good old days, like the sleepovers we'd have, with Dad telling us ghost stories while Mum chided him for scaring us so close to bedtime. Or the time we locked ourselves out of the house, and accidentally broke one of the windows whilst trying to get back in!

She's due in Blighty on the 17th but she's going to come a day early so that we can spend some time together before she heads off on her initial training – not that she's told me where that is, because the censors will only take it out. I must say, it all sounds terribly exciting.

Jack paused in his reading. Libby was understandably excited about being reunited with her old pal, but could that bring trouble for Jack? He was certain that Libby would have been a very different girl when Emma knew her last, and Emma's return might bring the old Libby back. He knew the two girls had often talked of their futures, and he very much doubted that in those days Libby's had included marriage to a carpenter. Libby had been a woman with ambition, and it had been her suggestion that her parents get a shop in Norwich rather than keep the stall on Petticoat Lane. She had probably had aspirations of marrying a banker or someone of equal standing.

He relaxed as the memory of a long-ago conversation came back to him. They had been in the kitchen of Gordon's flat when Libby had told them how her father had wanted her to marry a penpusher but she had refused, saying that she didn't want to be married to anyone who thought himself better than her. A small smile twitched his lips. He was letting his imagination run away with him. The death of her parents had changed her circumstances, but not her character – she was too strong to allow that to happen. He continued to read, then briefly wished he hadn't as he took in the next few words: *I did toy with the idea of joining up so that we could serve together . . .* he held his breath as he read the rest of the sentence: *but that would never happen, as she's already way ahead of me in the process.*

Jack felt himself relax. If Libby had decided to join the services, the chances of meeting up with her would have been nigh on impossible.

I suppose it goes to show how much I've grown up, the letter went on, *because there was a time when I'd have joined up anyway in the hope that our paths might coincide at some point, but I don't live my life on whims any more. Although that could be down to my haring across the country only to find that my Liverpudlian relatives weren't much better than the one I'd left behind! Talking of which, we've devised a plan with Suzie for this Saturday . . .*

Jack read the rest of the letter with interest. He'd only met Jo and Donny once, and quite frankly once had been enough. They were nothing like Libby and he hadn't liked the way they'd taken advantage of her and Margo when the girls had been bombed out of their first flat, or the way they viewed their niece as some kind of windfall.

Chapter Four

Libby grinned as Emma's words came down the line.

'Libby! I can't tell you how good it is to hear your voice.'

'Same here,' said Libby, 'cos there was a time when I thought I may never hear from you again!'

'You and me both,' breathed Emma. 'I bet you've changed heaps since I saw you last.'

'Only that I'm a little bit older and a whole lot wiser,' said Libby. 'How about you? You didn't say much about your life in Ireland.'

'It's not for me,' said Emma plainly. 'I'm like a fish out of water over here. No matter how hard I try, I just don't fit in.'

'Oh, Em, I am sorry. Is that why you chose to join the services?'

'Yep. Dad wasn't exactly thrilled, but he came round to our way of thinkin' in the end.'

'Our way?'

'Mum doesn't really like it over here either, but she's determined to see it through if only for the sake of the family.'

'Does this mean they'll be movin' back to Blighty once the war's over?' Libby asked.

'Like a flash. Dad's been strugglin' to find work. Even though he's a fully qualified builder he can only get labourin' jobs, and even that's not regular.'

'I'd love to see your parents again, as well as Cathy, of course.'

'And they you,' said Emma. 'Mum says she's goin' to give you the biggest hug when she sees you next. They were devastated to hear about yer parents, and even though there's nothin' he could've done to save them Dad wishes he'd hung on just till he knew they were safe, cos that way you could've come with us.'

Libby was shaking her head fervently. 'That's very kind of him, but who knows what would've happened had you not got on that train?'

'I s'pose you're right; we never know what's around the corner,' said Emma. 'I wish I could lay my hands on that rotten git what stole yer parents' stuff, cos I'd ring his flamin' neck. As if things weren't bad enough without him doin' that to you? And what was the point in him stealin' the stuff in the first place if he was just goin' to sell it as a job lot, cos I bet he didn't get much for it. Fancy takin' such a big risk for a few pennies; a couple of quid at most.'

Libby opened her mouth to respond and closed it again. Now she came to think about it, why *had* the thief stolen the van for a bunch of old furniture, some of which was so rickety they'd thought it might not survive the journey to Norwich. 'Whoever it was must've thought there was more in the van than furniture.'

'Like what?' snapped Emma. 'The deeds to a country estate?'

'Well, if they thought that they were in for a bit of a shock.' Libby fell silent as a memory of her father, packing his briefcase into the van along with his furniture, came into her mind. Shrugging it off, she continued to chat with her friend. 'I just hope they get their comeuppance one of these days.'

'And aren't you lucky you just happened across that photo album as well as the diaries.'

'About that,' Libby began, but the operator cut across her, letting them know their time was up.

'Typical!' said Emma. 'It hardly feels as though we've been on the phone for three seconds, let alone three minutes.'

'Blimey, we haven't even talked about meetin' tomorrow. What time does your ferry get in?'

'Eight thirty,' said Emma promptly.

'I'll see you there. And Emma?'

'Yes?'

'It's bloomin' good to have you back!'

'Ain't it just—' Emma began, before being cut off by the operator.

Libby sighed happily as she replaced the handset. This time tomorrow she would be with her friend, talking about old times as well as everything that had transpired since they saw each other last. Striding out through the kitchen door, she headed back to the barn where Margo and Suzie were waiting to hear the news.

'How was she?' Suzie asked, as soon as Libby appeared.

'Just as I remembered her,' Libby replied. 'Her ferry gets in at eight thirty tomorrow, and quite frankly I can't wait!'

'You've got an awful lot to catch up on,' said Margo; 'hopefully even more so after this evenin's events.'

Suzie clapped her hands together. 'I'm really lookin' forward to this. I've never done a stake-out before – the closest I've come is keepin' a look-out for scuffers, which wasn't very excitin'.'

Margo giggled. 'I s'pose it's kind of the same thing, which is good cos at least it means you've had some practice. I keep thinkin' that we're goin' to stick out like a sore thumb, cos I don't know how you can look inconspicuous when you're up to no good.'

Suzie rolled her eyes. 'It's easy. Stick to the shadows, and pretend you're waiting for a friend to arrive.'

'Is that what you used to do when yer dad was on the rob?'

'I didn't have to, cos I was only lookin' out for scuffers. As soon as I seen them I'd tell Dad, and we'd skedaddle before they could collar us.'

'With your experience you should apply to be one of them policewomen. They say it takes a thief to catch a thief.'

'Could you imagine what yer dad would say if you did?' Libby laughed.

'He'd have a heart attack if he seen me in a scuffer's uniform,' said Suzie. 'It would be worth it to see the look on his face, though.'

'Jokin' aside, are we still goin' ahead with the same plan?' Libby was eager to get started.

'Yes,' said Suzie. 'Margo and I will hide round the back whilst you go and see your aunt. We'll wait for your uncle to come out, and go from there.'

'As in?'

'I either know them or I don't, but we can discuss that on the way to the cinema,' said Suzie. She stopped speaking as she saw Margo fingering a pale yellow frock. 'I thought the idea was to be inconspicuous? You'll stand out like a sore thumb wearin' a frock like that. You need dark clothes, to blend into the shadows.'

Margo screwed her lips in thought. 'I've got a navy blue frock that Tom bought for me. Would that do?'

Suzie nodded. 'Perfect. It doesn't matter what Libby wears, cos she doesn't have to worry about being seen.'

Libby clapped her hands together. 'Let's get this show on the road!'

The girls chattered excitedly the whole time they were getting ready to go out, and it was with great enthusiasm that they headed into the city later the same evening.

'You don't know how good it feels to go for a wander around the city without fear of bumping into the scuffers,' said Suzie. 'I used to dread going out and

177

about when I were living with me dad, cos I was for-ever looking over me shoulder.'

'I was the same with my dad,' said Margo. 'I used to tell him you never know who's watchin', and it would only take one person to see him pickin' someone's pocket for the game to be up.'

'But wouldn't that happen there and then?' asked Libby.

Margo shook her head. 'Not necessarily. Not many people like to say anythin' at the time for fear of reper-cussions, but if they see you out and about on yer own they might well grab a passin' bluebottle and tell them what they saw; next thing you know you're up to yer neck in strife.'

'I couldn't live my life like that,' said Libby. 'I'd be a nervous wreck!'

'It's horrid,' said Suzie, 'which is why I'm glad I don't have to worry about it any more.'

'I very much doubt any of them would recognise you,' said Margo, who was eyeing Suzie with approval. 'You look totally different with your hair up and a dab of makeup.'

'Eating three square meals a day whilst working on the farm has filled me out nicely. I didn't even know I had a waist till today,' said Suzie, smiling sheepishly. 'Did you hear them fellers whistling at us when we got off the bus?'

Libby laughed. 'I certainly did – I thought you were goin' to do a runner at first.'

'I thought it was the scuffers blowing their whistles to say they'd spotted me,' Suzie chuckled. 'This being innocent thing is going to take some getting used to.'

'You won't have to give it a second thought when you come to London with me.'

'It will be a whole new lease of life,' agreed Margo; 'take it from one who knows.'

'Made all the sweeter by the war being over,' said Suzie. 'I'll never have to worry about anything ever again.'

Margo raised her brow fleetingly. 'There's always summat to worry about, cos that's just life.'

Suzie placed a hand to her stomach. 'My guts are doing cartwheels; it must be all this talk about scuffers!'

'Mine too,' admitted Margo. 'I reckon it's all this cloak and dagger stuff.'

'No one wants to get caught with their trousers down . . .' Suzie started, much to the amusement of her friends.

'I *beg* your pardon?' Libby chortled.

'No one wants to get caught doing summat they shouldn't be doing,' Suzie explained, 'and no matter the reason it's wrong to spy on people.'

'Which is why I'm kind of hopin' we'll bump into one of them whilst we're walkin' down the street,' said Libby.

'It would be far easier,' agreed Margo, 'but since when has life ever been easy?'

'Do you both mind awfully if we go to the chippy *after* we've been to the Murphys'?' asked Suzie, still clutching her stomach. 'Only I'm too nervous to eat anything.'

'I'd rather get this over and done with, then go for summat to eat afterwards,' Libby agreed.

'I know, let's talk about the film we're going to see,' suggested Suzie. 'That should help take our minds off things. What was it called again?'

'*The Wizard of Oz*,' supplied Margo, 'and I guarantee you'll love it. It's about a girl called Dorothy who winds up in the land of Oz, where she meets a scarecrow, a tin man and a cowardly lion.'

Libby wagged a warning finger. 'Careful. You don't want to give too much away.'

'Very true,' said Margo. 'As we're gettin' close, how about we go through the plan one more time, make sure we're all singing from the same hymn sheet?'

'Best had,' said Libby. 'I'll wait until you and Suzie are in position round the back of the property before knockin' on the door. I'll pop in for no more than five minutes then make my excuses and meet the two of you on the corner.'

'Only how will we know when you're done?' asked Margo.

'Good point,' said Libby, adding after a moment's thought, 'I'll go to the corner and cough loudly three times.'

'Perfect,' said Suzie.

Libby stopped as they neared the bottom of the street. 'Best foot forward. I'll see you both in a bit.' Taking a deep breath, she began to walk up the court.

Suzie looked sceptical as she stared at the house at the far end, and seeing the expression on her face Margo spoke in lowered tones. 'Did you think we were comin' somewhere different? Only you look a tad confused.'

'I am a bit,' confessed Suzie, as they began to make their way round the back of the houses. 'When Libby said her aunt lived at the top of the court opposite the lavvy, I thought we must have our wires crossed.'

'Why? It seems pretty simple to me.'

'Only it *can't* be,' said Suzie as they took up their position. 'Either that or I've remembered it wrong.'

Margo appeared to be somewhat bewildered. 'Remembered what wrong?'

'The Murphys I knew—' Suzie began, but was hastily shushed into silence as Margo pointed at a man and a woman who'd emerged from the back of the house and stopped on the opposite side of the street.

Unable to speak in case they were heard, the girls stood in silence, shooting each other occasional furtive glances. Margo wondered what had made Jo and Donny come outside when their niece was presumably at the front door waiting for them, but they didn't appear to be doing anything other than standing there. For one heart-wrenching moment she did wonder whether they'd seen her and Suzie and had come out to take a better look, but then she saw they weren't looking in the right direction.

It was too dark for Suzie to see properly, but she could just make out the man taking something from his jacket pocket, and the woman accepting something he offered her. *Cigarettes!* she thought. Leaning forward, she concentrated with all her might as she waited for one of them to light a match. *I'll only have a few seconds to get a good look, so I can't afford to even blink*, she told herself.

Donny lit the match and Suzie gasped as both his and Jo's faces were illumined. Hastily covering her mouth with her hand, she cursed herself inwardly for making a noise. How could Libby have got things so terribly wrong?

Margo was holding her breath, hoping that Suzie hadn't drawn attention to their whereabouts, but it was clear by the way the Murphys kept looking back to the house that they were more bothered by Libby's presence than anything else. If she didn't know any better, she'd think them to be hiding from Libby; and that's when the penny dropped. *They're pretendin' to be out so that they don't have to speak to her. Just wait till we tell her* . . . She froze as another more sobering thought struck her. If Libby thought her aunt and uncle were out she might well come round the back to tell her and Suzie, and that wouldn't bode well for any of them. She gently nudged Suzie to gain her attention before putting a finger to her lips and jerking her head in the direction of the way they'd come. Suzie followed her back down the alley and it was only when they turned the corner that Margo dared to speak.

'Did you get a good look?'

'Yes.'

'And?'

Suzie was about to reply when she was interrupted by Libby, who was coming towards them. 'Trust them to be out . . .' Margo cut her short.

'They weren't out, Lib; they were hidin' from you. Either that or they just happened to step outside for a fag moments before you knocked on their door – which is too big a coincidence for my liking.'

Libby tutted irritably. 'They smoke in the house, so they were obviously tryin' to avoid me, which is a bit rich all things considered.' She looked at Suzie. 'Did you manage to get a proper look at either of them?'

'As soon as they lit their fags.' Libby waited patiently for her to continue, but Suzie appeared lost in thought.

'And?' prompted Margo. 'Did you recognise them?'

'Well, yeah,' said Suzie, 'but we seem to have got our wires completely and utterly crossed somewhere along the line.'

Libby rolled her eyes. 'Let me guess. They've lied about their name.'

'Not at all,' said Suzie, much to the girls' surprise. 'They're definitely Murphys.'

'Then how could you not know who they were when we first told you about them?' asked Margo, somewhat confused. 'They are Jo and Donny, aren't they?'

'I haven't a clue what their Christian names are. I've only ever known them as the Murphy—' She was cut short as Libby interrupted without apology.

'You mean they're livin' in sin?' said Libby. 'Though I can't say as I'm surprised, cos I can hardly see Donny forkin' out for a weddin'.'

Suzie gave Libby a quizzical look. 'What makes you think they're a couple?'

'Because Jo refers to Donny as my uncle, of course.'

Suzie sighed. 'She might well do, with him being her brother an' all.'

Suzie's statement was so outlandish, Libby burst out laughing. 'We've definitely got our wires crossed, because there's no way Jo and Donny are siblings.' She blew her cheeks out. 'I know they might be a couple of rum 'uns, but incest? Not on your nellie!'

'Not only are they siblings, they're twins,' said Suzie firmly, 'and I'm not the one with my wires crossed, you are.'

Libby gawped at her. 'You can't be serious?'

'That's why I didn't click when you referred to them as Jo and Donny. Everyone round these parts knows them as the Murphy twins.' Seeing that Libby was at a loss for words, Suzie threw her arms up in a questioning manner. 'What on earth made you think they were married?'

Libby blinked. 'Jo said summat about my not rememberin' my Uncle Donny and I assumed she meant because they'd got together after we left Liverpool. But I was knee high to a grasshopper when I last saw any of my mum's family, so I really don't remember much at all.'

Margo stopped walking abruptly. 'Don't you remember your aunt sayin' that Donny slept in a separate room because he snored?'

'Well, yeah, but that's not surprisin', cos we could hear him from our room,' said Libby.

'I have no idea as to whether Donny snores or not, but that ain't the reason for them not sharing a bed,' said Suzie bluntly.

At that point Libby came up with the only explanation she could think of. 'Have you thought they might be lyin' to everyone else, but not to us?'

'I wish I could tell you different, Lib, I really do, but the truth of the matter is that the Murphy twins are well known around Liverpool, as are their parents, uncles and aunts – not to mention cousins, of which there are many.'

'But why lie?'

Suzie shrugged. 'Why do folks like them do half the things they do?'

Libby looked to Margo, who had been keeping relatively quiet. 'Was it definitely them?'

'No two ways about it.'

Libby continued to walk whilst she tried to think things through. 'Let's look at this logically. What's the difference between them bein' my aunt and uncle by marriage and my aunt and my uncle by blood?'

'None that I can think of,' said Suzie.

Libby turned to Margo, who was being unusually quiet. 'Margo?'

'Maybe we're lookin' at this all wrong,' said Margo wretchedly.

'How do you mean?'

'Maybe they're not your aunt and uncle at all.'

'Of course they are!' cried Libby.

But Suzie didn't look so certain. 'But you've already said you can't remember seeing your aunt the last time you were in Liverpool, and as you've never seen your uncle, how can you be sure? Not just that, but why were you looking for your family down the market and not where they lived?'

'My Uncle Tony said they lived on the Scottie, but – as Tom informed us – so do a lot of people by the name of O'Connell. It was his suggestion that it might be quicker to search the market where they would be well known. We asked around for quite some time, but no one seemed to remember who they were, or anything about them, and I was beginning to think we'd got the wrong market when I bumped into my aunt. She recognised me from the moment she saw me, and how could she have done that unless she knew who I was? Not only that, but she was chatting to the woman who ran the stall about the market stall she ran with her family back in the day, and that was before she'd laid eyes on me.' She hesitated as she spied the cynical look on Suzie's face. 'Why are you lookin' at me like that?'

Suzie relented slightly. 'I'm sorry, Libby, truly I am, but if you knew the Murphys like I do, you'd know what they were capable of.'

'Only how could they have possibly known who we were lookin' for, never mind be in the right place at the right time?' said Margo, who even though she believed Suzie was right to be suspicious still thought it too incredible for words.

Suzie barely paused before replying. 'When you were asking if anyone knew your grandparents, did anyone say or do summat that seemed odd or unusual to you?'

'Not at all,' said Libby. 'They were all really helpful, or as helpful as they could be.'

But Margo's face had clouded over. 'There was that one bloke,' she said, 'you must remember him, he asked more questions than the others. You even asked whether he had a problem with you lookin' for your relatives, cos he were bein' that nosy.'

'That's right,' agreed Libby. 'But I don't see what he has to do with anythin'.'

Suzie had a sinking feeling that she was beginning to get the picture, and it wasn't at all pretty. 'What did he look like?'

Margo shrugged. 'He was around the same age as Jo and Donny, but unlike them he was well dressed, I suppose you could say a typical spiv, and he had a weird-soundin' name, proper Irish.'

Suzie rubbed her chin thoughtfully. 'Darragh? Cillian? Oisin . . .' She stopped speaking as Libby and Margo exchanged glances.

'That last one rings a bell,' said Libby.

'Oisin Murphy is one of their cousins,' said Suzie. 'He's always smartly dressed, cleanshaven apart from an awful pencil moustache, and he wears a fedora.'

'That's the one,' said Libby, her heart sinking into her boots. 'That must be why he was askin' so many questions, so he could go back and tell Jo who we were and what we looked like.'

'I'm afraid there's not a doubt in my mind,' said Suzie. 'It's what my father referred to as baiting the line. You find yourself someone who's particularly vulnerable and meet their needs.'

'Meet their needs?'

'You were lookin' for your mum's family and they supplied it,' said Margo.

'But how did they know my Uncle Tony?'

Margo was ticking the list off on her fingers. 'Jo told Libby that Tony had always been no good and she'd wager he'd kept his distance when she was growin' up. She couldn't possibly have known that unless she'd met him, and what's the likelihood of that happening when they live at opposite ends of the country?'

'Birds of a feather flock together,' said Suzie simply. 'Tony must've come up this way at some point or other.'

Libby spoke dully. 'He used to stay in Liverpool when he was visiting my parents. Don't you just bet he probably dabbled in hooky gear whilst he was here.'

'Flippin' Nora . . .' was all Margo could manage.

'How often did we say we found it hard to believe that Jo and Donny were related to me?' said Libby.

Margo rolled her eyes. 'Too many times to count.'

'They might've lived on the Scottie at one point, which would explain how they knew about your parents and grandparents,' said Suzie. 'Gossip's always rife in that part of Liverpool.'

Libby clapped a hand to her forehead. 'And *that's* why they said they'd moved to Ireland, when they'd really gone to Blackpool. Jo knew my mum's family had gone overseas, which was how she knew she was safe to pretend to be my aunt.' She stopped speaking as something else hit her. 'My grandparents might still be alive!'

Margo's eyes rounded. 'Oh, Lib, surely they wouldn't have lied about that?'

Libby shrugged. 'They've lied about everythin' else, why would they tell the truth about my grandparents? Particularly when they knew I'd want to get in touch with them. Far easier for Jo to pretend that they were dead, and that she was my mum's sister, especially when she thought she might benefit from some inheritance. Why on earth did I take her at her word?'

Margo put her arm around Libby's shoulders. 'Because you wouldn't expect anyone to make summat like that up.'

'You didn't believe her, not at first,' Libby reminded her.

'I did when she started talkin' about Tony.'

Libby clutched a hand to her stomach, which was beginning to feel decidedly queasy. 'I've just remembered the conversation we had with that woman on the market stall.'

'The one I was talkin' to when we found yer aunt?'

'She said the O'Connells would rather cut their own throats than deal in dodgy gear. We thought it odd at the time, but it makes perfect sense now.'

'I'm sorry to say they literally saw you coming,' said Suzie.

'So what now?' said Libby hollowly. 'Do I confront them? Tell them that I know they're lyin'? Or walk away and never see them again?'

'Only you know the answer to that question,' Suzie told her.

'I wish Jack were here.'

'Why don't you talk to him first?' suggested Margo. 'See what he has to say?'

'He'll go spare,' said Libby. 'He never did like them.'

'Look on the bright side,' said Margo, a wry smile poised on her lips. 'At least they're not your real aunt and uncle.'

A small chuckle escaped Libby's lips. 'There is that, I suppose. Although that does bring me on to another, more pressing thought. Who is my real aunt, and where is she?' Her eyes grew round. 'I came to Liverpool to tell my mother's family what happened, and they're still none the wiser, and all because of those cheatin', lyin', greedy . . .' She stopped speaking, too angry and upset to continue.

Margo linked her arm through Libby's. 'Try not to let them get to you. Even if you'd known the truth you could hardly have gone all the way to Ireland to search for them, because believe you me, if you think lookin' for someone by the name of O'Connell is hard in Liverpool, just you try it in Ireland.'

'Like lookin' for a needle in a haystack, but at least I'd have known the truth.'

'Emma!' cried Margo, from out of the blue. 'Why don't you ask Emma's family to put summat in one of the local rags?'

Libby dismissed this without hesitation. 'Maybe when I first arrived, but that was before I read Mum's diary. Anyone who can turn their backs on their own daughter the way they did doesn't want to know the truth. We've been at war for a long time now, and not once have my grandparents tried to get in touch to see how we are, and whether we're all right.'

Margo dropped her gaze. 'Sometimes you're better off without yer family.' Another thought occurred to her. 'Do you realise we spent weeks livin' with complete strangers?'

'And we paid their bleedin' rent, as well as buyin' them food, cookin' an' cleanin' . . .' Libby's eyes rounded with trepidation. 'Thank Gawd I never asked her if she knew about the stuff my mum wrote in her diary. Could you imagine if I had? The very thought leaves me sick to my stomach.'

'They're hardly in a position to judge,' said Suzie, 'not after what they've done to you.'

'They wouldn't have judged me, but they would have found a way to use it against me,' said Libby sternly, 'and what's more, I'd have handed it to them on a plate! Talk about bein' my own worst enemy. Thank goodness I kept my mouth shut, cos this way it's me what's got them over a barrel and not vice versa.'

Suzie was looking decidedly nervous. 'What do you mean by that?'

'I deserve to know the truth about my grandparents, and I reckon the Murphys can give it to me, or if not they'll know someone who can. And if they don't tell me what they know I'll threaten to tell the scuffers how they've been pretendin' to be my relatives so they can diddle me out of my money!'

'You mustn't do that,' said Suzie earnestly. 'Donny mixes with the types of men that make my dad look like a saint. He won't take well to you turning up on his doorstep demanding answers. In fact, he'll be keen for you to keep your mouth shut, and he knows a very good way of ensuring that'll happen. I don't blame you for wanting to have a go, but what good will it do? It's not as if they're decent people who'll apologise for lying to you.'

'The least they can do is tell me the truth. They owe me that much!'

Suzie gave her a disbelieving look. 'And do you really think they'll tell you out of the goodness of their hearts?' Seeing Libby shrug she pressed on in exasperated tones, 'Not a cat in hell's chance. People like that don't do something for nothing. If you want to know the truth you'll have to pay them for it, and seeing as it's going to end their hopes of an inheritance that information won't come cheap, so I certainly wouldn't advise you to go down that path, because even if they haven't a clue they'll make up any old nonsense and keep you dangling for weeks if not months, or at least until your money runs out. If you take my advice, you'll steer well clear.'

'Why should I pay them a penny when I know where to send the scuffers?' said Libby. 'They'd have a field day with the amount of contraband them two've got stashed in their house. It's them with summat to lose, not me!'

Suzie spun round to face Libby. 'Have you lost your mind? Just look at what my father did to his own mother, then ask yourself what Donny would do to you if you threatened to report him to the scuffers?'

'I won't breathe a word as long as they tell me what they know,' said Libby reasonably.

'Only you're not thinking like them,' said Suzie. 'From their point of view, there's nowt to stop you from doing just that as soon as they've given you the answers you're looking for. If anything, they've got more hope of you not going to the police whilst they still have summat you want. Not to mention what it would do to their reputation should word get out that they gave in to blackmail; let's not forget that's why Donny had to go to Blackpool in the first place.'

Margo stared at her. 'You know about that?'

Suzie nodded darkly. 'Enough to know that one of the fellers he dealt with went missing the day before he left.'

'But he's not been arrested . . .' Libby began, but Suzie was shaking her head.

'There's probably as many bent scuffers in Liverpool as there are criminals.'

'That feller must've had a family,' said Libby. 'Surely they reported him missin'?'

Suzie eyed her cynically. 'Even if they did, plenty of people go missing in big cities.'

'But surely they could tell the scuffers that their loved one had fallen out with Donny?'

'If they wanted to go the same way as their loved one, then yes they could,' Suzie said bluntly.

'Then why did Donny bother goin' to Blackpool if he knew nothin' would come of it?'

'Because tensions would've been running high,' said Suzie, 'and you never know when someone such as yourself will come along to stir the pot.'

'So, what do you suggest I do? Walk away without speakin' my piece?'

'No, because I know how good it is to get this stuff off your chest, but don't ask them for anything because that's when the trouble will start. Tell them what you know and what you think of them and walk away.'

'Or don't even bother to waste yer breath,' said Margo, 'because I very much doubt they'll care that they've been caught in a lie.'

'Jo will,' said Libby, 'because I reckon she's the drivin' force behind this whole thing. Not just that, but she'll know she's never goin' to see a penny of any inheritance whether it exists or not.'

Margo was still dubious. 'But do you think it's wise to confront them when we've been to their house and know so much about them?'

Libby sighed wretchedly. 'I want them to know that I know, but if it makes you feel any better I'll talk to Jack first and see what he says.'

Margo hoped Jack would talk some sense into her friend, because there was no point in trying to appeal to the Murphys' better nature when they simply didn't have one.

'Do you want to grab some chips and forget the cinema?' Suzie asked. 'That way you can call Jack straight away.'

'Thanks, Suzie, but I don't see why we shouldn't continue as planned. If we see a telephone box on the way to the chippy I'll call him, but no matter what he says I shan't be goin' back to the Murphys' until I've had a good chance to think things through.'

When they eventually found a telephone box that was in working order, Margo and Suzie waited outside whilst Libby made the call.

'Hello, Treacle. To what do I owe the pleasure?'

Libby felt as though a huge weight was being lifted from her shoulders as she quickly explained the situation, ending with, 'I don't know whether to go back and have it out with them or leave well alone.'

'I *knew* they couldn't be trusted!' Jack snapped.

'So, what do you think I should do?'

'What would you like to say, given the chance?'

'That I know what they've done and they're never goin' to get a penny of my money – not that I've got any, but they don't know that.'

'And if I say I think you should walk away?'

Libby paused, but only briefly. In truth she'd made her mind up from the moment she'd heard the truth. 'I respect your wishes, and you're probably right, because that's what I should do, but . . .'

'. . . You can't,' said Jack.

'Knowing that they tried to take advantage of me when I was at my lowest will never leave me unless I confront them. I know Margo and Suzie agree with you in thinkin' I should leave sleepin' dogs lie, but it's not in my nature.'

'I know that from seein' you with yer Uncle Tony,' said Jack. 'I don't suppose you can wait until I get some leave so that I can come with you?'

'It wouldn't have the same impact if I had you with me,' said Libby. 'I was the one they took advantage of, and I want them to see that I'm stronger than they thought.'

'Will you at least take one of the girls with you?'

'I could, and I daresay they'll want to come, but this is summat I need to do on my own, if only to prove to myself that I don't need someone to hold my hand every time summat goes wrong.'

'When, then?'

'I'm not sure yet. I'd like Emma's visit to be over first.'

'That sounds like a sensible plan. You will let me know when you're goin' to go though, won't you?'

'Of course, and I'll call you to let you know how Emma's visit went.'

'I wish I was going to be there to meet her.'

'Me too, but I'm sure there'll be plenty of other times – not to mention our weddin'.'

The operator cut across, letting them know their three minutes had come to an end.

'Take care, Jack,' was all that Libby managed before being cut off. Replacing the receiver, she headed out to the girls, who were eager to hear Jack's thoughts.

Margo folded her arms across her chest. 'Well?'

'He thinks I should leave well alone, but I told him as I'm tellin' you that I need to get this off my chest, and what's more I'll be goin' on my own.' Margo immediately began to shake her head, but Libby was adamant. 'I have to do this for myself as much as anything else. I know I'm more than capable of standin' up to people like them, but I can't prove that unless I actually do it.'

Suzie also folded her arms across her chest. 'But what if things take a sinister turn?'

'They won't,' said Libby confidently. 'Because I shall speak my thoughts then leave. I'm not goin' to mention my real aunt or grandparents, just the fact that I know Jo and Donny to be liars and they'll never see nor hear from me again.'

'I hope you know what you're doin',' said Margo.

Libby turned to Suzie. 'You told yer father what you thought of him when you could easily have kept shtum – tell me that didn't feel good!'

'Of course it felt good,' said Suzie, smiling.

'You was with the scuffers at the time, though,' Margo objected.

'But she knew that wouldn't always be the case,' Libby shot back.

'I can see why Libby feels she has to do this,' said Suzie, much to Margo's surprise, 'but there's no reason why she can't have some sort of safety net.'

'When I do go, I'll be on me own,' said Libby firmly.

Margo arched a hopeful eyebrow. 'So you're not goin' any time soon then?'

'Not for a few days at least, so let's forget about the Murphys and enjoy the rest of our evenin', startin' with some fish and chips!'

'Sounds good to me,' said Margo, hoping against hope that her friend would see fit to leave the Murphys well alone given the fullness of time.

***

It was the morning of Emma's arrival and Libby had left the girls to load the cart while she went off to change out of her dungarees.

'Bernie says he's ready whenever you are,' said Margo as she entered the barn a few minutes later.

Libby gave her the thumbs up before stifling a yawn beneath the back of her hand.

Margo's brow rose. 'I'm not surprised you're tired, cos I could hear you tossin' and turnin' in yer sleep last night. If I were to guess, I'd say this whole Donny and Jo business is still playin' heavily on yer mind.'

Libby grimaced as she ran a comb through her hair. 'Every time I shut me eyes I see Jo grinnin' like the cat that got the cream, thinkin' that she'd put one over on us. All I could think about was wipin' that smug smile off her face.'

'I know how hard it must be for you, and I'd dearly love to go round there and give them both a piece of my mind – and a few other things besides – but I know I'd just be wastin' me breath, as well as puttin' meself in danger.'

'Which is why I don't intend on goin' there until I've thought it through thoroughly,' said Libby.

'I'm glad to hear it.'

Suzie popped her head round the door. 'Are you ready? Only Goliath's chomping at the bit for the off.'

Libby chuckled softly. 'You make it sound like he's rarin' to go when in truth he's only eager to get back to his hay net.'

'What are your plans for today, Lib, or have you not made any?' Suzie asked as they made their way out of the barn.

'I thought I'd take Emma to do a bit of sightseein' before bringin' her back to the farm later on this afternoon.'

'It'll be nice for her to see where you live,' said Margo. 'Have you asked Bernie about her stoppin' overnight?'

'Not yet. I thought I could ask him on our way into the city.'

'He'll not say no,' said Suzie. 'Mam said the barn was full to the rafters during the May blitz.'

'That's what I thought; they've hearts of gold have the Lewises,' Libby agreed. 'It'll be the icin' on the cake if he does say yes; havin' Emma spend the night will be just like the old days.' She waved to Bernie, who was ready for the off. 'Wish me luck, not that I'll need it.'

The girls bade her goodbye and good luck as she hurried off to join Bernie. 'Sorry to keep you waitin',' she said as she raised her foot to board the cart.

Bernie gave her an approving glance, which turned into a grin as his eyes settled on her wellington boots. 'Are you sure they match your outfit?'

Following his gaze, Libby rolled her eyes. 'I swear they're so comfy I forget I'm wearin' them half the time. Shan't be a mo!'

She raced back to the barn and quickly donned her kitten heels. *Not as comfortable as my boots*, she thought as she picked her way back across the cobbled yard, *but I'd have looked pretty rum walkin' through the streets of Liverpool in a frock and wellies!*

She held Bernie's hand as he helped her onto the cart, thanking him as she did so. 'It's difficult to board in a ladylike fashion when you're wearin' a frock,' she said as she took the space beside him.

'I'm sure I wouldn't know,' chuckled Bernie, and clicked his tongue, signalling Goliath to walk on.

Libby twisted to face him as the cart rumbled its way down the drive. 'Can I ask a favour?'

'Of course!'

'As I've not got much time with Emma, I was wonderin' if she could sleep in the barn with the rest of us, just for tonight?'

Bernie steered Goliath onto the main road before replying. 'I sort of assumed she was going to, so in answer to your question, then yes, of course she can.'

Libby beamed. 'Thanks, Bernie. This is goin' to be the best night ever.'

'What time's her ferry due in?'

'Eight thirty, so we've plenty of time.'

Bernie glanced at the watch on his wrist. 'Do you want to go straight there? You'll have to wait a couple of hours until your friend gets here but at least you'll keep your frock clean.'

'I'd quite like to deliver the milk with you, if that's all right?' She gazed at the road ahead. 'I'd rather keep myself busy.'

Bernie raised an eyebrow. 'Any particular reason?'

'I've got a lot on my mind at the moment, what with the Murphy twins and—'

Bernie cut her off without apology. 'How on earth does a nice girl like you know the likes of them?' he spluttered.

Libby relayed the events of the previous evening, finishing with: 'I want to give them a piece of my mind. The girls think I should leave well alone, but how can I do that when my principles won't allow me to?'

Having pulled Goliath to a halt and jumped down to the road, Bernie began pouring milk into the various vessels which were offered to him by his customers. 'You make it sound as though you intend to punish them somehow.'

Libby joined him and took a tankard from one of the housewives. 'Wouldn't you?' she asked. Barely pausing for breath, she pressed on. 'I reckon they deserve to suffer for what they've done to me, but Suzie's made it quite clear that any threats I make will be met with violence, so bang goes any idea I had of payback, which if you ask me is jolly unfair.'

Bernie walked Goliath further up the road as they continued to talk. 'You're right, it is unfair. But what's the point in going to see them if you can't make them rue the day they lied to you?'

'I just want them to know that I know that they're a pair of liars and that I've seen right through them.'

'That's understandable,' said Bernie. 'No one likes to think someone's got one over on them, and by telling them you know the truth you'll have taken that away from them.'

'And I'll be the one in control, not them, so they'll have lost – not that there was anything to lose, mind you, but they don't know that – as far as they're concerned, they'll have lost the chance to diddle me out of me parents' life savin's, which was their plan all along.'

Bernie arched an eyebrow. 'You have life savings?'

She laughed. 'No, but for some reason they're convinced I'm sittin' on a small fortune, which is why they lied to me in the first place.'

'And I take it you're not going to say anything to put them right?'

'Nope. I'm goin' to leave them wonderin' what might've been!'

'So when do you intend to put the record straight?'

'Revenge is a dish best served cold,' said Libby, 'so I shall take my time and let them stew, wonderin' what's happened to stop me callin' by.'

Bernie grinned. 'They'll probably think you've come into your inheritance.'

Libby chuckled mischievously. 'They might, mightn't they?'

'I think you're taking the right form of revenge,' said Bernie as they moved to the next street, 'cos Suzie's right: people like the Murphy twins don't take kindly to threats.'

She eyed him curiously. 'How do you know them – or am I bein' nosy?'

Bernie shrugged. 'I don't know them, I know *of* them – I think everyone in Liverpool does. They're notorious for their dealings, and I don't think there's anything they don't dabble in.'

Libby shook her head ruefully. 'If I'd known who they were I'd've told them to sling their hook from the off.'

'Hardly your fault when you were new to the city. Besides, they're good at what they do,' Bernie told her. 'They know the right things to say and do to win someone's trust – as well as their money.'

'Well, I'll be the one that slips the net,' said Libby, 'and I shall enjoy tellin' them so, too, when the time is right.'

'You've certainly got a lot to tell your pal.'

'Poor Emma,' said Libby. 'She'll be fed up to the back teeth of hearin' my woes by the time I've told her everythin'.'

'That's what friends are for,' said Bernie. 'We all need a good whinge every now and then, even me.'

'Granted, but seein' as I haven't seen her since losin' me parents, she'll be subject to a full-on whinge with extra whining on top!'

Bernie smiled. 'I expect she'll be just as bad.'

'What makes you say that?'

He pulled a face. 'Her parents moved her to Ireland to keep her safe, yet she's chosen to join the ATS. I should imagine that didn't go down too well with her folks.'

'You're right. Her father was furious when he found out.'

'And I bet there's more to it than meets the eye,' Bernie added. 'There often is with these things.'

'She was desperate to come back to Britain,' said Libby. 'It must be rotten to be stuck somewhere which makes you unhappy.'

'Like you in Liverpool, you mean?'

'It's not Liverpool that's made me unhappy – or the people in it, for that matter.'

'Then why the urge to go back to London? Mam says that's your intention once the war's over.'

Libby watched Goliath's ears bob up and down as he plodded down the road to their final stop. 'It isn't so much that I don't like Liverpool, but more that I shouldn't have left London. You see, I'd convinced myself that I had to tell my grandparents of their daughter's passin', but I realised much later that I was usin' them as an excuse to run away from my problems. Had I met Jo and Donny in an ordinary way, I would've told them the news and left, because it was glaringly obvious that they were just as bad as my Uncle Tony, but I was so desperate to be part of a family I turned a blind eye, kidding myself that they weren't as bad as they appeared.'

Bernie blew his cheeks out. 'They say love is blind.'

'Exactly! I'd have done anythin' to have that feelin' of family back.'

'But if your Uncle Tony's as bad as them, why go back?'

'My uncle more or less bullied me out of London because I wasn't strong enough to fight my corner, but I am now, and I want to give it to him the way I'm goin' to give it to the Murphys. I gave up too easily last time, but after talkin' it through with the girls I now know what to do to get my parents' stall back and send him off with a flea in his ear.'

'Good for you!'

'Once he's heard what I've got to say he'll have no choice than to hand me back what was rightfully mine in the first place, and once he's done that I shall restore the Gilberts' good name.'

'And is that the only reason why you're going back – so that you can give him what for?'

'No. I'm also goin' back because I lived there quite happily until my uncle turned on me.'

Bernie eyed her curiously. 'If you were happy, why were you going to start a new life in Norwich?'

Libby replied without hesitation. 'Because of the war.'

'But the war's not just happening in London.' He glanced pointedly to some buildings ahead which lay in ruins. 'As well you know.'

'Granted, but it's where I grew up,' said Libby, 'which makes it my home.'

Bernie jumped down from the cart to serve the gathering women and children. 'Home is where the heart is, or at least that's what they say, but in my opinion home isn't always a place.'

'How do you mean?' said Libby, confused.

'Home can be your family rather than a place. Take your fiancé, for example. He was happy to call Liverpool his home because you were here; he wouldn't have done so otherwise.'

Libby thought of Gordon in London, and of Jack's reluctance to go back because he would be far away from her. She spoke slowly. 'His heart's with me, so home is wherever I am?'

Bernie grinned. 'Spot on.'

'And you think that because my heart's with him, that could be the drivin' force behind me wantin' to go back to London, and I'm usin' my Uncle Tony as an excuse?'

Bernie performed a small bow. 'Talking does wonders, doesn't it?'

Libby blew her cheeks out. 'It does, but it also leaves me confused, as well as feelin' slightly guilty.'

'Guilty? Why would you feel that?'

'I've promised Suzie that she can come back to London with me, but what if I don't end up goin' back?'

'You have to do what's right for you,' said Bernie. 'Just make sure you talk it through with your pals first. For all you know, moving to London could be the wrong thing for Suzie, cos I'm guessing she only wants to go there so that she can run away from her name.'

'She does indeed, and I don't blame her, cos she won't find it easy if she stays here.'

'She'll find it a lot easier with friends by her side, but if you change your mind and come haring back to Liverpool, what will happen to Suzie then?'

Libby was about to say she wouldn't do that when she remembered Margo. 'Maybe I should go back for a visit before settin' anythin' in stone.'

'I think that would be wise, and you've the perfect excuse with Jack in Biggin Hill.'

Libby glanced pointedly at Bernie's wrist. 'How are we doin' for time?'

'Not bad at all. We'll finish off here and I'll drive you over.'

Libby was shaking her head. 'It's ever so kind of you, but . . .'

'But me no buts, as Mam always says,' said Bernie. 'We can't have you late for the big reunion.'

'Thanks, Bernie. You're goin' to make some woman a good husband one of these days!'

Chapter Five

Emma craned her neck as she tried to catch a glimpse of Libby amongst the throng of people going about their daily business. Hearing the sound of horse's hooves, she saw her pal approaching on a cart driven by the most handsome man she had ever seen.

'Emma!' Libby cried as she jumped down from the cart. 'You're early!'

The two friends took each other in a tight embrace, with Emma staring wide-eyed at Goliath over Libby's shoulder. 'Blimey, Lib, you sure know how to travel!' She glanced to Bernie, who smiled down at her.

'You can't be Jack, so you must be Bernie?' said Emma, smiling shyly back.

'I am indeed!' he confirmed, adding, 'Can I give you ladies a ride anywhere?'

It was clear from the look on Emma's face that she would very much like Bernie to give her a ride just about anywhere, but Libby had other plans.

'Thanks for the offer, but I'm goin' to take Emma for a look round the city and maybe a spot of lunch before heading home to get changed for a night of dancin' in the Grafton.'

'Perhaps later, though?' said Emma hopefully.

Bernie held Emma's gaze as he spoke. 'How about I pick you up when you're ready, save you getting the bus back?'

Libby was about to say that it was a kind offer, but would be asking too much, when Emma spoke first. 'That would be lovely, Bernie,' she said, staring at him dewy-eyed.

Since she could hardly refuse his invitation after Emma had accepted it, Libby said hesitantly, 'I suppose it can't harm as long as you don't mind? Cos it's a big faff gettin' Goliath suited and booted as it were, and we could just as easily catch the bus . . .' She fell silent as Bernie raised his hand.

'The pleasure would be all mine. What time would you like me to pick you up?'

'I was plannin' on catchin' the three o'clock bus, so any time around then would be fine.'

'Splendid. Shall we say three o'clock outside St George's Hall?'

'Sounds good to me. And thanks again.'

With a wave and a click of his tongue, Bernie moved Goliath on, leaving the girls behind.

'No wonder you like life at the farm,' breathed Emma as she waved back.

'I've got Jack, remember?' Libby reminded her.

'And who's Bernie got?' said Emma as she linked her arm through Libby's.

'No one,' said Libby, 'but he's broken his fair share of hearts if you're thinkin' what I think you're thinkin'.'

Emma waved a dismissive hand. 'What's the point in havin' a heart if you don't get it broken once in a while?'

Libby eyed her friend affectionately. 'Gawd, I've missed you, Emma Bagshaw.'

'And I you,' said Emma. Casting her eye around the grand buildings surrounding them, she added, 'My goodness, it's good to be back in Blighty.'

'I was sorry to hear that you didn't like life in Ireland,' said Libby. 'It can't have been easy startin' somewhere new.'

'I felt like a foreigner,' said Emma, 'because that's how the locals made me feel. I wish I could say it was my imagination, but they made it quite plain that I wasn't welcome.'

'Then they must have rocks in their heads,' said Libby, 'cos you're one of the sweetest, kindest girls I know.'

'I'm not the only one who's had it tough, though. You said summat about findin' your mother's diary, and I got the impression that all was not well, am I right?'

'Probably the worst thing I ever did; and whilst I hate to burden you with my woes, I think it's important you should know everything that happened to me after you left London, because that's the whole reason why I came to Liverpool in the first place.'

'I thought you came to tell your relatives about your parents – may they rest in peace?'

'I thought that too, but when I look back . . .' She sighed. 'I'll start at the beginning.'

As they walked, Emma listened without interruption, only speaking when Libby had finished. 'I don't know whether you're the unluckiest person alive, or the luckiest,' she said bluntly.

Libby pulled a doubtful face. 'I don't know about bein' the luckiest.'

Emma began to tick the list off on her fingers. 'You escaped the clutches of that vile man, got rescued from drownin' by your future husband, and found a good friend in Margo, not to mention escapin' two more bombin's. If that ain't lucky I don't know what is!'

'What about me mum's diary? Had I not found that I'd still be none the wiser, which quite frankly I think I'd prefer.'

'You can't change what your mother did, but at least you know why the rest of her family treated her like an outcast – although I find it hard to believe she had an affair, no matter how brief. Or that you're the product of that affair, I might add.'

'Even after three years of tryin'?' said Libby cynically.

Emma studied Libby's face. 'You've got yer dad's eyes and mouth, and yer mam's hair and cheekbones. Unless the man who had an affair with yer mum was a dead ringer for yer dad, I don't see how you *can't* be his.'

Libby stood in stunned silence as she took Emma's words in. 'You're right. I *have* got my father's eyes. Why on earth didn't I think of that before?'

Emma shrugged. 'Cos you're on the inside lookin' out and I'm on the outside lookin' in. Not only that, but unlike Jack and Margo I actually knew your parents, very well in fact, which is why I can see the resemblance. Not just looks, either. You've also got yer father's impulsive nature, cos dashin' off half-cocked is the sort of thing he'd do too.'

'Granted, but that doesn't change the fact that me mum did what she did with another man.'

Emma eyed Libby in a cynical fashion. 'Are you certain you've read the diary right?'

Libby replied without hesitation. 'You can read it for yerself if you like.'

Emma shook her head fervently. 'No thank you. The written word can usually be interpreted in more ways than one, and I don't want to draw a conclusion without speakin' to the writer first.'

'Bit hard under the circumstances,' said Libby.

Emma wagged a reproving finger. 'Which is all the more reason for you not to be jumpin' to conclusions. If you want my advice, you should leave sleepin' dogs lie and forget you ever read that bloomin' diary.'

'Do you know what? You're right. I've wasted too much time worryin' over summat that's beyond my control. I'm goin' to forget about the past and concentrate on the future.' She slid her arm through Emma's. 'You've only been here two minutes and you're already makin' me feel heaps better about things.'

'Good, because I don't like to think of you tyin' yerself in knots when there's really no need.' Emma eyed Libby studiously. 'We've not seen each other in over a year, yet I don't feel as though any time has passed at all.'

'It's like we've just picked up where we left off,' said Libby. 'I reckon it's because we're like peas in a pod.'

'We are that,' Emma agreed. 'I must say, I'm really lookin' forward to seein' where you live and work.'

Libby chuckled softly. 'And I suppose Bernie has nothin' to do with your desire to see the farm?'

Emma tried to swallow her telltale smile. 'He has a certain charm.'

'Well, he'd better have his wits about him if he thinks I'm goin' to let him break yer heart,' said Libby. 'I seen the way you was lookin' at each other earlier!'

'Can you blame me? The man's a god!'

Libby laughed out loud. 'I wouldn't go that far, but I'll admit you'd have to be blind not to be drawn to that smile, and he certainly has a good hand to offer any potential bride.'

'I reckon I'd rather enjoy bein' a farmer's wife,' said Emma dreamily.

'You can help me muck the pigs out later, see how keen you are then,' said Libby. 'Bernie might be devilishly handsome, but farmin's hard work.'

'Worth it, though, if you've got him to come home to,' said Emma.

'Honestly, Emma, you're incorrigible!'

'Are you sayin' I'm wrong?'

'Far from it! Not only is he devilishly handsome, but he's got a good head on his shoulders an' all,' said Libby, before relaying the conversation she and Bernie had had regarding the Murphys and her decision to go back to London.

'Wise as well as wonderful,' sighed Emma. 'Can he get any better?'

'Emma Bagshaw! What has come over you?'

'I need to catch up with you!' said Emma, tucking her arm through Libby's. 'When I last saw you, you'd never been kissed, yet here we are not much more than one year on, and you're betrothed to a man I've never even met!'

Libby fished around inside her handbag, pulling out a copy of the photograph she'd given to Jack on the day of their parting. 'There you go. Meet Jack!'

Emma admired the image with approval. 'I can see why you fell for him. What colour are his eyes?'

'Green,' said Libby promptly, 'and they sparkle like emeralds.'

'I hope I'm lucky enough to find a man who makes me as happy as Jack makes you,' Emma sighed, 'although I think I might well be on my way.'

Libby tucked the photograph back into her handbag. 'You're makin' it sound as though you've fallen in love at first sight.'

'He certainly makes me go weak at the knees,' said Emma. 'Is that love?'

Libby thought of Jack and how he had made her feel the last time he had kissed her goodbye. 'I'd say so.'

'Do you reckon he feels the same way?' asked Emma eagerly, but quickly dismissed the idea out of hand. 'Forget I said that. A man like Bernie will have his pick of the bunch.'

'From what I've heard Bernie's had a lot of women fall at his feet, but as far as I'm aware he's not been serious about any of them apart from Roz.'

Emma pricked up her ears. 'Who's Roz?'

Libby told her the saga of Roz, Felix, Bernie and Suzie. By the time she had finished Emma was staring at her open-mouthed. 'That farm of yours is worse than Petticoat Lane when it comes to gossip!'

'It certainly makes for an interesting life,' said Libby. 'Not that I approve of idle gossip, mind you. Having said that, had I not told Suzie about the Murphys I'd still be oblivious of who they really are.'

'I'd like to get my hands on them, the filthy rotten scoundrels,' snapped Emma. 'Scum of the earth, that's what they are.'

'And that's what I shall tell them, only perhaps not quite in that fashion,' said Libby.

'Well, I certainly wouldn't leave Liverpool on their account,' said Emma, 'and I'm not just sayin' that cos I want to come and visit you at Hollybank every time I have a bit of leave.'

Libby smiled at her friend affectionately. 'Why do I get the feelin' Bernie might get to see more of you than me?'

'What are you tryin' to say, Libby Gilbert?' Emma giggled, feigning shock.

Libby wagged a chiding finger. 'You know full well what I meant.'

Emma lowered her voice. 'Have you and Jack done anythin' other than kiss?'

'Emma!' gasped Libby. 'What sort of a question is that?'

'An honest one,' said Emma plainly. 'You and Jack have been through a hell of a lot together. It wouldn't be unheard of for a girl in your position to have succumbed to her womanly needs.'

Libby laughed until the tears formed. *'Womanly needs*? What *have* you been reading?'

'Gone With the Wind. Have you read it?'

'No, and I'm not sure I should. Is it any good?'

'Tediously long,' said Emma, 'but with nothin' else to do than sit in my room, it helped to while away the hours.'

'As well as fill yer head with all kinds of notions,' noted Libby.

'Bernie can be my Rhett Butler any day of the week, and I'll be his Scarlett O'Hara,' said Emma, adding dramatically, 'and he will kiss me like someone who knows how.'

Libby's brows couldn't get any higher. 'Flippin' 'eck. I hope Bernie knows what he's lettin' himself in for!'

Emma giggled. 'Trust me, if Bernie came towards me with his lips pouted, I'd either pass out or run away.'

Libby burst out laughing. 'What happened to wantin' to be kissed by a man that knows how?'

'Talkin's one thing, but doin'?' She puffed her cheeks out. 'I'm not sure I'm ready for that yet.' She paused briefly. 'How did you know when you were ready, and what was your first kiss like?'

'I didn't have a clue, which is the best way if you ask me,' admitted Libby. 'Had I thought about it, I'd have been a bit like you, but as it was it was totally out of the blue. As for what it was like? It was wonderful.'

'Where did he kiss you?'

'On the lips.' Libby chuckled as Emma rolled her eyes. 'He kissed me at Euston station, on the night I left for Liverpool.'

'Kissin' by moonlight,' breathed Emma. 'How romantic!'

Libby smiled. 'I suppose it was. Although we'd nearly kissed in his father's bedroom a few days before, so I guess things had been building up from there.'

Emma stared at her agog. 'His father's *bedroom*?'

Libby wagged a chiding finger. 'It's not what you're thinkin'. Jack was loanin' me some of his mother's dresses.'

'You said you *nearly* kissed, so what stopped you?'

'Jack's father. I swear he nearly had a heart attack when he came back to find us in the bedroom.'

'I bet he did! And whilst you were quick to quash my earlier suggestion, do you think it's just as well he came home when he did?'

'If you were to ask me now, then I'd say yes, but we barely knew each other back then. We weren't even boyfriend and girlfriend, let alone engaged to be married.'

'So, you've thought about it then?' said Emma, waggling her eyebrows suggestively.

'Of course I have! And you needn't look at me like that, because I know the thought's run through your head and you haven't even got a boyfriend!'

'You'll be gettin' married soon enough. Are you nervous about yer weddin' night?'

'Terrified!' admitted Libby. 'But I know that Jack won't rush me, because he's a gentleman through and through.'

Emma was eyeing her wistfully. 'You're ever so lucky to have a man like Jack in yer life.'

'I know, and there's not a doubt in my mind that it was fate that brought us together, cos I'd literally be dead if it hadn't.'

'Who'd have thought it, eh? All those conversations we had about the sort of man we'd like to marry, and you actually found your very own knight in shinin' armour when you wasn't even lookin' for one!'

'He's perfect in every way,' Libby agreed.

'Have you thought about what you're goin' to do for a weddin' dress? Cos I can't imagine they're goin' to be easy to come by what with the government takin' all the silk to use as parachutes.'

'I'm not really bothered what I get married in,' said Libby truthfully, 'I just want everyone to be happy.'

Emma nudged her friend with a wink. 'Can Bernie be my plus one?'

'Of course he can!' Libby laughed, and it suddenly occurred to her that she'd laughed a lot since Emma's arrival. 'And I hope it goes without sayin' that you'll be my bridesmaid?'

Emma gave a small squeal of delight. 'Of course I will!'

Libby beamed. 'Perfect! Now, what do you say to a ginger beer and a penny bun at Lyons?'

After lunch the girls took a stroll around the rest of the city, with Libby pointing out various landmarks, finishing with the Liver Building and the tale of the liver birds that sat atop it.

Emma looked to one of the clock towers that adorned the building. 'It's nearly quarter to three. How far are we away from St George's Hall?'

'Not far,' said Libby, 'but we'd best get a move on if we're not to be late.'

Emma tucked her arm through Libby's as they hurried off in the direction of the hall. 'You know all them things I was sayin' about Bernie earlier?' she puffed.

'Yes?'

'You know I'm goin' to be as quiet as a mouse when I see him, don't you?'

Libby chuckled. 'Yes, but don't worry. Bernie's a good conversationalist; he'll soon put you at ease.'

'I might like to think I'm Scarlett O'Hara,' confessed Emma, 'but I'm more like the cowardly lion in *The Wizard of Oz* – have you seen it?'

'Yes, I have.' Libby smiled. 'And you're nothin' like the cowardly lion. Shy, yes, but cowardly? Never!'

Emma clasped the stitch which had formed in her side as they came to a halt outside the hall. 'All that farm work's made you as fit as a fiddle,' she told Libby, who was barely out of breath. 'I dread to think how I'm goin' to cope in the army.'

'They'll soon whip you into shape,' said Libby. She waved to gain Bernie's attention as the cart came into view.

Emma rolled her eyes. 'Either that or kill me.'

Bernie frowned at Libby as he jumped down from the cart. 'What on earth have the two of you been doing?'

'Runnin',' said Emma, trying not to wince as the stitch objected to her speech.

'Just as well you don't have to run back to the farm, then,' said Bernie. He hopped back onto the cart and held his hand out. 'Let's be having you.'

Emma eyed the height of the cart dubiously. 'I dunno if I can get my leg that high,' she confessed.

'Not to worry,' said Libby. 'Bernie can pull you up and I'll give you a shove from behind if necessary.'

'It's goin' to be necessary all right,' mumbled Emma as she held on to Bernie's hand.

Bernie lifted Emma onto the cart without any help from Libby, much to Emma's relief. 'Thanks, Bernie. That was a bit more dignified than havin' a shoulder ride in order to get on.'

Bernie waved a dismissive hand. 'It's like everything in life: practice makes perfect.'

'No amount of practice will make my legs grow,' said Emma ruefully.

'You've got beautiful legs,' said Libby warmly. 'Hasn't she, Bernie?'

Emma's face flushed scarlet as Bernie eyed her legs with approval. 'A fine set of pins,' he confirmed, before adding conversationally, 'How would you like a tour of the farm when we get back, Emma?'

Emma prayed that the colour wasn't deepening in her cheeks as she took him up on his offer. 'I'd like that very much, but are you sure I'm not puttin' you out?'

'Positive! Now how about you tell me what you did in the city. I trust it went well?'

'Swimmingly! I didn't get to see much the last time we were here, because we got straight off the train onto the ferry, which was a real shame, because Liverpool is beautiful. It quite reminds me of London, what with all the grand buildings – and the river, of course, which is much wider than the Thames.'

'I've never been to London,' mused Bernie. 'I'd like to go, though.'

'If you ever need a guide, then Emma's your girl,' said Libby loyally. 'She knows London like the back of her hand, don't you, Emma?'

'Lived there all me life, practically. But I'm sure Bernie's far too busy . . .'

Bernie cut in. 'Some things are worth making time for. Besides, everyone deserves a break every now and then. Do you know if you're being posted close to London?'

'I won't know until I've completed my basic trainin' in Pontefract.'

'That's a fair old trek,' said Bernie, the disappointment clear to hear in his voice.

'Too far for me to pop back for a visit,' said Emma ruefully, 'but I did hear someone say that they give you a week's leave before you get your first postin'.'

'You're welcome to come and spend your week's leave on the farm, if you'd like to,' said Bernie.

The smile on Emma's face said it all. 'That would be marvellous. Are you sure you don't mind?'

'Not at all. The more the merrier.'

'I'll show you how to milk the cows, and find where the chickens have laid their eggs,' said Libby. 'You'll just love life at the farm, I know you will.'

Bernie pulled Goliath to a halt and passed Emma the reins, something which she had not been expecting. 'You can even help me deliver the milk, if you like.'

Protesting at having been given full control of the largest horse she'd ever seen, Emma tried to give the reins back, but Bernie placed his hands over the top of hers, saying calmly, 'Don't worry, Goliath won't do nothing. Now, tell me if you can you feel the connection between the reins and the bit?'

She mumbled, 'Ummhmm,' too frightened to speak in case she said something that would make Goliath move.

'Perfect! You don't have to do anything other than maintain that tension, so that he knows you're there, and the rest is easy. You pull gently to bring him to a halt, and click your tongue to get him to walk on.' He demonstrated the latter and Goliath obediently broke into a slow walk. 'Now, try pulling him back to a halt.'

At first Emma pulled the reins so gently that nothing happened, but with a little encouragement from Bernie she placed more tension on the reins and Goliath came back to a complete halt.

'I did it!' she gasped, quietly so as not to alarm him. She turned to Bernie, her eyes dancing with delight. 'Isn't he a good boy?' Bernie's blue eyes twinkled back at her as he instructed her to walk Goliath on.

Clicking her tongue, Emma was disappointed when the horse failed to respond, but Bernie told her she was doing it too softly, and after a few more attempts Goliath broke into a walk.

'How does he know what to do?' Emma asked as he plodded slowly on.

'Years of practice,' said Bernie. 'Are you enjoying yourself?'

'Lovin' every minute,' she said, and the smile on her face made it clear that this was the case.

As they made their way out of the city Bernie taught Emma how to guide Goliath onto a new road, and when they eventually arrived at the farm he showed her how to take him through gates.

Jumping down from the cart, Bernie walked over to the second gate they came to and opened it wide. Emma clicked her tongue for Goliath to walk on, and Libby waited until they were on the other side before whispering, 'I've been here since December and Bernie's never taught any of us how to drive the cart – not even Roz! Or not that I know of.'

Misunderstanding, Emma made to hand her the reins. 'I'm sorry. Did you want to have a go?'

Libby shook her head, but before she could say anything Bernie came back. Swinging himself up onto the cart, he smiled at Emma. 'Ready when you are.'

Emma clicked Goliath on before asking Bernie the question she'd been wondering about since going through the first gate. 'Libby said that the farm was big, but just how big is it?'

'Eighty acres.'

Emma gave him a look of awe. 'There was a farm in the village where I lived in Ireland; the farmer said they had twenty acres, which quite impressed me till now.'

'That's why we need so many land girls,' said Bernie, who appeared pleased to hear that he'd managed to impress Emma. 'We couldn't possibly manage it on our own, and with petrol being in short supply we have to rely on manual labour far more than we did before the war.'

'Well, you're certainly doin' yer bit to feed the nation, and then some,' said Emma.

Smiling proudly, Bernie continued their tour of the farm – some of which even Libby hadn't seen – until they arrived back in the yard. After helping the girls to get down from the cart, he unhitched Goliath whilst Libby and Emma looked on. 'Would you like to help me turn him out, Emma?' he asked. 'You can ride him back to his field if you like.'

Emma's smile couldn't have got any broader as she gratefully accepted his offer. 'I've always wanted to ride a horse!' Seeing the obvious look of disappointment on Libby's face, Bernie arched his brow.

'Sorry, Lib, do you want to ride as well? You could go two up, if you like.'

Libby nodded enthusiastically. 'We'll have to put summat else on our feet, though, cos I ain't traipsin' through the mud in these.' She glanced pointedly at her kitten heels.

Emma looked down at her own shoes, which were equally unsuitable for anything but city wear. 'Oh heck. I think I'll have to give it a miss.'

'Nonsense,' said Bernie. 'We're bound to have some wellies that'll fit. Libby will help you find some, won't you, Lib?'

'Of course. Come with me, Emma, and we'll see if any of the girls have got owt that'll fit you.' Taking her pal by the hand, Libby led her to the barn, chattering excitedly all the way. 'First teachin' you to drive and now takin' you for a ride? I reckon a certain young farmer's rather keen on you.'

'Are you sure he's not doin' it out of politeness, what with the two of us bein' friends an' all?'

But Libby was shaking her head fervently. 'I seen the way he looks at you, and it's the same way Tom looks at Margo and Jack looks at me.'

Emma began to blush. 'Are you sure?'

'Positive,' said Libby. She opened the door to the barn and began to rummage through the available footwear whilst hastily introducing Emma to the girls. She glanced at Emma's feet as the others exchanged greetings.

'What *are* you doing?' queried Suzie as she strolled towards them.

'Lookin' for a pair of wellies to fit Emma,' said Libby. 'Bernie's givin' us a ride on Goliath.'

Margo gaped at them. 'How come?'

Libby looked up from her search with a large grin etched upon her cheeks, and jerked her head in Emma's direction. 'Cos he's got the hots for Emma.'

Emma gave an embarrassed giggle. 'I'm sure he hasn't.'

'Blimey, he doesn't let the grass grow!' said Suzie.

Emma fixed Suzie with an inquisitive gaze. 'Oh?'

'I told you he has a reputation for breakin' hearts,' Libby reminded her. 'Not that I think he's goin' to do that to you, mind you, or at least he'd better not!'

'I think Libby might be on to summat,' said Margo approvingly, 'cos I don't think he's ever offered any of the other land girls a ride on Goliath, not even Roz.'

Libby stood up. 'Damn and blast, Emma Bagshaw. Why have you got such small feet?'

'It doesn't matter,' said Emma. 'I'll wait here.'

Libby looked at her sharply. 'Oh no you won't! I ain't missin' my chance to have a ride on Goliath, so you're comin' too, whether you like it or not.'

Emma looked down at her shoes. 'I can't walk through the mud in these.'

'It's OK, I'll give you a piggyback.'

Margo came over with a pair of slacks and a jumper for Emma. 'You can wear these.'

Thanking Margo for her kindness, Emma quickly changed out of her dress, and Libby followed suit. Suzie, Margo and Adele donned their boots, so that they could go with the girls to watch them have a ride.

'You're ever so lucky,' said Suzie as they made their way over to Bernie and Goliath. 'Closest I've come to riding a horse is when I sat on Thor by accident.'

Margo laughed. 'Not that he noticed, the great lump.'

'Who's Thor?'

'Margo's dog,' explained Libby. 'He's a bullmastiff.'

Bernie chuckled softly as he watched the girls approach. 'Let me guess. Everyone wants a go?'

'We've come to watch,' said Margo, 'although I wouldn't say no if you're offerin'.'

Bernie jerked his head, indicating for them all to come over. 'I reckon he can take three, but . . .'

Adele was waving her hands in denial. 'I'm happy enough to keep both feet on the ground, thanks all the same.'

Suzie stared at her in disbelief. 'Don't you want to ride him?'

'I like to be in control,' said Adele. 'I don't mind the cart, because I can't see Goliath tanking off with that thing strapped to him.'

Bernie burst out laughing. 'If it's Goliath doing a runner that's worrying you, I wouldn't give it a second thought. It'd take a rocket to get him going.'

'That may be so, but I'd still prefer to keep both feet on the ground,' said Adele firmly.

'Suit yourself. Come on, ladies, who wants to go at the front?'

After a lot of laughter and near misses, Bernie managed to get Emma at the front, with Suzie sandwiched between her and Libby. 'We'll have to swap on the way to the field so that Margo can have a turn,' said Libby. 'I don't mind sharin' my go.'

'Does he even know they're on him?' Adele asked as she watched Goliath move forward at his normal pace.

'Probably not,' said Bernie.

'He's lovely and warm,' remarked Libby. 'Quite soft, too.'

'I wish I could take a photo,' said Adele.

'Maybe when I come back for my next visit?' said Emma.

'Definitely,' said Bernie. 'I'll put his old show bridle on.'

'I didn't know you used to take him to shows,' Libby exclaimed.

'Before the war,' said Bernie, 'and he used to get placed every time.'

'That's because he's the best Suffolk Punch in the whole wide world,' said Suzie loyally.

'C'mon, Margo, it's your turn,' said Libby, sliding off the horse's back. There was a lot of squealing and giggling as Margo nearly pulled Suzie and Emma off in her effort to get on. When they were all settled, Goliath walked stoically on.

'Isn't he lovely?' said Libby.

'The best,' said Margo. 'I'm definitely goin' to have horses when I get a smallholdin'.'

'That's the end of the track,' Bernie told the girls. 'I'll get Margo and Suzie down first, because they've got wellies on.'

'I'll help Margo release Goliath,' volunteered Suzie.

'And I'll give Emma a piggy back,' Libby began, but Bernie was shaking his head.

'I'll carry Emma, as long as it's all right with Emma of course?'

Blushing madly, Emma nodded shyly as Bernie scooped her up and carried her back down the track as though she weighed nothing at all. When he reached the cobbles, he gently placed her down, his hand lingering on her shoulder as he twinkled at her. 'What time's your train tomorrow?'

'Ten a.m.' said Emma promptly. 'At Central Station.'

He pushed his hands into his pockets. 'If you fancy coming with me to deliver the milk, I can take you to the train after we're through, as I did with Libby this morning.'

'Are you sure I wouldn't be puttin' you out?'

'Not at all; in fact it'll be my pleasure.' He looked over to the other girls, who were feigning disinterest. 'Good night, ladies.'

There was a chorus of general good nights as he set off for the main house, before the girls hurried over to Emma.

'I don't know why I'm blushin', cos it's not as if he's asked me out on a date!' she said, fanning her face with her hand. 'So why do I feel as though he did?'

'Because it's obvious he likes you,' said Libby, 'and if you were going to be here any longer he'd *definitely* have asked you on a date.'

Emma pulled a rueful face. 'Why oh why didn't I apply to join the Land Army?'

'Coulda, woulda, shoulda,' said Libby. 'Think how much happier we'd be if only life worked on that premise.'

'Everything happens for a reason,' said Suzie, 'or at least that's my theory, and I think I prefer that to regret.'

Libby grimaced apologetically. 'I'm glad you said that, cos me and Bernie had a chat this mornin' and I've decided not to jump in with both feet when it comes to goin' back to London.'

'What did he say to make you change yer mind?' asked Margo.

Libby relayed the conversation she'd had with Bernie, and her subsequent decision to visit the city rather than up sticks and move back. 'I've been flyin' by the seat of my pants ever since losin' me parents,' she told them, 'and I do think he might be right, because I'm not sure I'd be as keen to go back if Jack wasn't down that neck of the woods. I really am sorry, Suzie, cos I know you had your heart set on London.'

'Don't worry about it,' said Suzie at once. 'I'll work summat out.'

'Why don't you join the services, like me?' suggested Emma. 'That way you get a home and a trade – or as I like to call it, a new start.'

'But I wouldn't know anyone,' said Suzie.

'Neither will anyone else,' said Emma, 'and as we'll all be in the same boat, I should imagine makin' friends would be easy; or at least I hope so, cos that's what I'm countin' on.'

Suzie looked doubtful. 'But what about after the war?'

'You could have a proper trade under yer belt by then,' said Libby reasonably. 'You could be a driver, or a typist—'

Suzie cut her off before she could go any further. 'With my spelling? They'd chuck me out on me ear before I'd learned to spell knife!'

'Maybe not a typist, then,' said Libby, 'but I bet you could drive.'

Suzie brightened. 'Dad taught me to drive the lorry after he chucked Roz out. It's quite easy once you get the hang of it.'

'There you go then! And if not, there's cookin', cleanin', all manner of jobs. They won't ask you to do summat unless you're suitable.'

'Libby's right, and you'll have far more options with a career under yer belt,' said Margo, 'so what d'you reckon? Are you goin' to give it a go, or sit tight and see what happens?'

'If I stay here, I'll have no choice but to take whatever's available when I leave,' said Suzie. 'I liked the idea of running a market stall with Libby in London, but that's no good if she decides to stay in Liverpool, whereas if I join the services it sounds as though I'm more or less guaranteed a trade.'

'Is that a yes?' asked Adele tentatively.

'I think so, but I won't make enquiries until I've spoken to me mam.'

Adele smiled approvingly. 'She'll appreciate you taking her thoughts into consideration.'

'I want her to be proud of me,' said Suzie.

'She is proud of you!' cried Adele. 'She knows how hard it was for you to stand up to your father, never mind the effort you've made to put things right ever since.'

'Which is why I wanted to be with her when we show him Sheila's ration book,' said Suzie, 'and I won't be able to do that if I'm in the services.'

'You'll get leave,' said Emma.

'But it would be ideal if we show him the book the day he gets out of the nick. That won't be for another six months, and I could be anywhere by then.'

Libby shrugged. 'One of us could go with her, or all of us even.'

'Which is very good of you, but I want to show him that me and Mam aren't going to be bullied and that we stand together against him.'

'Which is understandable, but you can't base your whole life around one day,' said Margo. 'None of us know if we're goin' to make it through the night, never mind what tomorrow might bring.'

'You're pretty safe here though, surely?' asked Emma, glancing up at the roof above their heads.

'As we can be, although I guess nowhere is one hundred per cent safe,' Libby told her. 'I'm sure the bombs don't always land where they were intended, and the shrapnel from the SS *Malakand* landed three miles away from where she was docked. If you're in the wrong place at the wrong time, it's goodnight, Vienna!'

Suzie gave a reluctant sigh. 'When you put it like that, I suppose you're right. I can't put my life on hold on account of "what ifs"; if I was going to do that I might as well wait for Libby to make her mind up about London. I'll still speak to Mam first, though, so that she knows of my intentions.'

'Well, I for one think you're doin' the right thing,' said Libby, 'and who knows? The services might well suit you down to the ground.'

'Do you know, I rather think they might,' said Suzie, sounding a little more cheerful, 'and whilst I'd give anything to be with me mam on the day she gives me dad his marching orders, maybe there's summat else planned for me.'

'Such as?' said Adele.

'Maybe that'll be the day that I do summat that'll win us the war,' said Suzie optimistically.

'And that's the best way to look at it,' said Libby, before being corrected by Suzie.

'It's the only way to look at it. Because no matter how much you want to be, you can't always be in control of your own life.'

'But aren't you taking control by deciding to join the services?' mused Adele.

'Not really,' said Suzie. 'I've been steered onto that path by other events, and it's easier to go with the flow, cos it makes no sense to fight against the tide.'

'If you look at things the way Suzie does, it actually makes sense,' said Adele with approval. 'Everything we've done has brought us to this moment, and even though there've been a few bumps along the way, look at how much happier we are for the journey.'

'Hear, hear!' cried Emma. 'And just in case any of you are wonderin', then no, I'm not just sayin' that because I'd not have met Bernie otherwise!'

'Talking of which, are you looking forward to tomorrer?' asked Suzie.

'If you're askin' whether I'm lookin' forward to helpin' Bernie deliver the milk and startin' a new life then the answer is yes,' said Emma plainly, 'but I shall be ever so sad to leave Libby.'

Libby gave her a hug. 'At least we're in the same country, and we'll have a whole week together once you've finished yer trainin'.'

'Which is a lot more than some folk get,' Margo commented.

'I know you talked about goin' dancin' at the Grafton earlier, Lib, but do you mind awfully if we stay in?' Emma asked. 'Not that I want to be a party-pooper or anythin' like that, but I'm rather enjoyin' our chat. It's somethin' I've sorely missed over in Ireland.'

'It's your evenin',' said Libby, 'so we'll do what you want to do.'

Adele clapped her hands together. 'Who's going to give me a hand with the scouse?' There was a chorus of 'I will's as the others set about preparing the ingredients, but Emma frowned. 'What's scouse when it's at home?'

'It's a stew of vegetables with meat,' Libby explained, 'unless it's blind scouse, of course; then it has no meat in it. It's a traditional Liverpudlian dish.'

'Sounds delish,' said Emma, adding, 'I've really missed doin' stuff like this with you,' as she took a carrot and started chopping it ready for the pot. 'We must make sure that we never lose touch again.'

'We won't,' said Libby firmly. 'I'm certain of it.'

With everyone pitching in, it didn't take them long to prepare the scouse, and then Adele chose to stay behind to keep an eye on their meal while the rest of the girls took Thor for a walk around the farm.

'You're ever so lucky gettin' to live here,' Emma told Libby. 'I don't think I'd have ever contemplated goin' back to the city if I were in your position.'

'It's an idyllic life, but I don't think I'd be brave enough to take on a smallholdin' or anythin' like that without havin' the Lewises to hand.'

'You could always try gettin' a stall on this Paddy's market you've told me about,' Emma supposed.

'It's certainly summat to think about,' agreed Libby. She gave Emma a playful nudge as they passed the main house. 'Don't look now, but you're bein' watched.'

Emma immediately looked towards the house before hastily looking away. 'Why did you tell me not to look?'

Libby chuckled. 'Why did you look, when I told you not to?'

Emma shrugged. 'It's instinctive. Is he still there?'

Libby side-glanced to the window. 'Yes, he's wavin'.'

Thinking her friend was teasing, Emma looked over to the window, then blushed before waving back. 'I thought you were pullin' me leg,' she hissed from the corner of her mouth. 'I'd not have looked over if I'd known he was still there.'

Libby tucked her arm through Emma's. 'I know you're shy, but you really can't afford to hang about, not in this day and age.'

'Is that why you and Jack are gettin' married toot-sweet?'

'Yes,' said Libby simply. 'I'd like to think we have all the time in the world, but we'd be silly to put off until tomorrow what we can do today.'

'Then why didn't you get married before he left for London?'

'Because I wanted to see if I could get in touch with you first, plus he didn't have sufficient leave.' She hesitated before adding, 'I also wanted to get married in London so that Pete and the others could be there, but over the past few days I've realised just how good my friends are here in Hollybank, and now I'm not so sure.'

'Torn between two worlds,' said Emma.

'Definitely, and I'm not even sure how much of my old world exists, or how I'll feel if I go back.'

'I've been wonderin' that too,' said Emma. 'It'll be awful to see a pile of bricks where your old house once stood. Havin' said that, our house might've gone the same way. Our old school too, come to that.'

Libby grimaced. 'I'd hate to see that reduced to rubble, cos I enjoyed our time there, and I don't want my last memory to be seein' it in ruins.'

'But you have to go and take a look, otherwise you'll be forever wonderin', don't you think?'

'Or is it best to remember things how they were? Keep the memories and never go back?'

'Maybe. It makes me think of our earlier conversation when you told Bernie that I knew London like the back of my hand, cos thinkin' about it now, I very much doubt that's still the case.' She shook her head angrily. 'Mum says it's wrong to hate, but I don't care. I hate the Nazis for what they've done. They've no right to destroy our lives like this, and for what?'

'It's why I no longer attend church,' admitted Libby. 'It would be hypocritical for me to pretend to put my faith in God, when I haven't got any. It's not like I can ask him to watch over those I love, because I did that every night when Mum and Dad were alive, and look what happened to them!'

'I can't argue with you,' said Emma bluntly, 'but that won't stop you from worryin' about Jack and his father.'

'Terribly so,' Libby said. 'There's not a day goes by that I don't fear a phone call tellin' me the worst.'

'I know we've said that it doesn't look as though the war's goin' to end any time soon, but I hope it does, for all our sakes,' said Emma. There was a general murmur of agreement, and the girls made their way back to the barn.

After a delicious meal of scouse, served with fresh bread that Helen had made that morning, Emma helped with the washing up before announcing that she was ready for her bed. 'I think it must be all this fresh air,' she said, sliding between the sheets.

'Or happiness,' said Libby. 'After all, you got plenty of fresh air in Ireland.'

'I definitely made the right decision to leave Ireland,' said Emma. 'Havin' the girls welcome me as if they'd known me for years was proof of that.'

'Aren't you worried it might be different in the services?' asked Margo, as she budged up to make room for Thor.

'Nope. I figure birds of a feather flock together, and we've all chosen to sign on the dotted line for one reason or another, which must make us like-minded.'

Suzie gave a short sharp approving grunt. 'It means we're all running away from summat.'

Emma was about to say she thought that probably wasn't the case, but then she thought again. 'I suppose you might well be right. You're runnin' away from your surname, I'm runnin' away from a miserable life in Ireland, and most of the others will be doin' the same, whether it be to get a better job, or a way out of poverty.'

'The runaways, that's us,' said Suzie sleepily.

Libby sat up on one elbow. 'You've hit the nail on the head, Suzie, and no mistake! Just look at me! I've been runnin' for the longest time, and I didn't even know it.' She yawned audibly before pressing on sleepily,

'Maybe it's time I should stop, because all this runnin's fair worn me out.'

Settling down to sleep, Suzie imagined herself wearing air force blue in front of a bomber with an airman by her side, Emma envisaged herself in the arms of Bernie, and Libby saw herself and Jack with nothing behind them. *A blank canvas*, Libby thought to herself, *and that's fine for now.*

The next morning all the girls were up betimes, including Emma, who'd managed to find a pair of wellies in the old tack room.

'I can't believe you took to milkin' straight off the bat,' said Libby, as she watched Emma deftly handling one of the cows. 'It took me a long time before I was as good as you.'

'It's a knack,' said Adele. 'You've either got it or you haven't, and Emma's got it.'

Beaming proudly, Emma continued with her milking. 'My day couldn't be more different,' she said. 'I'll have gone from milkin' cows this mornin' to sleepin' in a Nissen hut tonight.'

'At least you'll get a lie-in tomorrow,' said Suzie, 'and not be up at five o'clock as you were this morning.'

Emma grimaced. 'Maybe so, but it'll be star jumps before brekker, or so I've been told. If that doesn't get me fit, I don't know what will.' She looked to Suzie. 'When you join up, you'll have an advantage over the rest of us, what with you havin' lived on the farm for as long as you have. I bet you're as fit as a fiddle.'

A slow smile etched Suzie's cheeks. 'And I already know how to drive a lorry, which means I'll be ahead of the game for once as opposed to bein' the one what's runnin' to catch up, as I usually am.'

Bernie appeared in the doorway. 'Good morning, ladies. I trust you all had a good night?' There was an anwering chorus of 'good morning's, and he looked at Emma with approval. 'I see you've taken to milking like a duck to water,' he said.

Emma blushed. 'Probably more down to luck than skill,' she said shyly.

'Not from where I'm standing,' said Bernie. 'Would you like to help me harness Goliath? I've got him in ready.'

Emma looked to Libby, who nodded. 'Go on, we'll be fine here.' Speaking from the corner of her mouth, she added, 'Don't do anythin' I wouldn't.'

Bernie looked down at Emma's footwear as they walked towards the stable where Goliath was munching on some hay. 'Ah, good. I see you've found some wellies. If you give them to me before you go, I'll make sure to keep them safe for your return.'

Emma thanked him as she stroked Goliath's velvety nose. 'I can't believe how wonderfully soft his muzzle is.'

'Everyone thinks horses have tough muzzles, but they really don't,' said Bernie. 'Would you like to feed him a carrot?'

Emma looked doubtful as Bernie handed her the carrot. 'He won't bite me by accident, will he?'

Bernie held his hand out flat, indicating for Emma to copy him. 'Not if you hold your hand like this he won't.'

Emma held out the flat of her hand with the carrot balanced on her palm. 'Are you sure . . .' she began, but Goliath had snuffled the carrot from her hand before she could finish the sentence. 'I barely felt him!' she cried delightedly as Bernie passed her another carrot.

'A gentle giant, that's our Goliath,' he said as Goliath munched down the last of his carrots. 'Now I'll show you how to put his bridle on.' He demonstrated how to open the horse's mouth to receive the bit.

'He's ever so good, considerin' you're shoving' a great big lump of metal in his mouth.'

'You'll find that most horses are good-natured,' Bernie told her, 'although of course you do get the odd one that doesn't like being told what to do.'

'A bit like us humans, I suppose.'

Bernie laughed. 'That's summat you'll have to get used to in the ATS.' As he spoke, he placed the heavy yoke over Goliath's neck and backed him between the shafts of the cart before fixing the traces into place, explaining as he did so the various parts of the harness and their purpose.

'Is that it?' Emma asked. 'It looks as though the shafts are just restin' in them leather hoops.'

'Togs,' supplied Bernie, 'and I promise you it is secure, although I'll grant you it doesn't look it.'

'There's a lot more to farmin' than you'd think,' said Emma. 'I doubt I'll have scratched the surface even after a week.'

'It won't be all work and no play,' said Bernie. 'I noticed that you didn't go out last night, so I thought it might be nice to take you to the Grafton when you come back, by way of thanking you for helping out here. Unless you'd rather not . . .'

'I'd love to,' said Emma, 'but it's really not necessary. I enjoy helping Libby and the girls.'

'I can see that,' Bernie said, smiling, 'but I'd still like to take you out.'

Emma felt a warmth enter her neckline, and prayed the blush would disappear before it reached her cheeks. *He's not actually asked you out on a date*, Emma told herself, *or at least I don't think he has.*

Bernie leaned against Goliath's shoulder. 'Would it be too forward to ask if I could write to you whilst you're away?'

Delighted that he wanted to keep in touch, Emma spoke without hesitation. 'Not at all – in fact I think that would be lovely. I've not got many pals, except for Libby of course.'

Bernie appeared perplexed. 'How could a lovely girl such as you not have many friends?'

'It's a long story, but in short I'm English, not Irish.'

He blew his cheeks out. 'You'd think they'd leave those thoughts behind them, seeing what's going on in the world right now. You can't afford to hate someone because of something that happened years and years ago, or where would it end?'

'Exactly! Holding a grudge does you no good in the long run. You can't keep blamin' the present for the past.'

'I like your way of thinking, Emma . . .?'

'Bagshaw,' supplied Emma. 'What a pity it is that you and I don't rule the world, eh?'

His eyes twinkled at her. 'I know I said I'd like to take you out to say thank you for helping out on the farm—'

'And I said it wasn't necessary,' Emma reminded him.

'So how about if I take you out on a date instead?'

Emma stared at him as the words sank in. 'That would be lovely, but you do know that I won't be back for a long time, don't you?'

'I'll still be here,' he said casually. 'Besides, I rather think you're worth waiting for.'

Blushing madly, Emma replied shyly, 'In that case, how can I refuse?'

Bernie beamed. 'Excellent! I shall take you out to dinner as well as dancing.'

Emma felt as though she'd gone from a little girl to a woman fully grown in a matter of seconds. 'I think you should know that I've never been taken out to dinner before – in fact, I've never been on a date either.'

'I find that hard to believe, because I'd have thought a woman like you would have them queuing around the block,' said Bernie, before being interrupted by the girls calling out to see if he was ready for them to load the cart.

Bernie beckoned them over, and Libby handed Emma her belongings whilst casting her quizzical glances. 'What's tickled your fancy,' she hissed as Bernie jumped down to fetch another churn. Emma glanced at Bernie, who had his back turned to them, and Libby followed her line of sight before looking back at her pal's broad smile. 'Oh my God!' she hissed. 'He's asked you out on a date.'

Emma gaped at her. 'How on earth did you know that?'

'We've known each other all our lives,' whispered Libby. 'I can tell by the grin on yer face that he's either kissed you or asked you out on a date, and seein' as you're not flat out on the floor I presumed it was the latter. I take it you said yes?'

'When I eventually found my tongue, I thought it only fair to remind him that I'd not get any leave for quite a while, but he said that some things are worth waitin' for.'

'Didn't I say he liked you!' said Libby excitedly.

'And it seems you were right.'

Suzie wandered towards them, oblivious of what had gone on. 'I'm not very good at writing, but I'll get one of the girls to help me so that I can let you know whether I've been accepted into the services or not.'

'Good luck with everythin',' said Emma. 'You never know yer luck: we might be stationed together at some stage or other.'

Margo was staring at Libby. 'Why are you grinning like the cat that got the cream?'

Libby tried to swallow her smile, but she was too happy to banish it completely. 'I'll tell you later.'

Adele pointed to Emma's wellies, which were still on her feet. 'You might get a few odd looks if you turn up for duty wearing them.'

Emma struck a hand to her forehead. 'Honest to goodness, I've a head like a sieve at times!' Holding on to the cart, she trod out of her wellies and pushed her feet into the shoes which Libby had brought for her. 'Good job you noticed; I'd have looked a right 'nana turnin' up for duty in these!'

Leaning down, Bernie twinkled at her as he helped her aboard.

Pretending that she was pink-cheeked from the effort of mounting the cart and not from holding Bernie's hand, Emma sat down next to him. 'I should be able to do this with ease by the time I see you both next,' she said as Libby joined her on the seat.

'You'll be the one helpin' us onto the cart by then,' Libby quipped. 'It's amazin' how quickly things change in a short amount of time.'

'Talking of things changing quickly, did Suzie say she might be joining the services, or did I mishear?' asked Bernie.

Libby relayed the previous evening's conversation, asking him not to mention anything to Joyce until Suzie had had a chance to tell her mother of her intentions. 'My lips are sealed,' he promised, 'but didn't I tell you not to worry and it would all come out in the wash, or words to that effect?'

'You certainly did, but not for one minute did I think it would work out as well as it has,' Libby admitted. 'I reckon this could be the makin' of Suzie.'

'I think it's the best thing that could've happened to her,' said Bernie as he pulled Goliath to a halt at the first stop on the round. 'Some folk just need a little nudge.'

Emma watched Bernie and Libby doling out the milk and began to do the same, although she had to ask

Libby to tell her how much to charge. 'How on earth you can work it out when the containers are all different sizes is beyond me,' she said, 'and I'm sure you charge some of the women less than you do others anyway. Or am I imaginin' things?'

Not wanting to drop him in it, Libby glanced at Bernie, who answered for her. 'Some of them have less money than others, so we charge what they can afford,' he said.

Emma looked at him approvingly. 'That's awfully decent of you, but how do you explain that to the authorities? Libby was tellin' me how you have to account for every drop of milk and every laid egg.'

He shrugged. 'We do, but eggs get cracked, and milk gets spilt. It's impossible to account for every drop,' he said with a wink.

'You've a good heart, Bernie. There're plenty who are sticklers for the rules.'

'Some rules deserve to be broken,' said Bernie sternly. 'It'll be a cold day in hell before I see a child go without just because their mother wasn't born with a silver spoon in her mouth.'

Emma gazed at him thoughtfully. Bernie would make a very good father one of these days.

They continued with the rest of the round, with Bernie keeping an eye on his wristwatch to make sure Emma wasn't late for her train.

'Time flies when you're havin' fun,' said Emma as she got down from the cart outside Central Station.

'I hope all goes well with your training,' said Bernie, resting the reins on the seat to join her. 'You won't forget to write, will you?'

Emma glanced fleetingly at Libby before locking eyes with him. 'Not a chance. You'll all be sick of my letters by the time you see me next.'

Libby came forward to hug her friend. 'That will *never* happen. You must write every day if you can.'

'I will,' said Emma, smiling shyly at Bernie before turning her attention back to Libby. 'I've already got heaps to tell you.'

Bernie lowered his head to hide the smile which was forming on his cheeks. He knew from working with the girls on the farm that they liked to discuss the ins and outs of their personal lives in great detail, so he had no doubt whatsoever that his proposal of a date would also be discussed at length as soon as Emma had the opportunity.

They heard the squeal of a train's wheels as it pulled in to one of the platforms, and Emma sighed ruefully. 'I'd better go and see if that's mine,' she said.

Bernie glanced at his watch. 'If it is then it's on time, which makes a change.'

Taking her satchel in hand, Emma gave Libby a one-armed hug. 'It's been so good seein' you again, Libby Gilbert; I can't wait until the next time.'

'Take care of yourself, Emma, and make sure you don't leave anythin' out when you write!' said Libby quietly.

Emma giggled softly before turning to face Bernie. 'Goodbye, Bernie. Thanks for lettin' me stay.'

He waved a nonchalant hand. 'It was my pleasure.' He winked. 'Take care of yourself, and good luck.'

'Yes, best of British,' Libby added hastily. Emma gave them a small wave before hurrying up the steps. Once at the top she turned to wave again before disappearing from view. Libby felt her lower lip tremble. 'I ain't half goin' to miss that girl.'

'She'll be back before you know it, with tales aplenty,' said Bernie, hopping back onto the cart. Libby took her place next to him.

'I hear you've got a date planned,' she said.

Bernie gawked at her. 'How the bleedin' hell do you know that? Are the two of you telepathic or summat?'

Libby laughed. 'It feels like that at times, but no, I guessed, and Emma confirmed it while we were loadin' the cart with the girls.'

'And do you approve?' he asked, clicking Goliath to walk on.

'You're a lovely feller,' said Libby, adding somewhat guardedly, 'I just hope you're not on the rebound.'

He turned his gaze from the road ahead to regard her solemnly. 'I can see why you'd think that, but no, for the record I'm not on the rebound.'

'Only I thought you were head over heels with Roz. Isn't that why you and Suzie had such a falling out?'

'We fell out because Suzie was being vindictive,' said Bernie. 'She set me up for a fall, and made me look stupid in the process.'

'So, you weren't hurt by Roz's affection for Felix?'

'My pride took a heck of a battering,' admitted Bernie, 'but it's not as if we were in a relationship or owt like that. In fact, before Suzie came along and twisted things, I had already resigned myself to the fact that Roz was out of my reach.'

'But that didn't stop you fallin' for her?'

'This is like the Spanish inquisition; they should get you a job interrogating Fritz,' he said with a wry smile.

Libby laughed. 'She's my friend. I'm bound to have some concerns.'

'You're a good friend, and I can see why you have your reservations, but I promise you I wouldn't be asking Emma out on a date if my intentions lay elsewhere.' He shrugged. 'It's not as if I was going to stay single for the rest of my life.'

'I know, but you've not had time to get over Roz.'

He eyed her shrewdly. 'You do know that Roz and I never kissed?'

Libby blushed. 'No, but then I don't really know the full story behind what happened.'

He turned Goliath towards home. 'There's not much to tell. I found Roz attractive, and hoped for a relationship, but that's where it ends. I'd agree with you had we become an item, but Roz was never my belle. We only ever went out as friends.'

Libby cocked her head to one side. 'I know Roz should have told you the truth, but—'

'There are no buts,' said Bernie. 'Roz wasn't honest with me, end of story.'

'You're not nursin' a broken heart, then?'

He laughed. 'The only thing I'm nursing is my bruised pride.'

Libby relaxed. 'Sorry for all the questions, but I needed to be sure. Emma's never had a proper boyfriend before, and I'd hate to see her bein' used.'

He placed his hand over his heart. 'I'd never do that to anyone, not after having had it done to me.'

'She's a good girl with a generous heart,' said Libby. 'Much like you – apart from the girl part, that is.'

'Then maybe we're a match made in heaven.'

'A bit like me and my Jack,' said Libby. 'I can't wait to tell him everythin' that's happened.'

'Shall my ears be burning?'

'Definitely!'

Chapter Six

Suzie followed her mother into Rose Cottage so that they could have their lunch together whilst Suzie broke the news of her intentions.

'What do you think?' she said after she had finished explaining. 'I know it's a bit unexpected, but I really want to do this.'

Joyce smeared Marmite onto a round of bread. 'I think it's a marvellous idea, if that's what you want to do. I'd feel a lot happier with you in the services than working the markets down south, even if you would have been with Libby.'

'I'll get a proper career this way,' said Suzie, 'and I might even meet someone special, who knows?'

Joyce smiled. It was heart-warming to hear her daughter talk of her future with such positivity. 'That truly would be the icing on the cake,' she said. 'And you needn't worry about me confronting your father on my own; I'll make sure that he gets the message loud and clear.'

'I wanted him to know we were a united front,' said Suzie sadly, 'but perhaps I could write to him before he gets out? Tell him I've moved on, but that I support you one hundred per cent.'

'You don't need to do that,' Joyce assured her. 'I'll make sure he gets the gist.'

'If I can be there I will,' said Suzie loyally, 'but as I said to Libby, everything happens for a reason, so I shall let the cards fall where they may.'

'Speaking of Libby, did you have a good time at the cinema on Saturday?'

Suzie described the events of that memorable evening, starting with the Murphy twins. Joyce's face had clouded over at the mere mention of their names, but as soon as she was told the full story her features darkened further. 'I know it's wrong to hate, but I can't help myself when it comes to the likes of the Murphys,' she said. 'Imagine them doing that to an innocent girl like Libby.'

'I didn't know you knew them,' said Suzie, surprised.

Joyce rolled her eyes. 'Better than I'd care to admit.'

Suzie was intrigued. 'I take it this has summat to do with Dad?'

To her surprise, her mother shook her head. 'You'd think so, but no.'

'Do you mind if I ask how you know them?' Suzie ventured, curious to learn more.

Joyce handed Suzie the Marmite sandwich. 'I didn't have any dealings with them personally, but . . .' She bit into her own sandwich as she took her place at the table opposite her daughter. Chewing thoughtfully, she swallowed before continuing,

'. . . I know enough to know they're vile people who'll take advantage of anyone who's down on their luck.' She hesitated. 'What made you think they had summat to do with your dad?'

Suzie told her mother how Libby and the others had seen Donny apparently doing business with Callum in the Grafton, and Joyce tutted beneath her breath. 'I don't know why I asked; it was obvious really. Birds of a feather and all that.'

'Aren't they just?' said Suzie. 'I'm just glad that Libby found out before things went any further.'

'I thought she didn't have any money, anyway,' said Joyce.

'She doesn't but she's got plenty of love, and the idea of her loving people like them makes my skin crawl.'

'They don't know the meaning of the word,' said Joyce angrily. 'Unless it comes to money, of course; they certainly love that.'

'I feel really sorry for Libby,' said Suzie, in between mouthfuls. 'She's been pushed from pillar to post as far as her relatives are concerned. Her poor parents would be turning in their graves if they could have seen the way her uncle treated her.'

'Her uncle?'

Suzie nodded. 'Her father's brother – he lives down south.'

'He can't be much of an uncle if she's chosen to stay up here.'

'She's better off without him, that's for sure,' said Suzie.

Joyce watched her daughter curiously from across the table. 'I've never really asked Libby about her past, because you don't like to, do you, not when things have obviously gone awry back home. I know she's lost her parents, but I never really understood what she was doing up this neck of the woods.'

'Her mam was a Liverpool girl born and bred,' said Suzie, and was immediately interrupted by her mother.

'If that was the case, then how could she not know that Jo wasn't her aunt?' she asked, her brow wrinkling.

Suzie licked her fingers before taking her plate over to the sink. 'I'm not entirely sure, but I do know she was a small child the last time she saw her Scouse grandparents.'

Joyce tutted beneath her breath. 'What is it with families? They reckon that blood's thicker than water, but I've yet to see proof of that.'

'I'm so lucky to have you in my life now,' said Suzie. 'I'll miss you when I go away – or rather *if* I go away.'

'They'll be glad to have a hard-working girl like yourself in the services, so you needn't worry about being turned down,' said Joyce confidently.

'I'm so used to people flinching when they hear the name Haggarty, I find it hard to believe that any employer will welcome me with open arms.'

'They won't care what you're called as long as you're willing to do your bit,' said Joyce. 'Don't forget, the real criminals – folk like the Murphys and your dad – wouldn't dream of signing on the dotted line. It says a lot that you're volunteering for the forces when you could quite easily have become a land girl.'

A small smile tweaked Suzie's lips. 'I hadn't thought of it like that.'

'It's true though,' said Joyce, 'and they'll know that when they ask you what skills you have.'

Suzie laughed. 'I don't reckon there'll be much call for shovelling manure, or milking cows.'

'Granted, but it shows you're not afraid to get your hands dirty,' said Joyce, 'not to mention getting up at the crack of dawn to see to the animals before you've so much as had your first cup of tea.' She rinsed the plates under the tap. 'I'm really going to miss you, and it's a shame that you're going to be leaving so soon after us finding each other again.'

'I know, but this is summat I have to do if I'm to break away from the name Haggarty.' Suzie hesitated. 'Does it never bother you?'

'I use my maiden name,' said Joyce simply.

Suzie pouted. 'I wish I had that luxury.'

There was a brief knock on the door to the cottage before it opened and Libby walked in as Joyce called her through. 'Well, that's Emma off to a new life in the services,' she said wistfully.

'What was she looking so pleased about before she left?' asked Suzie. 'Talk about the cat that got the cream.'

Libby relayed her conversation with Bernie, finishing with: 'I know he's a lovely feller, and I'd love for them to be an item, but not if he breaks things off further down the line.'

'I'm sure he won't do that to her,' said Joyce. 'He's a good lad is our Bernie, not like them Murphys. They're rotten to the core, them two – especially him.'

'Suzie told you?'

Joyce nodded.

'I always thought that she was the driving force behind their deception,' said Libby, somewhat surprised that Joyce saw things differently. 'She certainly seemed to call the shots whenever we went round for a visit.'

'He hasn't got a caring bone in the whole of his body,' said Joyce. 'Besides, it would have made more sense for her to take the lead on this one since she was the one posing as your aunt; but believe me, it's him that wears the trousers in that family.'

Suzie was regarding her mother curiously. 'You must've had some kind of run-in with him, because you seem to know an awful lot about him.'

'I'm not about to dredge up the past, but I will say this: Donny's an evil so-'n'-so who couldn't give a monkey's about anyone bar himself. Libby's lucky she found out when she did, cos believe you me, he's got more than one trick up his sleeve when it comes to extorting money out of folk, and he doesn't care who gets hurt in the process as long as it's not him!'

'That's why I said Libby should think twice before threatening him with the scuffers,' said Suzie.

Joyce turned sharply to Libby. 'I hope you listened to her.'

'Albeit reluctantly,' admitted Libby.

'Thank goodness for that,' said Joyce, breathing a sigh of relief, 'cos I know first-hand how he deals with threats.'

Suzie stared at her mother. 'I thought you said you hadn't—'

Quickly, Joyce waved her into silence. 'When I say first-hand, I mean through others.'

Libby stifled a yawn with the back of her hand. 'I hardly got a wink of sleep last night what with one thing and another, and I've still to tell Jack that I've changed me mind about London, as well as everythin' else.'

'You're going to need longer than three minutes, that's for certain.'

'I'm hopin' to go and see him just as soon as he gets a twenty-four-hour pass,' said Libby, 'or forty-eight for good measure, cos it's too far to go for a quick hello.'

'I hope they give him leave soon, cos it would be better for us if you saw him before Suzie leaves to do her basic training.'

'And Roz,' said Libby, but Joyce was shaking her head.

'Roz has decided to stay and do her bit, which is commendable, all things considered.'

'What about her father?' asked Libby, dumbfounded to hear of Roz's change of heart.

'She said her mother's got a good lead as to his whereabouts, so they're hoping it won't be too long before he's in Britain.'

'How can they know where he is, if he's not already here?' Libby wondered.

'They have their ways and means of finding these things out,' said Joyce. 'I'm guessing they must have their fair share of spies overseas.'

'I really enjoyed spying on the Murphys,' said Suzie, 'but I wouldn't want to spy on the Nazis. That must take some real nerve.'

Joyce held a hand to her forehead. 'I'm just glad I only found out what you did *after* the fact. I'd have had kittens otherwise.'

'So might I, had I known it was the Murphys I'd be spying on,' said Suzie. 'As it was, I thought it was a husband and wife who I didn't know, so I hadn't the foggiest.'

Joyce looked disgusted. 'They really thought this through, didn't they? The lengths some folk will go to astounds me.'

Libby glanced at the clock above the mantel. 'I only came in to tell you I was back; I'd better get to work or the girls will be wonderin' what's become of me.'

'That makes three of us,' said Joyce. 'C'mon, girls, let's get crackin'.'

**

Libby smiled as she heard Jack's voice come down the phone.

'Hello, Treacle. How's tricks?'

She drew a deep breath before telling him of her decision to leave London on the back burner until she'd thought things through more thoroughly.

'And what about the Murphys? Have you come to any decision about them?'

'I have, and you'll be pleased to hear that I've decided to keep my distance and let them stew over what's happened to keep me away.'

'They'll probably think you've come into your inheritance and are unwillin' to share,' chortled Jack.

'That's exactly what Bernie said,' cried Libby, glancing at the kitchen clock, just visible from where she was standing in the hall. 'And I thought it only fair to tell Suzie of my decision rather than have her hang on, and she's decided to join the services.'

There was a short pause before Jack replied, 'Good for her!'

The operator cut across, letting them know their time was almost up.

'I knew three minutes wouldn't be long enough!' said Libby sullenly. 'Do you have any idea when you're eligible for some leave?'

'Yes. I've got a forty-eight on the fifteenth of May. Will you be able to make it?'

'Wild horses couldn't stop me,' said Libby happily.

'I'm afraid you'll have to find a B&B to stay in, cos Dad's rentin' my old room out to make some extra money.'

'Not to worry, we'll sort summat.'

The operator's voice came sharply down the line, letting them know she was about to terminate the call.

'Tell Suzie good luck from me!'

'I will; cheerio, Jack.'

'TTFN—'

The line went dead, but Libby was smiling. She had a firm date, and she couldn't wait to start making arrangements for her trip back to London.

***

APRIL 1942

Standing in line outside the recruiting office, Libby looked at those around her. 'I didn't realise it would be this busy,' she told Suzie as they moved slowly up the queue.

'Me neither,' agreed Suzie. 'Do you think I'll get in, given the number of volunteers?'

A girl standing ahead of them in the queue answered the question. 'They won't turn you away unless you're medically unfit, or in a reserved occupation such as farming.' She glanced from Suzie's wellingtons to her dungarees in a pointed fashion.

Suzie followed her gaze. 'I've been helping out at Hollybank, but I've not signed on as a land girl or owt like that.'

The woman held out a hand. 'I'm Babs Higgs.'

Suzie introduced herself and Libby. 'Do you know what you want to do?' she asked.

Babs cast a reproving glance at the buildings nearby. 'I'm not bothered as long as I get out of this dump.'

Suzie frowned. 'Liverpool's not that bad.'

Babs grimaced. 'Maybe not if you're livin' on a farm, but if you're sharin' a two-room flat with your mam and dad and six siblin's . . .'

'Six?' cried Suzie and Libby together.

'You not got any brothers or sisters?'

'Only child,' said Suzie.

'Me too,' said Libby. 'In fact, most of our friends are only children.'

Babs rolled her eyes. 'I think my parents took the phrase "the more the merrier" to heart.'

Suzie smiled. 'And is it?'

Babs laughed softly. 'I share a bed with my five sisters, whilst my brother gets a bed to himself. What do you think?'

'I used to sleep on a bed of straw before our old place got hit, but I think I'd prefer that to sharing with five other people.'

'I can't wait to have a bed to meself, with no one tryin' to pull the covers off me; it'll be like heaven! Do you want to join any service in particular?'

'I'm not bothered as long as I get out of Liverpool,' said Suzie as they moved up the line.

'I thought you said Liverpool wasn't that bad?' said Babs, who was feeling somewhat confused.

Suzie laughed without mirth. 'I did. It's not the city I'm trying to get away from.'

Babs nodded wisely. 'Boy trouble, eh?'

'My dad,' said Suzie, 'or rather . . .' She paused before coming clean. 'I'm a Haggarty.'

'What's one of them?' Babs asked innocently.

Realising the name meant nothing to the other girl, Suzie brightened. 'It's my surname.'

'Oh,' said Babs, still looking slightly perplexed. 'I like the WAAF uniform – not to mention them handsome young men in their flyin' machines . . .' Suzie

259

listened in silence as Babs talked about her dreams of marrying a pilot. It was the first time she'd had a conversation with a fellow Scouser who wasn't trying to accuse her of anything or asking where her father was so that they could have a word in his shell-like.

It was a good hour later before Suzie and Libby emerged onto the pavement.

'That was easy enough,' said Suzie. 'All I have to do now is wait.'

Libby stood on tiptoe as she scoured the area for a sign of Bernie and Margo, who were going to pick them up. 'What did you make of Babs?'

'I thought she was wonderful,' said Suzie, 'probably because the name Haggarty meant nothing to her. I just hope she doesn't ask someone who the Haggartys are when she gets home.'

'I don't think she'll give it a second thought,' said Libby. 'All she seemed bothered about was findin' herself a rich husband so that she can get out of the courts.'

Suzie cast her a shrewd glance. 'I suspect half if not three quarters of the women in the queue were there for the same reason.'

'Good luck to them, I say.'

Suzie spotted the cart in the distance. 'Here they are.'

'Goliath's such a good boy,' Libby remarked. 'He doesn't bat an eye at the trams or the buses, just plods on regardless.'

'A gentle giant,' agreed Suzie. 'I'll miss him when I'm away.'

Libby raised a single eyebrow. 'Not havin' second thoughts already?'

Suzie shook her head, smiling. 'Not a chance. I'm really looking forward to a fresh start.'

'I never did ask what your mother made of you wantin' to join up.'

Suzie greeted the others before climbing into the cart. 'She was quite pleased that I'd changed my mind.'

'You've done it, then?' Margo said approvingly.

'Easy as falling off a log,' said Suzie. 'The hardest part was standing in that bloomin' queue.'

'The services are certainly popular,' said Libby. 'Far more so than I ever realised.'

'All looking for rich husbands,' Suzie laughed, 'and there I was thinking I'd be the only one.'

Bernie grimaced. 'I wonder how many of them will be nursing broken hearts before the war is out?'

'Because the men can have their pick?'

'Because a pilot's life expectancy is pretty low compared to those on the ground, and if a woman is after a rich hubby it's a pilot she'll be after,' Margo told her grimly.

'That's horrid,' said Suzie, with a look of disgust.

'Maybe so, but it's fact,' said Bernie.

'Do the pilots know?' asked Suzie tentatively. 'Or is that a stupid question?'

Bernie heaved a sigh. 'They probably think that they'll be one of the lucky ones, and as at least some of them will make it to the end in one piece they might well be right.'

'They must be awfully brave,' said Suzie quietly.

'Incredibly so,' agreed Libby. 'I'm just glad my Jack's a mechanic.'

'Any idea when you'll get your papers?' asked Margo.

'A couple of weeks,' said Suzie. 'It'll probably take them that long to get through the sheer number of women wanting to sign up.'

They sank into silent contemplation as Goliath plodded steadily on.

'It makes you realise how small your own problems are when you think of the men in the planes,' said Libby, finally breaking the silence. 'The Murphy twins might be the scum of the earth, but my issue with them seems trivial when you look at the bigger picture.'

'They're insignificant in the scheme of things,' agreed Bernie. 'Not worth the time of day.'

'You're right, and I'm not goin' to waste my time on people that aren't worth the effort. If I ever bump into them on the street I'll cross over, and if they call to me I'll ignore them.'

'And what about if you're face to face?' said Margo. 'What then?'

'I shall walk straight past, and if they try to waylay me I shall tell them I know who they really are, and have no interest in speakin' to them,' said Libby simply.

Margo grinned. 'Glad to hear it. It's the only way to deal with people like them.'

'And I feel better for it too,' said Libby. 'As if a weight's been lifted from off my shoulders.'

'Life's too short to be bitter,' said Bernie. 'Concentrate on yourself and those who matter and to hell with the rest of them.'

They spent the rest of the journey discussing what jobs they would like to do if they were joining the services, with Bernie saying he'd like to be a pilot – despite the dangers – because he thought it would be wonderful to fly like a bird; Margo saying she'd like to join the Wrens because she loved the sea, and Libby settling for the WAAF because she'd have more chance of being stationed close to Jack.

They arrived at the farm to find Joyce and Adele crossing the yard.

'How did it go?' Joyce asked Suzie as she helped her down from the cart.

'I'm to wait for my papers, which should arrive in the next two weeks,' said Suzie happily. 'The women in the queue seemed like a nice bunch, especially one called Babs, who had never heard the name Haggarty before.'

'A rare find indeed,' said Joyce, slipping her arm through Suzie's and calling over her shoulder as she led the way to the cottage, 'Are we all up for a cuppa?'

'You go ahead,' said Margo. 'I'll be along as soon as I've helped Bernie to put Goliath away.'

They trooped into the kitchen, where Joyce listened eagerly to Suzie, who was excited to tell her mother everything from talking to the women in the queue to the moment she had signed on the dotted line.

'I must say it all sounds very exciting,' said Joyce. She smiled at Libby. 'I'm glad you changed your mind about going to London.'

'Me too,' said Libby.

Suzie scooped the tea leaves into the pot, saying absent-mindedly, 'Mam wasn't keen on me working down the market.'

Embarrassed by her daughter's forthrightness, Joyce said quickly, 'Not that there's anything wrong with markets per se . . .' but Libby cut in.

'Petticoat Lane used to have a bad reputation, but those days are long gone. I wouldn't have asked Suzie to join me had that still been the case.'

'It's not to do with the market's reputation,' said Joyce.

'Then what?' asked Libby, somewhat guardedly. She didn't know Joyce as well as the others, but surely the older woman didn't think the role of a stallholder not good enough for her daughter?

'My folks used to run a stall down the market,' confessed Joyce, 'and even though London is a far cry from Liverpool, I didn't want Suzie to follow in their footsteps.' She held up a hand in acknowledgement that she was being petty. 'I know it's silly, but even so . . .' She shrugged helplessly, leaving Libby to fill in the rest.

'Too many bad memories of a time you'd rather forget,' she said. 'I get that, because it's the way I feel about my uncle takin' over my parents' stall. I thought I wanted it back so that I could right his wrongs, but it wouldn't be the same knowin' what he'd done.'

'Exactly,' said Joyce.

Margo entered the kitchen in time to hear the end of the conversation. 'Who's he, and what's he done?'

'My Uncle Tony,' said Libby.

'Oh, *him*,' said Margo. 'No further explanation needed.' She poured herself a cup of tea whilst Joyce filled her in on the rest of the conversation, ending with: 'So whilst it may seem silly, I can't help the way I feel.'

Margo looked from Libby to Joyce. 'What was the name of your stall?'

'Brannagan's Emporium. Why?'

'I'm just wonderin' whether your folks knew Libby's grandparents.' She turned to Libby. 'Where's the photo album – the one you came across down the market?'

'In the barn. Why?'

'I'm sure there was a photo of your parents standin' in front of a market stall. We didn't think much of it at the time because we couldn't make out all the people in the picture, what with it bein' so badly faded an' all, but what if they were Joyce's folks?' said Margo, her voice rising as she spoke.

'What if they were?' said Libby, who couldn't see why Margo was getting so excited.

'They might have known your mum and dad!'

Libby looked doubtful. 'It's a bit of a long shot, don't you think?'

'I don't mind taking a look, if it helps,' said Joyce.

With Margo eager for her to produce the photograph, Libby put her cup of tea to one side. 'I shan't be a mo.' She left the cottage and made her way to the barn, wondering if there was really any point in her doing so. *Even if she does recognise them, it's not as if it's goin' to change anythin'*, Libby told herself as she retrieved the album from amongst her possessions. *If my grandparents are still alive they're probably in Ireland, and that's all there is to it.*

She returned to the barn and sat down to flick through the album until she found the relevant photograph. Her eyes settling on the sign for Brannagan's Emporium, she turned the album to face Joyce. 'Well, I'll be blowed! They're standin' outside your parents' stall.'

Joyce paled as she pulled the album towards her. Staring at the photograph, she looked Libby square in the eye and pointed to Orla. 'That's your mam?'

Libby nodded. 'Orla O'Connell.' Seeing Joyce's grief-stricken expression, she spoke softly. 'Was she a friend of yours?'

Joyce gazed at the photograph through unseeing eyes. 'Orla's my sister.'

Libby stared at her, dumbfounded. 'She *can't* be.'

Joyce never took her gaze from the photograph as she spoke in a monotone. 'She can and she is . . .' Her lower lip was trembling; silent tears tracked her cheeks. 'Or was . . .'

Suzie placed a comforting arm around her mother's shoulders, but Libby was staring at Joyce with a steely expression. She very much wanted to protest, to say that Joyce must have got it wrong, but it was clear from the older woman's face that Joyce was speaking the truth. Under normal circumstances the news would've rocked Libby to her core, but she could only think of how Joyce had deserted her own sister when she needed her most, and Libby wasn't shy when it came to voicing her thoughts.

'I don't wish to sound unsympathetic, but why the tears when you turned yer back on her for the best part of fifteen years?' she said coldly.

Joyce dabbed at the tears with the handkerchief Suzie handed her. 'I can see how it must look, but I swear to you I didn't have a choice.'

Libby tutted irritably. 'Don't give me that! Everyone has a choice, and you chose to abandon her because of what she did.'

Her eyes growing wide, Joyce addressed the other girls whilst holding Libby's gaze. 'Could you give us a minute? Only I think it best if Libby and I talk in private.'

Libby watched Adele, Margo and Suzie walk silently out of the room whilst casting them both sympathetic glances. *She's asked them to leave because she's ashamed of my mother, and she doesn't want them to hear about the affair*, Libby thought to herself.

Joyce waited for the door to close behind Suzie before getting to her feet and putting the kettle back on to boil. 'Let's start with you telling me how much you know.'

Stony-faced, Libby relayed the story of how she'd found her mother's diaries and read the content within. 'So, you see, I know all about the affair, and I think it's despicable that you sided with your parents, especially after the way they treated you!'

Joyce was staring at Libby in utter amazement. 'Your mother never had an affair,' she said. 'I don't know what Orla wrote in her diary that could make you think

267

that, but believe you me, she was never unfaithful to your father – or not in that sense, at any rate.'

'Yes, she was. It's all there in black and white. You can read it for yerself if you don't believe me.'

'You've put two and two together and come up with five,' said Joyce. 'Your mother did do something she was ashamed of, but it wasn't lying down with another man.'

'If not that, then what? And you still haven't explained why you turned your back on her!'

Joyce poured the water into the teapot before adding more leaves. 'I'll start at the beginning, when Orla and Reggie were still the apple of my parents' eyes.'

'I very much doubt that,' Libby remarked sullenly.

Joyce pressed on, choosing to ignore the comment. 'My parents were extremely proud of the fact that Brannagan's Emporium had been in the family for generations. You'd swear it was some kind of empire the way they talked about it. I'd often hear Dad bragging to his customers that we'd still be trading long after the likes of Lewises and Blacklers had closed their doors – providing one of his daughters married a man worthy of continuing their good name, of course.'

Libby interrupted, her impatience getting the better of her. 'What had marriage got to do with it?'

'Our father thought women were incapable of running a business, believing them to be only fit to serve behind the counter. So when his new son-in-law expressed an interest in keeping the business going, Dad couldn't have been more thrilled.'

Libby couldn't help but interrupt again. 'Why was the stall called Brannagan's and not O'Connell's?'

'Connor Brannagan was my great-great-grandfather, and it was he who founded the stall. Just like my parents, he was keen for the stall to remain in the family, as long as it remained under the name of Brannagan's – it was my father who added Emporium, because he thought it made the stall sound more upmarket; grand, if you will.'

'So that's why no one knew of a stall called O'Connell's,' breathed Libby. 'Talk about barkin' up the wrong tree.'

'A bit like you with this affair business.'

'But what's the stall got to do with my mother's affair?' asked Libby, utterly perplexed.

'Nothing,' said Joyce plainly. 'Everything was going swimmingly except that your mother failed to conceive despite years of trying.'

'Which is why she had an affair,' insisted Libby. 'I know you don't believe me.'

Joyce rolled her eyes. 'I don't believe you because it's not true. Your mother was desperate to have a baby, but she sure as heck didn't have an affair in order to do so.'

'Then how do you explain me?'

'I'm getting to that,' said Joyce somewhat irritably. 'Your mother tried all the tricks in the book, but no matter what she did, or how meticulously she followed the doctors' advice, nothing seemed to work. So when she was offered some so-called miracle pills she grasped the opportunity with both hands. But of course that sort of thing never comes cheap and the pills were expensive – very expensive. After living with Callum for so long, I could smell a rat from a mile away, and I knew the pills weren't kosher, so unbeknown to your mother I nicked a couple to give to one of Callum's dodgy associates for testing.' She shook her head sadly. 'They were nowt but painkillers, although I don't know why she expected them to be anything other when she was buying them off of Donny Murphy.'

Libby gaped at her. 'As in . . .?'

Joyce grimaced. 'The very same. He knew how desperate she was to have a baby so he sold her a bunch of useless pills telling her that they were guaranteed to work if she took them for long enough, knowing that she'd keep buying them in the hope she'd fall pregnant.'

'But surely I'm livin' proof that the pills worked.'

'That had nowt to do with the pills. Your mam stopped taking them way before you came along.' Joyce fell momentarily silent as she tried to remember where she was in the story. 'I knew that Orla would want to confront Donny if I told her about my discovery, so I didn't say anything until after she'd had you.'

'She must have been furious. What did she say?'

'Very little to me. She stormed off and confronted Donny, saying she wanted her money back and that she'd tell the police if he refused to comply. Donny told her she didn't know what she was talking about, and if she even thought about going to the police he'd make sure Reggie never saw the light of day again. Your mam couldn't take the risk that he'd be true to his word, so she kept quiet. But that didn't get her out of the hole she was in.'

'What hole?'

'She'd been using the rent money to pay for the pills, and everything else was bought on the never-never. In short, she was up to her eyeballs in debt, and your father knew nothing about it, of course.'

'And all because she wanted a baby,' said Libby thickly.

'And that's not all. Just when she thought things couldn't possibly get any worse, Mam and Dad confronted her, saying that they'd heard rumours about her seeing some man behind your dad's back, and they believed you to be his child and not Reggie's.'

'Surely she put them straight?'

Joyce gave a short, sarcastic laugh. 'By telling them what? That she'd been buying drugs off some back-street dealer? If that wasn't bad enough, she didn't have any proof to back up her story.'

'She had you!' cried Libby. 'You were the proof.'

Joyce gaped at Libby. 'You think they'd trust the woman who got pregnant out of wedlock by a crook? As far as they were concerned, I was the devil incarnate, and anyone who associated with me should be tarred with the same brush.'

'So what happened?'

Joyce shrugged. 'Orla had to pick her poison. Face the music and tell Reggie she'd practically bankrupted them for a handful of painkillers – and that by doing so she'd also put his life in danger – or leave Liverpool and never look back.'

Libby wiped the tears with the backs of her hands. 'So they left, but how could you have stopped talkin' to her when she needed you the most?'

'I didn't want to, but your mother was desperate to make things right with our parents, and she'd never have been able to do that with me in the picture. Not just that, but I came with problems of my own, and your mother had enough on her plate without worryin' over me.'

Libby nodded slowly. 'She wasn't much better off in London, what with my Uncle Tony treatin' the two of us as though we were lepers. I had no idea why he treated us so badly, until I found the diaries. I instantly assumed he must have known about the affair, but seein' as there was no affair I'm now flummoxed as to his reasoning.'

Joyce pulled a disgruntled face. 'Tony never liked your mam because he thought she took your father off him. Bloomin' ridiculous for a man of his age, but there you go.'

'Do you not think my grandparents said summat to him?'

Joyce looked genuinely shocked. 'Good God no! They didn't want anyone finding out their suspicions; as far as they were concerned summat like that could ruin the reputation of their precious emporium. If Tony knew anything it was probably through his association with Donny, because he used to have dealings with Donny himself.'

Libby's mouth rounded as the penny dropped. 'That's why he hated her so much. Because he knew she was judgin' him when from his point of view she wasn't much better herself. But there's a deal of difference between being so desperate to get pregnant you buy some hooky pills and makin' a livin' from sellin' stolen goods.'

'Where is the utter delight living now?' asked Joyce, her voice heavy with sarcasm.

'London,' said Libby, 'runnin' my parents' stall which he stole from under them the day they died.'

Joyce's face turned thunderous. 'Now why doesn't that surprise me?' She hesitated, a line creasing her brow. 'Only if you knew he'd stolen it, why didn't you report him to the scuffers?'

Libby went on to tell Joyce everything, including Suzie's advice to trace the money back to the bookies.

'And now you know that you can expose him, what are you going to do?'

'I'm not sure he's worth my time,' said Libby, 'besides which I daresay there won't be a stall to salvage after he's run it into the ground.'

'How that man can sleep at night is beyond me,' said Joyce. 'His brother would be turning in his grave if he knew what Tony had done.'

Libby tried to recall something Joyce had said earlier in the conversation. 'How did Donny know my mum was desperate to get pregnant?'

Joyce shrugged. 'I don't know – word of mouth mebbe? You know what awful gossips folk can be.'

But Libby was shaking her head. 'My mother wouldn't associate with the sort of people that knew Donny. He must have heard it from someone else.'

Their eyes met and both women instantly knew the answer. 'Tony,' breathed Joyce. 'I'd bet a pound to a penny that Tony told Donny of their troubles.'

'So it's his fault that Donny sold them pills to me mum,' said Libby.

Joyce's features became wooden. 'That's not all. Jo and Donny took you in knowing full well whose daughter you were.'

Libby held a hand to her forehead as the truth hit her. 'Jo knew she could pretend to be you without fear of repercussions because she believed that Callum had bumped you off! She and Donny were goin' to try and fleece me the same way as they did me mum.' Her jaw flinched angrily. 'Well, they're not goin' to get away with it, not this time!' She stood up so sharply her chair danced precariously on its back legs before settling. 'I'm goin' to the police to tell them everythin' they've done to me and my family, and to hell with the consequences.'

'Hold your fire,' said Joyce. 'You don't want to go running off half-cocked; you need to think about this sensibly.'

'What's there to think about?' steamed Libby. 'My mother was forced to leave the city, her family, and everything she loved because of *him.*'

'I know,' said Joyce, 'but think about it, Lib. What good will going to the scuffers do without proof?'

'I've you.'

'And do you really think they'll listen to me when my husband's Callum Haggarty? Because in case you'd forgotten, your uncle hasn't the best reputation around these parts.'

'Uncle Tony?' asked Libby, confused.

'Callum. Like it or not, he's your uncle.'

'Oh, great! Talk about out of the fryin' pan into the fire.'

'My point exactly. Plus, we've not got any evidence: the pills are gone, and we've no proof as to who sold them to Orla. As far as the scuffers are concerned, you reap what you sow if you deal with the likes of the Murphys. Not only that, but your mam left the city owing Gawd only knows how much, and that won't go down well in the eyes of the law.'

Libby sank slowly into her chair. 'We can't let Donny get away with it. Not after everythin' he's done.'

'I understand you want to get him back for what he did to Orla,' said Joyce, 'but sometimes you just have to admit defeat.'

'Never!' said Libby, her jaw jutting out defiantly. 'I'll make that man pay for what he did to my mum if it's the last thing I do!'

***

Libby was sitting cross-legged on her bed reading the latest letter from Emma.

Hearing about Donny has made my blood boil. How one human can do that to another is beyond me, it really is. Our parents always taught us to cheer people up when they were feeling down, not take advantage of them.

Libby smiled as she continued to read her friend's opinion of the Murphys and what she would like to do to them. *Good old Emma*, she thought, *she'll always have my back.*

She paused in her reading and cast her mind back to her telephone conversation with Jack soon after finding out that Joyce was her aunt.

'I can't believe she was under yer nose the whole time,' breathed Jack. 'What are the odds?'

'I reckon it's the magic of Hollybank,' said Libby. 'Remember, it's where Suzie found her mum, too.'

'I think you're right,' agreed Jack. 'You can't tell me fate doesn't exist.'

Libby laughed softly. 'I wouldn't dream of it.'

'And how do you feel about them bein' your true relatives?'

'My aunt had to be someone, and I'd much rather that be Joyce than Jo Murphy! The hardest part is knowin' that Callum's my uncle. A bit like jumpin' out of the fryin' pan into the fire as far as uncles are concerned.'

'And Suzie?'

'Not only is Suzie a diamond in the rough, but I'm proud to have her as my cousin, especially as I never even knew I had one!'

'I'm so glad things have worked out for you, Lib. Have you cleared your diary for the fifteenth?'

'I have indeed, and I'm countin' down the days.'

'Me too,' he said. 'I thought we might take a trip into London so that you can see what it's like first-hand.'

She felt her tummy jolt unpleasantly. 'As long as we don't bump into that bloomin' uncle of mine, cos I won't be able to hold meself back from givin' him a piece of my mind.'

'Does it matter if you do? Give him a piece of your mind, I mean?'

'Yes, because I want to have a nice relaxin' time with my fiancé, not get banged up for assaultin' that scumbag.'

Jack laughed. 'Fair comment.'

Now, she turned her attention back to the letter.

I must admit, at the start I felt a tad awkward about writing to Bernie because I didn't know what to say, but his letters are full of interesting chat about Liverpool and his plans for when the war is over. He's told me about the Grafton and the bands that play there, and how he's going to take me to see all the sights as soon as I get back, but you mustn't worry that I shan't have time for you, because I shall!

Margo entered the barn, washbag in hand. 'You readin' that letter again?'

Libby nodded happily. 'I worried she might be lonely when she joined the ATS, but she's made heaps of friends already.'

'It's certainly perked Suzie up,' said Margo. 'She can't wait to start her new life.'

'It seems strange to think of her as my cousin,' said Libby.

'Good strange or . . .?' said Margo, purposely leaving the last bit hanging.

'*Very* good strange,' said Libby, 'cos I've finally found the family I was lookin' for, and it's far better than I could have imagined.'

Margo pulled a guilty grimace. 'It just goes to show you can't always believe what you read.'

'I still feel terrible about that,' acknowledged Libby. 'Why couldn't I have been more like Emma, instead of jumpin' to conclusions without any proof? She refused to believe my mother would do anythin' like that.'

'Don't beat yerself up about it,' said Margo. 'You weren't the only one who got hold of the wrong end of the stick.'

'I know, which is why Jack feels guilty too, but I've already told him he can't blame himself, cos he wasn't the one who put the words into my head. I did that when I read it for myself.'

'We're all guilty as charged when it comes to that diary,' said Margo, 'but at least we know the truth now, although that's not much of a consolation when you think about it.'

'I can't wait to see Jack next month; it'll be a real break from all that's gone on,' said Libby.

'Ooo! I was havin' a word with Tom about that.'

'Oh?'

'Tom's always been keen to know more about where I grew up, and what London's like compared to Liverpool, so when I mentioned that you were goin' down on the fifteenth, he suggested we might go with you – if that's all right with you?'

'Of course it's all right! Blimey, Margo, I'd love to have you along for the company, and it'll be fun showin' Tom your old stompin' ground.'

'Then that's settled,' said Margo gleefully, 'or at least it will be when I've had a word with the Lewises, cos they're the only stumblin' block I can foresee.'

Libby shrugged. 'As we'll only be away for a couple of days, I can't see them sayin' no. After all, they'll be no worse off than they were before we came to Hollybank.'

'I s'pose so, and it's better we go before Suzie leaves for her initial trainin'.'

'Exactly!' said Libby. 'And now that we've got that sorted out, how do you feel about goin' back home? Are you worried about bumpin' into yer dad at all?'

Margo laughed sarcastically. 'I'll be all right as long as I steer clear of the bookies and the track.'

'But aren't you goin' to show Tom your old home in Blendon Row?'

'From across the way,' said Margo. 'I don't particularly relish meetin' any of my former neighbours because . . .' She fell into silent contemplation. It wasn't so much that she was ashamed of the folk who lived in Blendon Row, or of the fact that she used to live there, but seeing some of the young boys still working as shoeblacks would be a stark reminder of what her life would be like had she stayed in London. '. . . because I've moved on from that life, and I have no desire to return.'

'You want him to see where you came from,' said Libby, 'but skimmin' over the surface, not in depth. Hearin' that you used to work as a shoeblack is very different from seein' it first hand, only with the lads on every street corner it's not really summat you can hide from.'

'Granted, but seein' them from afar is very different from seein' them face to face,' Margo glanced at her fingernails, which were no longer stained black from years of polishing boots, 'and I'd prefer to keep it that way.'

'When are you goin' to see the Lewises?'

'Now's as good a time as any,' said Margo, turning back to the door. 'Strike whilst the iron's hot!'

'Good luck!' Libby called after her as she disappeared, then glanced at the letter in her hand. If only Pontefract were close to London!

***

Libby, Margo and Tom were waiting for their train on the platform at Lime Street Station as the warm sunshine poured through the few panes of glass which had survived the May blitz.

'It's been ages since I last went on a train,' said Libby. 'Not includin' the overhead railway, of course.'

'At least you'll be sittin' in seats this time round,' said Tom, 'and not bundled in amongst the mail sacks.'

'It's amazin' how much your life can change in such a short period of time,' remarked Margo. 'When I came to Liverpool I had barely two ha'pennies to rub together, whereas now I can afford to buy me own ticket!'

'It's been one heck of a ride,' said Libby, 'but well worth the trip!'

'Do you include your new uncle in that statement?' asked Margo mischievously.

'No I do not!'

'Not to worry. All families have their black sheep,' said Margo. 'At least yours is behind baaahs.' She grinned at her own joke, but Libby and Tom both groaned.

'That was awful!'

'Made me smile,' said Margo.

Tom glanced along the track to an approaching train. 'Do you think this one's ours?'

Libby followed his gaze. 'I hope so. It's already runnin' half an hour late, and I'm not goin' to ask the guard when it's due, cos I'm gettin' fed up of hearin' the same answer.'

'You do realise there's a war on?' said Margo and Tom in unison.

'Exactly!'

The train had come to a standstill and the passengers were pouring out of the carriages. 'Flippin' 'eck, how many can they fit on one train?' said Tom as the already crowded platform became swamped with people who were all trying to leave the station at the same time.

Margo grimaced as waiting passengers began to surge towards the train. 'It looks as if there's as many gettin' on as there was gettin' off!'

'I don't fancy standin' up all that way,' said Libby. She cast an eye towards the back of the train. 'I don't suppose we could sneak in amongst the luggage?'

Tom began to stride towards one of the carriages in a determined fashion. 'No, we could not! Sittin' amongst cushy mailsacks might be one thing, but hard suitcases? No chance.'

Libby wrinkled the side of her nose. 'I wish I'd worn me wellies.'

Margo laughed. 'Why? Do you think the smell would empty the carriage?'

'No! I meant they're comfier than heels.'

'I'm surprised you don't wear them for dancin',' remarked Tom as he helped the girls to board the train.

'I would if I could,' said Libby, as she held on to his hand, 'but I don't think Jack would be best pleased.'

'I think Jack would love you no matter what you wore,' said Margo, as she joined Libby.

'Considerin' I looked like a drowned rat when we first met, I'd say you're probably right.'

Tom lifted the bags onto the rack above the seats whilst the girls settled into their places. 'Blimey, it's hot in here,' said Libby, shrugging her arms out of her jacket.

'It's all these people squeezed into a small space,' said Tom as he slid the window next to Margo open. 'I'll close it once we get goin'.'

'I bet Jack won't get a wink of sleep tonight knowin' you're on your way,' said Margo, handing Tom her jacket.

'I was the same,' said Libby. 'Tossin' and turnin' all night, I was.'

Margo raised her brow. 'I know. I could hear you tryin' to be quiet.'

Libby grimaced. 'It's a good job I don't share a bed with Thor, or he'd have been on the floor.'

Tom rolled his eyes. 'How you can have that filthy great mutt in the same bed as you is beyond me.'

'He is *not* filthy, *or* a mutt,' Margo pouted.

'Mebbe he's not a mutt,' conceded Tom, 'but you can't tell me he's clean when he's hangin' around the farm all day.'

'That's why I put an old sheet on the bed for him,' said Margo.

'Well, you'd best get him used to the floor, cos I ain't havin' no dog on the bed once we're married.'

Libby chuckled softly. 'You can't blame him, Margo. Sharin' with Thor must be like havin' another person in the bed – and a big person to boot!'

Margo eyed Tom accusingly. 'Just where do you expect him to sleep when we get our smallholdin'?'

'I thought we could get Jack to make us a nice kennel, what with him bein' a carpenter an' all . . .' Tom began, but Margo could scarcely believe her ears.

'Kennel? You don't seriously expect him to sleep outside?'

'He's a dog; he's meant to sleep outside,' said Tom reasonably, adding, 'and what sort of guard dog sleeps on someone's bed?'

'A lucky one,' Libby giggled.

'I can't ask him to sleep outside when he's been sharin' me bed. You wouldn't like it if I did that to you.'

'Because I'd be your husband!' said Tom. 'There is a difference.'

'I don't know why we're even botherin' to discuss it,' said Margo stubbornly. 'It's not as if we've even got a smallholdin' to move into yet!'

'And I can't believe I'm havin' to persuade my future wife to kick the dog out of the marital bed we haven't got yet either,' said Tom pointedly.

Margo mumbled, 'If anyone's gettin' kicked out of bed it won't be Thor,' before changing the subject to the scenery which was passing them by. 'I didn't realise we were on the move. Only another six hours to go before we hit London – if we're lucky.'

As if on cue, the train began to slow. Tom peered out of the window as he tried to see the reason behind it. 'We've another train ahead of us,' he told the girls. 'I hope we don't have too many hold-ups.'

'Do you suppose the B&B will still let us in if we turn up late?' asked Margo anxiously.

'Of course they will,' said Tom confidently. 'I'm sure they must be used to people arrivin' at all sorts of hours with the transport system bein' the way it is at the moment.'

To their relief the train quickly began to gather speed and they were on their way once more. Leaning against the window, Libby idly watched the fields go by and found that she was wondering how many head of cattle each farmer had, and whether their farm was as big as Hollybank or a collection of smallholdings.

It'll be very different scenery once we start the approach to London, she thought. *I wonder how much of it I'll recognise?* She glanced down at her fingernails. She was very much looking forward to seeing Jack, but she wasn't sure how she'd feel about the city itself. Her thoughts reverted to the conversation she'd had with Emma regarding their old school. *I don't know how I'll feel if they've bombed the school*, she thought now, *or Petticoat Lane for that matter, but I do know one thing: it won't be the London that I once loved if they're gone!*

By the time they arrived in Biggin Hill some eight hours later, the three of them were ready for bed.

'Don't bother wakin' me if there's a bleedin' air raid, cos I'm stoppin' in bed,' Margo told the others as she plodded along beside Tom.

Remembering what life had been like before they left the city, Libby made a suggestion. 'Maybe we should find the nearest shelter and kip down there for the night, save gettin' woken up later?'

Tom yawned audibly. 'Whilst I could probably sleep on a clothes line, I'll settle for a nice comfy bed, keep my fingers crossed and hope for the best.'

'Crossed fingers,' said Margo sleepily. 'The answer to all our problems!'

Tom pointed at the sign above the pub door. 'This is us: The Old Jail.'

'Thank goodness for that,' said Libby, as Tom opened the door for them to pass through.

'You should feel right at home, what with your family ties,' Margo chuckled as she followed Libby.

Libby rolled her eyes. 'Oh, ha ha.'

Tom checked them in at the bar and ordered a round of drinks whilst they waited for the landlord's wife to fetch the keys to their rooms.

'I hope we don't face delays like that on the way back,' said Margo, who'd chosen to stand rather than sit down with her drink. 'My backside's pretty sore after bein' sat on the whole time.'

'And there we were worried we mightn't get a seat,' agreed Libby, who was standing beside her. 'I hope they have soft beds here.'

'Are you goin' to give yer aunt a quick call to let her know we've arrived safely?'

'I said I would,' said Libby, and spoke to the landlord. 'May I use your telephone, please?'

In answer he jerked his head towards the phone in the hallway behind the bar. 'Pay Ivy when you've finished,' he said, indicating the barmaid, who was writing their names down in the register.

Libby had expected to leave a message with Helen, but when she got through to the farm she was pleasantly surprised to find that Joyce was awaiting her call. 'I was beginnin' to worry,' she confessed, 'I know London's a long way, but even so . . .'

Hearing a voice that sounded very like her mother's caught Libby off guard. 'You sound like my mum,' she said softly.

'All mothers worry, even if they're not your actual mother,' said Joyce, who hadn't quite grasped Libby's meaning.

'I meant you actually sound like her,' said Libby. 'I didn't realise how much until just now.'

There was a long pause. 'Does that upset you?'

Libby smiled. 'No, it's lovely. I did wonder whether I might forget what Mum sounded like, but I don't have to worry about that any more.'

'What about your dad?'

Libby tutted beneath her breath. 'Uncle Tony sounds just like my father, but I don't particularly want to hear owt he has to say.'

'Well just you forget about him, and enjoy your break away,' said Joyce. 'And say hello to the others for me.'

'I will.' They said their goodbyes and Libby walked back to the bar, where she gave the money for the call to Ivy, who in return handed her two keys.

Having chosen a table at the far side of the pub, Margo waved to get her attention and waited for Libby to join them. 'Did you get through?'

Libby took a sip of her drink before replying. 'I did. My aunt sounds just like my mum on the phone.'

Margo and Tom exchanged glances. 'How did that make you feel?'

'Good,' said Libby. 'I know I'll never hear my mum's voice again, so this is the next best thing.'

Margo brightened. 'That's wonderful, Lib.'

Libby hid a yawn behind her hand. 'I don't know how much longer I can keep my eyes open!'

Margo drained her glass. 'C'mon, sleepy-head, it's time we hit the hay.'

'We'll see you bright and early for breakfast, Tom,' said Libby as she hooked her arm through Margo's. 'Jack said he'd be here at nine o'clock sharp – or, as he put it, zero nine hundred hours.'

'The twenty-four-hour clock always confuses me,' said Margo as she followed Libby to their room. 'Why can't people say p.m. or a.m.?'

Libby closed the door before hanging her coat up on the hook. 'Cos they don't like to make things easy for the rest of us.'

Margo took the jug of water which the barmaid had left for them and poured some of it into the wash bowl. Flinching as the cold water hit her face, she gasped, 'Stone the flamin' crows!'

'Cold, is it?' Libby giggled sleepily as she stripped to her vest and knickers.

Margo spoke thickly as she rubbed the circulation back into her cheeks with the hand towel. 'Just a tad.'

'So, what do you fancy doin' tomorrow?' said Libby, taking her turn at the bowl.

'I'm easy. What does everyone else fancy?'

'I can't make up my mind what I want to do first,' said Libby, 'so I thought I'd probably play it by ear, and see what Jack wants to do.'

'Fair enough. When are you goin' to see Gordon?'

'Ah, now that's easy. We're goin' to have supper with him at his tomorrow, and he's invited you and Tom along, unless you have other plans?'

'We'd love to come,' said Margo. 'Tom's been sayin' he'd like to meet Gordon, and this is a good opportunity.

'I'm glad you said that, cos he's got some feller stayin' with him. When Jack joined the RAF, Gordon let his room out to help make ends meet, which is why we aren't stayin' over at his.'

'Sounds sensible,' said Margo.

'Jack says he rents the room out a bit like a B&B, so he never knows who's goin' to be there from one day to the next.'

'So how do you know it's a feller stayin'?'

'He'd not let the room to a woman. Tongues might wag.'

'True,' conceded Margo, sliding between the covers, 'but what's his lodger got to do with you bein' pleased that Tom and I are joinin' you for supper?'

'I don't want to be sat on me tod listenin' to men's talk,' said Libby. 'I had enough of that when I was down the market. Dad and Pete would stand around for hours talkin' about stuff I hadn't got a clue about, or any interest in for that matter.'

Margo grinned. 'What's men's talk when it's at home?'

Libby put her toothbrush back in her washbag before swilling her mouth out with fresh water. 'Mostly politics, or fishin', or the right tool for the right job.'

Margo grimaced. 'I can see why you want me to tag along. I'll let Tom know we're joinin' you for dinner.'

Libby waited for Margo to get into bed before blowing the candle out. 'Thanks, Margo. I knew I could rely on you.'

Libby snuggled down beneath the blankets, hoping against hope that the Luftwaffe would stay away. *I've not felt this fearful since we moved to Hollybank*, she thought as she closed her eyes. *I can't say I've missed it. I love Jack with all my heart, but I won't be sad to get back on that train. I just wish he were comin' with me!*

Chapter Seven

Eager for the day ahead, Libby and Margo were seated at the breakfast table waiting for Tom.

'By George, you two are bright-eyed and bushy-tailed!' he said, taking the seat between them.

'It was all that travellin' yesterday. I was out like a light as soon as my head hit the pillow.' Libby smiled at the barmaid who'd come over to take their order before continuing. 'Is it always this quiet here?'

'I wish! Livin' close to an airfield means we spend most nights down the cellar, which is why we keep mattresses down there.'

Libby frowned. 'My fiancé hasn't mentioned anything, and he's stationed at Biggin Hill.'

The barmaid's cheeks coloured. 'Ignore me. I shouldn't have said anythin'!'

'Don't worry about it. I probably got hold of the wrong end of the stick.' She glanced back at the menu before making up her mind. 'I'll have the porridge, with a pot of tea . . .' she raised her brow expectantly to Margo and Tom, who both nodded, 'for three, please.'

The others placed their orders, and Libby waited until the barmaid had left before voicing her concerns. 'I didn't want her to feel awkward, but if you ask me, Jack's been keeping this from me on purpose, cos he hasn't said anythin' about nightly air raids.'

'Maybe the barmaid's exaggeratin',' said Tom. 'The sirens used to go off all the time when the war first started, but that didn't mean the Luftwaffe were comin'.'

Margo was in full agreement with Tom. 'If it was as bad as she suggests, there'd be nowt left of the airfield, so I'd take what she said with a pinch of salt.'

Thinking that her friends were probably correct, Libby relaxed a little. 'You're right, they probably have lots of false alarms. Have you made up your minds what you want to do today?'

'I'm takin' Tom to see Blendon Row, Buckingham Palace, St Paul's Cathedral,' Margo waved a nonchalant hand, 'the usual stuff. You?'

'Whitechapel Road and Petticoat Lane, then on to Gordon's.' She opened her handbag and passed Margo a piece of paper. 'This is his address.'

'What time is he expecting us?' asked Margo, leaning back so that the barmaid could place the breakfast tray on the table.

'Any time after five thirty,' said Libby. 'Jack says Gordon's doin' a cold supper so it doesn't matter if any of us are a bit late, though I expect we'll try to get there earlier so that we can spend some time with him.'

'Did I just hear my name bein' mentioned?'

Libby twisted round to welcome Jack, who was approaching from behind. 'You're early!' she cried, half rising out of her seat.

'I've been on leave as of midnight last night,' said Jack, pulling up a chair. 'You're damn lucky I wasn't here at six o'clock this mornin'.'

'I wouldn't have minded,' said Libby.

Jack gestured towards the barmaid. 'I don't think the staff would've welcomed me with open arms.'

Tom pushed the toast rack towards Jack. 'Have you had brekker?'

Jack waved a hand to decline the offer before changing his mind and taking a slice. 'So what's the plan of attack for today, then?' he said, opening a jar of blackberry jam.

Libby reiterated their plans, finishing with, 'If it's all right with you, of course?'

'Course it is! I take it we're all up for supper at Dad's?'

There were murmurs of agreement, muted by mouthfuls of toast or porridge.

'Libby says your dad's been rentin' your old room out,' said Margo, after swallowing her mouthful.

Jack wrinkled a nostril, showing his displeasure. 'He has, and I must say I'm not too happy about it.'

Tom paused, a slice of toast poised at his lips. 'Why not?'

Jack glanced at Libby. 'You know what my dad's like for takin' in waifs and strays. He's a real softy when it comes to sob stories, and I'm worried he might get taken advantage of.'

'I can see your concern, but what can you do?'

'Nothin', and that's the point,' said Jack. 'He's a grown man who knows his own mind; I just hope he'll be sensible and not get taken in by some hard luck story and let them stay for free.'

Libby pulled a sideways grimace. 'Like he did with me.'

'Only you were genuine,' said Jack.

'Libby thinks we'll get to meet his latest guest this evenin'?' said Margo. 'Does your dad often supply tea to his boarders?'

'Probably, because it's company, and nobody likes to eat on their own.'

'I hate to think of him bein' lonely,' said Libby. 'I know you're concerned, but if it makes him happy then where's the harm?'

'I s'pose.'

Libby remembered the barmaid's words as she wiped her mouth on the corners of her napkin. 'The barmaid reckons Biggin Hill's been the target of the Luftwaffe nigh on every night. Is that right?'

Scowling, Jack glanced towards the bar before answering. 'It's nothin' we can't handle.'

Libby's brow rose. 'So it's true then?'

He gave a half-shoulder shrug. 'Some of the sirens are false alarms, so it's not *every* night.'

Margo looked around her. 'Are we safe here?'

'As safe as anywhere close to the capital,' said Jack. 'Which has changed a lot since you were here last, by the way.'

The barmaid spoke absent-mindedly as she collected the empty bowls. 'It changes every day. I got lost the last time I went into the city.'

'It's hard to get yer bearin's when buildin's disappear overnight,' said Jack, 'but you know that after livin' through the May blitz.'

'Is the Petticoat Lane market still there?' Libby asked the barmaid, crossing her fingers.

The woman smiled broadly. 'They'll never stop the market from openin' up, I don't care what they chuck at 'em.'

Libby gave an inward sigh of relief. 'Thank goodness for that.'

Jack glanced at the watch on his wrist. 'If you're ready to leave we should make it in time to catch the next bus.'

Libby looked at the holdall Jack had brought in with him. 'Do you want to put that in your room before we go?'

'Can do.' He looked at Tom, who jerked his head for Jack to follow him.

'I must admit I'm feelin' a tad concerned about goin' into the city,' said Libby as she and Margo waited for the boys to return.

'We knew it would've changed,' said Margo, 'just not how much.'

'I think once a place stops bein' how you remembered it, it's time to move on,' said Libby. 'Do you agree?'

'I do. I've felt that way about the city ever since I left. Liverpool's my home now, and comin' back here just confirms that.'

'But you've not set foot in the centre yet,' said Libby reasonably.

'I don't have to,' said Margo. 'When I woke up this mornin', I automatically found myself lookin' for Thor.

When I remembered where I was, I started wonderin'
what they'd be doin' on the farm. Whether they'd finished
the milkin', and who was goin' on the round with Bernie.'
She pulled a downward grimace. 'I wished it was me.'

'It's your home,' said Libby. 'I didn't like to say anythin' first thing, but ever since we arrived I've found
myself doin' the same as you. Only I've been wonderin'
whether they'd had any incidents puttin' the cattle
back in the meadow, and if Thor was behavin' himself
or pinin' for you.'

Margo looked forlorn. 'Don't say that!'

'Say what?' asked Tom, who'd returned with Jack.

'Libby thinks Thor might be pinin' for me,' said
Margo as they left the pub. 'I don't like to think of him
bein' sad.'

Thoroughly regretting she'd brought the matter up,
in case Margo and Tom began bickering again over
where the dog was going to sleep when they were married, Libby swiftly moved on. 'The girls will take good
care of him, don't you worry.'

They made it to the bus stop in the nick of time, and
Libby spent the entire journey convincing Margo that
Thor would be just fine and dandy and was probably
enjoying having the bed to himself.

'I swear you care more about that dog than you do
for me!' said Tom as they stepped down onto the
pavement.

'He's helpless,' said Margo loyally, 'whereas you can
fend for yerself.'

'So can he,' Tom retorted. 'All he has to do is look at
you with them puppy-dog eyes and you're like putty
in his paws.'

Margo smiled, but didn't deny it. 'We'll see you later,' she said to Libby and Jack, and she and Tom went on their way.

Libby hooked her arm through Jack's. 'How did it feel when you first came back?'

'Horrid,' he said simply, 'because you weren't with me. How about you – are you glad to be here?'

'Much like Margo, I miss Hollybank,' said Libby. 'We've got a really good routine going there, and it feels odd not to have milked the cows, or done the milk round; a bit like I'm missin' out.'

'Did you feel the same way about not bein' on the market?'

'No, but that has more to do with Uncle Tony than anythin' else.'

Eager to move the conversation away from her uncle, Jack swiftly changed the subject.

'Where would you like to go first?'

'Whitechapel Road,' said Libby promptly.

'Is there any reason why you want to go back when you know your home's no longer there?'

'It may sound odd, but I'd like to say goodbye. It may be a pile of bricks and mortar now but it was my home, and I loved livin' there.'

'It's funny how somethin' like a house can almost take on a personality,' said Jack, as they made their way through the city. 'It may sound daft to you, but I feel that way about some of my tools.'

Libby raised a surprised brow. 'Your tools?'

He nodded. 'My chisel used to belong to me grandad, and it reminds me of him every time I use it. I'd hate for it to break, or go missin'.'

As they turned onto Whitechapel Road Libby squeezed Jack's hand. Glancing to where her parents' house once stood, she stared at the fire-blackened bricks. 'What I'd give to turn back the hands of time,' she said to Jack, who'd placed his arm around her shoulder. As she continued to gaze at the rubble, a familiar voice spoke from beside her.

'It's Libby, isn't it?'

Libby turned to greet the ARP warden who had been with her when they discovered her parents. 'Mr Bishop! Aren't you a sight for sore eyes!'

'No need for formalities,' the warden assured her. 'Please, call me Lionel.'

'Lionel,' said Libby, albeit a little shyly. 'Talk about long time no see.'

'It is that,' agreed Lionel, 'but am I ever glad to see you!'

Libby was surprised. 'Oh? Any reason in particular?'

'Yes. You see, I remembered somthin' about the day your stuff got nicked from outside yer parents' house not long after you left for Liverpool, but of course I had no idea how to contact you.'

Libby was intrigued. 'What was it?'

'I think I might know who stole the van.'

Libby eyed him sharply. 'Go on.'

'When we pulled yer dad out from the rubble, I got the distinct feelin' that I'd seen him somewhere before, but couldn't think where. I mentioned it to one of the fellers and they said how your father had a stall down Petticoat Lane. I figured that must be it, and thought no more about it – until recently.'

'Why, what happened recently?'

'I saw some feller down the market who reminded me of yer dad, and that's when it clicked.'

'It was the man who stole Dad's van,' breathed Libby. 'Are you certain it was him?'

'No doubt about it,' said Lionel.

'And he reminded you of Dad.' Libby was beginning to get excited until a thought entered her mind. 'But how do you know what the man who took the van looked like? I thought it was only Mrs Fortescue who saw him?'

He grimaced apologetically. 'That's what I thought at the time, but seein' the feller down the market jogged my memory and I remembered how I'd seen him leanin' against the side of yer dad's van only seconds after the bomb went off. He was talkin' complete and utter gibberish, which didn't surprise me too much because shock can do that to people. I thought he was goin' to try and drive the van away, so I made him come down to the shelter with me, explainin' that he was safer there than in his van.'

'What happened after the all-clear sounded?' asked Libby, with bated breath.

'He thanked me for takin' him to the shelter, sayin' that he hadn't been thinkin' with a clear head, and that he'd move the van so it wasn't in anyone's way.'

Libby gawked at him. 'Why on earth didn't you mention any of this at the time?'

He shrugged helplessly. 'People do all kinds of stupid things durin' air raids. I've had women try to go back to their house because they think they've left the kettle on, or because they can't remember whether they've locked the door or not. Some feller tryin' to outrun the bombin' in his van is not uncommon, besides which he didn't seem in the least bit suspicious. He even had the keys.'

'Dad kept misplacin' the keys, or packin' them away by accident, so Mum said it would be best if he kept them in the van so we'd know where they were.'

'He must've known,' said Lionel. 'Or just got lucky, one of the two.'

'Oh he knew alright, because he's my uncle and that's why he reminded you of my dad!' She shook her head angrily before continuing. 'So he *was* there when the bomb hit, yet he told me that he'd bought the business off them just before it happened,' said Libby. 'I distinctly remember him sayin' he wasn't even a street away when the bomb hit, but if he was just outside, then why not say so?'

'Because he was lyin',' said Jack grimly.

Libby racked her brains as she desperately tried to remember the conversation. 'I'd gone to the market to tell Mr Filmer – he's the market inspector – that I wouldn't be able to open up just yet, when I saw my uncle on the stall. I felt guilty for not tellin' him about my parents sooner and he said not to worry and that he was sorry to hear the news . . .'

Jack cut her short. 'That doesn't make sense. Why would he say he hadn't heard the news if he'd been there as it happened?'

Libby felt her heart sink. 'Because he didn't want me to think he'd been anywhere near. He only confessed to havin' seen them that day because I asked how he'd managed to buy the business off my father when I knew for a fact he'd not done so before I'd left for work that morning.'

The warden eyed her thoughtfully. 'I take it you told yer uncle about the van gettin' nicked?'

Libby nodded miserably. 'I chastised him for not comin' with me to report it stolen, but of course he wouldn't want to do that when he was the one that nicked it in the first place.' She fell silent as something Emma had said came to the forefront of her mind. 'Emma asked me why someone would nick the van just to sell the contents as a job lot for a handful of pennies, and that it wasn't as if my parents had the deeds to an estate in there. I thought at the time that summat didn't sit right, and now I know what it was. They didn't find my father's briefcase when they pulled him out of the house, so it must've been in the van, along with the bill of sale as well as all our other legal documents.' Her mouth ran dry as the enormity of what she was about to say hit her. 'Tony used them documents to forge me dad's signature.'

'It was him all along,' agreed Jack.

A memory came over her, leaving her sick to her stomach. 'He said he'd tried to persuade Mum to leave the house as soon as the siren sounded, and that she'd refused, insisting on waiting for me in case I came home. At the time I couldn't fathom why my mum had done that, because it was totally out character for her to do so – she was always the first out of the house, insisting that we hurry up and join her down the shelter because she was convinced Hitler was aiming for our house and our house alone.'

'So why didn't she run out that day, then?' supposed the warden. 'Cos yer uncle got out in time.'

'Summat must've happened,' whispered Libby, a tear trickling down her cheek, 'and he just drove away, leavin' them to die.'

'What are you goin' to do?' said Jack. 'Cos you can't let him get away with this.'

'I shall take a leaf out of my cousin's book and report him to the police, but first I need Lionel to make sure it was my uncle that he saw.' She turned to the warden. 'Are you able to come with us and take a quick gander?'

'Too right I am!' said Lionel vehemently. 'Wait here while I get one of the fellers to cover me.'

He soon returned and they began their walk to the market. Deep in thought, Libby tried to come to terms with the enormity of their discovery. She hadn't questioned it further when Mrs Fortescue had said the man in the van had looked like her father, because they'd quickly realised that the van had been stolen and not simply driven away by her parents. *It's because you trusted him*, Libby thought to herself. *Not only that, but you couldn't see a reason for him wantin' the stuff in the first place. If only I'd put two and two together, I'd have realised that the theft of the van was linked to him havin' the deeds to the business.*

Jack interrupted her thoughts. 'No wonder he didn't go to the funeral: guilty conscience.'

'It's a shame that we've got no other proof than my say-so,' said Lionel, 'but at least you'll know the truth.'

'There is one thing. My uncle told me he'd paid for the business with the money he'd won on the gee-gees. He'll have to come up with proof of that if he's to convince a jury of his innocence.' She looked to Lionel. 'Did he see you when you saw him last?'

'No, or at least I don't think so. He was talkin' to one of the Sykes family, which is why he caught my eye in the first place.'

Libby paled. 'I knew he was up to no good, but I didn't realise he was dealin' with the likes of them. I bet he got them to forge me dad's signature, cos they're well known for that sort of thing.'

'He's in deeper than any of us realised,' said Jack. 'I thought yer uncle was a spiv, but he's worse than that, much worse.'

She felt her heart quicken in her chest as they neared the market. Hanging back just before the entrance, she addressed Lionel and Jack. 'The two of you will have to go on without me, cos people are bound to recognise me and we can't afford for Tony to get wind that I'm back, and with an ARP warden in tow, because he'll realise the game is up. Jack's met my uncle, so he'll be able to confirm whether you've identified the right person, Lionel.'

Looking at the warden, Jack jerked his head in the direction of the market. 'Let's get this show on the road.' The two men disappeared amongst the stalls while Libby slunk into the shadows, hoping to remain unseen.

What are the chances of me bumpin' into Lionel the only time I'm back in London, Libby thought now. *I know he has to remain on duty to stop the kids from playin' silly beggars on the rubble, but even so he could've been on his break, or at the far end of the street, or even on his day off.* Her thoughts turned to her uncle driving off in the van leaving her parents to die, but the image was too much for her to bear, so she turned her attention back to the market. *Pete and the others have been workin' cheek by jowl with the man who betrayed two of their dearest friends, and they don't even know it. I knew Tony was lyin' from the moment he opened his mouth, but they all took his side—* she corrected herself: *or some of them did at any rate, sayin' that they felt sorry for me, and he should go easy on me because of everythin' I'd been through. He must've been cock-a-hoop when he realised he'd got away with it. Well, I wonder how they'll feel when they learn that I was right all along?*

'Libby?'

She froze as the unwelcome voice came from behind her. Keeping her fingers crossed, she didn't reply, hoping the voice had been a figment of her overactive imagination.

'Is that you?'

Libby reluctantly turned to face her uncle. Trying to keep her temper under control, she made to step around him, mumbling, 'I was just leavin',' under her breath as she did so.

This was so unlike the Libby Tony knew that he automatically put his arm out to stop her, taking a look around him. 'Who're you hidin' from?'

'I'm not hiding from anybody!' Libby snapped, her face turning beetroot as she tried to push past him. 'So, if you'd move out of my way . . .'

But Tony knew a liar when he saw one, being one himself, and he wasn't prepared to let Libby go without some kind of explanation. 'Any other time you'd have been swannin' round the market like you owned the place, so why not today?'

'Too many memories,' murmured Libby, in the hope that this would suffice.

'Then why come here in the first place?'

'I told you; I was just leavin',' said Libby. 'What's it to you anyway?'

'You're up to somethin',' said Tony, his eyes narrowing.

To her horror, Libby saw that Jack and Lionel were approaching, in animated conversation with her old friend Pete. *They haven't seen him*, she told herself; *they're goin' to walk straight over and the game'll be up. If Tony realises what's goin' on he'll scarper before Lionel has a chance to take a good look. I have to grab their attention before it's too late.*

Staring her uncle square in the eye, she raised her voice. 'You're a liar, Tony Gilbert! And what's more I can prove it!'

Tony hung his head in his hands. That was more like it. 'Oh, for Gawd's sake, not this again.'

'You lied about the money, the business and stealin' my parents' van, but I'm not surprised considerin' you hang out with the likes of the Murphy twins.'

'Eh?'

'You heard!' she shouted, pleased to see that the others had stopped close enough for Lionel to have a good look but far enough away to not spook Tony. 'You, Jo and Donny were as thick as thieves when you was in Liverpool. Extortin' money from me mum by sellin' her dodgy pills when you knew they were nowt

304

but painkillers. You led her to them like a lamb to the slaughter; even turned a blind eye when Donny threatened to kill yer brother.'

'No I didn't!' hissed Tony. He was pumping his hands up and down, indicating that he wanted Libby to lower her voice. 'Donny was the one what come up with the idea to sell her them pills, not me, and he wouldn't have actually done anythin' to Reg; he only said that to frighten her.'

Libby, who hadn't been expecting any type of confession, stared at him blindly. 'Frighten her? You scared the bloody life out of her! Everyone knows what the Murphys are like, includin' you! How could you do that to yer own family?'

'What was the harm in givin' her a little hope?' said Tony, looking truly dumbfounded that Libby should think him to be in the wrong. 'It's not my fault she didn't know when to stop. If anythin', you should be angry at her for gettin' yer dad into so much debt. He lost everythin' because of her.'

Fighting back the urge to throttle him where he stood, Libby felt silent tears of frustration lining her cheeks. 'At least she didn't leave anyone to die, unlike you.'

He looked truly perplexed. 'What the hell are you on about?'

'You were standing outside their house moments after the bomb hit.'

He rolled his eyes. 'I wasn't anywhere near the house when the bomb hit. If you want to blame anyone for their death, take a look in the mirror. Yer mum would've left as soon as the siren sounded if you'd come home like you should have.'

305

Bringing her hand back, she slapped him so hard across the face her fingers stung from the blow. 'How dare you blame me, when you know it's not true! Mum would've been out of that house in a flash, I know she would, which means you must've done summat to stop them from leavin'.' She barely hesitated before continuing vehemently, 'What did you do, Tony?'

Tony paled. 'I never done nothin'.'

'Yes, you did, it's written all over yer face. Dad never signed them papers, so I reckon you must've had a row.' Seeing the hunted look deep in his eyes, she spoke through her fingers, hardly able to believe what she was saying. 'You did, didn't you?'

'It was him what threw the first punch!' yelled Tony. 'All I did was protect meself, which I've every right to do!'

Libby's jaw dropped as the enormity of his confession overwhelmed her. 'Is that why they never got out? Because you attacked him?'

'I told you; it wasn't like that!' Tony insisted, but she could see the guilt in his eyes.

'I *knew* you were lyin'. Mum was paranoid when it came to air raids. I *knew* she wouldn't wait for me.' She fixed him with a look of pure hatred. 'You attacked my father, then left him to die.'

'I went back, but I was too late,' said Tony. 'I'd have got them out if I could, but . . .'

'They'd have got out if you hadn't attacked him,' cried Libby. 'It's your fault they're dead, not mine!'

Tony stared at her, his mouth opening and closing like a fish out of water. Stumbling backwards, he turned to run, only to find himself face to face with the warden.

'That's him,' Lionel said firmly. 'That's the feller what stole yer dad's van.'

Overwhelmed by the truth, Libby fell to her knees, whilst Jack rushed forward to catch her. Seizing his opportunity to escape, Tony fled the market with Pete in hot pursuit.

'He as good as murdered them,' she sobbed. 'We have to tell the police.' She looked wildly around her. 'Where's Pete?'

'He's gone after yer uncle,' said Lionel, 'although I doubt he'll have much luck. Yer uncle was out of here quicker than a dog out of the traps.'

'Which is what we shall have to be, if we want the police to stand a chance of catchin' him before he flees the country,' said Jack, who was already striding in the direction of the nearest police station.

'Like Donny did when he went to Blackpool,' said Libby, her voice still hoarse with emotion.

'Exactly.'

Several hours had passed before they finally emerged from the police station, and Libby felt as though she'd been put through a wringer and hung out to dry. Turning to the warden, she took his hands in hers. 'Thank you so much for everything that you've done. I can't begin to tell you how grateful I am.'

He twinkled kindly at her. 'I'm just glad I could be of help, although I wish I'd remembered somethin' sooner.' He took out a pencil and pad from his pocket

307

and wrote down his address. 'If you need me for any-thin' you can reach me here.'

She took the piece of paper and tucked it into her handbag. 'Thanks again.' They bade the warden a warm goodbye before heading back to the market.

Jack jerked his thumb over his shoulder, indicating the police station they'd just left. 'While they look for Tony, we really should try and see if we can find the people who witnessed his confession, so that it's not just our word against his.'

'It's goin' to be like lookin' for a needle in a haystack,' said Libby with a resigned sigh.

'It might not be as bad as you think. All we have to do is spread the word and hope that people come for-ward, and I rather think they will given the severity of his crimes.'

Back at the market they made straight for Pete's stall, where he was chatting to a small group of people. Slightly disappointed that he wasn't sitting on her uncle's chest waiting for the police to arrive, Libby walked over to him. 'I take it he got away?'

'He was too quick for me. Sorry, Lib.'

'Not to worry. We've reported him to the scuffers and they've put a warrant out for his arrest, so we're hopin' they'll have him banged up before nightfall. In the meantime we're goin' to start spreadin' the word to see if we can locate any of the people who witnessed his confession.'

Pete indicated the group in front of his stall with a sweep of his arm. 'They very kindly waited for you to return.'

Hardly able to believe it, she turned to the people gathered by his stall. 'You all saw what happened?'

'Saw it *and* 'eard it,' confirmed one of the men.

'Evil git,' said a woman, her hair hidden beneath a headscarf. 'I 'ope they bleedin' well hang him.'

'Would any of you be willin' to give a statement down the Commercial Street police station? Only it's our word against his otherwise.'

'Just you try and stop us,' said another woman. 'There ain't no way we're goin' to stand by and let him get away with what he done to you and yer folks.'

Thanking each of them individually, Libby waited until they'd left before turning back to Pete, who was eager to know how Libby had happened across her uncle.

'He found me. You could've knocked me down with a kipper when I saw him standin' there bold as brass.'

'That makes two of us,' said Pete, 'cos we ain't seen hide nor hair of Tony for weeks.'

'I reckon my parents must be smilin' down on me today,' said Libby, 'cos me bumpin' into Lionel and then Tony is too much of a coincidence.'

'And you've got yer parents' stall again,' said Pete, 'which means that you're back where you belong.'

Libby pulled a grimace. 'I'm not sure I want it, not after everythin' that's happened.'

Pete nodded wisely. 'It's all a tad raw at the minute. Give it a few days and you'll feel differently.'

But Libby was shaking her head. 'I don't fit in here any more, Pete. I'm the wrong piece for this jigsaw puzzle.'

'Of course you fit in here!' cried Pete. 'The Gilberts *are* Petticoat Lane.'

'Only they were never meant to be,' said Libby softly. 'If it hadn't been for Tony and his cronies my parents would still be in Liverpool, and had that been the case they might still be alive.'

Pete eyed her beseechingly. 'Don't let him win, Lib. Don't allow him to cheat you out of what's rightfully yours.'

She smiled gratefully. 'I'm not. This is my decision, and one that I'm happy with because it feels right. I'm a Scouser now, Pete, and I belong in Liverpool with my aunt and cousin, where I'm happy.'

He twinkled at her affectionately. 'I'm glad to hear you're happy, and if stayin' in Liverpool makes you that, then that's all anyone can ask for.'

'Thanks, Pete. I knew you'd understand. I do hope you'll come to the weddin' when Jack and I marry?'

Pete rubbed his hands together enthusiastically. 'Just you try and stop me!'

She turned to Jack. 'I know I said I wanted to get married in London, but would you mind awfully if we got married in Liverpool after all?'

He gently brushed her hair behind her ear with the tips of his fingers. 'I'd marry you in the middle of the desert if it would make you happy.'

She leaned into the palm of his hand as he cupped her cheek. 'Thanks, Jack.' Grasping his hand in hers, she looked back to Pete. 'We'll pay for your ticket—'

Pete held up a hand to stop her from going any further. 'No, you won't, cos you can't pay for everyone's and I know a lot of them on the market will want to come and wish you well.'

'The more the merrier!' said Jack. Responding to Libby's questioning look, he added, 'I know what you're thinkin', but don't worry, cos we'll manage somehow.'

Pete beamed. 'Glad to hear it, cos I know they'll be keen to see Reggie and Orla's kid tie the knot. Just you let me know when and where and we'll be there!'

Libby leaned her head against Jack's chest while gazing fondly at Pete. 'You're a star, do you know that?'

Pete's bottom lip appeared to quiver fleetingly as he waved a nonchalant hand. 'Give over, you're makin' me blush!'

Jack wrapped his arm around his fiancée's waist. 'We really should head off to me dad's, cos they're probably startin' to worry.'

Libby held a hand to her forehead. 'I completely forgot! What time is it?'

Pete glanced at his wristwatch. 'Just after five.'

Libby gave a small cry of alarm. 'We were meant to be there well before now.' She came round to Pete's side of the stall and kissed him on the cheek. 'Thanks for everythin', Pete. I'll let you know the date of the weddin' as soon as it's set.'

'Right you are. I'll put it straight in me diary.'

Bidding Pete a hearty goodbye, Jack and Libby left the market at a brisk walk. 'The others aren't goin' to believe what we have to tell them,' said Libby as they headed for the nearest tram stop.

'You were terrific back there, Lib. I hope you know how proud I am of you. Not only have you got yer uncle bang to rights, but you've also managed to put a nail in the Murphys' coffin.'

'I have?'

'The police will be eager to have a word with the Murphys regarding their part in all this.'

'They'll deny it,' said Libby.

'Probably, but that won't stop the scuffers from payin' Donny a visit, and seein' as he ain't got an inklin' that anythin's up he won't be expectin' their call, which means they'll find his house full of loot. They might even find him doin' a deal with some ne'er-do-wells down the docks. The important part bein' that none of it will come back on you, because you weren't the one who said anythin'.'

'Two birds one stone,' said Libby.

'And I know the policeman was dubious about securing a conviction, but you shouldn't have any problem doin' so with all them witnesses to back you up!'

'Hanged by his own words,' said Libby. 'I can't think of a better way!'

They alighted from the tram a short distance from Jack's father's flat, and as they neared the steps that led up to the door Libby asked, 'Do you think we should keep quiet about everythin' in front of your dad's boarder? Loose lips and all that?'

Jack scratched the back of his neck in a thoughtful manner. 'It might be sensible, given that we don't have a clue who he is.'

bottom of the Thames. To Tony the choice was simple. If he got rid of the loot, the police wouldn't be able to pin anything on him, and he'd just have to hope he could outrun the Sykeses. His mind made up, he hastened to his lodging and quickly gathered his belongings. *If Donny bloody Murphy had kept his mouth shut I'd not be in this mess*, he thought as he threw everything into two holdalls. *Trust him to drop me in it just to save his own bleedin' neck.* Glancing around the room to check he hadn't missed anything, he tried to work out how Libby had come into contact with the twins in the first place, and what had happened to make them spill the beans. He knew that Libby had gone looking for her grandparents, so he could only assume that they'd found out about Donny peddling pills to Orla. He rolled his eyes as he threw one of the bags over his shoulder and tucked the other under his arm. *I bet she went round there all guns blazin', threatenin' to shop him to the bluebottles, and Donny tried to cover his own back by sayin' it was all my idea. Of course she'd believe him over me, and I bet she couldn't wait to come back to London to have me arrested for somethin' I never even did. But how am I meant to prove my innocence when the twins are lyin' through their teeth?* He remembered what he'd said just before he'd run for it. *They can't do me for anythin', cos I was only defendin' meself. It's not my fault he didn't get out.* A treacherous inner voice spoke the truth. *If they couple what happened to Reggie with anything the Murphys might have to say, what then?* His cheeks paled. He'd only told Donny to make sure she didn't go to the bluebottles because he didn't want Reggie finding out that he had anything to do with it; he didn't realise Donny had got her to keep shtum by threatening to do Reggie in!

Seeing a policeman cross the junction in front of him, Tony held back, his heart hammering in his chest. He held his breath and counted to twenty before continuing with haste, glancing to the holdall in his fist. The Sykes family had given him the contraband to sell on, and they'd expect their cut of the profits. He briefly toyed with the idea of giving them the stuff back, but knew that if the police caught him trying to return it he'd be dropping the Sykeses in it as much as himself, and that didn't bear thinking about. *Either way, your goose is cooked*, Tony told himself; *you've only one real choice and that's to dump it in the Thames and get out of London.*

Reaching Tower Bridge, he made up his mind to dump the contraband halfway across and keep going until London was far behind him. *You can always start afresh elsewhere*, he told himself; *better that than the alternative.*

He had reached the halfway point and had put his bag of personal belongings down, ready to throw the contraband into the river, when a heavy hand landed on his shoulder.

'Well, if it isn't Tony Gilbert! I've been lookin' for you everywhere!'

***

Libby and Jack exchanged glances.

'Are you *sure*?' said Libby, unable to believe Gordon would agree to take in a sworn enemy of the country.

'As eggs is eggs,' hissed Margo, closing the door behind her. 'Does your dad know what a German sounds like, Jack? Only he's chattin' away like nowt's wrong.'

'Of course he does,' said Jack, albeit a tad uncertainly, 'but are you sure he's a Kraut and not from another country with a similar-soundin' accent?'

'I haven't a clue where he comes from,' admitted Margo, 'but I know a German accent when I hear one and he sounds just like Hitler!'

Libby grimaced. 'I think we'd best take a look for ourselves.'

They followed Margo and Tom up the stairs and into the flat, where they found Gordon and his boarder sitting by the kitchen table. Crossing her fingers that Margo had made a mistake, Libby greeted Gordon before turning to the other man.

'Hello. I'm Libby, Jack's fiancée and Gordon's daughter-in-law to be. You are?'

'Samuel,' said the man in a heavy German accent. 'Pleased to meet you, Libby.'

Libby immediately looked to Jack, who was staring wide-eyed at the man. Averting his gaze, he casually wandered over to the kitchen cupboard, and turned his back to the dresser so that he could remove a knife from the kitchen drawer unnoticed. Sliding it up his sleeve, he walked over to join the others, all of whom had chosen to remain standing.

'That's a bit of an unusual accent you've got there, *Samuel*,' said Jack. 'Do you mind my asking where you're from?'

Samuel glanced at Gordon before replying. 'Not at all. I come from Germany, but I am a Jewish refugee.'

'Bit old, aren't you?' said Tom. 'I thought refugees were kids.'

Gordon eyed Tom levelly. 'A refugee is someone who's fleein' from a war-torn country, regardless of their age.'

Seeing that further explanation was expected, Samuel pressed on. 'I can show you my visa if that would make you feel better?'

'Refugees don't have visas; that's why they're called refugees,' said Jack. 'That much I do know.'

'You're quite right,' said Samuel, 'but when the Nazis come to arrest you and your family in the middle of the night you immediately become a refugee, visa or not.'

Interested despite her concerns, Libby sat down. 'Where are your family?'

'We got separated at the train station,' Samuel began, but was interrupted by Gordon, who was eyeing them incredulously.

'Surely you don't think I'd harbour a spy?'

Libby's cheeks bloomed. She very much wanted to say no, but how could she when the man's story seemed too far-fetched to be true. 'Not knowingly,' she said, quietly.

Samuel put his hand in his pocket, and Jack readied himself to strike. Placing a document down on the table, Samuel raised an eyebrow. 'You can see for yourself.'

Libby picked up the visa and examined it. 'Very nice, but as I've never seen a visa before it could well be a fake for all I know.'

Tucking it back into his pocket, Samuel shrugged. 'Then you will have to take me at my word.'

Tom was rubbing his chin thoughtfully. 'You seem awfully relaxed for a man who's lost his family. Aren't you worried they're still in Germany?'

'My daughter came over on the Kindertransport,' said Samuel, 'and my wife . . .'

Margo gave him a look of smug satisfaction. 'We know all about the Kindertransport, *Samuel*, and they only took unaccompanied children, which makes you . . .' She had been about to say a liar when he interrupted her.

'You're correct, they did, which is why my wife pretended that my daughter was an orphan.'

Margo was about to congratulate him for thinking on his feet when something she'd heard one of the girls say came flooding back to her. 'She wasn't meant to be on the train,' she said, her voice barely above a whisper.

'Indeed, we were bound for another vessel,' Samuel agreed.

'I'm not talkin' about yer wife. I'm talkin' about Roz,' said Margo quietly.

Samuel fixed Margo with a penetrating stare. 'What did you just say?'

Margo sank down on the chair opposite his. 'Your daughter, what was her name?'

318

'Rozalin Sachs, or – as you just said – Roz for short.' He hesitated before going on cautiously. 'Do you know where my daughter is?'

Libby stared at him open-mouthed. 'Hang on a minute! Are you seriously expectin' us to believe that *our* Roz is *your* daughter?'

Samuel shrugged. 'It would appear so.'

'She's at Holly—' Margo began, but Jack cut in before she could finish.

'Don't say another word, Margo,' he warned. ''Cos I don't buy his story for one minute. Roz told us how there was Nazis on the train, and I'd wager he's one of them.'

Margo felt sick to her stomach. She had been on the cusp of giving Roz's whereabouts away to someone who might mean her harm.

'You think they'd send a soldier to retrieve one girl, who might not even be alive?' said Samuel incredulously.

'I'd find that more likely than you bein' here at the same time as us by chance,' said Jack fervently.

Samuel bent down and untied the lace of his left shoe before sliding it off his foot and lifting it up. Taking great care, he removed the inner sole and pulled something out. Holding it up for all to see, he said, 'This was taken when Roz was just thirteen years old.'

They all stared at the photo, which clearly showed Roz with himself and a woman they presumed to be his wife.

'She's workin' at Hollybank farm in Liverpool,' said Margo without hesitation.

Samuel stared at Margo as if he couldn't believe what he was hearing. 'How do you know this?'

'Because she's part of the Land Army, same as us,' said Libby. 'We all work on the same farm.'

Holding the photograph to his lips, Samuel began to weep. 'My bubala made it.'

Blinking back the tears, Libby laid a reassuring hand on his shoulder. 'Not only did she make it, but so did your wife.'

'You've seen Inge?'

'We haven't,' Libby admitted, 'but Roz has. Your wife's helpin' the British with their enquiries whilst lookin' for you.'

'I never dreamed it possible,' said Samuel. 'I hoped, of course I did, but. . .' He paused before adding, '. . . thank you, for giving me the news I've been longing to hear.'

Gordon stared at them in wonder. 'Talk about luck.'

'I don't think luck had much to do with this,' said Libby. 'Fate yes, but not luck. What with one thing and another, I reckon we were all destined to come to London when we did.'

Samuel nodded. 'I think you are right; you see, I wasn't meant to be here at all. The hotel which my friends had booked turned me away because of my accent. I thought I'd have to sleep on the streets until Gordon came along.'

Gordon took up the rest of the story. 'I'd nipped out to get stuff for tonight's tea when I bumped into Samuel in the greengrocer's asking if they knew of somewhere he might stay for the night.'

'When did you arrive in Britain?' asked Tom.

'Yesterday,' said Samuel. 'Had I not met Gordon, who knows how long it would've taken me to find my family?'

Libby folded her arms across her chest. 'Don't anyone try tellin' *me* there's no such thing as fate! Not when Samuel here bumped into the only feller in London who could lead him straight to his daughter!'

'It must be a million to one chance,' said Tom, 'if not more!'

'I can't wait to see her again,' said Samuel, his eyes glistening with tears. 'Has she had a happy life in Liverpool?'

'I think it's probably best if we let her tell you all about that when you see her for yourself,' said Libby, who had no desire to tell him how her uncle and cousin had used Roz as slave labour when she first arrived.

Samuel's smile broadened. 'I would like that very much.'

'Then it's settled,' said Libby. 'We shall take you with us when we go back to Liverpool.'

Samuel was looking hesitant. 'This is very kind of you, but I wouldn't want anyone to get into trouble on my account, and you'd be taking a massive risk by travelling with someone such as myself.'

'Not if we play our cards right,' said Tom. 'If we do all the talkin' for you, no one need ever know you're not true blue, which should make it a lot easier for you.'

'Are you sure?' asked Samuel doubtfully.

'Positive. I just wish we could tell Roz,' said Libby. She eyed Jack thoughtfully. 'Do you think we could let her know the good news without alerting the authorities?'

Having surreptitiously placed the knife back in the drawer, Jack sat down next to Libby. 'We could telephone the farm,' he suggested, 'and let her know that we've bumped into her dad, and that he'll be travellin' back to Liverpool with us. I don't see the harm in that.'

'Good idea,' said Libby. 'That way she can get in touch with her mother and tell her she needs to come back to Liverpool.'

'I wish I could speak to them,' said Samuel ruefully, 'but it would be taking too great a risk.'

'Not to worry. You'll be with them soon enough,' said Jack. He jerked his head at Libby. 'If you're ready, I suggest we shake a leg.'

Libby got to her feet. 'We shan't be long.'

As they descended the stairs, Libby called out to Jack, who was racing ahead of her. 'Where's the fire?'

Jack looked back towards the flat as Libby caught up with him. 'We may know that Samuel's kosher, but in the eyes of the law my father's harbourin' an enemy alien, and we gave the police this address in case they hear any news of Tony.'

Libby struck her forehead with the palm of her hand. 'Damn and blast, I'd forgotten about Tony. Do you think we should go back and warn them?'

'No, cos we'd have to explain everythin' first, whereas phonin' the farm shouldn't take more than a couple of minutes.' He opened the door to the telephone box and picked up the receiver to check it was in working order. Stepping back, he passed the handset to Libby.

Libby asked the operator to put her through and waited until she heard Helen's voice before speaking quickly.

'Hello, Helen. It's me, Libby.'

Helen sounded worried. 'Hello, Libby love. I wasn't expecting to hear from you. Is everything all right?'

'We're all good this end,' said Libby, 'but I haven't got long so I need to be brief. Can you pass on a message to Roz for me, please?'

'Of course.'

'She needs to get in touch with her mother and tell her to come back to Liverpool, because we've bumped into her dad, and he's comin' back with us for a visit.'

Helen gasped, ahead of a lengthy pause. Libby was just about to ask whether she'd heard her when the older woman responded. 'Message received and understood. I'll get on to it straight away.'

'Thanks, Helen. We'll see you as planned.'

'Right you are. Take care on the way home.'

'Will do.'

Libby hung up the receiver and joined Jack. 'Well, that's that done. I'm sure Helen'll be faced with a thousand and one questions when she breaks the news to Roz, but she knew better than to ask for any details.'

'This is goin' to be one heck of a reunion,' said Jack. 'I wish I could be there with you all.'

'I just hope we get there!' said Libby. 'It'd be awful for the scuffers to spoil things at the last hurdle.'

'It would indeed, which is why we need to speak to Dad post haste.'

'Forewarned is forearmed,' Libby agreed.

'You've got many hurdles to jump as yet,' said Jack. 'Hidin' Samuel at Dad's will be a darn sight easier than trekkin' him halfway across the country.'

'We can pretend he's deaf and mute,' said Libby. 'That should make things a bit easier.'

'That's a great idea, but we need to plan everythin' meticulously, right down to the last detail; so that we're prepared for all eventualities.'

He led the way up the stairwell, and when they arrived in the kitchen Libby told them about her conversation with Helen, finishing with: 'But I'm afraid that gettin' Samuel to Liverpool may be the least of our worries.'

Margo raised an inquisitive eyebrow. 'Oh?'

Libby went on to explain her encounter with Tony and all that had happened as a result of their meeting, finishing with: 'Which is why I said we were destined to come to London when we did, cos had we not I'd never have found out the truth regarding Tony *or* met Samuel.'

'Oh, Libby, that's just dreadful!' gasped Margo, hurriedly adding, 'About Tony, I mean.'

'The man needs bloody stringin' up if you ask me,' said Tom, briefly apologising for his bad language, 'although I don't see how any of this affects Samuel.'

Libby grimaced. 'We gave Gordon's address to the scuffers, in case they needed to get in contact with us while we're still here.'

Gordon appeared nonplussed. 'Not to worry. Should they call by, Samuel can hide in his room.'

'Which is all well and good,' said Jack, 'but the train journey back to Liverpool will be a tad harder than that. It only takes one person to raise the alarm and he'll be off that train before you can say knife, so we think it better if Samuel pretends to be mute; that way the three of them can do the talkin' for him.'

'It'll be tough goin',' said Gordon, 'but I have every faith in the three of you to pull it off.'

'I promise I shall not say a word,' said Samuel, pretending to clip his mouth closed.

'If we get to the station before the crowds have gathered, we might get a compartment to ourselves, which would make life a bit easier,' said Libby.

'If anyone should ask, we'll tell them he's my father,' said Margo helpfully, 'and that he's joinin' me and Tom in Liverpool where it's safer.'

Gordon got to his feet. 'Now that we've sorted that out, what say you we get these sarnies down us before they start to curl at the edges?'

'I can't thank you enough for all you've done for me,' said Samuel gratefully.

'I know how desperate Roz has been to know that you're safe and well, and if that means takin' a few risks then so be it, cos I know I'd do anythin' to see my parents again,' said Libby.

'You're good children – all of you,' said Samuel. 'Your parents would be proud.'

Margo chuckled wryly. 'You'd not say that if you'd met my father!'

Libby passed round the plates which Gordon had handed to her. 'What with one thing and another I forgot to ask you how your day went?'

Margo rolled her eyes. 'Wonderfully, until we bumped into Dad outside Harrods.'

'Oh dear – that doesn't sound good. I take it he didn't welcome you with open arms?'

'Open arms?' cackled Margo. 'All he wanted was his money back.'

'You're jokin',' said Jack as he helped himself to a couple of rounds of Spam and pickle sandwiches.

'I wish I was,' said Margo sadly, 'but they were the first words that came out of his mouth. He didn't even say hello!'

'Say hello? He didn't even ask how she was,' muttered Tom. 'No "where have you been?" or "welcome home darling".'

'What did you say to him?' asked Libby, a sandwich poised before her lips.

'Not much,' said Margo. 'I didn't see that there was much point, as he obviously hasn't changed in the slightest.' She brightened. 'But that's enough about him. What do you want to do tomorrow?'

'I haven't been to visit my parents' grave yet,' said Libby.

'We could come with you, if you like?'

'I'd be grateful, cos it will be very different goin' to see them now that I know that Tony was the one who put them there.'

'Do the police see it that way?' asked Tom. 'Or do they see it as bein' the same as Callum with his mother?'

'They think he won't be held responsible,' said Libby, 'but as they rightly said, they're not the judge, so they can't really say for certain.'

'I think it would be a good idea if we call in at the police station en route to the cemetery,' said Jack. 'Save them comin' here.'

'We can't take the risk that they might call here tonight,' said Libby, 'so I think it better if we drop in there on our way back to the B&B, to tell them that they can contact me there if need be.'

Margo wrinkled her brow. 'Why didn't you do that in the first place?'

'Cos I didn't want the scuffers turnin' up at the B&B, but that was before we knew about Samuel.'

'So, what's the plan of action from here on in?' asked Gordon.

Jack spoke up. 'I know you were all plannin' on goin' home the day after tomorrow, but I think it best all round if you leave late tomorrow evenin'. The train won't be as busy, which should make your journey back a lot easier.'

Samuel looked from Libby to Jack. 'You mustn't cut your time together short on my account.'

'Jack's leave finishes at midnight tomorrow anyway, so I may as well say goodbye to him at the station instead of the B&B,' Libby told him. 'We'll look at the train times and come round when we're ready to leave, so if you can make sure you're ready for the off?'

Samuel smiled. 'I'm already packed; you get into the habit of being able to flee at a moment's notice when you've got the Nazis on your tail.'

'And we can telephone the farm on our way back to the B&B so that they know we're comin' home a day early,' said Margo.

Libby raised her glass of lemonade. 'Now let's forget our woes for a while and enjoy this wonderful spread Gordon's prepared!'

***

Tony felt his heart hammering in his chest as he looked into the soulless eyes of the man who'd confronted him. 'I was just comin' to see you,' he gabbled. 'I'm goin' to be out of town for a bit . . .'

Arnie Sykes looked at the bag which Tony had been about to throw into the river. 'That's funny – you looked like you was goin' for a swim to me.'

Tony laughed in what he hoped was a relaxed manner. 'Swim? Not me. I never learned.'

'Then why was you goin' to throw that bag in?' asked Arnie, ripping the holdall from Tony's hands as he spoke.

'I wasn't. I was leanin' over for a better look.'

Arnie smiled, but only with his lips. 'Let me help you.'

Gripping Tony by the neck, he forced him off his feet, while Tony scrabbled around wildly in an attempt to find something to hold on to. 'I'm not an idiot. We know the bluebottles are buzzin' round lookin' for you, Tony Gilbert; question is, why?'

'I swear I won't mention no names,' squeaked Tony in a strangled voice.

'Like you done with the Murphys?'

Tony tried to push Arnie's hand away from his throat. 'I dunno what you're on about. I never done nothin' to them; it was them what dobbed me in!'

'But you were quick enough to set the record straight,' said Arnie. 'That's the trouble with bilge rats such as yerself: there's no loyalty. You're only bothered about savin' yer own skin, leavin' everyone else out to hang in yer stead.'

Tony knew what the Sykeses did to people who grassed; he only had a matter of seconds to act if he were to get out of this alive. He swung the other holdall straight onto Arnie's head. Still clutching the bag in his hands, Tony ran for it, only turning to look over his shoulder when he was nearly off the bridge. Seeing Arnie skid to a halt, Tony wondered what had made him abandon his pursuit until he ran full pelt into someone.

Sprawled on the ground, Tony was in cuffs before he could even look up. 'We knew you was doin' business with the Sykeses,' said the constable. 'All we had to do was follow 'em, and bingo!' With that he waved to someone on the far side of the bridge, and to Tony's horror he saw that Arnie had also been arrested, complete with contraband.

He turned frightened eyes to the constable. 'They'll kill me for this, you know they will.'

The constable shrugged. 'From what I've heard, your days are numbered either way.'

***

It was the following morning, and the four friends were heading for the cemetery where Libby's parents were buried.

'You could've knocked me down with a feather when that bluebottle showed up at breakfast this mornin',' said Libby. 'Anyone else would've fled the city, but not Tony; he was too greedy for that, and thank God too, otherwise he'd have got away scot-free.'

Tom strode behind them with Margo on his arm. 'D'you reckon he fessed up to the Murphys?'

'The copper never said much, but if his face was anythin' to go by then I'd say yes,' said Libby, 'cos even

329

though his lips were tellin' me he wasn't allowed to say just what had gone on, his eyes were speakin' volumes!'

'I do hope so,' said Margo. 'I'd love to be a fly on the wall when the scuffers turn up. They'll think they've stumbled into Aladdin's cave.'

'I wonder what excuse they'll use for havin' the best part of a brewery in their living room?' Tom put in.

'They'll have to think fast, because they won't have a clue they're expectin' visitors until the coppers turn up on the doorstep.' Libby gave a wistful sigh. 'I'm just disappointed that they won't know that I was the one that sent them their way.'

'It's certainly been an eventful visit,' said Margo. 'And not one that I'd care to repeat in a hurry – if ever.'

'You and me both,' agreed Libby. 'I wasn't sure how I'd feel about comin' back to London, but this visit has certainly helped me make up my mind.' She looked to Jack. 'What about you?'

Jack thought it through before answering. 'I don't mind where I live as long as I'm with you.'

She slid her hand into his. 'What about yer dad?'

'He just wants us to be happy.'

Libby felt her stomach drop as the gates to the cemetery came into view. Seeing the look on her face, Jack squeezed her hand. 'Are you all right?'

'I will be.' She swallowed as she regained her composure. 'I guess seein' the gates brought everythin' floodin' back. I can still see all the people from the market who'd come to pay their respects, whilst I hoped and prayed that Tony would do the decent thing and turn up.' A tear trickled down her cheek. 'If only I'd known the truth.'

'You do now, and that's what matters,' said Jack softly. 'When you think about it, it's a good job he never showed his face, cos you'd feel even worse about it now had he done so.'

'I made so many mistakes, none of which I'm proud of . . .' said Libby, her voice faltering as the cross which she and Jack had engraved came into view.

'But you put them right, no matter how difficult it was,' Margo told her, 'and that's what's important.'

'I'm glad Mum and Dad didn't get to see me at my lowest cos they've never seen me like that before.'

Jack put his arm around her and kissed the top of her head. 'They'd love you regardless.'

She smiled at him, her eyes glistening with tears. 'You always know how to cheer me up.' She kissed her fingers before touching the cross. 'I know they're still lookin' after me.'

Margo slipped her free arm round Libby's waist. 'They must be mighty proud to see what a wonderful woman you've grown into – I know I am.'

'Thanks, Margo.' Her gaze fell to the neatly cut grass in front of them. 'Someone's been tendin' to the grave. I wonder who?' She felt her stomach drop. 'Surely not Tony?'

'I doubt it,' said Margo. 'Perhaps Pete, or one of the others from the market?'

'Maybe. I wish I knew who, though, so I could thank them.'

Jack smiled at her. 'Do you really not know?'

Libby stared at him blankly before the penny dropped. 'Your dad?'

'He comes down once a week to tend to Mum's grave, so he does your parents' at the same time.'

Libby's cheeks bloomed with embarrassment. 'Oh, Jack, I can't believe I never thought to ask where your mother was buried.'

He gave a half-shoulder shrug. 'You had bigger things to worry about at the time.'

'I still should've asked.' She looked around her. 'Where is she?'

Jack pointed to the far end of the graveyard. 'She has a cross the same as yer parents', but dad couldn't afford anythin' but a pauper's grave.'

Cursing herself for making such a big deal out of having her parents buried in a purchased plot, Libby hung her head in shame. 'Why didn't you stop me from bleatin' on about a proper grave?'

Jack laughed softly. 'Because Dad wanted the same for Mum, and there's nothin' wrong with wantin' the best for your loved ones.'

'Can we go to her?' Libby asked him.

'Of course we can.' Turning, he led them to the far corner of the cemetery, where there stood just one cross.

Libby felt a shiver run down her spine as she looked upon his mother's grave. 'Brings it all into perspective, doesn't it?' she said quietly.

Jack nodded fervently. 'You have to make the most of every moment, cos you never know when it'll be yer last.'

'There's nowt like standin' in a graveyard to make you realise how precious life is,' said Margo, much to the amusement of the others.

'Flippin' 'eck, Margo, you've a rum way of puttin' things,' chuckled Libby.

'That's what I love about her,' said Tom. 'She comes out with some real corkers at times.'

'It's true, though,' Margo objected, although she too was laughing.

Libby turned to Jack. 'Ever since we arrived in London, it feels like I've leapt from one disaster to another. How about we do somethin' simple?'

'As I've a feelin' you won't be comin' back for a while, how about we go for a walk through St James's Park?'

'Perfect!'

Chapter Eight

It was the evening of their departure, and everyone had gathered at the flat to take Samuel to the station.

'I shall miss your company, Samuel, but I can't say I'll be sorry to see you leave,' said Gordon. 'I've been like a cat on a hot tin roof worryin' that somethin's goin' to go wrong at the last minute.'

'We're not out of the woods yet, Dad,' said Jack.

'Aye, so let's not count our chickens,' agreed Tom.

Samuel grimaced apologetically. 'I'm sorry for being such a burden—' he began, but they were quick to cut him off.

'You're nothin' of the sort!' cried Libby.

'This is our decision,' said Jack firmly, 'so don't you be apologisin' for nothin'.'

Gordon collected his coat from the peg by the door. 'I'll not rest if I don't see you've got on that train safely, so I'll come along to wave you off.'

'The more the merrier,' said Margo.

'It's goin' to be very different from the last time we were at Euston,' Jack told Libby.

'What, no kiss goodbye?' she teased.

He wagged a chiding finger. 'That would never happen.'

Gordon looked to Samuel. 'Have you got everythin'? Cos you mustn't say anythin' once we've left the flat.'

Samuel tapped his suitcase with the palm of his hand. 'It's all in here. I've checked and double-checked.' Stepping forward, he took Gordon's hand in a firm handshake. 'Thank you, Gordon. I appreciate all you have done for me.'

Gordon gave him a grim smile. 'I'm just glad I could be of assistance. Say hello to your wife and daughter for me.'

Samuel patted his hand. 'I shall tell them all about the man who made this possible,' he said, before placing his fedora on his head, and drawing a deep breath. 'Let's get this show on the road, as you English say.'

They began the short walk to Euston station, making certain not to inadvertently try to include Samuel in the conversation as they went.

Holding Jack's hand in hers, Libby looked up at him. 'I know what we were sayin' about my parents lookin' out for me, but I reckon this weekend was written in the stars.'

He curled his fingers around hers. 'What with Tony behind bars, the Murphys about to get their just deserts and Samuel on his way to see his daughter for the first time in over two years, I couldn't agree more. All we have to do is set a date for the weddin'.'

'I'll book the first available slot at the register office.' Her smile broadened. 'I can't wait to tell Emma; I just hope she can make it.'

'She'll make it all right,' said Jack.

'How can you know that?'

'Cos your guardian angels will make sure of it,' said Jack simply, 'just you wait and see. Suzie'll be there an' all.'

Libby sighed happily. 'All I have to do now is find myself a weddin' dress, cos there ain't no way I'm gettin' wed in dungarees!'

'I don't care what you're wearin' as long as we tie the knot,' said Jack. 'Grass skirt and a coconut bra would do for me!'

'I think you'd look much better in yer uniform,' Libby giggled as they entered the station.

'Oh, ha ha. You know what I meant!'

'Well, I'm certainly not goin' to get married in a grass skirt or a coconut bra!' She stopped speaking as her attention was drawn to an approaching train. 'I'm fed up with these trains bein' on time!'

'Not to worry. We'll have all the time in the world soon enough,' said Jack. He glanced over at the others, who were also looking at the train. Sliding his arms around Libby's waist, he leaned forward. 'The next time I see you, it'll be the night before our weddin'.'

'Oh no it won't!' cried Libby. 'I'm not havin' our weddin' get off to a bad start before we've even tied the knot.'

He chuckled softly. 'Fair enough. In that case . . .' He paused as the truth hit him. 'The next time I see you will be on the day of our weddin'.'

Libby felt her heart soar in her chest. 'It's goin' to be the best day ever!'

Leaning forward, he kissed her softly, causing her cheeks to bloom with embarrassment at such a public display of affection. 'We had our first kiss in this station,' she reminded him.

'We sure did,' said Jack. 'How apt it is that we have our last kiss as an unmarried couple here too.'

Margo, who had already boarded the train along with Tom and Samuel, leaned out of the carriage they were in. 'C'mon, Lib. We've managed to wangle a compartment to ourselves!'

Jack hugged Libby tightly before allowing his arms to fall. 'Take care of yerself, Libby Gilbert.'

Gordon stepped forward to give Libby a hug goodbye. 'Cheerio, Lib. Don't forget to keep me in the loop regardin' Samuel as well as everythin' else.'

Beckoning Libby to join her, Margo stepped back from the door. 'Quickly, Lib. You don't want the train to leave without you.'

Libby hurried reluctantly towards her friend, boarding just in time for the guard to close the door before moving on to the next. She slid the window down and leaned out so that she could continue talking to Jack and Gordon.

'I'll telephone your base as soon as we get home,' she told Jack, adding, 'I'm sorry we didn't have more time together, Gordon. We'll have to make up for it when you come up for the weddin'.'

'It'll be me first time out of London in donkey's years,' said Gordon. 'I'm rather lookin' forward to the break.'

Suddenly a whistle blew loudly, causing Libby to start. 'If I don't have a heart attack before I get there!'

she snapped, looking pointedly at the guard, who was standing a few feet away.

Jack grinned. 'You've gone soft livin' in the country!'

'I suppose I have,' said Libby. 'The loudest thing I hear is the bull bellowing for his girls.' As the train pulled forward, she gripped hold of the window to steady herself. Waving to Jack and Gordon until they were lost from view, she wiped the tears from her eyes, and gathered her composure before heading into the carriage to join the others. *A lot's happened in a short amount of time*, she told herself as she walked along the corridor to their compartment, *but it's all in the past now. In a few months' time you'll be Mrs Jack Durning with an exciting future ahead of you!*

***

By the time they arrived in Liverpool the next morning, they were glad that the longest and most difficult part of their journey had come to an end. Not being able to talk to Samuel had been far more of a problem than any of them could have imagined.

'I keep wantin' to include him in the conversation,' Margo had told Libby on one of their many toilet stops. 'I suppose it's only natural, but even so.'

'I shall be glad when we're back on the farm where we can all talk freely,' Libby agreed.

Now, as they sat in the taxi on their final leg of the journey, the group remained silent until they had been dropped off by the driver. 'Well, thank goodness for that!' said Libby as they watched the taxi head back down the drive.

Hearing a cry of euphoria, she turned to see Roz and Inge rushing towards them. Nearly knocking Samuel off his feet as they wrapped their arms around him, both women wept unapologetically.

'Seein' that makes it all worthwhile,' Libby said, her voice hoarse with emotion. 'I wish Gordon and Jack were here to see it too.'

'I hope they go easy on him when he turns himself in,' said Tom, 'after everything he's been through.'

Margo looked dubious. 'I don't think they see it like that, but you never know. They did bring the Australian lot back.'

'To fight in the war,' said Libby, 'not out of the goodness of their hearts.'

Having been silent for the last few hours, Samuel finally spoke his thoughts. 'I'd gladly join the war.'

'They won't try to send you back, will they?' sniffed Roz, holding on to his hand.

'They'll have a fight on their hands if they even try,' said Libby sternly.

'I have my visa,' said Samuel, 'so they should only detain me as an enemy alien at worst.'

Libby gave Roz and Inge a hug each as they came over to thank her for her and Jack's part in bringing Samuel back to them. 'It was our pleasure,' Libby assured them, 'but I promised I'd telephone Jack to let him know we'd got home safely, so if you'll excuse me?'

With everyone else heading into the barn, Libby made her way to the main house and gave the Lewises a weary smile as she entered the parlour.

'You're back!' cried Helen. 'Did you manage to bring Roz's father with you?'

'We did indeed.'

'You look worn out,' said Arthur. 'Why don't you get your head down for a bit?'

'Because if I sleep now I won't get a wink tonight, besides which I've still got a great deal to do.' She gestured towards the phone in the hall. 'Would it be all right if I made a couple of quick phone calls?'

Arthur took the pipe from his lips. 'Course it would, only make sure you don't say owt that could bring the authorities callin',' he said, glancing meaningfully towards the barn.

Libby tapped her forelock in mock salute. 'Don't worry. We've got quite good at talkin' about Samuel without talkin' about Samuel, if that makes sense.'

Bernie raised his brow fleetingly. 'No wonder you look worn out.'

'Travellin' with someone who's classed as an enemy alien certainly hasn't been easy,' said Libby. 'But worth it when you see him united with his family.'

'We'll let them have some time to themselves before poppin' over to say hello,' said Helen.

'I know Samuel's keen to thank you all for lookin' after Roz,' said Libby. Yawning behind her hand, she made her way into hallway and asked the operator to put her through to Jack's base. As soon as his voice came down the line, Libby could tell that he must have spent half the night awake with worry.

'Hello, Lib. Is everything all right?' he asked anxiously.

'Perfect,' said Libby. 'The journey was long and tedious, and not one I'd wish to repeat in a hurry, but all's well that ends well and we're back at the farm.'

'I bet they were pleased to see you.'

'Cock-a-hoop,' said Libby. 'Lots of tears, as you'd imagine.'

Jack breathed a sigh of relief. 'Dad'll be happy to know you're back safe and sound. Have you telephoned Emma to tell her about yer uncle?'

'I will in a minute; I wanted to speak to you first, to put yer mind at rest.'

'Thanks, Lib. I appreciate it, cos I can hear how tired you are, which is why I'm going to say goodbye.'

Libby smiled gratefully. 'Goodbye, Jack. Speak soon.'

She waited until she heard him hang up the receiver before asking the operator to put her through to Emma's base. She didn't have to wait long before her friend's voice came down the phone, full of concern. 'Libby? I thought you'd still be on yer way back from London.'

'It's a long story, all of which I can't tell you over the phone,' said Libby. 'But you were right about me mum not havin' an affair. It was all down to Tony and the Murphys.'

'The Murphys?' cried Emma. 'What on earth have they got to do with it?'

'Like I say, too long a story to tell over the phone,' said Libby. 'All you need to know right now is that Tony's behind bars, and I'm goin' to set the date for the weddin' as soon as the register office opens.'

Emma squealed excitedly. 'You must let me know as soon as you've done it, so I can book my leave.'

'Will do. Just so you know, we'll be gettin' married in Liverpool, and this is where I intend to stay.'

'I'm glad you've made up yer mind,' said Emma. 'No one likes livin' in limbo.'

'I'll let you know the time and date just as soon as I get back from the register office. And I'll write as soon as I can to fill you in on everythin' else.'

'Please do, cos I'm dyin' to know what's gone on.'

The operator cut across, letting them know their time was up. 'I'll speak to you soon,' was all Libby managed before the call was terminated.

She dropped enough coins in the box to cover the cost before making her way back to the parlour, which was empty. Heading outside, she went over to the barn, where she was greeted with a general cry of congratulations.

'Hold fire, I've not set the date yet!' she giggled.

'As good as,' said Suzie. 'I do hope I can make it. I've never been to a weddin' before.'

'Let alone as a bridesmaid,' said Libby with a grin.

Suzie's jaw dropped. 'Are you sayin' what I think you're sayin'?'

'That I want you to be my bridesmaid?'

Suzie squealed with excitement as she engulfed Libby in a hearty embrace. 'I *have* to make it now! Even if I go AWOL.'

Joyce made a gurgling sound in the back of her throat. 'Oh no you won't!'

Suzie smiled at her mother's response. 'Don't worry, Mother, I've no intentions of followin' in my father's footsteps.'

'Glad to hear it,' said Joyce. Glancing at Libby, she added, 'The sooner you get down the register office and fix a date the better.'

'Agreed,' said Libby. 'Does anyone else need to go into the city?'

Samuel nodded, much to the dismay of his family. 'I have to do the right thing if I want the authorities on my side,' he said reasonably, 'and it's unfair of me to stay at the Lewises' given the trouble they could get in for it.'

'But surely a few hours more couldn't hurt,' said Roz.

He chucked her under the chin. 'A few hours could be the difference between my being arrested and my walking into the police station a free man.'

'Your father's right,' said Libby. She looked to Margo. 'We could do with callin' in at the police station ourselves, see if there's any news regardin' the Murphys . . .' but Margo was shaking her head fervently.

'The Murphys might get wind that we've been asking questions, and we can't afford for that to happen, especially as we don't know for certain that Tony even blabbed.'

Joyce perked up. 'What's this about the Murphys?'

Libby explained everything that had transpired as a result of her run-in with her uncle at the market, finishing with, 'I'm convinced Tony spilled the beans as soon as they put him in cuffs, but we don't know anythin' for definite.'

'Flippin' Nora,' breathed Joyce. 'Talk about everything falling into place.'

'I wish we could find out what's goin' on without gettin' involved,' said Libby. 'I hate bein' kept in the dark.'

'I should imagine word will soon get round if they've been arrested,' said Suzie. 'You can't remove a big fish like Donny without causing a few ripples.'

'We're going to have to sit tight and be patient,' said Joyce, 'cos the last thing we want to do is give him the heads-up.'

'All good things come to those who wait,' agreed Suzie.

Tom yawned audibly. 'I didn't get much kip on the train, and as I've a shift tonight I'll be sayin' goodbye before I fall asleep on me feet.'

Margo smiled sympathetically. 'Sorry, Tom, I'd forgotten you'd got work tonight.' She jerked her head in the direction of the barn doors. 'C'mon, let's get you home. Are you coming, Libby?'

Samuel hugged and kissed his wife and daughter goodbye before going to join the trio waiting for him outside, Roz still clinging to his hand.

'Why can't we come with you?' she sniffed. 'It's not fair!'

'Because I don't want to risk either of you getting into trouble,' said Samuel reasonably. 'Have faith in me, bubala.'

'I do have faith in you,' insisted Roz. 'It's the system I don't trust.'

Inge smiled at her husband, who was finding it hard to see his daughter so distressed. 'She witnessed her fiancé being deported; you can't blame her for being cynical.'

'Felix is a young man who came over with no papers,' said Samuel. 'His situation was very different from mine.'

'I hope you're right,' said Roz, 'because I couldn't bear it if they took you away.'

Libby tried her best to reassure her. 'We're going with him to the station, so you needn't worry he'll be on his own when he walks in.' They said a final goodbye to the others and headed off down the drive.

'I hope you know that you can call on us if you need any character witnesses,' said Tom.

'Thank you, Tom, but I shall be asking for Mr Garmin to come to the station to speak on my behalf. He's a man of great importance, so I'm hoping they will listen to him.'

'Fingers crossed,' said Libby as she waved the bus down. They climbed aboard, and Tom paid their fares despite Samuel's objections.

'I have money,' he assured them.

'And you'll need to keep hold of it in order to telephone Inge and Roz to tell them what's going on. And with a bit of luck you'll need it to catch a bus back to the farm,' said Tom.

Libby looked at the clippie, who was staring suspiciously at Samuel. 'It's all right, he's with us,' she said sharply.

Samuel pushed his wallet back into his pocket. 'You can't blame people for being cautious,' he said. 'I'd be just as wary if I were British.'

'You might be German, but you're no Nazi,' said Tom firmly.

'I should get that in writing,' Samuel chuckled. 'It might save me a lot of time.'

'I've been anxious about a lot of things these past couple of years,' said Libby, 'but I don't think I've been this nervous about anything in my life!'

'They won't send me back to Germany,' Samuel assured them, 'not with my visa and the information I can give them.'

Tom leaned forward eagerly. 'Such as?'

Samuel tapped the side of his nose. 'Loose lips . . .'

Tom wrinkled the side of his nose in disappointment, while Margo stared at the older man in wonder. 'Golly, you have been living life on the edge.'

'It sounds a lot more exciting than it is in real life,' said Samuel ruefully. 'Living in cellars and only going out after dark is far from glamorous.'

'I'd be a nervous wreck,' admitted Margo.

The bus pulled to a halt and Tom got to his feet. 'This is us.'

They descended onto the pavement and began walking towards the police station, which wasn't far from the stop.

'I feel awful droppin' you off. It feels as though we're abandonin' you,' said Libby. 'Are you sure we can't come in to vouch for you?'

'They wouldn't believe you,' said Samuel bluntly. 'They'd think you were a naïve lot who'd fallen for a sob story, just as you thought Gordon had. Whereas Mr Garmin, on the other hand . . .'

Margo stopped outside the door to the station. 'Good luck, Samuel. I hope it all works out for you, I really do.'

'Best of British,' said Libby with a grim smile. 'You know where we are if you need us.'

Samuel doffed his cap. 'Thank you all. I hope to be seeing you very soon.' They watched him walk straight-backed into the station.

'I wouldn't want to be in his shoes,' sighed Libby as they continued on their way to Brougham Terrace. 'It was obvious what that clippie was thinkin'.'

Tom raised a chiding brow. 'Samuel's right, though, cos it was no more than what we thought when we first arrived at Gordon's.'

Libby rolled her eyes. 'Don't remind me. It just goes to show how easy it is to be prejudiced against some-one just because of the way they look or sound.'

'Why weren't Roz and Inge arrested for bein' enemy aliens?' Margo wondered.

'Because Roz was underage she wasn't seen as a threat,' said Libby, 'and I'm guessing that when Inge presented herself to the authorities she offered to tell them everything she knew in exchange for their help finding her husband, who could also give them import-ant information.'

'So Samuel might be all right, then?' said Margo hopefully.

'I should think so,' said Libby, 'especially with his wife already working for the government.'

'If that's the case, why on earth didn't he take Inge along to vouch for him?' asked Tom, sounding confused.

'Because if they don't trust him, they may lose their trust in Inge too, which could land them both in hot water,' said Libby simply. 'Strictly speakin', Samuel should've reported straight to the authorities as soon as he landed in Britain, not gone lookin' for his family first.'

'Softly softly catchee monkey,' said Margo. 'I bet poor Roz and Inge are a bag of nerves back at the farm.'

'If I were the Lewises I'd give them summat to do, to help keep their minds off things,' said Libby, continuing thoughtfully, 'I think Samuel might well be right when he says they won't send him back to Germany. After all, he made it across the Channel undetected, so if he went back he could tell other people what to do to remain undiscovered, which would be a danger in itself if it reached the wrong ears.'

'He could an' all,' agreed Margo.

Tom led the way onto Brougham Terrace and stopped in front of one of the buildings. 'Is this it?' asked Libby as she looked up at the sign above the door.

'Not as pretty as a church,' said Margo, 'but it does the same job.'

'I'm not sure you can compare a government building to a house of God,' chuckled Libby.

'I agree, cos this is much nicer,' said Margo. 'I wouldn't want to get married in a church surrounded by dead bodies.'

Tom stared at her wide-eyed. 'By heck, you have some funny notions!'

'I'm talkin' about all the gravestones,' said Margo indignantly. 'It's not exactly a cheery start to your new life.'

Libby smiled. 'I never thought of it like that before, but I suppose you're right.'

They entered the office as they talked, and Libby asked the registrar for the first available date. Her answer, when it came, was disappointing.

'August!' cried Libby. 'But that's months and months away!'

The woman looked down at the log book in front of her. 'It's either that or October.'

'But when I popped by last week, you told me that you didn't have anything free for the whole of the summer!' said Tom. 'How come you've got summat now?'

The woman's cheeks coloured sightly. 'We had a cancellation,' she said, her brow rising. She added, 'It seems some sailors really do have a woman in every port - much to his fiancée's dismay.'

'Looks like it's your lucky day,' Margo said to Libby, then suddenly frowned at Tom. 'Hang on a mo. What do you mean, you called by last week?'

Tom pushed his hands into his pockets. 'I didn't want to say owt until I'd got a date because I know how busy the registrar is, so I called into the office just before we went to London.'

A slow grin was etching Libby's cheeks. 'Tom! You dark horse!'

Margo blushed. 'I hadn't realised you'd given it any thought.'

He shrugged. 'I've wanted to marry you since the day we met, but I was hoping for a summer wedding. However . . .'

Libby cut across him without hesitation. 'You could always share our date. After all, you did call in first,' she said, looking to the registrar for confirmation.

The woman arched a beautifully shaped eyebrow. 'A double wedding?'

'Could we?'

'Lots of people do.'

'We couldn't intrude on your big day, Lib,' said Margo. 'It's all right, we'll just wait until next year.'

'You can't,' said Libby, 'cos none of us know what tomorrow might bring, remember?'

Tom's eyes were shining but he looked dubious. 'What about Jack? Shouldn't you ask him first?'

'How many times have you heard Jack say he doesn't mind where or when we tie the knot so long as we do?' said Libby.

The registrar looked meaningfully at the queue which was beginning to form behind them. 'I'm going to have to ask you to make up your mind, because if you don't want the date there's plenty who will.'

'But I haven't got the ring,' said Tom. 'Or not with me at any rate. I left it at home.'

Margo squealed sharply. 'You've bought an engagement ring?'

He gave her a sloppy smile. 'Like I said, I knew I wanted to marry you from day one.' The registrar cleared her throat, looking at them expectantly, and Tom beamed at her. 'We'd like to book a double weddin' for the twenty-fifth of August!'

**

'A double weddin' is just fine by me,' said Jack as he spoke to Libby down the phone, 'and with the weddin''

350

bein' so far off I reckon I might be able to wangle a week's leave for us to have ourselves a little honeymoon.'

'Oh, Jack, that would be wonderful!'

'At least with it bein' in August, there's more of a chance that everyone will be able to make it to the weddin'.'

'Exactly!' said Libby. 'And it gives us more time to save, as well as prepare.'

'Have you told Emma?'

'I'll do that next,' said Libby. 'I'm lucky the Lewises don't mind me usin' their phone as much as I do.'

'They're a good bunch,' said Jack. 'You fell on yer feet when you moved there.' Libby was agreeing when the operator informed them their time was up, so she said goodbye quickly and asked to be put through to Emma's base.

'Hello?' said Emma. Sounding slightly out of breath, she added, 'Is that you, Lib?'

'It certainly is. We've been to the register office and the closest date we could get was the twenty-fifth of August, so we've booked a double weddin' cos Margo and Tom couldn't get in till October otherwise.'

'I didn't even know they were engaged,' confessed Emma.

'Neither did Margo until they got to the register office,' Libby chuckled. 'So what d'you reckon? Do you think you'll be able to make it?'

'August will be just fine. I'll have completed all my training by then, so gettin' a forty-eight shouldn't be a problem.'

'Suzie's hopin' the same,' said Libby, 'and Jack's goin' to book a week's leave so that we can go on honeymoon.'

'Honeymoon,' said Emma dreamily. 'I wonder where me and Bernie'll go on ours.'

Libby burst out laughing. 'You've not had your first date yet!'

'I know, but he writes the most wonderful letters. I feel like I've known him my whole life.'

'Does he feel the same way?'

'He says he does,' said Emma, 'and we never run out of things to talk about when he calls me on the phone.'

'I've noticed he seems to have a spring in his step nowadays,' conceded Libby.

'I hope it's down to me. I know you warned me to be careful and what not, but it's hard to hold back when you think you've found the one.'

Once again, the operator told them to wind up their call.

'When you come back on leave, we'll go shoppin' for yer bridesmaid dress,' said Libby.

'Are you sure you don't want me to wear my uniform?' said Emma. 'If Suzie wore hers, we'd be matchin', and I'm rather proud of my role in the services.'

'What a fabulous idea!' said Libby. 'I'll have a word with Suzie and let you know what she thinks.' She said goodbye before the operator could cut them off and replaced the receiver, then headed outside.

'Did you get through?' Margo called from the orchard, where she was helping Suzie and Joyce to collect the eggs. Libby went to join them.

'Yes, and whilst they were both disappointed with the long wait, they realise it's for the best. I thought I'd send a telegram to Pete as it's quicker than writin'. Emma wants to wear her uniform, Suzie, so if you do the same you'd be matchin', but it's up to you. I'm easy either way.'

'I'll wear my uniform too,' said Suzie proudly. 'I can't wait to see people's faces when they see a Haggarty in air force blue!'

'Speaking of Haggartys, your father will be getting out in a little under two months' time; not long before the wedding,' said Joyce.

Libby froze. 'You don't think he'd turn up on the day just so that he could stick it to us, do you?'

'No, because I'm going to arrange to see him this Friday,' said Joyce determinedly. 'I want to make sure he's got the message loud and clear before getting out, cos if he finds out that you're my niece, I've not a doubt in my mind that he'd consider tryin' to ruin it for you.'

'My thoughts exactly,' said Libby.

'Which is why I intend to let him know we mean business,' said Joyce. She glanced to Suzie. 'They don't normally allow more than one visitor, but I reckon they'd make an exception to the rule if you tell them you're heading off to serve your country.'

Suzie crossed her fingers. 'I hope so, cos two voices are better than one, and if Dad sees how serious we are it might make all the difference. There's no way he's going to ruin Libby's big day – not on my watch.'

Libby smiled affectionately at her cousin. 'Thank goodness I have the two of you as my real family,' she

353

said. 'Could you imagine what it would've been like had the Murphys really been my relatives?'

'Fag stumps in the font,' Margo reminded her with a chuckle.

'Exactly! I wish I could come with you both, but I haven't exactly got a good excuse.'

'And have him know who you are before we've heard what's going on with the Murphys?' cried Joyce. 'No chance.'

'I know for a fact that those on the inside can pass messages to those on the outside,' said Suzie. 'One careless whisper and before you know it the Murphys'll be breathing down your neck.'

'Enough said. I shall keep my distance, and hope they do the same.'

***

Callum looked up at the prison officer who had entered his cell. 'What now?' he said in surly tones.

'Now, now, no need to be like that,' said the officer. 'I've come to let you know that you've a visitin' order for this Friday.'

'Who?'

'Your wife and daughter.'

Callum shook his head. 'You don't allow more than one at a time.'

'We're makin' an exception, what with your daughter joinin' the services.'

Callum gave a disbelieving grunt. 'What do they want?'

The officer laughed sarcastically. 'What do you think I am, a messenger boy? You want to know what they want, speak to them on Friday.'

'And what if I refuse?'

The officer glanced around the small cell. 'You can sit here starin' at these four walls, or use the opportunity to have a change of scenery. The choice is yours.'

Callum muttered that he would think about it, and the officer left.

What in hell's name do they want with me, Callum thought, until he remembered the officer's words about Suzie going into the services. A sly grin twisted his stubbled cheeks. *Suzie's worried that I'll go after Joyce whilst she's out of the way, so they're coming to beg my forgiveness, in the hope that I'll leave her alone.* He gave a contemptuous snort. *Fat chance of that after what they've done to me! I shall make her rue the day she ran away.*

***

It was nearly midnight when the girls were woken by a commotion in the yard.

'What's going on?' asked Suzie, blurry-eyed.

'I dunno, but I'll soon find out,' said Libby as she swung her legs out of bed.

Heaving her dungarees over her nightie, Margo frowned at Libby. 'You can't go out in yer nightie.'

'Oh yes I can,' said Libby. 'You two stay here, I'll be back in a mo.'

She heard her cousin give a derisive cough as she too got out of her bed. 'You ain't going nowhere on your

355

own,' said Suzie, hopping across the floor as she tried to put her wellingtons on. 'We either all go, or none at all.'

'But what if it's the Murphys?' said Libby.

Suzie rolled her eyes. 'Exactly! What if it *is* the Murphys?'

With all three women at the door in various stages of undress, Libby took the lead. Grabbing a gardening fork which was standing outside the barn, she waved for the girls to follow close behind.

Peering over Libby's shoulder, Margo heaved a sigh of relief. 'It's only Samuel!'

Hearing his name, he turned to face the girls apologetically. 'I'm so sorry, ladies, I didn't mean to disturb you.'

'It's all right,' Libby yawned. 'How did it go down at the police station?'

He spread his arms wide. 'As you can see, I've not been placed under arrest, and whilst I'm bound to stay in Liverpool, I'm free to enjoy the city.'

'That *is* good news,' said Margo. 'Definitely worth gettin' up for.'

'Are you not stoppin'?' asked Libby, indicating to the taxi which was parked in the yard.

'Mr Garmin's offered to let me stay at his, and Inge's coming with me. Roz too, if she'd like.'

Roz smiled at him lovingly. 'You and Mum need some time alone. I'll come and see you tomorrow evening after work.'

Inge came out of Rose Cottage, her suitcase in her hand. 'We can't thank you enough for everything you've done for us,' she said.

'It was our pleasure,' said Libby. 'I hope you'll both be able to attend the wedding?'

Inge handed her suitcase to the taxi driver. 'Wouldn't miss it for the world!'

***

'Have you got the ration book?' Suzie asked her mother for what felt like the millionth time.

'It's in my handbag,' Joyce confirmed. 'I've checked and triple checked, because we wouldn't have much of a case without it.'

'What are we going to do if he tells us to give it to Bill?' hissed Suzie, glancing anxiously around her.

'He won't,' said Joyce, but in truth she had been wondering the same thing, because if Callum did call their bluff, their plan for a quiet future would be in ruins.

'He might,' muttered Suzie, seeing the uncertainty on her mother's face.

'Well, if he does, we shall have no option other than to hand it to Bill and hope for the best,' said Joyce.

An officer came to take them through to Callum. 'I did wonder whether he'd agree to see you,' he told them conversationally, 'as he wasn't what you'd call keen when he heard about your visit.'

'He'll probably wish he hadn't by the time we're through with him,' said Suzie.

The officer led them through. Callum barely raised his head as they walked towards him.

'I'll make this brief,' Joyce began.

'Don't bother beggin' for forgiveness, cos you'll be wastin' your breath,' snarled Callum, keeping his eyes averted. 'You might think you have the upper hand with me bein' locked up in here, but when I get out . . .' he chuckled softly, a wicked grin forming on his cheeks, 'there'll be nowt to stop me from payin' you a visit.'

'That's where I beg to differ,' said Joyce coolly. She unclipped the clasp of her handbag and withdrew Sheila Derby's ration book. 'Do you remember givin' this to Roz?'

'Never seen it before in my life,' Callum snapped. 'If that's the best you've got then go ahead, give it to the scuffers. It'll be your word against mine.'

Joyce eyed him dispassionately. 'Oh, I won't be giving it to the police, cos you're right, it would be a complete waste of time.'

Callum tutted irritably. 'Talkin' of a complete waste of time . . .' he began, only to be shot down by Suzie.

'We'll give it to Bill Derby,' she said. 'What's more, we'll tell him exactly who we got it from, and what you asked Roz to do with it. And before you say he won't believe us, remember that you were the one he sent in to search for her possessions, and it would be most unlikely for us to find it after you'd failed to do so, don't you think?'

Callum shot his daughter a look of pure hatred. 'And they reckon that I'm the bad 'un.'

'I learned from the best,' said Suzie, adding sarcastically, 'You should be proud.'

'Fine!' he growled. 'I'll leave you alone.'

But Joyce was shaking her head. 'I want you out of the city as soon as you're released.'

'Do you now?' He laughed scornfully. 'I'll agree to leave you be, but as for leavin' the city . . .'

Joyce got to her feet. 'Either you go, or I hand this to Bill. I'd actually prefer the latter, because I know you'd never be able to threaten me again once Bill got his hands on you, but you're still Suzie's father, and that is the *only* reason why I'm hanging fire.'

'Where the hell am I supposed to go?'

She shrugged. 'There're ships leaving port all the time, and they're always looking for more hands.'

'Thanks to your daughter, I now have a prison record,' Callum reminded her.

Suzie gaped at him. 'Thanks to *you* you've got a prison record. If you hadn't been picking pockets none of this would have happened.'

Joyce gazed at him icily. 'We're really doing you a favour when you think about it, cos I know for a fact that the scuffers are keen to search through the building for that loot of yours.' She held up the ration book. 'I wonder what they'd say if they found this amongst the rubble?'

'You wouldn't,' he said in hollow tones.

'I could and I would,' said Joyce firmly. 'You will leave Britain as soon as you are released, and if you ever try to return I shall make sure the long arm of the law is there to greet you.'

'And let's face it,' Suzie put in, 'I bet Sheila's won't be the only piece of contraband you stole from the deceased, am I right?'

Callum looked to the officer, who was standing some distance away. 'I'm ready to go back.'

Joyce narrowed her eyes. 'Do I have your word?'

'Does it matter, if you're goin' to hide that book for the scuffers to find?' said Callum dully.

'It's the difference between me handing it over to Bill or you leaving the country,' said Joyce. 'Your choice.'

He stared at the ration book in her hand. 'I'll go.'

'I shall be there to make sure you get on one of the boats,' said Joyce. Lowering her voice, she continued, 'Strangely enough, I don't take you at your word, which is why this . . .' she held up the book for his benefit, 'will be going into safe keeping, and should *anything* happen to me or Suzie, or Roz for that matter, it will be handed to Bill before you can say knife.'

He looked at the book, as though he'd dearly like to rip it out of her hands and tear it to shreds, and Joyce with it. Joyce smiled at the officer, who'd walked over to escort them out, then looked back to her husband.

'Until we meet again.'

He shot her a look of pure loathing as she left.

Only when they were outside did Joyce reveal her true feelings. 'I need a drink, and a stiff one at that,' she told Suzie.

'But I thought you hated alcohol,' said Suzie, as she jogged to keep up with her mother, who was walking at a fair pace.

'I do, but I need to steady my nerves,' said Joyce. 'My heart's going that fast I thought I was going to faint.'

'You didn't show it,' said Suzie, clearly impressed by her mother's ability to put on a strong front. 'I certainly don't think Dad realised you were nervous – far from it.'

'I don't know why I said I'd be down the docks to make sure he left,' said Joyce ruefully. 'Perhaps I felt braver knowing there were scuffers to hand should he lose his temper, but that won't be the case when he gets out.'

'If you don't go ahead with it now, he'll think you've lost your nerve,' said Suzie. 'If I can I'll come with you, and if not I know the girls will . . .' She brightened. 'Thor!'

'What about him?'

'Take Thor along. Dad doesn't know he's as soft as butter.'

'I don't know whether Margo would like that idea, not when she thinks he came from the docks in the first place. She might worry his old owner would claim him back.'

Suzie screwed her lips to one side. 'It's been months since Thor came to us. Nobody could prove he was theirs now.'

'I s'pose not,' said Joyce. 'But we'll have to run the idea past Margo, see what she thinks.'

'And where are you putting the ration book for safe keeping?'

Joyce laughed. 'My handbag. Your father won't take the risk that I've left it with a solicitor. Not that I could, of course – they'd want to know where it came from in the first place.'

'I don't think it matters,' said Suzie. 'I reckon he'll be on the first boat out of port.'

Joyce gave her daughter a sidelong glance. 'That comment you made, about the ration book not being the only form of contraband he'd stolen from the dead: do you really believe that?'

Suzie nodded. 'Not a doubt in my mind. I'm sure that's why he got so fractious with Gran.'

'And is that the only reason you think it's true?'

'He went out bombcombing every time there was an air raid. Most of the time he'd be pleased as punch when he came back, but I can remember at least two occasions when he came back in a bad mood, despite the fact that he had a bag full of loot,' said Suzie slowly. 'When we asked if everything was all right he jumped down our throats, so we kept shtum. But I know for a fact that some of the jewellery he stashed up the chimney had blood on it.' She heaved a sigh. 'I feel so ashamed of myself at times.'

'Why should you be ashamed?' said Joyce indignantly.

'Because I continued to live with him, knowing what he'd done. What sort of person does that make me?'

'A child, who had no other choice except to be homeless, or worse still go to the workhouse.' She clasped Suzie's hand in hers. 'Don't ever be ashamed of who you are. I'm proud to call you my daughter, Suzie Haggarty. Don't you ever doubt that.'

Suzie wiped a tear from her cheek. 'I won't.'

***

Libby, Margo and Adele watched in amusement as Joyce fussed over Suzie whilst they waited for her train to arrive.

'Are you sure you've got everything?'

Suzie patted her satchel. 'Sarnies, a bottle of ginger beer, and my papers.'

'What about underwear?' said Joyce. 'I know they'll provide you with a uniform, but you still need your—'

Suzie laid a reassuring hand on her mother's arm. 'Stop fretting. I've got plenty of clean underwear.'

Joyce fell momentarily silent, until another thought struck her, and fixing her daughter with an enquiring look she said, 'Washbag? Hairbrush? Handkerchiefs?'

'Mam!'

Joyce held her hands up in a placating manner. 'I just want to make sure you've not forgotten anything.'

'I know you do, but I'll be fine, and even if I have forgotten something I'm sure I'll be able to buy it from the stores.' She stopped speaking as a familiar face came into view. 'Well, look who it is.'

'Morning, Suzie,' said Charlie, his eyes on her satchel. 'Where are you off to?'

'I've joined the WAAF,' said Suzie proudly. 'I'm off to do my basic training in Innsworth.'

'You really have turned over a new leaf,' he said approvingly. 'Let's hope your dad does the same.'

Suzie gave a derisive snort. 'I'll not hold my breath.'

He pulled a downward grimace. 'If rumours are to be believed, he's talking of setting sail to pastures new the moment he gets out.'

Libby and Adele exchanged glances. 'Where did you hear that?' asked Suzie cautiously.

'General murmurs amongst the prison staff,' said Charlie.

'Perhaps he's decided to go on the straight and narrow,' said Suzie.

He gave a short mirthless laugh. 'Or maybe he's tryin' to escape the hangman's noose that's waitin' for him further down the line.'

Eager to change the subject, she cast an eye around the crowded platform. 'Are you on the lookout for pickpockets?'

He held his hands behind his back. 'As well as suspicious persons. It's part of my beat now.'

'If you're after suspicious persons, you need look no further than the courts, cos they're full of them!' she said with a wry smile.

He laughed. 'Quite true, although they're not as full as they used to be.'

'The war's been the perfect escape for a lot of people,' agreed Suzie.

'I was actually referring to the recent arrest of the Murphy twins; the crime rate's already halved with them two out of the picture.'

'About time too,' said Joyce. 'Everybody knows how shady they are. What took you so long?'

'They're very good at covering their tracks, and they've got lots of friends in low places,' said Charlie simply.

'So what changed?' asked Libby, who couldn't help herself.

He eyed her sharply. 'Some cockney feller grassed them up for an old crime. There's not a lot we can do about that, but it gave us the perfect excuse to pay them a visit.' He stared straight at Libby. 'Is that a cockney accent I detect?'

Meeting his eyes, Libby said nothing. Suzie cleared her throat. 'If you can't do much about this old crime they committed, how come they're under lock and key?' she asked.

'Cos unlike your father they hadn't a cat in hell's chance of fittin' their stash up a chimney.'

A smile curved Libby's lips, but she was careful not to let the constable see.

'At least no one can blame me this time,' said Suzie.

Charlie smiled. 'I'm pleased you've managed to turn things around for yourself, Suzie. I hope it works out for you, I really do.'

'Thanks, Charlie. Just think, the next time you see me I'll be in air force blue.'

'Now won't that be summat to celebrate?'

A young boy was pulling earnestly at Charlie's sleeve. ''Ave you seen me mam?'

Charlie twinkled down at him. 'What does she look like?'

'She's old, and she's wearin' an 'eadscarf.'

'With a description like that, how can we go wrong?' Charlie chuckled. He bade the girls goodbye and he and the youngster wandered off hand in hand, the constable pointing out various women while the boy shook his head. Only when they were out of earshot did the girls discuss their encounter.

'I thought he was on to me there for a minute,' gasped Libby. 'I knew I should've kept me mouth shut, but I just couldn't help meself.'

'He's as sharp as a tack is Charlie,' said Suzie, 'but if you ask me he knows when to use his discretion, which is why he never pushed you for an answer.'

'He's just glad that they managed to pin summat on them, much like the rest of us,' said Margo. 'It's criminal that they won't get done for what they did to Libby's mum, but without her here to testify we have to be grateful for what we can get.'

'And just like Suzie said, they haven't got anythin' on any of us,' said Joyce, 'so all's well that ends well.'

'And what about Callum?' Adele interjected. 'It sounds as though Callum's took your words to heart, what with him telling people that he's leaving the country.'

'I won't believe it till I see it with me own eyes,' said Joyce. 'Only then will I feel free to truly celebrate!'

Adele started as the approaching train blew its whistle to alert the waiting passengers to its presence, and Joyce's bottom lip began to tremble. 'This must be you,' she said to Suzie, who nodded.

'I thought I'd be nervous, but I'm excited beyond words,' she said gleefully. 'I'm saying goodbye to Suzie Haggarty, and hello to who knows?'

'Sergeant Haggarty given time,' said Libby loyally. 'Imagine that, eh? My cousin the sergeant!'

'I really could, couldn't I?' said Suzie excitedly.

'I hear the WAAF has female pilots,' said Margo conversationally. She grinned. 'So the sky really is the limit.'

Everyone laughed apart from Joyce, who was holding a hand to her tummy. 'I admire your ambition, but I don't think I'd ever sleep again if you became a pilot!'

'I'll be happy with whatever I end up doing, although I'd quite like to be a cook. That way I'll have a skill when I leave.'

'Maybe even start yer own café,' said Margo enthusiastically. 'It could be the next Lyons.'

Suzie's grin was growing ever wider. 'Now that would be summat to be proud of.'

Joyce looked on glumly as the passengers began to board the train. 'I hate to say it, but you'd best get going.'

Suzie hugged each of them goodbye, saving her mother and Libby until last.

'I shall book the date of your wedding off as soon as I know where I'm based,' she told Libby. Taking her friend in a tight embrace, she whispered, 'I know I've said it a thousand times already, but thanks, Lib. Not just for being the best pal a girl could ever have, but for standing by me when I was at my lowest.'

Libby pecked her on the cheek. 'Take care of yerself, Suzie. It won't be the same at Hollybank without you.'

Joyce dabbed her eyes before taking her daughter in her arms. 'Have you got the telephone number of the farm?'

Suzie rolled her eyes. 'Yes. And I'll call you as soon as I have the chance.'

Joyce cupped Suzie's cheek in the palm of her hand. Gazing at her daughter, she sighed, 'I love you, Suzie Haggarty. Don't ever forget that.'

'I won't,' said Suzie, smiling at her mother with equal affection, and turned to board the train. The guard blew his whistle and Suzie stayed by the window, mouthing the words 'I love you too, Mam' as the train began to move slowly away from the station.

***

JUNE 1942

Summer had well and truly arrived and the women at Hollybank were making the most of their time before the busy harvest. 'Is that another letter from Suzie?' Libby asked Joyce as the older woman looked at the writing on the front of the envelope the postman had just handed her.

'It certainly is,' Joyce confirmed. Reading the first few lines, she gave a small cry of triumph. 'She's only gone and landed a job in the officers' mess!'

Libby walked over to join her. 'That's fantastic news. She must be over the moon.'

'You can say that again. She reckons they get much better ingredients, and it's nowhere near the same pressure as the girls have in the cookhouse.'

'I knew she'd do well,' said Libby. 'She's got a real air of determination about her has our Suzie.' Her eyes fell to the other letters in Joyce's hands. 'Anythin' for me?'

Joyce glanced at the envelopes before handing two of them to Libby. 'Sorry, Lib. I almost forgot. One's from Jack, of course, and I think the other might be from Emma.'

Libby gave a squeal of excitement. 'I bet it's to let me know when she's having her week's leave.'

Joyce nodded absent-mindedly. 'She phoned him first thing this mornin' to say that she'd be back on the twenty-ninth.'

Libby grinned. 'That's brilliant news! Bernie must be cock-a-hoop!'

'He's a smile as broad as the Mersey, that's for sure!,' agreed Joyce. 'It wouldn't surprise me if it turned into a triple wedding.' She hesitated. 'Can you even have a triple wedding?'

But Libby, who knew her friend better than the others, was shaking her head. 'Emma wouldn't dream of gettin' married without her family there. Her little sister Cathy would never forgive her if she didn't get to be bridesmaid.'

'Maybe it's just as well; I doubt she'd get in at such short notice.'

'It was good of the Lewises to suggest we could hold the reception in the barn,' said Libby, 'although I suppose it's hardly surprisin' given their generosity.' She opened Jack's letter as she spoke.

'How's he getting on?' asked Joyce, gesturing towards the letter in Libby's hands.

Having scanned the first few lines, Libby read them out loud.

Dear Libby,

I hope you get this before Callum gets out of jail, because I wanted to remind you to be careful. I know he made out that he was compliant with Joyce and Suzie's request for him to leave the city, but a lot of time has passed since then, and he might well have changed his mind. If he tries to approach any of you – I'm assuming you'll go down to the docks en masse, at least I hope you will – then walk away. He'll only be trying to wheedle his way out of his agreement, and you don't need to hear that. And whatever you do, don't take the ration book with you, because if he knows you've got it, he'll try and take it back by fair means or foul.

Libby looked at Joyce for her thoughts.

'I'm glad he said that about the ration book,' said Joyce, 'because I fully intended to take it with me to show him that I was serious. But Jack's right – Callum would take it from me as soon as he saw me get it out of my handbag.'

'And without that you have nothin',' said Libby.

'When you write back, please thank him for his advice, and let him know that we'll do as he suggests.'

'Will do. Have you managed to get a date for Callum's release yet?'

'I'm going to give the prison a call later, see what's what,' said Joyce. 'I know it won't be until after the twenty-eighth of June, so we've a little breathing room as yet.'

Libby tucked Jack's letter into the pocket of her dungarees with Emma's. 'I'll read the rest of it after we've checked the cattle.'

Roz and Margo came over to join them and the women walked down together to bring in the cows.

'Good for Suzie,' said Margo, after Joyce had finished telling them her daughter's news.

'She's a credit to you,' said Roz, 'and who ever thought I'd be saying that?'

'Not me,' said Adele, 'but she's like a different woman since getting out from under her father's shadow.'

'I can't wait to see the back of that man,' said Joyce. 'I don't like to go on about it when Suzie's around, because he's still her father, and it must be hard for her to think that she'll never see him again.'

'I think she's wise enough to know he'll never change,' said Roz, 'so she either has to accept him as he is, which we all know she's not prepared to do, or say goodbye.'

'Did she say goodbye to him when you left the prison?'

'No, because she thought it would antagonise him when we were the ones telling him to leave the country.'

Margo grimaced. 'I see what she means.'

Roz was shaking her head sadly. 'What sort of man chooses a life of crime over his daughter?'

Margo laughed hollowly. 'One like my dad.'

'My dad would *never* do summat like that,' said Roz in bewilderment.

'Nor mine,' said Libby, 'but there's plenty of bad parents out there who don't give a fig about their kids.'

'Did she mention him in her letter?' Roz asked Joyce.

'Not a dickie bird,' said Joyce. 'She never does, but neither do I. Although I will drop her a line after he's out to let her know whether he's stayed true to his word – if he does, it'll be the first time he ever has.'

Margo opened the gate to the cows' meadow and held it wide as the others trooped through. 'Have you planned what you're goin' to do when he gets released?'

'I'll wait across the road outside the jail,' said Joyce, 'and follow him down to the docks.'

'But what then?' Libby wondered. 'Will you wait for the ship to set sail?'

She shrugged. 'I haven't thought that far ahead, but when push comes to shove I really don't know, because even if I see him get on the ship how will I know he's not going to jump overboard as soon as they're clear of the docks?'

Roz had been deep in thought whilst the others talked. 'Give Bill the ration book,' she said finally. 'Tell Callum you're going to give Bill the ration book as soon as his ship sets sail. He'll not come back once he knows you've done that.'

Joyce's heart was hammering in her chest. 'What if Bill doesn't believe me? Everyone knows I've got beef with Callum; Bill might think I'm lying about where I got the book from.'

'Not if I give it to him,' said Roz. There was a chorus of protests from the other women, but she insisted, 'It can only be me, because Bill will know that I'm telling the truth.'

'Do we have to give it to Bill, though?' said Margo. 'Callum will never know the difference.'

'But I will,' said Joyce, 'and if I'm ever to get a good night's sleep, Roz is right: this is the only way to do it.'

'And Callum will know I'm not bluffing,' said Roz. 'Not after the way he treated me.'

Margo closed the gate behind them. 'So, it's decided then?'

'He'll rue the day he ever crossed a woman!' said Joyce with satisfaction.

***

It was the day of Emma's return, and Libby and Bernie were on their way to pick her up from the station.

'Joyce told me of your plans to confront Callum when he gets out of prison tomorrow,' said Bernie, as Goliath plodded along the road. 'I asked her if I could tag along but she was adamant I should stay behind. Do you think you could persuade her otherwise?'

'Sorry, Bernie, but no. We want to show Callum that women united are a force to be reckoned with.'

'But aren't you taking Thor with you?' he asked reasonably.

'You can't count Thor!' cried Libby. 'He's the biggest coward out!'

'So why take him, then?'

'Because Thor has nothin' to lose by comin' with us, whereas your family have a good reputation around Liverpool and people might change their minds if they think you knew about the ration book all along.'

'And I suppose Emma has to go too?'

Libby's brow shot towards her hairline. 'I wouldn't be able to stop her if I tried. Emma's a real musketeer when it comes to her pals.'

'Can I at least arrange to meet you somewhere after-wards, if just to give you a lift home?'

Libby mulled this over for a short while before reaching a conclusion. 'I can't see the harm in that, but I'll have to clear it with Joyce and Roz, because this was their plan, not mine, and—' She broke off with a cry of delight as Emma came into view. She was jogging towards them, and when she was close enough she threw her bag onto the cart and climbed aboard without any assistance. 'Fitter than a butcher's dog, that's me,' she said, giving Libby a one-armed hug.

'You are that,' said Libby, making room for Emma between herself and Bernie, who was grinning at Emma like the cat that got the cream.

She gave him a shy smile. 'Hello, Bernie.'

He put his hand out to shake hers, then changed his mind. 'Do I get a hug too?'

Blushing slightly, Emma opened her arms to welcome him in. 'I don't see why not. How's the bull?'

Libby laughed. 'What do the two of you talk about when you're on the phone?'

'Everythin',' said Emma, 'and believe me, bulls are more interestin' than mountains of spuds!'

'Are you trying to suggest that our Gregory's not interesting?' Bernie asked Libby, tongue-in-cheek.

Libby held her hands up in a placating manner. 'There's nowt wrong with Gregory. I'd certainly not criticise a ton of bull, or not to his face at any rate.'

'He weighs a ton?' asked Emma, aghast. 'I wouldn't fancy him steppin' on me toes!'

'That's why you have to be quick on your feet,' said Bernie. 'Cos when a bull decides he's going some-where, he's going, whether you like it or not.'

'Maybe we should take him with us tomorrow?' said Emma, a grin forming on her lips. 'I can't see *anybody* causin' us bother if we had Gregory in tow.'

'I don't think a rampagin' bull would be quite the look that we're after,' Libby chuckled.

'It'd certainly get his attention,' said Emma. 'So what's the plan of attack, then?'

Libby told her of their plan, while Emma listened without interruption.

'I have offered my services,' said Bernie, once Libby had finished, 'but they've been turned down point blank.'

'Sometimes a girl has to do what a girl has to do,' said Emma. 'Where does this Bill live?'

'That's the only stumblin' block,' Libby admitted. 'Suzie doesn't know where he moved to after his house got bombed.'

'Do we even know that he's still alive?' Emma won-dered. 'And do you not think it will get Bill's back up when you tell him that you waited for Callum to leave Britain before handin' Sheila's ration book over? I know I'd be spittin' feathers if someone gave me infor-mation like that, when it was too late for me to do anythin' about it.' She fell into silent thought before adding, 'I'd probably take it out on the messenger, cos they'd be protectin' Callum, in a way.'

'But it's not like that at all,' Libby protested. 'We're protectin' ourselves, not Callum.'

'So, you're usin' Bill?' She cast her friend a chiding glance. 'That will just add fuel to the fire, or it would for me at any rate.'

Libby had an image of Roz handing the ration book to Bill while explaining that Callum had left the country. Even if she didn't tell him where Callum had gone, Bill would soon learn the truth and they'd be worse off than they were before.

Bernie pulled Goliath to a halt whilst they waited for the traffic to clear and laid out their position as he saw it. 'If I were Bill, I'd be tempted to march you down to the police station and tell them how you'd been holding on to my daughter's ration book knowing that Callum had stolen it.'

'I wouldn't want that to happen,' conceded Libby. 'Why can't these things ever be simple?'

Emma pulled a sideways grimace. 'I hate to say it, Lib, but it's only difficult cos you're not goin' into the situation with clean hands. Roz has had that book for ages, and she knew Callum had got hold of it by foul means not fair.'

Libby tutted irritably. 'I'll have a word with Joyce when we get back, cos we need to have a rethink.'

'Good job we talked it over prior to goin' to Bill's,' said Emma, 'else Callum would be the least of yer problems.'

***

The women stood outside the prison entrance waiting for Callum to appear.

One of the men who was guarding the door had come out to see why the small crowd had gathered, and the girls had explained they were there to see that Callum left the country as promised.

'And they reckon that women are the fairer sex,' the officer chuckled as he walked away.

When Callum eventually appeared, all six women walked towards him in a determined fashion.

Callum stared at the small posse in disbelief. 'You have to be joking?'

'Do we look like we're laughing?' replied Joyce tartly.

He pushed his hands into his pockets. 'I want to see the book; I never got to examine it last time and for all I know it might not even be Sheila's.'

Roz stepped forward, a sarcastic smile flashing on her lips. 'I'm afraid you can't do that.'

Callum's face lit up. 'Oh aye? Lost it, have you?' he said, sniggering nastily.

Joyce treated him to a confident smile. 'I'm afraid not. You see, we've already given it to Bill.'

Callum's face dropped in an instant. His eyes narrowing, he spoke directly to Joyce. 'That wasn't part of the deal.'

'You're right, it wasn't,' agreed Joyce, 'but that was before I weighed up our options, and it seemed to me that you'd only take us seriously if we got the ball rolling before you left Britain.'

'You evil bitch,' Callum seethed.

'So I was right,' said Joyce. 'You had no intention of leaving for good; you'd not be so angry otherwise.'

Callum said nothing, but if looks could kill Joyce would soon be pushing up daisies.

Roz pretended to tap an invisible watch on her wrist. 'Tick tock, time's a-wasting.'

'You didn't think Joyce was serious when she told you to leave, did you?' said Libby, her tone heavy with spurious sympathy.

'Of course I didn't,' he spat. 'She doesn't own the city!'

Joyce arched a beautifully shaped eyebrow. 'I think you'll find that we do, at least as far as you're concerned.' She held out her arm in the direction of the docks. 'After you.'

Callum took a step forward, his fist raised, but quickly stepped back when Thor pulled Margo forward while emitting a blood-curdling noise like that of a hellhound.

'Temper, temper,' said Joyce coolly, but her heart was hammering in her chest as if it was trying to break free. None of the women had heard Thor emit any kind of sound other than whining for food or snoring in bed.

Alarmed by the large dog's show of aggression, Callum spat in Joyce's direction before hastily turning on his heel and walking away.

'I didn't think Thor had it in him,' Libby whispered to Margo, impressed.

'He doesn't,' Margo confessed. 'I'm afraid I stood on his paw.'

Libby giggled. 'So that's why he rushed forward? He was tryin' to get away from you?'

Margo smiled guiltily. 'I would've apologised to him, but Callum might've guessed what had truly happened had I done so.'

Emma, who had been listening to the confession, nudged Libby. 'Pretendin' that Bill already had the book was a stroke of genius, don't you think?'

'I had my doubts that he'd swallow the lie, but he fell for it hook, line and sinker. You could tell that by the look on his face.'

With Callum striding ahead, it didn't take them long to reach the dock, and as he headed towards a ship by the name of the *African Goddess* Joyce called out to him.

'Aren't you going to say goodbye?'

Failing to break his stride, Callum threw them a two-fingered salute over his shoulder whilst swearing a loud response.

Joyce arched her eyebrow as she watched her husband pace the yard speaking to various seamen. 'I suppose that's a form of goodbye,' she said, before turning back to the others. 'I think we're safe enough to leave him with the rest of the rats.'

'How can you be sure they'll take him on?' said Libby, who was watching Callum dubiously. 'Cos he was right when he pointed out that he had a prison record.'

'Beggars can't be choosers,' said Joyce simply. 'There probably wouldn't be a single ship leaving port if they didn't take criminals on board.'

Margo laughed before asking, 'What will you do with the book?'

Joyce looked over to Callum, who was already boarding the *African Goddess*. 'I reckon my safest option is to throw it away cos I'd hate to get caught with it. But you saw the look on his face; what do you think?'

'I think you're one cool customer, Joyce Haggarty,' said Libby. 'You don't need that book, not any more.'

Margo indicated the ship with a jerk of her head. 'No goin' back now.'

They turned to see the ship's crew drop the gangplank as they prepared to weigh anchor.

She smiled satisfactorily. 'Good riddance to bad rubbish!'

***

Emma's leave was coming to an end, and she and Libby were walking the cattle back to the meadow.

'Why does time always go so quickly when you're havin' fun?' Emma pouted.

'It hardly seems as though you've been here for more than five minutes, never mind five days!' Libby agreed. She winked at her friend. 'Especially when I've had to share you with Bernie.'

Emma blushed apologetically. 'I'm sorry about that, and if it's any consolation I do feel awful about spendin' so much time with him, but . . .'

'Young love is time consumin',' smiled Libby, 'and there's no need to apologise because I was the same with Jack, as Margo was with Tom.'

'I really regret joinin' the ATS,' said Emma, 'but I don't think they'd have allowed me to join the Land Army – not when I was livin' in Ireland.'

'And if you'd not joined the ATS you wouldn't have reason to be over here in the first place.'

'There is that,' agreed Emma, 'and if you'd not joined the Land Army, I'd never have met Bernie regardless.'

'I never thought of it like that,' said Libby. 'I hope they post you somewhere closer to Liverpool.'

'I'd never even heard of Devizes before I got me papers,' Emma admitted. 'I thought it sounded rather foreign, and I did worry I might be goin' overseas until someone told me it was in Wiltshire.' She smiled wistfully. 'Bernie's hopin' I might get posted to Liverpool when I qualify for the ack-acks.'

'It's only natural for him to want to spend more time with you,' said Libby. 'I know it's still early days, but even a blind man could see the two of you have hit it off.'

'We get on like a house on fire,' said Emma. 'I feel incredibly fortunate to have met him.'

'Have you told yer folks about him yet?'

Emma laughed. 'Dad says he's sick of hearin' the name Bernie.'

'And yer mum?'

'She can't wait to meet him, and neither can Cathy.'

'I reckon yer dad will change his mind when he sees Hollybank for himself,' said Libby, winking.

Emma rolled her eyes. 'You're probably right, but there again I suppose every father wants the best for their little girl.'

'Do you remember the conversations we used to have about our weddin's when we were growin' up?'

Emma smiled. 'We always picked the grandest churches in which to say "I do", and the most lavish venues to have our weddin' breakfasts.'

'I'd have been so upset if you'd told me I were to get married in a register office and that I'd be holdin' my weddin' breakfast in a barn,' said Libby wistfully, 'but things like that don't matter when you're in love.'

'Love changes everythin',' said Emma. 'I'd happily follow suit if it meant me and Bernie would be together for ever.'

Libby tucked her arm through Emma's. 'I'm so glad you'll be able to make it. Cos barn or Buckingham Palace, it wouldn't be the same without you there.'

Chapter Nine

Libby admired her reflection for what felt like the hundredth time. She hadn't had high expectations when it came to her wedding dress, and with time running out she had begun to worry she might not be able to find anything suitable in time for the big day. Margo, on the other hand, had been lucky enough to stumble across a smart blue two-piece suit down Paddy's market.

'You lucky so-'n'-so,' said Libby, as they left the market with the dress. 'At this rate I'm goin' to have to get wed in me own old clothes.' And that might well have been the case had Helen not come to her rescue with a lavender frock she had worn to her sister's wedding many years ago.

'We'll soon have it fitting you like a glove,' Helen had said thickly, a row of pins between her lips; she had continued to nip and tuck the dress as she went on, 'By the time I'm done it'll look like it was made especially for you.' Hearing Libby sniff, she had looked up to see tears cascading down her cheeks. 'Oh, Libby luv, I *promise* . . .'

But Libby was shaking her head. 'It's not that. I was just thinkin' about me mum and how different things would be if she were here.' Her bottom lip quivered. 'I can't tell you how glad I am to have all of you in my life.'

Helen sat back on her haunches. 'I thought you'd been coping remarkably well given the situation. It's times like these that you miss family the most.'

Libby wiped her tears with the backs of her hands. 'All this business with Callum, Tony and the Murphy twins has been a brilliant distraction, but now that's all over and done with I've got nowt to divert me from the here and now, and I can't stop thinkin' about me mum, and how Dad's not goin' to be the one who walks me down the aisle. I know there's no sense in wishin' things were different, but I just can't help meself.'

'It's only natural,' said Helen. Leaning forward, she continued to pin the dress into place. 'But do you really think they won't be there?'

'You mean in spirit?'

Helen nodded. 'They were certainly with you when you went to London, because you being in the right place at the right time was surely no coincidence.'

Libby fielded another tear with the crook of her finger. 'I think they've been with me all through my journey, but it's not the same as havin' them there to hug and hold.'

'You've got Gordon,' said Helen.

'Very true, and Dad would be so pleased to know that I had a father figure like Gordon to take over his role.'

'You may have lost your parents, but you're not short of people who love you, Libby Gilbert, don't ever forget that.'

Leaning down, Libby took Helen in a tight embrace. 'Thank you, Helen. Your words mean a lot, they really do!'

***

It was the day of the wedding and Libby twisted her hips to get the full effect of the lavender skirt which flared so beautifully around her. 'Stunning,' said Margo simply. 'That's the only word for it.'

Libby regarded Margo's blue-clad reflection in the mirror. 'That makes two of us.' She cast a concerned eye in the direction of the yard. 'Do you know if Suzie's managed to do the flowers?'

In answer, Margo brought her arms from around her back, revealing two bouquets of wild flowers, each tied with a ribbon. She handed Libby hers before lifting her own to her nose and taking in the scent.

'They're beautiful,' breathed Libby.

'A florist couldn't have done a finer job,' Margo agreed.

Emma briefly knocked on the door to the barn. 'Are you decent?'

The girls called for her to come in, and were delighted by the look on her face as she gazed admiringly at them.

'You both look beautiful,' she said, smiling at Libby through tear-brimmed eyes. 'Your parents would be so proud of you, Lib.'

Libby fanned her face with her hand in an attempt to repel the tears. 'Not now, Em. I've only just reapplied my makeup from the last lot.'

'Sorry!' Emma glanced at the flowers held by both girls. 'Them bouquets are the icin' on the cake.'

'They certainly are,' agreed Libby, who was looking out of the window. 'How are they gettin' on with Goliath?'

Emma wagged a reproving finger. 'You're not allowed to see until Bernie picks you up outside the register office.'

Margo clutched her bouquet to her chest. 'How much longer until we leave?'

Emma was about to reply when Gordon knocked on the door and asked everyone to make their way outside. Taking a deep breath, Libby let it out slowly and Margo did the same.

'I swear my tummy's doin' a jive,' Margo said as they gingerly picked their way across the cobbles to the waiting car.

'I was just about to say that mine's doin' the jitterbug,' chuckled Libby.

Looking very smart in his suit, Gordon smiled broadly at the two women. 'You'd never guess the two of you got ready in a barn,' he said, opening the back door of the cab.

'And I'm not wearin' me wellies neither.' Libby gestured to the cream shoes which she'd managed to find down the Greatie.

'Not for want of tryin',' quipped Margo as she got into the back of the taxi. 'Not that I blame her; I hate wearin' heels.'

Taking his place next to the driver, Gordon twisted in his seat. 'Are you both sure that you've got everythin'?'

Libby nodded confidently. 'Margo's dress is blue and new, her shoes are old and she's borrowed my lippy.' Barely pausing for breath, she added, 'Some of the flowers in my bouquet are blue, my dress is both borrowed and old, and my shoes are new. I think that's everythin'.'

'Thanks for agreein' to walk us both down the aisle,' said Margo. 'It's very kind of you.'

'My pleasure,' said Gordon. 'As you know, everyone's there, bar Bernie, Emma and Suzie, who are followin' on with Goliath.'

'What about Thor? Please don't tell me they've forgotten him?'

Gordon smiled. 'As if they'd do that! Thor's sittin' on the cart ready for the off.'

'Are you sure they'll make it to the weddin' on time?' asked Libby anxiously. 'I love Goliath to pieces, but he's not the speediest of beasts.'

'We're arrivin' ahead of time so that we can get the two of you out of sight whilst Bernie deals with Goliath.'

'And are you sure that the boys are already there?' Margo was also getting anxious. 'I don't want Tom or Jack seein' us until we walk down the aisle.'

'Don't worry. The boys know that you're on yer way, and they're already in there waitin' for you.'

Libby felt her tummy flutter. 'What about Pete and the rest of them from down the market?'

Gordon laughed. 'Blimey! How many times? Everyone's present and correct, so stop worryin'.'

'I hope we don't get an air raid,' said Margo absent-mindedly.

'Margo!' Libby cried, 'Don't go sayin' things like that!'

Margo shrugged. 'You never know, though.'

Gordon chuckled quietly. 'I think we're safe for today, cos the sun is out and the sky is blue . . .'

'And there ain't no Krauts to spoil our view,' said Margo happily.

Gordon laughed out loud. 'I didn't realise poetry was one of yer strong suits.'

Libby wound down the window just a tad to allow a cool breeze in. 'Is it hot in here or is it me?'

'I'm boiling. I reckon it's nerves,' said Margo.

Libby gazed around as they entered the city. 'I wish I'd asked my mother more about her weddin' day.'

'Unfortunately, we normally only remember to ask these things when it's too late,' said Gordon wisely.

'I hope I do find the rest of her diaries,' said Libby, 'because I'd dearly love to know what her day was like.'

'I thought you was goin' back to the stall for a gander?' said Gordon.

Libby shook her head. 'I've not had the time, but I will soon, cos who knows what I might unearth?'

Margo pointed to the register office ahead of them. 'We're here!'

Libby smiled nervously as the taxi came to a halt. 'Here goes nothin',' she said as Gordon came round to open the door for them.

'I'm glad I'm doin' this with you,' said Margo as she ran a hand down her frock to eliminate any creases. 'I'd be a nervous wreck if I were on me own.'

'That makes two of us,' said Libby.

'Silly really,' said Margo, 'cos we ain't got owt to be nervous of. We're marryin' two smashin' fellers that . . .'

Libby pulled her friend to one side, hissing in her ear, 'That we'll be expected to do you know what with tonight.'

Margo's face crumpled in incomprehension. 'Eh?'

Libby glanced at Gordon, who was going ahead of them to make sure the boys were out of the way before they entered the building. '*Sex*,' said Libby, her voice barely above a whisper.

'Oh, that!' Margo giggled. 'I don't see why you're worried about that. It's easy.'

Libby stared at her open-mouthed. 'You mean you've already done it?' she asked, aghast.

'Of course not!' said Margo, irritably, 'but I've watched the cows and they seem to find it simple enough.'

Libby laughed until the tears came. 'But Margo, you're not a cow, and Tom's not a bull.'

'True, but the pigs are the same, and the sheep . . .'

Libby's sides were beginning to ache with laughter. 'But they've all got four legs!'

Margo's brow furrowed. 'What's yer legs got to do with it?'

Seeing Gordon walking back towards them, Libby hushed her friend into silence. 'Gordon's comin'.'

'Everyone's where they're meant to be, and as I'm sure I can hear Goliath, I think we should get you both inside.'

As she moved towards him, Libby heard the clip-clop of hooves growing ever nearer. 'Blimey, Goliath was quick! Are you sure it's them?' she asked Gordon as they walked with him into the building.

Leaning out of the doorway, Gordon waved to someone before hurrying back inside. 'It certainly is, so if you'd like to follow me . . .' He led them into a small room and closed the door behind them. After several minutes of anxious waiting, Emma came in to join them, followed by Suzie.

'Bernie's gone straight in,' said Emma.

Beaming proudly, Suzie gazed affectionately at the girls. 'You both look beautiful!'

'As do you in yer smart uniform,' said Margo. 'Have you seen Thor?'

Suzie's eyes danced with delight. 'I have indeed. He's outside with Goliath, and they both look fit for a king.'

'Goliath looks like one of them show horses,' Emma agreed. 'He's got hoof oil on and everythin'.'

Gordon placed a finger to his lips, warning the girls to keep quiet. 'Don't go lettin' the cat out of the bag. You don't want to spoil the surprise.'

Suzie nodded wisely. 'My lips are sealed!'

The registrar appeared in the doorway, clearing his throat. 'Are we ready, ladies?'

Libby and Margo looked at each other before replying. 'As we'll ever be,' said Libby, tucking her arm into Gordon's as Margo did the same on the other side. Proud as a peacock, Gordon walked them out of the room.

*

Libby thought she had never been happier than she was when she signed the register. 'Did you see Mrs Fortescue?' she asked Jack. 'She was the elderly lady sittin' next to Pete.'

'The one blubbin' like she was fit to burst?' said Jack.

'That's the one! She took me in the day Mum and Dad died; she was an enormous help and I know she very much wanted me to go to Scarborough with her.'

'Why didn't you?'

'Because she was goin' to live with her daughter, and I still had a score to settle with Tony. Mrs F was worried that things were goin' to go drastically wrong between me and Tony, and how right she was!'

'Did you manage to see her last night at the B&B?'

'I did, and I'm glad that Pete had already filled her in about Tony, because I didn't relish tellin' her that she'd been right all along.'

'I'd wager even she hadn't realised the extent of his treachery.'

'Gosh no. She was furious beyond words,' said Libby.

'Did Pete mention who'd taken over the stall?' asked Jack.

'His wife,' said Libby simply. 'Deb's always been a brilliant cook and so she's opened it up as a cake and pie stand.'

'Does that make you happy?' asked Jack hesitantly.

'As Larry,' said Libby. 'I couldn't have thought of a nicer couple to take it over. They're honest, hard-workin' people who've striven to make a livin' for themselves. I couldn't be happier for them, I really couldn't, and I know my parents would be pleased to know that they were doin' well for themselves.'

'So all's well that ends well,' said Jack, as they made their way out of the office behind Margo and Tom.

She looked at the small band of silver which encircled her wedding finger. 'And I couldn't think of a better endin' than this.'

He brought her hand up to his lips and kissed her fingers. 'Me neither: surrounded by our friends and family, in the city which we'll be calling home.'

'I just wish your father would agree to come up north,' said Libby, 'cos we'd be like a proper family then.'

'Funny you should say that,' said Jack. 'Dad's been havin' a chat with Bernie, and what with Bernie's contacts it looks very much as though Dad will be joinin' us after all.'

Libby's eyes sparkled. 'Oh, Jack, that's wonderful!'

'Carpenters are in short supply what with the war an' all, and Bernie said he's got a heap of jobs for Dad to do, as have his farmin' friends.'

'So when's he thinkin' of makin' the move?' asked Libby eagerly.

'As soon as he can. He'll have to finish what business he has in London, as well as make arrangements to bring up his tools, all of which might take some time, but other than that he's as good as here already.'

'This day just keeps gettin' better and better,' said Libby.

Margo gave a cry of delight as she stepped outside.

Eager to see the cart which awaited them, Libby hurried after her and was pleased to see that Goliath had been washed and brushed to within an inch of his life, and that someone – possibly Suzie – had woven flowers into his mane and tail. The cart itself had been adorned with ribbons and bows, as well as the meadow flowers which matched their bouquets. Perhaps realising that so far he'd escaped her attention, Thor gave a friendly woof, and Libby laughed to see that his collar had been replaced with a bow tie and his normally dull coat was glossy and free from the muck and dirt of the farm.

'What do you reckon?' asked Suzie, who was beaming proudly at her cousin. 'Did I do good?'

'You did brilliantly,' said Libby approvingly. 'How did Thor like his bath?'

'He didn't,' said Suzie, adding guiltily, 'It's a good job Margo never heard him. He was howling like a babby when we got the soap out.'

'Worth it, though,' said Libby, tucking her arm through Suzie's. 'I couldn't be prouder to have you as my cousin, you do know that?'

Suzie blushed. 'I never thought I'd hear anyone say them words – and not just because I never knew I had a cousin, neither.'

'Well, I hope they praise you in the WAAF,' said Libby sternly, 'cos I for one know how much you deserve it.'

'They reward you with promotions, and my corp reckons it won't be long before I'm climbing the ladder,' Suzie said proudly.

'That's wonderful news. I don't suppose you've heard owt about that rotten father of yours when you've been on yer travels?'

'Nah, he's long gone,' said Suzie, 'and I don't even feel sad about it. Have you heard owt about the Murphys?'

'Not a lot. We know they've been sent to jail, but not for how long. We can't go askin' too many questions because we don't want to arouse suspicions.'

'They've got their punishment, and that's all that matters,' said Margo. 'It's very rare that people get their comeuppance in this world, so it's nice to see it happen now and then.'

Jack and Tom walked over to join them. 'They're asking if we're ready to make a move.'

Libby nodded. 'I shall feel like royalty, bein' driven through the streets with everyone starin' at us.'

Margo hopped onto the back of the cart with ease and was joined by Tom, with Libby and Jack bringing up the rear.

'What about Emma and Suzie?' asked Libby, sitting carefully on one of the hay bales. 'Surely they're riding with us?'

Jack jerked his head towards the front of the cart. 'Too right they are. They'll be sittin' next to Bernie.'

Libby kissed him on the cheek, causing the wedding guests to cheer. 'I do love you, Jack Durning.'

'Glad to hear it,' chuckled Jack as Emma and Suzie took their places next to Bernie.

With a click of his tongue, Bernie coaxed Goliath into a trot to the cheers of the wedding guests as well as many passers-by.

Libby thought she had never danced as much as she had the evening of her wedding. Gazing lovingly into Jack's eyes, she smiled softly. 'This has been the best day of my life.'

'It's worked out perfectly,' agreed Jack. 'It was nice to see Emma havin' a catch-up with Mrs Fortescue.'

'Two of my favourite people,' said Libby, 'and they both managed to make it to our big day.'

'You always said that gettin' married wouldn't be the same without Emma by your side.'

'It wouldn't,' said Libby simply. 'Havin' Emma there made all the difference; I feel like the luckiest girl alive.'

He leaned in to kiss her. 'You do know she can't be with you for *everythin'*.'

Libby blushed. 'Of course I do, but you do realise that I'm as nervous as a kitten?'

He gently kissed her lips. 'Don't be. You know I'd never do anythin' to hurt you,' he murmured.

As he traced a line of kisses along her neck, Libby felt herself relax under his touch. 'I love you, Jack Durning.'

His hand located the small of her back, and pulled her in close. 'I love you too, Mrs Durning.'

His eyes twinkled down at her as their lips met, and Libby knew that she had nothing to fear.

Epilogue

Libby gazed out of the window as Jack drove them to Hollybank for their annual reunion; it had been eight years since the war in Europe had ended, but she still couldn't look at the skies on a clear night without hearing the words 'bomber's moon'.

Suzie had proved them all right, progressing to sergeant by the end of the war, and they hadn't been altogether surprised when she told them of her intention to stay on in the WAAF.

'I don't want to leave,' she had told Libby during the VE Day celebrations. 'I'd feel like a fish out of water on the outside. I love the routine, the discipline, but most of all the stability. You've always got a home in the WAAF, and . . .' there had been an audible pause, 'Derek's hoping to make it to air crew now that so many men are leaving.'

Libby had smiled as she recalled the photograph Suzie had sent of her beloved beau Derek, his arm around Suzie, both of them beaming broadly.

397

'You're incredibly lucky to love what you do,' Libby told her cousin. 'Don't give it up for anyone or anything.'

'That's what Mam said, but I can't help worrying about her now that the war's over.' She gave a short mirthless laugh. 'More so than I did when the war was on.'

'Because her future's unsettled?' Libby had guessed.

'Exactly.'

'Don't worry about yer mam,' said Libby. 'We'll keep an eye on her; make sure she's all right.'

'I know you will,' said Suzie, 'but a smallholding's a big responsibility . . .'

'Which is why Tom and Margo are going to help her out.'

'But I thought Margo was after a smallholding of her own?' said Suzie, sounding puzzled.

'She is. They've got their eye on somewhere close to the place yer mam's hoping to get—'

Suzie interrupted without apology. 'So how are they going to be able to help me mam, if they're getting a place of their own?'

'They're goin' to help each other out,' said Libby. 'You scratch my back, I'll scratch yours type of thing. Yer mam's goin' to be doin' mainly arable farmin', and Margo and Tom will be farmin' livestock; mainly pigs, sheep and chickens from what Margo's told me.' She chuckled. 'Margo's even hopin' to train Thor up as a sheepdog.'

Now, as Libby looked out across the familiar countryside, she turned her mind to how things had worked out for all concerned.

Joyce, Margo and Tom had all worked well together, and their smallholdings had grown in size when more land became available. Joyce had hired a farmhand by the name of Ben, whom she later married, and Margo and Tom had gone on to have two children, Isobel and Ivor, both of whom loved their life in the country, with Thor acting as their trusted companion.

Suzie had continued in the WAAF until marrying Derek, when she had given up her career in order to bring up their only son, Arthur. With Derek having been recently posted to Gibraltar, Suzie had the unenviable task of breaking it to her cousin that her small family were unable to attend the reunion.

'I wish we could be there with you, because I love our little get-togethers, but it's impossible, what with Derek's job, and Arthur's aversion to flying – summat which the RAF boys continue to rib Derek over to this day!'

'I've never been on a plane in my life, so I don't know as I'd be any better than poor little Arthur,' confessed Libby, 'but even so, you'll be sorely missed.'

Now, as the fields of Hollybank came into view, Libby smiled as she envisaged her oldest friend rushing around as she got their anniversary lunch in order whilst keeping an eye on her wayward son, Dylan.

'Bernie tells me I worry too much, but I just can't help meself,' Emma had told her as they searched for Dylan one dark autumnal evening. 'There's so much that can go wrong on a farm, and Dylan treats the whole place like one big playground. I've asked Helen for advice but she says he's just like Bernie when he was a kid and not to worry.'

'How did she cope?'

Emma held up her crossed fingers. 'Did a lot of that and hoped for the best.'

'Sounds about right.'

Emma was shaking her head. 'Since when did crossed fingers keep a child from goin' under a cow, or the wheels of a tractor?'

'You did marry a farmer,' said Libby. 'You've only got to see how carefree Bernie can be to know what he'd be like around kids.'

Now, as Jack turned up the driveway to Hollybank, Libby watched their daughter Orla – now five years old – in the rear-view mirror of the car. 'Make sure you change into yer wellies before you go off with the other children. Patent leather shoes are not meant for climbin' muckheaps!'

Orla grinned mischievously. 'I know, but muckheaps are so much fun to jump around on, don't you think?'

Libby rolled her eyes. 'You're a tomboy, that's what you are, Orla Durning.'

'Which is why I shall marry Dylan when I'm older,' said Orla primly. 'No one will call me a tomboy when I'm a farmer's wife.'

Jack snorted with laughter. 'Does Dylan know about this?'

'Of course he does!' cried Orla. 'I told him last time we was here.'

'You know your own mind, I'll give you that,' said Jack. 'Just like yer mam.'

'Did you always know that you wanted to run a market stall?' Orla asked her mother curiously.

'Of course,' said Libby. 'I wanted to carry on the family tradition, just like your gran and grandad, God rest their souls.'

Orla pouted sadly. 'Do you think they'd be pleased to know that you did?'

Libby laughed. 'I think your grandfather wanted me to be a penpusher . . .'

'Do people really push pens for a livin'?' asked Orla, wide-eyed.

'It means to work in an office,' said Jack, chuckling.

'Oh, that doesn't sound much fun.'

'Exactly!' said Libby. 'I'd far rather be down the market than stuck in some stuffy office answerin' to them in command.'

Jack glanced lovingly at his wife as he addressed his daughter. 'Your mam's always been a woman with a wild heart who knows her own mind, which is why I fell in love with her.'

'I'm like that,' said Orla proudly, 'an' that's why I told Dylan we'd get married when we were old enough.'

'And what did Dylan say to that?'

Orla shrugged. 'Not a lot.'

Jack grinned. 'There's not a lot he *could* say.' He brought the car to a halt outside Rose Cottage.

'Dylan!' cried Orla. She rushed out of the car, but quickly came back as Libby called for her to put her wellies on.

Arriving at the car, Dylan flashed them a dazzling smile, his teeth made all the whiter by the grime which covered most of his face. 'We're goin' to play roundheads and cavaliers,' he said by way of explanation for the sword he'd fashioned out of sticks, and the saucepan on his head.

'Let me guess. You're one of the roundheads?' teased Jack.

Dylan's grin broadened. 'Don't be daft,' he said, pointing to his tin hat. 'I'm one of the cavaliers; can't you tell?' He continued without waiting for a reply. 'The others can be the roundheads, and me and Orla will be the cavaliers.'

They turned to see Emma coming out of the front door to Rose Cottage, followed closely by Bernie, who was already grimacing at the thought of his wife's reaction when she saw her son's recently clean face now caked in dirt.

'I don't know why I bother naggin' him to wash behind his ears when he goes and smears dirt on every patch of bare skin he can find!' she complained, but her lips were twitching.

Libby greeted her friend with a warm embrace. 'You can't be a warrior without a bit of dirt. We were always covered in muck when we was kids,' she reminded her friend.

'Usin' the dustbin lids as shields whilst we threw sticks at each other, pretendin' they were arrows,' said Emma. 'I'd forgotten about that.'

Dylan produced two crudely fashioned bows, one of which he handed to Orla. 'I made you this.'

Beaming with delight, Orla gave the piece of baling twine an experimental twang. 'Have you got any sticks we can use as arrows?'

Nodding, Dylan jerked his head back the way he'd come, gesturing for her to follow him. 'I'll help you with your camouflage, and after that we can make a den whilst we wait for the others to get here.'

Suspecting that by camouflage Dylan really meant mud, Emma would have spoken had not Libby intervened. 'I don't mind a bit of mud when she comes here,' she told Emma as they watched the children run off together. 'It's good for them.'

'Don't be tellin' Dylan that,' said Emma. 'I'm sure he spends most of his day endeavouring to get dirtier than the day before.'

'And quite right too,' said Jack, with Bernie agreeing wholeheartedly.

'Have any of the others arrived, or are we the first?'

'You're the first.'

'I always thought Roz would go back to Germany when the war was over,' Libby commented as she followed Emma into the cottage.

'She might well have done had her parents returned, but goin' back would be a bitter pill to swallow when yer friends and neighbours had treated you as badly as they did.'

Libby shuddered. 'Not to mention them awful concentration camps . . .'

'Do you think the war would have ended any quicker had they known about the camps sooner?' Emma wondered.

'No,' said Libby flatly. 'Felix reckons they all knew summat bad was goin' on when they started cartin' Jews off to those so-called "camps".'

'It's impossible to comprehend how anyone could do what they did. I'm just glad the Sachses decided to make Britain their home,' said Bernie.

'I'll never understand how Adele could have even contemplated goin' back to Germany,' said Libby stiffly. 'I know her parents wanted her to join them, but even so.'

'They're stayin' as a matter of principle,' said Emma, 'which I can kind of understand. After all, why should they leave when they never did anythin' wrong?'

'That's all well and good for them,' Jack supposed, 'but Adele's made a good life for herself here. I don't blame her for wantin' to stay put.'

'Roz and Felix have the right idea, by not wanting their children growin' up in a community what once turned against them,' said Bernie, adding, 'How many kids have they got now? I'm sure they have a new one every time I see them!'

'Four,' said Emma promptly, 'but don't you go thinkin' it's some kind of competition, Bernie Lewis, cos one's plenty.' She took the kettle from the stove and poured most of the water into a teapot. 'It's a shame Adele hasn't found someone.'

'I should think watching her friend have four kids within as many years has probably put her off,' Bernie chuckled. 'One's bad enough.'

'Our Dylan's a pleasure – most of the time.'

Bernie gestured to the yard with his hand. 'Fancy taking a gander at the new tractor, Jack?'

Libby rolled her eyes as Jack followed Bernie outside. 'Men and their machines, eh?'

'He spends more time fiddlin' with that thing than he does with me!' said Emma, before gasping out loud as her words caught up with her and both she and Libby began to giggle.

'Speakin' without thinkin' first is a speciality of mine!' said Emma as soon as she could speak at all.

'Always has been,' said Libby. She took a cup of tea from her friend before asking her next question. 'How's yer mum and dad?'

'Grand,' replied Emma. Sitting down with her own mug, she went on, 'Mum said they'd have loved to come and join us, but Dad's busy at work and she's the same with her WI meetings. We've said we'll take Dylan to visit them in the summer hols, as we do every year.'

'I need to go back too, if just to tend to Mum and Dad's grave. Perhaps we could all go together, make a proper holiday out of it?' suggested Libby.

'That would be fabulous,' said Emma, her eyes shining. 'Dylan loves goin' to see his grandparents, but it's not the same when you're the only child in a house full of adults.'

'I'll have to check with Jack,' said Libby, 'but I can't see why we wouldn't be able to join you.'

Hearing the crunch of car tyres on gravel, Emma looked out of the window. 'Here's the rest of them!'

Libby got up from her seat to open the door. Speaking straight to the men, she said, 'Bernie's showin' Jack his new tractor,' and smiled as Tom, Felix, Gordon and Ben promptly strode off in the direction she indicated.

Appearing in the doorway behind her, Emma made sure her friend's children had donned their wellingtons before telling them where to find Dylan and Orla. She watched them hasten towards the meadow as she welcomed Roz, Margo, Adele and Inge into the house.

'Here, let me take your coats,' said Libby, whilst Emma set about making more cups of tea.

'We left Thor at home this year, cos he's gettin' too old to play the trusty steed!' said Margo, and turned to Emma. 'Do you need a hand with anythin'?'

'You can help with the sarnies if you like, but the sausage rolls, quiche and Scotch eggs are already done.'

'You've turned into a domestic goddess,' said Libby approvingly as she fetched the bread from the pantry. 'Not surprising, I suppose, considerin' your mum was an excellent cook.'

'I try my best,' said Emma as she fetched Spam, corned beef and cheese from the larder. 'Can you get the tomatoes and onions from the pantry please, Roz?'

Roz did as she was asked and the women set about making the sandwiches. 'I miss my days on the farm,' Roz said, as she helped to butter the bread. 'Everything seemed a lot simpler back then.'

'I love our smallholdin',' said Margo. 'I couldn't imagine doin' anythin' else.'

Adele, who was working as a lady's companion in one of the big houses in London, couldn't have agreed more. 'The cattle don't go off and whisper in corners, or tut reprovingly because the two and a half teaspoons of sugar tasted more like two and a quarter!'

'How do you find tutoring children, Inge?' asked Emma. 'I bet it must be tryin' at times, especially if they're like my Dylan.'

'I only tutor the older ones. It's far easier on a one-to-one basis than trying to control a class full of children...' The women continued to chat about the education system and how it had changed since the war until they had used up every slice of bread.

When she had finished arranging the food on plates, Libby placed her hands on her hips to admire their work. 'Shall I call everyone in?'

'Please,' said Emma. 'I'll put the kettle on for anyone who wants a cuppa, and make squash for those who don't.'

Libby stepped outside and headed over to the men, who were fiddling with the tractor's engine. 'Emma wants everyone in.' She jerked her head in the direction of the fields. 'D'you fancy helpin' me hunt for roundheads and cavaliers, Jack?'

Jack wiped his hands on an old rag which had been laid on top of one of the tractor's wheels. 'It'd be my pleasure,' he said, touching his forelock in mock salute.

Libby heaved a reminiscent sigh as they walked down the grassy track which led to the meadow. 'I remember the day you brought Margo and me to the farm as if it were yesterday!'

He slipped his hand in hers. 'You still believed the Murphys to be yer relatives, and hadn't a clue that Suzie and Joyce were actually yer aunt and cousin.'

'I remember everyone warnin' me off goin' to see Donny while he was in jail, but I knew I had to speak my piece.'

'Like you did with yer uncle.'

'Exactly!' She turned her thoughts to the day she had gone to the jail to visit Donny. He had eyed her with a surly expression as she sat opposite him. She had waited for him to speak first, but it seemed he had nothing to say, so Libby had done all the talking.

'Just for the record, I know what you done to my mother,' she had said in hushed tones. 'You do know that you ruined her life?'

He'd shrugged. 'It was her own fault.'

'For wantin' a family so badly, she'd listen to scum like you?' Libby hissed. 'She wasn't the one in the wrong – that was you, and you alone.' She paused momentarily. 'I say you alone, but of course my Uncle Tony had summat to do with it.'

She smiled as she saw the penny drop.

'You!' he said, his piggy eyes boring into hers with a look of such hate, Libby could actually feel it.

'Of course it was me,' said Libby smugly. 'You didn't seriously think my uncle had walked into the nearest police station off his own bat to confess all? Not a chance. I was the one who put the idea in his head that you and Jo had dropped him in it.'

He had pounded his fists against the table, causing the officer nearby to step forward.

Libby tutted sarcastically as Donny lowered himself back into his seat. 'Temper, temper.'

'Just you wait until I get out of here, then you'll know what my temper's really like,' he seethed.

She had smiled sweetly. 'I'm not scared of you, Donny Murphy, or Jo for that matter. You're nowt but a couple of bullies who thrive on their reputation, half of which you've made up. You see, I've been doin' some diggin', and all that stuff about you doin' someone in was a cock and bull story to hide the real reason behind your leavin' Liverpool.'

Donny's face fell. 'You don't know jack sh—'

'Oh, but I do,' said Libby. 'You left Liverpool cos you'd bitten off more than you could chew and you were scared that Bill Derby was goin' to rip yer throat out, so much so you agreed to let him peddle his goods out of yer house. Bill Derby lost an awful lot of money when you got arrested; how do you think he'd feel if he knew it was your fault that you got arrested in the first place?'

'How . . .' Donny began, before changing his mind and keeping quiet.

'How do I know?' asked Libby. She leaned forward. 'Cos when you're on the right side of the law you get to learn all sorts, certainly enough to know that you're nowt but a bag of hot air!'

'I can make an exception . . .' growled Donny, but Libby just laughed.

'I've eaten bigger than you for breakfast! Thanks to me not only are you and your dreadful wife behind bars, but so is my uncle and the Sykeses.' She saw the hunted look cross his face. 'I see you've heard of them.'

Donny stood up to leave, but Libby wasn't going to allow him to go without finishing what she had come to say.

'If you *ever* consider gettin' on the wrong side of me or mine, just remember one thing. I make prisoners out of men that once walked freely.'

Donny had sworn at her beneath his breath, but despite his cursing he'd left Libby alone from that day onwards.

Startled by Orla and Dylan who jumped out at them whilst brandishing their swords, Libby held a hand to her chest. 'It's the cavaliers, Jack!' she yelped in mock terror. 'Whatever shall we do?'

'I'll save you, m'lady,' said Jack as he swept her up into his arms. Seeing several cherub-like faces peeping out at them from behind the blackthorn hedge, he cried, 'Never fear, the roundheads are here!'

Laughing, Libby held on tightly as Jack rushed her back up at the track with the children in hot pursuit.

Arriving back at the cottage, he gently lowered his wife to the ground before sweeping Dylan up in one arm and Orla in the other. 'Over here!' he called to Ivor, who was pretending to be cantering round on his horse.

Libby thrust the cottage door open and ushered the children inside, telling them to go and wash ready for lunch.

The queue for the bathroom was long, and Emma quipped that the men were as bad as the children when it came to getting their hands dirty. Bernie nipped across to the main house to tell his parents that lunch was ready, while Emma got everybody seated on various stools, chairs and benches around the three differently sized tables, with the children sitting at the lowest.

After everyone had eaten their fill, the women cleared the tables and washed the dishes whilst the men retired to the parlour of the main house.

'Eight years,' said Adele softly as she gathered the empty plates, 'is a long time, but at the same time it seems like no time at all.'

'Fifteen years since we left Frankfurt,' noted Inge.

'Are you ever tempted to go back?' asked Margo tentatively. 'Just to see what it looks like now?'

Inge stared into space as though deep in thought. 'It's not my home any more,' she said simply. 'It hasn't been since the day they turned on us, and quite frankly I don't care what it looks like now.'

'But some people have moved back,' said Libby.

'Only because they're looking for loved ones, or because they don't see why they should've been forced out of their homes in the beginning, but I don't want to fight any more, not after having done so for so many years. I could never look any of my neighbours in the eye again, because I have no idea whether they or their children played a part in murdering my people.'

'I find it incredibly difficult to understand how my mother and father could stay there, for that very reason,' said Adele. 'I know that I wouldn't want to stand in a queue not knowing whether the man in front of me drove the train to one of the camps. I don't care if he was only doing it because he feared for his own life. If more people would've stood up to Hitler sooner, think of the lives that could've been saved.'

'It can never happen again,' said Margo, but Inge was smiling at her in a sympathetic fashion.

'I don't wish to appear cynical, but history has a habit of repeating itself, the good *and* the bad.'

Roz wiped a plate dry as she gazed out of the window to the meadow where the children were playing. 'I hope our children never see it in their lifetime.'

'Me too,' agreed Inge, 'but let's not forget the Great War ended in nineteen eighteen, just twenty-one years before the start of World War Two.'

'There can't be a World War Three,' said Emma hollowly. 'There just can't.'

Libby laid a reassuring hand on her friend's forearm. 'We must make sure that people never forget the atrocities of what we went through, in the hope that others will take heed.'

'And if they don't then we must be ready for them,' said Helen, 'not like we were last time around.'

'Even if the kind of awful men who like to dictate haven't learned anything, the rest of the world has,' said Margo, 'and with Europe united we'll never be in the same position again.'

'Men,' tutted Joyce. 'Why can't they be happy with their lot?'

'We only go to war on the say-so of men,' agreed Inge, quickly adding, 'Not that I'm tarring every man with the same brush, you understand.'

'We should put the women in charge,' said Libby. 'There'd be no war if we did that.'

'Boadicea?' ventured Joyce.

'Only cos she fought the Roman empire,' said Margo reasonably. 'She didn't start it.'

As they tidied everything away, they continued to speak of how the world would be if they, or women like them, were in charge. Once the last plate had been placed in the dresser, Emma hung the tea towels over the Aga rail and they headed over to the main house to join the men.

Seeing Jack on one of the armchairs, Libby headed over to join him.

'I would say for you to pull up a pew,' said Jack, glancing around the crowded room, 'but as it stands you're goin' to have to settle for my lap.' He patted his thighs.

Smiling, Libby did as he suggested, and leaning her head against his chest she looked round at all the friends who were gathered in the cosy parlour.

'Penny for them?' asked Jack.

'Just thinkin' how I came to Liverpool lookin' for a family, and nearly returned to London, believing I hadn't found one. Yet look at the evidence.' She gestured round at the assembled people. 'I've got the biggest family a girl could wish for.'

He kissed the top of her head. 'Glad you stayed?'

She lifted her head so that they were gazing into each other's eyes. 'Comin' to Liverpool was the best thing I ever done, and I wouldn't change a single thing.'

His brow rose in surprise. 'Not even the Murphys?'

'Not even the Murphys,' Libby confirmed. 'Everythin' happens for a reason, Jack, and had I known about them from the start I really think I'd have left before I found my mother's diaries, and before I'd learned who my real family were. And if that had been the case Donny and Tony would've got away with everythin' scot-free, and I couldn't stomach the thought of that. Knowin' that Tony got banged up for manslaughter wasn't the outcome I wanted, but at least it brought me a small amount of justice. Comin' here and findin' out the truth was one of the toughest things I've ever done, but it's made me into a stronger woman, and our children will only benefit from that.'

He eyed her steadily. 'You mean child.'

Libby smiled, a hand to her stomach. 'I mean children.'

Jack's eyes danced as the news sank in. 'I didn't know you'd been to the quack.'

'I didn't want to say owt until I knew for sure, and I don't want to tell Orla yet, because it's still early days and you know how excited she can get. She's bad enough on car journeys! Askin' if we're there yet when we're still hours away is one thing, but can you imagine what she'll be like when I'm months away from givin' birth?'

Jack nodded fervently. 'Smart thinkin'.'

'This has been the first opportunity I've had to talk to you without worrying that a roundhead or a cavalier might jump out on us and accidentally overhear the truth. You know what little gossips kids can be.'

He held his hand to her stomach. 'I'm goin' to be a daddy all over again,' he said blissfully.

'Wait until you tell yer dad,' said Libby. 'He didn't stop smilin' for a week when we told him he was goin' to be a granddad.'

He ran his forefinger down the side of her face. 'You're the most beautiful, wonderful woman in the whole wide world, Libby Durning, have I ever told you that?'

She laughed softly. 'Only on a daily basis.'

'And quite right too,' said Jack.

She gazed at him adoringly. 'I love you, Jack.'

He leaned in for a kiss, murmuring, 'I love you too, Libby Durning.'

Dear Readers,

First, let me start off by saying that I hope you all had a wonderful Christmas and New Year! It hardly seems as though any time has passed since I wrote to you all in *Winter's Orphan*, yet here we are gearing up for warmer days ahead – hopefully!

The best part about writing trilogies is that you get to spend more time with certain characters and follow their life journeys for far longer than you would in a one-off. Indeed, I sometimes get so attached to the characters that I find it hard to let go. There were so many questions left unanswered in both *Winter's Orphan* and *White Christmas*; and with all the characters winding up on the same farm, *A Mother's Secret* seemed the perfect book in which to complete their stories. I found revisiting the Haggartys after such a long time very interesting, especially as their lives had changed such a lot. Watching Suzie develop a relationship with her mother while out of her father's control was both encouraging and heart-warming, as well as proof that anyone can turn their life around, no matter their upbringing.

Writing this book has kept me busy over the last year. But life has also been very full outside of my writing schedule. As many of you know, we were heartbroken to lose our dear lurcher Snoopy last year. With Sparky being eleven years old, we had no intention of getting another dog, but poor Sparky missed his buddy terribly, and went from a happy, outgoing dog, who was full of life and vitality, to a shadow of his former self. We heard through the grapevine that a local rescue centre was looking to rehome a lovely nine-year-old lurcher called Tara who'd lost her owner through a bereavement and was struggling to find a new home due to her advanced years. With both dogs being mature we knew it might not work out, but Sparky welcomed Tara into his home with open paws, and they soon became inseparable; reminding us of an old married couple! It's been wonderful to see him come out of his shell, and enjoy life once more, not to mention the warm fuzzy feeling you get when you rehome an elderly dog, whose choices were running out!

Although I was sad to leave old characters behind, I'm really excited to be at the start of a brand new trilogy. It's interesting to meet a whole new set of characters, who I shall introduce you to when the time is right. But for now I shall continue to work away at developing their personalities and watching them grow.

Before I sign off, I want to quickly remind you all to sign up to my newsletter, where I run giveaways, offer exclusive extracts from upcoming books, and provide notes on my writing process. The link to subscribe can be accessed through my Facebook page: Katie Flynn Author.

Thank you all for reading *A Mother's Secret* and for being the best readers I could ever ask for! Wishing you all a wonderful 2024. Until next time.

Lots of love,

Holly Flynn xx

DISCOVER THE LATEST
HEARTFELT READ FROM

Katie Flynn
The Winter Runaway

COMING OCTOBER 2024
AVAILABLE TO PRE-ORDER NOW

KATIE FLYNN

If you want to continue to hear from the
Flynn family, and to receive the latest news about
new Katie Flynn books and competitions,
sign up to the Katie Flynn newsletter.

Join today by visiting
www.penguin.co.uk/katieflynnnewsletter

Find Katie Flynn on Facebook
www.facebook.com/katieflynn458